Sins of the Fathers

Historical Fiction by Herbert J. Stern
and Alan A. Winter

Sins of the Fathers
Wolf

Non-fiction by Herbert J. Stern

Diary of a DA
Judgment in Berlin
Trying Cases to Win: 5 Volume Series
Trying Cases to Win: in One Volume

Novels by Alan A. Winter

Island Bluffs
Savior's Day
Snowflakes in the Sahara
Someone Else's Son

Sins
of the
Fathers

A NOVEL

HERBERT J. STERN AND ALAN A. WINTER

*You shall have no other Gods before me . . . For I, the LORD your God
am a jealous God, visiting the iniquity of the fathers upon the sons . . .*
—Deuteronomy, Chapter 5

Skyhorse Publishing

Skyhorse Publishing books may be purchased in bulk at special discounts for sales promotion, corporate gifts, fund-raising, or educational purposes. Special editions can also be created to specifications. For details, contact the Special Sales Department, Skyhorse Publishing, 307 West 36th Street, 11th Floor, New York, NY 10018 or info@skyhorsepublishing.com.

Skyhorse® and Skyhorse Publishing® are registered trademarks of Skyhorse Publishing, Inc.®, a Delaware corporation.

Visit our website at www.skyhorsepublishing.com.

10 9 8 7 6 5 4 3 2 1

Library of Congress Cataloging-in-Publication Data is available on file.

Cover design by Kai Texel

Print ISBN: 978-1-5107-6942-7
Ebook ISBN: 978-1-5107-6943-4

Printed in the United States of America

Ceux qui peuvent vous faire croire à des absurdités peuvent vous faire commettre des atrocités.

—*Voltaire (Questions sur les Miracles, 1765)*

TRANSLATION
Those who can make you believe absurdities can make you commit atrocities.

In honor of

Ludwig Beck
Dietrich Bonhoeffer
Hans Dohnanyi
Wilhelm Canaris
Ewald von Kleist-Schmenzin
Hans Oster
Werner Schrader
Erwin von Witzleben
and
Fabian von Schlabrendorff

Many will recognize the names of these German officers and citizens who lost their lives participating in the July 1944 assassination attempt of Adolf Hitler to end the war Germany could not win.

Few, however, are aware that six years earlier these same men risked their lives to prevent Hitler from starting that war.

Fabian von Schlabrendorff survived unimaginable cruelty at the hands of the Nazis and was spared death at the last minute when Judge Freisler died from Allied bombing in February 1945, with Schlabrendorff's file in his hand.

This book is dedicated to our wives, Marsha Stern and Lori Winter, for their patience, understanding, support, and love.

Prologue

Munich, 1936

It was left to me to bring justice to the two black-uniformed Dachau guards who beat Max Klinghofer to a bloody pulp. When I found Max, his face was unrecognizable. He was caked in his own excrement. Max died in my arms, and I am thankful that in those last precious moments he knew I was there. I wept over Max's body, stroking his hair, wiping the blood away from his cheeks with my tears, promising to avenge his needless death.

I had already dealt with Felix Querner. Now it was Konrad Jüttner's turn.

Drastic measures were required to get Querner to reveal Jüttner's name. In the end, he told me what I needed to know. Everybody talks in the end. Both guards were members of the *Schutzstaffel-Wachverbände*—the *SS* Death's Head Units—that ruled Dachau with the brutality demanded by their commandant, Theodor Eicke. Eicke graduated from a mental institution the year before he took over Dachau. That was one of two qualifications to run Dachau in the eyes of *Reichsführer* Himmler, head of the *SS*. The other? The ability to inflict pain and suffering without remorse . . . and train others to do the same.

As I waited in the shadows, a thunderclap rumbled to the west. I counted the seconds before a bolt of lightning flashed like a photographer's bulb. A spark of blue-white flickered, only to be swallowed by the darkness and disappear. Puddles turned into ponds. Branches scattered across the road. Driving on the rutted road would be treacherous.

I had planned for such a night.

The din of the driving rain was soon exceeded by the throbbing of a tuned engine. I glanced at my watch. Right on time.

As Jüttner's car rounded the bend, two white headlights bobbed over fallen debris, casting bleached beams helter-skelter. I leaped to the middle of the road and waved my arms. I knew my *SS* general's uniform would force the driver to stop. Moreover, he would see my car off kilter in the ditch by the side of the road.

Jüttner slowed to a halt and cranked down the window of his black Ford Rheinlander sedan.

"That's quite a car you have," I said, marveling at its sleek look despite the rain pounding off it like the rat-a-tat of a Maxim machine gun used in the Great War. "It's the first one I've seen."

"Only been made for a couple of years. Got it the other day. But you didn't stop me to admire my car . . ."—he double-checked my insignias—". . . *Herr Obergruppenführer.*" He brushed crumbs off his tunic from the buttered *brötchen* in his hand, sat taller behind the wheel, and pointed. "I see your car in the gulley. How did that happen?"

"The more I tried to drive it out, the more the rear tire spun deeper into the mud. I was waiting for someone to come along to help steer if I pushed from behind. Lucky for me it was an *SS* man."

I plumbed his eyes for a flicker of suspicion. There was none. I peered at his uniform crests. "A *Sturmbannführer*, I see."

I was a general officer, five ranks above him. He had to help.

Jüttner opened the car door, stepped into the mud, and sized me up. "You look big enough and strong enough. It just might work."

I was six-foot-seven and well over two hundred and fifty pounds. Pushing my car while he steered was more than plausible.

"Aren't you going to pull your car to the side?"

He shook his head. "It's fine right here. I make this trip every night. I'm the last one on this road 'til the morning shift."

This confirmed what I knew from previous reconnaissance.

Jüttner was a beefy man who did not restrain himself at the table. He lumbered around his car, surveyed my back tire buried in mud, sized up the incline of the ditch, and then gave a thumbs-up. "We should be able to do this."

He slipped onto my front seat while I sloshed to the rear and leveraged my foot against a small boulder I had strategically planted earlier. I signaled I was ready; he put the car in gear. I gritted my teeth as I drove my leg into the rock. With both hands cupped around the bumper's rim, I lifted with all my strength. Joints cracked. Muscles quavered. The car budged. I struggled for traction as the car continued to move. Jüttner goosed the gas pedal enough to coax the car over the hump and onto the road.

Jüttner slid out of the car smiling, proud that he had helped an *Obergruppenführer*. "That was easier than I thought it would be."

When he turned to close the door, I smashed the crook of his left knee with a truncheon. Jüttner screamed. He toppled to the ground, clipping his head on the way down. He grabbed his leg with his left hand.

"What the hell did you do that for?" Blood gushed down his face. As his left hand levered him up, his right hand groped for his pistol. I smacked his arm with the club; it cracked. His half-drawn gun flew into the foliage.

With both hands, I yanked him by the collar onto his good foot. "You're not going anywhere, Jüttner."

Pain rocketed through his body. Jüttner grimaced. His breathing grew shallow. He struggled to gain control, to make sense of what was happening.

"Are you crazy!" he shouted. "I don't care if you are a general. When I tell my commandant, he will go right to the *Führer*. You're as good as dead."

I snorted. "Your Commandant Eicke will stand idly by and do nothing. Do you know why? Because no one in the Reich is closer to the *Führer* than me."

Hearing this, the whites of his eyes widened. He shot furtive glances this way and that, hoping for someone to come along . . . knowing no one would.

Desperate, he barked, "What do you want?"

"Let me refresh your memory. August '34. A Jew was tortured so badly in Dachau that he was unrecognizable. Remember?"

"There were so many . . . I . . . can't recall . . ." He gasped for air. "We had our orders to mete out severe punishment at the slightest infraction." Gasp. "Prevent the others from stepping out of line."

"His name was Max Klinghofer. Do you remember Max?"

There was a flash of recognition. "The fat little Jew? I remember. He was a wiseass. Spoke back to us."

Max had been like a father to me. Without a blink, I punched Jüttner in his gut. He doubled over. I held him until he stopped puking, angled him up, and smashed him again.

Jüttner clawed for air. I was in no rush. He could take all the time he needed.

When his chest and shoulders stopped heaving, he raised his good hand. "Enough. No more."

I held him up by his jacket collar or he would have collapsed. Our eyes met, fear in his. Without a word, I belted him again. "That was for Max's friend, Kitty. She loved him very much." Then I unleashed the hardest blow of all. Bones snapped. A rib. Probably two. "That was for me, you piece of shit."

The driving rain slowed to a light drizzle. The wind died down. Jüttner's sour stench of fear coupled with the stink of shit and piss sliding down his leg made me gag. I swallowed hard.

"Who gave the order to kill Max?"

"There was no order. Felix and I did what was expected of us." Then he turned, wide-eyed. "Felix," he whispered.

"What about Querner?" I spit his name out.

"We never found his body." Jüttner was barely audible. His eyes flitted everywhere but at mine. Then a look of recognition crossed his face. "It wasn't a boating accident, was it? You killed Felix."

"Good for you. Now someone knows what happened to Querner. For the last time, who gave the order to kill Max?"

"I told you. There was no kill order. The moment an inmate breaks a rule, any rule, we have the right to punish them as we see fit."

The rain stopped. A sliver of moonlight painted a silvery cast on his face. Jüttner knew he was as good as dead. He managed a defiant smile. Blood covered his front teeth, rendering the final ghoulish touch to his façade. "You don't want to understand, *Obergruppenführer* . . . if, indeed, that is what you are. Your Jew, Max, was the lucky one. He didn't last long compared to some of the others. He was weak. The weak go fast. If you ask me, that is a blessing in disguise."

Infuriated, I wrapped my left arm around his head, a quick jerk, and he was dead.

I dragged Jüttner to his car, shoved him behind the wheel, pulled out the choke, and started the engine. Next, I grabbed a thick branch that had fallen in the storm, snapped it over my knee to the size I needed, and wedged it between the seat and the gas pedal. Then I stretched to reach the clutch and shift the car into gear. I stood on the running board and steered through the open window, pointing the car down the middle of the road. The car gathered speed. When I no longer felt safe, I jumped off, catching myself before I tumbled to the ground. Just when I began to wonder how far it could go straight, the car veered into the ditch that paralleled the road, teetered on two wheels, and then flipped into a tree. There was a whoosh as the gas tank exploded. Soon flames engulfed the car. I waited a moment to assess the damage before I turned away.

Back in my rented Mercedes, I pressed hard on the accelerator, secure that the investigation would conclude that Konrad Jüttner died in a terrible accident on a dark, stormy night.

*

Days later, I found the newspaper article that announced Jüttner's accidental death.

All seemed in order.

I no sooner put the paper down than my office phone rang.

"Hello." No one answered. I hung up. Not ten seconds later, the phone rang again. "Hello." No one.

It was a prearranged signal. I left the Chancellery building and headed for the lobby in the Hotel *Kaiserhof* on *Wilhelmplatz*. I found an empty phone booth.

When the call went through, the man on the other end said, "What were you thinking?"

"Hello to you, too, Bernhard. How's the weather in London?"

"Not as stormy as it could be for you. I gave you Querner's name so you could report him to the Ministry of Justice for killing Max. Then I discover he goes missing in a boating mishap. I don't believe in coincidences, but I didn't say anything. Now I read about Jüttner. Have you gone mad?"

"Querner gave up Jüttner."

"That's obvious. Friedrich, you promised not to do anything rash." Usually calm and in control, Bernhard Weiss spoke faster, his voice pitched higher. "Look at what you did: not one, but two! How long do you think it will take before Heydrich or Himmler link you to these murders?"

Bernhard Weiss had been the deputy president of the Berlin Police before the Nazis ordered the Jewish policeman's arrest. That's when I helped him escape to Prague.

"No one saw me. Both deaths appear as accidents. That is how the final reports read. It's over. Justice has been served."

"You would be wise to trust my instincts, Friedrich. They have served me well over the years."

"And my instincts tell me it's time to leave Germany, Bernhard. I can't stay any longer. You have no idea how crazy it is getting. Hitler grows less stable by the day."

"It can't be that bad! Most foreign papers applaud all he is doing for Germany."

"At what price? The outside world sees Hitler's picture the way Goebbels paints it. The real Hitler, the Hitler I see, has all but withdrawn from the Party leadership since becoming chancellor. If you can believe it, he left Hess in charge of the Party . . . and you know how much of a fool that one is. Day-to-day operations are in disarray as Hitler builds a war machine in defiance of the Treaty of Versailles. Rather than hold cabinet meetings, he consults with a vicious gang of the worst sort that elbows each other for power. Then there is his master plan to restore all of Germany's lost territory."

"In a way, I understand that."

"That's where everyone underestimates him. Hitler intends to expand Germany's borders well beyond what we lost in the Great War. The man is unstable."

"Friedrich, words matter to you. What are you trying to tell me?"

After all of these years, I was reluctant to unmask myself in order to explain how dangerous Hitler had become.

"Friedrich . . . Friedrich are you still there?"

"I am. It is time someone else knew."

"What? You're talking in circles," Bernhard said.

I drew in a deep breath. "Bernhard, do you remember that day in the *Düppel* neighborhood? The park bench. Do you recall what we talked about?"

"That was before Hitler took power, right? I was investigating you. Your background. When I discovered that Friedrich Richard died in Pasewalk Hospital in 1918 . . . I stopped the investigation because, well, I didn't know what I would discover. The last thing I wanted was to compromise you. I needed you to remain safe and stay in place."

"You might never have trusted me had you continued that investigation."

"What would I have learned?"

"That I am a victim of amnesia. That I was blown up in the Second Battle of the Marne, during the summer of 1918. That I had multiple broken bones and burns on my back and arms. A plastic surgeon at Charité Hospital repaired my face. While my injuries healed, my memory never returned. That is why they sent me to Pasewalk Hospital. For psychiatric treatment."

"At least you're better now."

"I'm not. Dr. Edmund Forster was unable to restore my memory."

"Are you telling me you have *no* memory since before your injuries? You seem so . . . normal."

"I'll take that as a compliment."

"I'm confused. What does this have to do with Hitler?"

"Hitler was in the bed next to me at Pasewalk. He claimed to have been blinded in a gas attack."

"No surprise there. It's in *Mein Kampf*," Bernhard said.

"I helped him navigate through the hospital. Cut his food. Took him to the toilet. Think about it. Two people who spend that amount of time together become connected. Friends. For us, Pasewalk was the cornerstone of our relationship. Here's the point: We shared the same psychiatrist. Dr. Forster diagnosed Hitler as suffering from hysterical blindness. He labeled him a psychopath."

"I was following, until now. You are telling me that a psychiatrist restored Hitler's sight?"

"Forster used hypnosis. It worked."

I heard breathing, but nothing else. It was my turn to ask, "Bernhard, are you there?"

He cleared his throat. "*Mein Gott.* You are saying that Germany is in the hands of a psychopath."

"Now you understand."

"If this is true, those records must be retrieved to expose the man for what he is. Before it's too late."

I gulped. "There are no records. Soon after Hitler became chancellor, he sent me to Pasewalk to destroy his medical records. If I knew then what I know now, I never would have done it."

"What about your records?"

"What do you think? When I destroyed Hitler's, I also destroyed my file along with the real Friedrich Richard's record."

"What was your name before you took his?"

"I was called Patient X."

"Then where did Friedrich Richard come from? Whose idea was that?"

"Dr. Forster gave me the name of a dead patient."

"Can't Forster confirm Hitler's pathology?"

"If only he could. Forster was found shot in the head a few months after Hitler became chancellor. They found the gun by his side, but his wife claimed he never owned one. They ruled it a suicide."

"You don't think it was?" Bernhard asked.

"Unlike Hitler's half-niece, Geli, who did commit suicide, it is hard to believe Forster would have taken his own life."

"We both know Hitler had nothing to do with her death."

"Not in the literal sense. But his overbearing control drove Geli to it. Her death left him more unhinged. Then look what he did to his present girlfriend: Eva Braun."

"I was in Berlin for *her* suicide attempt in 1932," Bernhard said.

"He keeps her caged up in the Berghof like a pet. Last year, she tried to kill herself, again. Moreover, he is a hypochondriac. He keeps a phony doctor in tow to pump medicine into him every morning. That is just a fraction of what I put up with because I promised you I would remain close to Hitler."

"You were able to soften those first laws that removed Jews from their civil service jobs," Bernhard said.

"How long did *that* last? I want you to know that before I killed those two beasts, I did go to Minister of Justice Gürtner. I wanted them prosecuted. He told me that *SS* brutality in the camps was out of his jurisdiction. Bernhard, the rule of law does not exist in Germany today."

"Friedrich," Bernhard paused to collect his thoughts, "that is why you must stay. Save lives when you can. On top of that, continue to record what happens. Your firsthand account is invaluable. No one sees Hitler or his machinations with your perspective."

I tossed my head back and laughed into the phone. "Why would anyone care what an amnesiac—who still doesn't know his true name—says about Hitler and the Nazis?"

"Let me put it to you a different way. The French are afraid of Hitler. Half the British Lords support him. The Americans bury their collective heads in the sand believing they are protected by two great oceans. And the Jews? My people are crushed between a tyrant determined to force them to leave and an indifferent

world that refuses to accept them. Friedrich, when war comes—
and we both know it will—there must be someone inside to help
save those who can be saved, to help defeat Hitler any way we
can. If not you, then who?"

PART I

PART 1

Chapter 1

Berlin 1934

The last months of 1934 were the worst of my life, or at least for the sixteen years that I could recall. Every night I sat in the house Max left me, ruminating on my role in Hitler's rise to power. I did what I did then in the belief that it was the only path to restore Germany to greatness. The fact that I never harmed a Jew—to the contrary, I did all I could to protect them—provided no solace. Max was dead, and that was that. I went home each night to an empty house, eating little and drinking more scotch than I should. I experienced fits of melancholy. Before I found myself in a black hole too deep to climb out, I paid a visit to the only person who gave a damn about me.

*

"Friedrich, it's been too long. I didn't know when I would see you next."

Kitty Schmidt owned the best brothel in Berlin: Pension Schmidt. I found her behind the bar inspecting crystal glasses for smudges. Kitty was bedecked in a low-cut red gown trimmed with black fringes. She made no effort to hide her ample figure. For me, Kitty was ageless. Both mother and mistress to men who entered her salon, Kitty listened to their stories, heard their confessions, consoled them, nurtured them, and provided pleasure as they wanted . . . and needed. Her "staff" of young women was among Berlin's best. Years back, I worked here as a bouncer in a job Max had arranged for me.

"Every time I thought I would stop by something got in the way."

"That is a poor excuse, Friedrich. You and I know each other too long to make up stories."

"The truth is that there are too many memories here."

"Speaking of which, have you visited the cemetery? It helps. When I go, I talk to Max. Tell him how much I miss him. How the business is doing. How Marta is managing the Nightingale. Before I leave, I place a rock on his headstone. That's a Jewish custom, you know. It feels good. Like leaving a piece of me to let him know I was there."

"I tried once. I got as far as the entrance but turned around. In a way, living in his house, I feel trapped in his coffin."

Kitty touched my arm. "He wanted you to have it because he loved you."

"I'll visit his grave one day. Just not now."

I looked at the piano in the corner and felt a pang of nostalgia. "Anybody play it?"

"A few wanted to, but I discouraged them. They weren't you."

Then she added with a mischievous twinkle, "You know, Friedrich, the ones from the early days miss you, too."

"It's been almost fifteen years. Who would remember me?"

We both knew the answer: Marta Feidt. Marta and I were a number back then. Kitty should have known better than to try to open that door. When I didn't express an interest, she said, "Friedrich, you can hardly keep your eyes open. Your face is drawn. Haggard. From the looks of it, I bet you're not sleeping much. And you are certainly not eating. Your ribs are poking out. Wait here."

"Ever the Mama Hen. When are you going to stop taking care of me, Kitty?"

"When you find yourself a *Fräulein*, and not a minute before," she said over her shoulder.

In no time, a plate of cheese and crackers appeared before me. I nibbled something dry. Without thinking, I washed it down with scotch. I stared at nothing. Lost in memories that were no longer relevant.

Sitting there, I realized that only Kitty remained from the few I held dear. Max was gone. Lilian Harvey, whom I deeply loved, abandoned Germany and me for Hollywood the month Hitler became chancellor. Not three months later, Bernhard Weiss fled to Prague and then on to London. The fact that I might not see the smallish man with his big spectacles again—who performed giant-sized acts of courage standing up against the Nazis when few dared—left a big hole in me. Kitty snapped me back.

"Friedrich, what is eating at you?"

What is eating at my soul is that Max was tortured to death and his murderers have gone unpunished.

I pulled myself together.

"I'm concerned about you, Kitty. About the salon. About the Nightingale. How is it doing?"

"Business could not be better. Max's club is busier than ever, though I must admit, I don't much care for the clientele these days. And as for Pension Schmidt, brothels never go out of style."

We touched glasses.

"Your successes are a testimony to your business skills." As I said it, something nagged me. Then I remembered. "What are you doing with your money these days?"

"What I've always done: turn it into foreign currencies and send it to banks in safe countries."

I took her hand. "*Who* is taking your money to those banks? Jews, right?"

"They're the only ones I trust."

"Those days are about to end. You need to rethink this."

She pulled back. "What are you talking about?"

"Can't you see the handwriting on the wall? Jews can no longer work for the government."

"You made them keep the ones who served in the war."

"Only until Hindenburg died. Then they were out, too. Now Jews cannot own or work on farms. Germans treated by Jewish doctors will no longer be covered under national health insurance. The future is here, Kitty. There are more laws being written to push the Jews out of Germany as we speak. It is only a matter of time before they won't be allowed to travel. Carrying your money will be out of the question."

The more I described the plight of German Jews, the tighter she gripped the bar until her knuckles turned white.

"Will they send them to the camps like the Communists and the Jehovah's Witnesses?"

"That's not in the plans. Hitler's goal is to make the Jews so miserable that they leave."

Then, ever practical, Kitty turned to the future. "If the Jews are on the way out, who can I trust with my money?"

"That's why I brought it up."

As she heaved a sigh, her ample bosoms rose and fell. "There's no choice then. I will have to start moving the money myself."

I was afraid she would say that . . . but held my peace.

Chapter 2

Berlin, 1935

When Max died, I promised to avenge his death. Yet there I was, a few months later and I had not lifted a finger to even get the names of the men who murdered him. The talk with Kitty helped. It spotlighted what bothered me: I had not moved on my promise. That was about to change. It was time to visit Franz Gürtner, the minister of justice.

Gürtner was a throwback to the nineteenth century in both manner and dress. He wore a black, three-piece suit. His starched, white shirt sported wing-tip collars usually reserved for formal wear. A patterned tie peeked out from under his vest. Frameless pince-nez glasses with round lenses, perched over a graying mustache, gave him an owl-like appearance.

"What can I do for you, *Herr Obergruppenführer?*"

"Franz, I'm not in uniform. Besides, we've known each other a long time. Friedrich works just fine."

He smiled. "What brings you here, Friedrich?"

"I never commended you for standing up to Goebbels and Göring. If they had their way, the Reichstag Fire Trial would have been moved to a court that would have delivered the verdict they sought."

Gürtner shrugged. "The law is clear. Matters of treason against the state must be before the Supreme Court. But you didn't come here to compliment me. What's bothering you, Friedrich?"

"It's the guards in the concentration camps. Especially Dachau. Their commandant, Eicke, encourages them to take the law into their own hands. He allows them to beat prisoners without limits. If they die, no one is held accountable. Their criminal conduct is under your jurisdiction! What can be done to stop them?"

Gürtner steepled his fingers. "I share your concern, Friedrich. But there is nothing I can do."

I leaned closer. "Franz, how can you say that? You are the minister of justice. This is under your dominion. You must stop this brutality."

"Don't you think I tried? I am as sick of this as you are. When I became aware of the situation in the various camps, I wrote Deputy *Führer* Hess. Here . . ." He fumbled through the papers on his desk. "Here it is."

He read the letter out loud.

> There are numerous instances of mistreatment which have come to the Administration of Justice that can be divided into three different causes. Beating as disciplinary punishment in concentration camps. Beating political prisoners to make them talk. And cruel treatment of internees for sheer fun or sadism.

"All three describe Eicke and his men at Dachau," I said.

"If it were only just Dachau. It's pervasive in all the camps."

The letter wobbled in his fingers before he resumed reading. "'The tormenting of prisoners for fun is an insult to every German sensibility!'" Gürtner flung the letter aside.

"You could not have been clearer. What happened?"

Gürtner turned solemn. "Reinhard Heydrich is what happened. He paid me a visit." Referencing the feared and hated Heydrich brought back a host of memories. I was at Heinrich Himmler's chicken farm in 1931 when Himmler offered Heydrich a position in the SS. The fact that I was reluctant to support Himmler's decision created a tension that still exists between Heydrich and me. I will never forget the last day of the Röhm Putsch when Heydrich insisted that I accompany him to the Lichterfelde Military Academy. Delight danced in Heydrich's eyes as he explained how scores of Brown Shirts were lined up, four at a time, before a firing squad against the courtyard wall. When I puked at the clumps of flesh and bone stuck to the brick wall, Heydrich laughed as he offered his handkerchief to wipe the retch from my mouth. The man was an enigma: a skilled musician, world-class fencer, and accomplished sailor cloaked in civilized clothing that delighted in inflicting pain.

"I know Heydrich," I replied dryly.

"Well, *Gruppenführer* Heydrich made it perfectly clear that *SS* judges appointed by *Reichsführer* Himmler would deal with all questions of wrongdoing in the camps."

"What about past cases?"

Gürtner threw up his hands. "Closed. Friedrich, I did all I could. The Gestapo runs the camps and German law does not apply to them. It is that simple."

I left Gürtner with a new clarity: If the men who beat Max to death were to be held accountable, I would have to do it. But first, I needed their names. I reached out to Bernhard Weiss, the former head of the Berlin Police, now exiled in London where he ran a printing shop.

*

It took three tries before I succeeded.

"Where were you this morning?" I asked.

"I can't be expected to be in my shop every minute of the day," Bernhard answered. "I had to deal with a vendor who wants me to pay for inventory that arrived damaged. Now what was so important that you tried to reach me three times before noon?"

I explained that no matter what avenue I pursued, I could not discover the identity of the guards that killed Max.

"Why not go to Himmler?"

"And ask him what? 'I need the name of the guards involved in the death of a Jew so minister of justice Gürtner can prosecute them?' That is the last thing he would ever do. Please help me, Bernhard."

What choice did I have? I had to lie to one friend to avenge the death of the other.

"It won't be easy, you know. I like to save my currency for bigger matters, but . . ." he sighed, "since this is about Max . . . I may be able to get one name, if that."

*

Life went on while I waited to hear from Bernhard. One win-ter's night, settled in my favorite chair before a blazing fire with a glass of *Lemberger* wine, I was about to crack open F. Scott Fitzgerald's *Tender is the Night*—I had begun reading books in English during my many transatlantic crossings—when the phone jangled.

"Why aren't you here with me?" The woman's voice was soft and sultry. And very familiar.

"Maybe I prefer reading a good book."

"Is that any way to treat an old lover? You'd rather be between the pages than between the sheets?"

"Marta, I know we barely spoke at Max's funeral . . ."

"Barely?" she cut me off. "You didn't even say hello. You rushed past me like I had leprosy."

"I'm sorry."

"You should be." She cleared her throat. "Friedrich, I took a chance calling you. You could be with someone. If you are, please excuse me."

The last time Marta and I were an item was thirteen years ago. Her fury still stung after I left her for the film star, Lilian Harvey.

I stroked the book cover and glanced at my wine. "My friends won't mind. To what do I owe the pleasure of this call?"

"I know how much you love music. There's a private club located in a factory that used to be owned by a Jew who left Germany. Tonight, they are highlighting fantastic musicians you would appreciate. Come with me. It will be like the old days when the great performers put their shows on in the underground cafés. That's how Max got his start. Remember?"

I was torn between wanting to go . . . and not giving her false hope.

"Who are the musicians?"

There was a time when I was as familiar with musicians tour-ing Germany as I was those featured in New York's Cotton Club or other city nightspots.

"Let that be a surprise. Are you game?"

I was.

As it turned out, the abandoned warehouse was near the famous UFA studios where I had worked scripting movie scores. UFA was Germany's answer to Hollywood. Those were happy days, rubbing shoulders with actors and directors, and making my small contribution to the burgeoning film industry.

I found Marta standing under a lamppost near the entrance. Shadows cast across her face made her more exotic than I remembered. Still lithesome, she wore a colorful, silk flower print, with a revealing neckline. "Time has been kind to you," I said.

"Is that supposed to be a compliment? I will pretend it is . . . otherwise, we are starting off on the wrong foot."

I hugged her. "It's been too long."

She looked up at me. "Whose fault is that?"

The club door opened at that moment and a jazz riff escaped, punctuated by a soaring clarinet.

My head snapped back at Marta. "Is that who I think it is? Stefan Weintraub, Horst Graff, Friedrich Hollaender? I know them and the rest of their gang! I was at the studio when the Weintraub Syncopators performed in *The Blue Angel* with Dietrich. They're amazing. I would never imagine them still in Germany."

Marta slipped her arm through mine. "This is their last performance. Then they leave for good. Now you understand why I called."

The night was glorious. Everyone in the smoke-filled room stomped and clapped and hooted as the band members, outfitted in black tuxedos, took turns soloing and stoking notes with unbridled passion. They were musical gladiators, challenging each other to do better.

Then a gunshot exploded from the back. The musicians stopped playing; the audience froze; some dropped to the floor. I popped out of my chair to see three drunk, black-clad *SS* men near the back wall, weaving on rubbery legs.

"Shame on you!" one shouted. "Shame on all of you for listening to this *Juden Negermusik*!" He fired another shot in the air. "*Raus!*" he shouted, "Everyone out!"

I touched Marta's shoulder to stay low. I whipped out my *Ausweis* bearing my photo in my *SS* general's uniform and stepped toward them. I stopped in front of the lout with the pistol. He was an *Oberscharführer*, a staff sergeant. His sidekicks were *Rottenführers*. Corporals.

I yelled, "*Obergruppenführer* Richard! Attention!" I thrust my card into his face. When the gun-wielding *SS* man leaned for a better view, I let my *Ausweis* slip to the floor. As he reached, I wrenched the weapon out of his hand and drove a left into his jaw. He collapsed like a sack of potatoes.

I wagged the gun at the other two. Bleary-eyed, they clicked their heels and made a feeble attempt to salute. They slurred, "Heil, Hitler!" I ejected the clip, vacated the round in the chamber, and pitched the pistol to the closest one, who fumbled it and had to pick it up off the floor.

"Help your Sergeant stand," I thundered. "Get the hell out of here before I take your IDs."

I signaled for the band to start playing . . . which they did. But the mood was broken; joy had left the room.

*

When we got to her front door, Marta took my hand. "Care to refresh your memory?"

Marta was beautiful. Her skin was candescent; she needed little makeup. Her smile was warm and inviting. It had been too long since I had been with a woman. I was tempted. But I knew it would be a mistake to go back. It could never be the same.

When I made no effort to step toward her building, she squeezed my hand. "We had a good thing, Friedrich. I know we could have it again . . . if we just tried."

I took her by the shoulders. "Now is not the right time."

She frowned. "The Nazis ruined it before for us. Don't let that happen again."

"As much as it would be easy to blame the Nazis, it's me. I am not in a good place."

"You can't mourn Max forever. Or is it Lilian?"

I hiked up my shoulders. "I wish I knew."

She touched my face, kissed my cheek, and walked away without another word.

*

Bernhard Weiss delivered. He had a name: Felix Querner. "I was told he didn't act alone," Bernhard said. "But this will get Gürtner started."

I did not like keeping up the deception, but that ship had sailed.

My next step was to request the file of every guard at Dachau under the pretext that I was looking for a personal driver . . . one that was tough. The next day, four boxes were delivered to my office. I thumbed through the personal folders until I came across Querner's. Querner had a violent past. He fought in the trenches during the war, rising to sergeant, and then joined the Freikorps and the Brown Shirts after that. He stood six-foot-five, almost as tall as me, with a thick purple scar that ran from his jawline to the corner of his right eye.

Most importantly, I had his address. Querner lived alone.

I flew to Munich the next day, rented a car, and drove straight to the Hofbräuhaus where I ordered schnitzel and a stein. As I ate, I mulled over where and how it would be best to confront Querner. I spent the next three days reconnoitering and studying his habits. By the fourth day, I was ready.

Querner lived in a small cottage on a dead-end street bounded by woods. I parked my rented car where I would need it later and made the long trek to his house. As I circled to the rear, I saw a light burning in the kitchen. According to his routine, I would not have long to wait. On schedule, a splash of light erupted when the back door swung open. His large silhouette plodded onto the grass. He struck a match. Embers from a cigarette blazed orange. Querner took a long drag before snatching the bag of garbage at his feet as he had done each night before.

Querner dumped the bag, stamped out the cigarette, and slipped inside. Only after I heard the click of the lock did I bang on the door with my gun drawn.

The door cracked open. "What the hell do you want?" He opened it wide enough for me to see part of his head but all of his gun.

I holstered my pistol and stepped back. "I didn't mean to startle you, but no one answered when I knocked on the front door. I saw the light and came around back."

"Now that you found me, who are you and what do you want?"

I flipped open my ID. "I am *Obergruppenführer* Friedrich Richard."

He compared the picture to me. Satisfied, he said, "An *SS* General . . . at this hour?"

"May I come in?"

He lowered his gun and pulled the door open. The moment I stepped over the wooden threshold, I lowered my shoulder and knocked him down. His gun lay beside him. I kicked it out of reach, flipped the door closed with one hand, and leveled my pistol at him with the other. "Don't do anything foolish, Querner. Get up. Slowly. Keep your hands where I can see them."

I motioned to a kitchen chair; he glared as he sat down.

"What's this about?" His eyes flitted about, searching for something he could use as a weapon.

I edged back. Out of reach.

"How many have you killed at Dachau, Felix?"

"You got it wrong, *Obergruppenführer*. We don't kill inmates at Dachau."

I tapped my forehead. "I forgot. You call them 'escapees.'"

"'Attempted escapees.' None succeed. What about them?"

"What do you call beating a man to death? Thwarting an escape?"

Querner grinned. "Rest assured, if we beat them, they deserved it."

"Max Klinghofer. Do you remember him?"

"The fat man that waddled like a penguin. What about him? Why the questions?"

"He was my friend."

"He was a Jew." He chewed his lower lip. Squinting. Calculating.

Without warning, he rammed the table toward me and cannonballed for my legs. I jumped to the side, pressed against the wall for leverage, and kicked hard. My boot caught his ear, tearing the bottom free. Blood poured down his neck. More agile than he looked, he lunged up like a coiled spring. I stiff-armed him with my left hand and clocked him on the temple with the gun in my right. He went down in a heap.

I leveled the gun at his face. "No more stupidity, Querner. Stand up!"

He gripped the edge of the porcelain sink and pulled himself up. As he did, he gazed at a kitchen knife alongside a half-sliced apple.

"Don't even think about it."

With my pistol aimed at his chest, I retrieved his gun and slipped it into my waistband. I righted the table and arranged the chairs in place. He watched me housekeep with a puzzled expression. I snatched his house and car keys off a wall peg and ordered him to turn around. "Right hand on your head. Open the back door with your left. Nice and slow."

"Where are we going?"

I shoved the gun into the small of his back. "For a ride. Now march." As we passed out of the driveway, I ordered, "Stop!" I locked the back door. "Okay. Move!"

When he got to his car, he asked. "Now what?"

"Either you squeeze into the trunk or sit in the back, cuffed."

"I'm too big for the *der Kofferraum*." He started toward me. I cocked the gun hammer. "There is a third choice."

He backed off.

"Wise decision. Hands."

Querner stuck his hands out to be handcuffed. "Behind you." I cuffed him, then guided him onto the back seat. "Do you have rope?"

"In the boot," he muttered.

I tied his feet in a figure eight, and then looped the end through the springs in the seat. When he complained it was tight, I tugged harder. I gagged him with a dirty rag from the boot. Fifteen minutes later, I parked next to the rental car I had left at Lake Walchensee . . . which happens to be one of the deepest lakes in Germany. I untied Querner's legs and maneuvered him out of the car. It was close to midnight. Not a soul in sight.

I pointed to a nearby rowboat tied to a post, jabbed the gun hard into his back, and ordered him to get in.

*

Still handcuffed, Querner faced me. I rowed, guided by the light of an almost full moon. Soon, my arms and shoulders burned from fatigue. At the center of the lake, I eased the oars into the boat. With gun in hand, I tugged the gag out of his mouth.

He tried to spit at me but only managed a string of drool onto his chin.

"What the fuck is this about? Why did you bring me here?"

"I want to tell you a story, Felix. It's about my friend Max Klinghofer."

"You could've told me at my house. There's no need for all of this . . . this . . . drama."

"I wanted to make certain I had your attention, Felix. Do I? Do I have your attention?"

He grunted.

"I will take that as a 'Yes.' When I'm done, Felix, there is one question you must answer."

"Fuck you."

"Good. I am glad we agree on something."

Whether Felix listened or not, I explained how wonderful Max had been to me. "He was like a father."

Felix jerked straighter. "Enough with your bullshit. What are you going to do to me?"

"I wanted you to hear how much I loved and respected Max Klinghofer."

"Okay, you sonofabitch. I listened. Had your jollies? Now take the fucking cuffs off."

"It's your turn."

"To do what?"

I waived the key. "Answer my question. Tell me what I want to know."

He huffed. "Get on with it."

"What is the name of the other guard who worked Max over with you?"

"Why do you want to know?"

"Because I want to have a private conversation with him . . . the same as I'm having with you."

"Do I have to sit like this on the way back, too?"

"You do . . . if you don't tell me what I want to hear."

"If I tell you, promise to undo the cuffs?"

"I said I would."

Once he gave me Jüttner's name, I helped Querner to his feet, careful not to rock the boat . . . which was a bit of challenge. With an abundance of caution, I grabbed his right hand in a vise-like grip, unlocked the cuffs, and then in a swift motion shoved him out of the boat. By the time he surfaced, his house and car keys were sinking to the bottom of the lake and I had rowed ten feet away.

"Help me, you bastard! I told you what you wanted to know!"

Even a champion swimmer could not avoid the hypothermia that would soon overwhelm his systems. His cries for help and gurgled coughs diminished with each stroke of the oars. Finally, the shrieks stopped.

I eased up on the rowing, content to let the boat glide through the water. Aided by the moon's blue-white light, I aimed for the parked cars. As I neared, I snagged the mooring post, stepped out, maneuvered the boat around, and pushed it back toward the middle of the lake. I grabbed a bottle of scotch from my car, emptied it into the lake, and ditched it on Querner's front seat. Whenever his car was discovered, the report would say Querner was a fool for taking a boat out late at night, especially after polishing off a bottle of liquor. The conclusion: Querner fell overboard and drowned.

An unfortunate accident.

I searched about for prying eyes before I slipped into my rental car. Comforted that I was very much alone, I returned to Munich knowing I was halfway to avenging Max's death . . . and was equipped with the other name I needed. Prudence counseled that I wait until Querner's "accident" was old and cold. That did not trouble me at all. In fact, I was quite content, for the time being.

Chapter 3

When I returned to my office in the Reich Chancellery, I found a note on my desk that my name had come up during a Gestapo interrogation. The message was three days old. I called Gestapo Headquarters to learn that Lilian Harvey had returned to Germany and been detained overnight. She had since been released to her room at the Hotel Adlon.

I called the hotel not knowing if she would be in. She answered.

"I heard about the questioning."

"That's how you say hello after all these years?" she said.

"Sorry. Hello. Are you all right?"

"I am. Thanks for asking." Then she explained. "They were fishing for names. Which actors and directors were Jewish, which were homosexuals, which were not."

"What did you tell them?"

"Hadn't the foggiest. Then they had the audacity to ask about any I might have slept with. At least *then* I would know which of them were Jewish. The pigs!"

"I'm glad it was nothing more serious than that."

"That's serious enough. I had to spend the night in the basement prison. A certain *SS* general I know was apparently in no hurry to get me out of Gestapo hands."

"Do you really think I would have abandoned you if I knew you were there? I was out of town when they picked you up. More to the point, why didn't you call to tell me you were coming back? If you had, none of this would have happened."

"If you can bear the truth, I thought about calling . . . for at least five seconds. I decided it would be a mistake."

"Avoidance is no way to treat an old friend."

She made a scornful sound. "Friend? I can't be a friend to a high-ranking Nazi. Those days are over."

"Are you forgetting that I never joined the Party? I have never been a Nazi and never will be."

"Friedrich. You always were delusional. People are judged by the friends they keep. When you associate with the likes of Himmler, Heydrich, Göring, and Goebbels, and the pack leader is your pal Adolf, how do you think people view you?"

"I'm no Nazi, Lilian." To prevent a snippy retort, I added, "You know I've followed your career in Hollywood."

"There wasn't much to follow."

I glanced at my watch. "Look. If you're not doing anything, how about a drink at the hotel bar?"

"Why not? For old time's sake."

*

I left the Chancellery building, went home, changed out of my uniform, showered, and slipped on a white shirt, gray gabardine slacks, and a navy cashmere blazer. I checked myself in the mirror. I wanted to look my best. I still adored her.

I hopped out of the taxi and saw the boutique next to the Hotel Adlon. I wondered if the Jewish owner was still there. After two years, Lilian could wait a few minutes.

"Excuse me," I said to the salesperson, "is *Herr* Oser-Braun available?"

"Whom shall I say is asking?"

"Friedrich Richard. We had dinner together one New Year's Eve. He should remember me."

She gave me a thorough once-over before smiling, "I am sure he will. Please wait here, *Herr* Richard."

Moments later, a smallish man in his thirties, balding, and sporting black-rimmed glasses, approached.

"Friedrich Richard," he said, "of course I remember you. It was at Max Klinghofer's Nightingale Club." Then he made a ticking sound. "Too bad about Max. He was a dear friend."

"I didn't see you at the funeral."

"I couldn't chance that the Gestapo lurked about taking names. What brings you here?"

"Lilian Harvey. She's staying next door."

"She's already been in. Her order will be ready tomorrow."

"Tell me, *Herr* Oser-Braun, is Hermann Kaufmann still in business?"

Oser-Braun made a sour face. "I don't know for how much longer. When the Nazis took over, the Gestapo put pressure on him to sell. Kaufmann was *Theaterkunst* and *Theaterkunst* was him. No one could support the film industry with costumes the way Hermann did. He wouldn't sell out to the Nazis, so Goebbels installed a crony of his, a man named Stahlberg, to run the domestic side of Kaufmann's business. Kaufmann was left to supply foreign films."

"How did that work out?"

"To Goebbels's embarrassment, not a year later, the domestic side faltered."

"Did Kaufmann get his business back?"

"Not exactly. Goebbels picked a trade executive to run the business with Kaufmann's wife. She's a Gentile. I donated plenty of money to Hitler's elections. I thought he would leave businesses like Kaufmann's and mine alone. But that's not the case. One-by-one, we are forced to sell and leave Germany. Remember Martin Breslauer? The antiquarian? He was the smart one. He got out with his inventory *and* money. Made it to America. I wish I had listened to him that night."

I remembered Breslauer. "What about you, *Herr* Oser-Braun? Do you have a plan?"

He shrugged. "Stay, until I can't take it any longer."

I wanted to tell him to get out while he could. It was going to get worse. But I didn't have the stomach to help the Nazis drive him out . . . even if it would be doing him a favor.

"I understand." We shook hands. "Stay safe."

*

I found Lilian at the hotel bar and as beautiful as ever. "Sorry I'm late."

I leaned to kiss her; she pulled back.

"Were you delayed by one of your goose-stepping pals? Run another errand for the *Führer?*"

"Come on, Lilian. We haven't seen each other in over two years and the first thing you do is antagonize. Why the animus? You know they are not *my* people."

"The truth hurts, doesn't it, Friedrich? You may not be a card-carrying member but in my eyes, you are. When it finally sunk into my thick skull that you were going to jump every time Hitler called, I knew there was no hope for us."

I stood there trying to decide if she was playing tough or really meant what she said.

Lilian had a glass of bubbly. I motioned to the bartender. "Scotch, please. Neat." I slipped onto the seat next to her. "Why did you come back? Your pictures did okay."

"Okay doesn't hack it in Hollywood. They had their own stars. Jean Harlow. Carole Lombard. Ginger Rogers. Then there's the gal right behind them that took my part when I balked at doing another movie: Fay Wray. The competition in Hollywood is fierce. I was no one special there. Not like in Germany."

"Is there a project for you here?"

She nodded. "I have the lead in *Schwarze Rosen.* Are you familiar with *Black Roses?*"

"Lilian?" I touched her hand; she moved it away.

"Don't try to start anything. I loved you. We were great together. But you didn't love me enough to stop pandering to your *Führer's* whims."

"I . . . I . . ."

"Let me finish. I seriously doubt anything has changed. In fact, I know it hasn't. So, should we cross paths again, please say hello. Kiss me on the cheek, if you want, but know that my feelings for you can never be rekindled. Not ever." She eased off the stool. "Don't ever forget, Friedrich, you were the one who destroyed us. You blew a good thing."

Chapter 4

Two weeks later, an agitated Adolf Hitler called me to his office.

"What do I have to do to get the army's support?" His arms flapped in frustration.

I stood by as Hitler paced back and forth in his expansive office in the Chancellery building, hands clasped behind him.

He pivoted toward me as if pleading before a judge. "The general staff wanted me to get rid of Röhm, one of my oldest followers. I did. They wanted me to strip away the power of the *SA*, so the army did not feel threatened. I did that, too."

He paced again. Mumbling. Waving his arms.

He stopped. "The German people elected *me Führer*. The army leaders swore their oaths to *me*, not to Germany." He struck his chest; it made a loud thump. "To *me*! And now they question *my* judgment!" he thundered. "Can't they see that *my* judgment has been perfect!?"

I remained motionless, hands at my sides. When he got this way, it was best to let his wrath run its course.

Everything he said was true. Two hundred Brown-shirted *SA* heads did roll. All opposition to Hitler and the army were eliminated. The fact that Hitler added a few other names to settle old scores from the past did not spoil the satisfaction the army got in bringing the *SA* to heel.

And it was also true that, five weeks later, when President Hindenburg died, Hitler demanded a plebiscite to validate his position as leader of Germany. The result was a near-unanimous election of Hitler as dictator, with the right to be called *Führer*. It was then that every member of the armed forces swore a personal oath to him . . . rather than to Germany.

I waited for the *Führer's* tantrum to end. When it did, his look softened. He smiled. "Come, Friedrich. Sit with me."

I slid onto one of two upholstered club chairs; Hitler took the other.

He wiped sweat from his brow. His flushed face returned to its normal pallor. He took a sip of water.

I knew what this was about. Soon after becoming the *Führer*, Hitler began to restore lands taken from Germany by the Treaty of Versailles. He regained the valuable Saar Valley with its coal mines through a successful vote of its people who wanted to return to German rule. Then, against the advice of his military leaders, Hitler ordered the German army to march into the Rhineland, calculating that little more than noise would be raised by the victors. Again, he was right. But his adventurism was not over. He miscalculated the general staff's reaction to his wanting to increase the size of the army plus other ambitions they knew he harbored.

Then, in his everyday voice, which few knew was barely above a whisper, he said, "We will soon announce that we have reinstated conscription. The German army must be comparable in size to other European powers, if not larger. I could not help reacting the way I just did. The two Werners balked at how many divisions I expect them to create. 'Too soon,' they said. 'Too many. The French will object to our violating the Versailles Treaty. They could possibly attack.'" He mimicked their voices as he spoke. Few knew Hitler was a great impersonator.

General Field Marshal Werner von Blomberg, minister of war, and Colonel General Werner von Fritsch, the Army's commander-in-chief, were cautious, thoughtful veterans of the Great War. They knew war's horrors firsthand and wanted to avoid them.

"What did you tell Blomberg and Fritsch?" I asked.

"Leave foreign diplomacy to me."

"*Mein Führer*." The days of informally calling him Wolf were far and few between. "The French surround us with a ring of security to protect themselves. They continue to negotiate a Non-Aggression Pact with Russia. We will be pressed from both directions."

Hitler shook his head. "It will be a token piece of paper between two nations that amounts to nothing. Mark my words, Friedrich: Germany will soon be on top again, as long as the military lets me do what I want."

"Why wouldn't Blomberg and Fritsch want the *Reichswehr* to grow? They've supported you until now."

"For reasons I can't explain, they've turned into old ladies afraid to venture a toe into the cold water because it might sting a bit."

"They'll come around."

"One way or another . . ." Hitler motioned me closer. "I have two things to tell you. Both delicate." I leaned toward him. "In the event anything happens to me, I have named Göring as my successor. It can be no other."

"Why do this now? You're only forty-five."

Every time his voice grew hoarse, Hitler feared he had throat cancer. No matter how many times his doctors reassured him he did not, Hitler doubted them.

He loosened his collar. "I don't know how long I have. I need to know that I left a succession plan that guarantees the Reich will continue for one thousand years."

"Did you consider any of the others?"

"Who else is there? Himmler is basically a policeman. Goebbels would be a reasonable choice but cannot keep his fly buttoned. That is no way for a leader to behave."

What was that about glass houses and throwing stones? How many scrapes had I gotten Hitler out of with teenage girls? Even now, he pretended to be celibate while carrying on with Eva Braun. The man lived within clouded and false optics.

Hitler continued. "Then there is Rudy Hess. He has the title of deputy *Führer* but we both know Rudy is incapable of doing anything meaningful."

"That leaves Hermann," I said.

"Precisely," Hitler answered.

Hermann Göring *was* the logical choice. He had exhibited great organizational skills from the moment he joined the Party in 1922. Over the years, Göring amassed titles like an avid car collector. As he gained weight, his ostentatious uniforms became a broader and broader canvas for his many decorations. He, more than anyone else in the Nazi inner circle, had the ability to follow Hitler's grand scheme.

"Let's hope none of this comes to pass," I said.

He cleared his throat and swallowed. "There *is* something else. As we discussed, the general staff has turned timorous. I will not let them stand in my way."

"What do you want from me?"

"Poke around, Friedrich. Spend time with them. Find out who is truly loyal and who is going through the motions."

I raised my hand. "Say no more. I will need some official position . . . or the generals won't deal with me."

"They have already been informed," he smiled. "Liaison to the *Führer*."

For the first time in a long while, I left Hitler with a lighter step. In the early years when I believed in him, I raised money from wealthy industrialists for his cause. I helped avert scandals that could have ruined Hitler and the Party. But once Hitler's agenda became a reality, I could no longer rationalize my participation and, instead, carried a burden of guilt. Now, Hitler handed me the means to help defeat him.

I ignored the flourish of *Sieg Heil's* by the guards as I exited the Chancellery building, lost in how pleased Bernhard Weiss would be when he learned of my new position.

*

That evening, sleep eluded me. I tossed and turned as I played out possible encounters my dual roles now opened to me. When the black of night yielded to hues of dark purple, its edges tinged with reds, there was no longer any point to remaining in bed. During my convalescence in Pasewalk Hospital, I learned I was a marksman. Shooting had become a tonic for me. I slipped on pants and a shirt and headed for the firing range.

Wannsee, a suburb of Berlin fenced in by lakes on one side and Düppel Woods on the other, offered boating marinas, beaches for swimming, a golf course, and a shooting range where I kept a Walther PP under lock and key.

By the time I left the clubhouse, the sky had given way to the warm glow of an early, yolk-colored sun. The air was filled with the scent of pine and the chatter of birds. Just then, the tranquil setting was punctured by the *pop-pop-pop* of what sounded like a 9mm Luger. Apparently, I wasn't the only one who wanted to use the range before it got busy.

I snatched a small pair of binoculars from my leather case and saw that the shooter flirted around the edge of the bull's-eye . . . but never a clean hit within. Respectable, but nothing more.

Instinct took over. I raised my gun and fired five rounds at the stranger's target from where I stood. When I neared the station, I was surprised to find Reinhard Heydrich.

"I didn't know you shot, Friedrich."

Reinhard Heydrich, the prototypic Aryan, tall, blond hair, blue eyes, lean of torso, but too wide on the bottom—projecting the image of an oversized gourd—was now Himmler's trusted right-hand man. His leadership in the "Night of the Long Knives" massacre earned his promotion to *Gruppenführer*, just one rank below me. A rabid anti-Semite, he intended to rise much, much further. And from my perspective, at just thirty-two years of age, he would.

He motioned to my hits on his target. "Five rounds, three in the bull's-eyes and one dead center. Impressive . . . except for the fifth. That one missed entirely."

Without a word, I hopped around the safety barrier. Then, standing so Heydrich had a clear view of what I was doing, I took out a penknife and dug the dead-centered bullet from the bull's-eye. Then I removed another . . . from the same hole. I handed Heydrich both bullets, gloating as his condescending grin faded from this effeminate face.

"There is your missing one, Reinhard. For the record, I was five-for-five." I glanced back at the target, "You, on the other hand, need more practice."

"My shots were close enough to do damage."

"I was never satisfied with close enough. But why here? There are shooting ranges nearer where you live."

His frown vanished. "You know I'm in charge of the '36 Olympics. The shooting events will be held here at Wannsee." He pointed. "The running part of the pentathlon will take place on the golf course next door."

I could not let him have his moment. "What about Jewish athletes? I hear we must have them."

His poise faltered. "That's a bit touchy. We are trying to work something out that satisfies all parties."

"You mean you've been told 'No Jews, no Olympics'?"

"We're not at that stage yet. We'll come up with something." Reinhard continued. "In the meantime, I understand you are the new liaison between the *Führer* and the *Wehrmacht*."

"Now that you bring it up, what can you tell me about the *Abwehr*? I've had little experience with them."

"The *Abwehr* is the *Wehrmacht's* department that deals with espionage and counterespionage."

"You deal with spies and traitors as head of the *SD*. How is the *Abwehr* different than the *Sicherheitsdienst*?"

Heydrich's thin lips curled upward in what was, for him, a smile. "The lines are pretty clear: internal versus external. My *SD* functions as the intelligence agency for the *SS*. We investigate all internal matters in Germany. The *Abwehr*, on the other hand, has the sole responsibility for all military installations, military espionage, and counterespionage. Essentially, everything outside of Germany that pertains to our integrity, our enemies, and our defense."

"If you and Himmler run the *SS* and the police, who runs the *Abwehr*?"

"Admiral Wilhelm Canaris. He and I go back to the time I trained as a cadet in the Navy; he was first officer on the ship. He's good at his craft."

"Now that I'm the special liaison, the admiral sounds like someone I should meet."

"You're in luck, Friedrich. The admiral's wife, Erika, has a string quartet. Next Sunday, I am filling in as second violin chair. We're playing Hadyn and Mozart. I know you're an accomplished pianist. I'll make certain you are invited. You'll meet Canaris and enjoy the concert at the same time."

"I just might be there."

___

Chapter 5

Bernhard Weiss was delighted to learn that I had been appointed special liaison to Hitler.

"This is the break I have been praying for," he said. "As liaison, you have permission to poke into every corner of the military, ask questions, and learn if there are others who share our view."

"Heydrich has unwittingly given us a shove in the right direction by getting me invited to Admiral Canaris's house."

"Canaris is smart. Crafty. Never underestimate a man who heads a spy agency."

"But is he a man of honor?"

"As in 'honor among thieves'? I can't answer that. I never met him. Keep in mind that he is the master of espionage. Use caution until you take measure of the man yourself."

*

As fate would have it, I arrived late. I stood on the front steps of Canaris's sumptuous house in the Charlottenburg section of Berlin, not wanting to interrupt the finale to Haydn's String Quartet Opus 76 Number 3 that seeped into the street. The music was superb.

When the piece ended, I reached for the brass knocker. A butler ushered me inside. Erika Canaris greeted me with her violin cradled under her left arm.

"I am so glad you could make it, *Herr* Richard. Unfortunately, your timing was a bit off. We just finished. But we will do this another evening."

"And I will make certain to be on time. I got derailed by a project that took longer than expected. Please accept my apology."

"It's the world we live in. Let me introduce you to the others." She grabbed my hand. "Of course, you know Reinhard."

I nodded. Heydrich stood next to a man shorter but with similar features. Erika continued, "This is his brother, Heinz. Heinz plays the viola but considers himself more a composer. And here is the last member of our quartet, the esteemed Hugo Becker." Becker bowed as we shook hands. "Hugo is the cello professor at the *Hochschule für Musik* in Berlin. Look at his beautiful cello. It's a Stradivarius."

"From 1719," added Becker. He cradled the fingerboard with his right arm, as if he and the cello were a couple.

Frau Canaris was quick to add, "He has two Strads."

The fact that anyone had one Stradivarius was monumental. Two boggled the mind.

Wilhelm Canaris ambled to my side. He was small. No more than five-foot-two. His head came up to the middle of my chest. He had silver-white hair and a narrow face with a nose that tilted upward, as if he were sniffing secrets from thin air. As a student, he was nicknamed *Kieker* (peeper) because he had an insatiable curiosity and an encyclopedic knowledge of all things obscure. A keen observer, his eyes flitted about, absorbing the way people stood, spoke to each other, made eye contact or didn't.

"It is an honor to meet you, *Herr* Richard. Please, join me in my study. Reinhard will meet with us there." Canaris turned away before I could answer. When I trailed him, I found Heydrich had already entered and, drink in hand, was perusing titles on the book-laden shelves.

"Now that you are here," Canaris began, "perhaps you can help settle a discussion we had earlier. I don't like Jews any more than the next fellow. But, in my opinion, Reinhard here has gone too far."

Heydrich stood straighter. "Wilhelm objects to my new ruling: anyone that has left Germany after the *Führer* became chancellor cannot return. Those who do try will be treated as émigrés and sent to concentration camps. Could anything be simpler or more straightforward?"

"Not if you intend to prevent Jewish businessmen from returning to Germany," I said. "Would you incarcerate Aryans, too?"

"Of course not! True Germans can always return."

"What if a Jew needs to visit a sick relative in another country?" I asked. "You wouldn't let them return to their home in Germany?"

"Isn't our aim to rid Germany of all Jews? Once they leave— for any reason—why let them return?"

"I, too, told Reinhard that this was a bit harsh." Canaris selected a pipe from one of the six nestled in the rack of his tobacco humidor.

Heydrich downed the rest of his drink. "Those people are nomads. They stay a while, suck whatever they can from the host nation as leeches do, and then move on to their next victim. They must be stopped once and for all. As a matter of fact, I have instructed my men to arrest the leader of every Jewish organization in Germany. We'll teach them that they can't stay here. Don't you agree, Friedrich?"

I chose my words with care. "If you know anything about me, then you know I have never embraced the Aryan notion of superiority. However, as a matter of common sense, if you want to get rid of Jews, order your men to leave the Zionists alone. In fact, do the opposite. Order your men to help them."

Heydrich postured. "That's absurd. Have you lost your mind? You're talking about Jews! You want me to help them?"

"Reinhard," it pained me to say his name, "Think about it. What is the Zionists' mission? To leave Germany for Palestine. Help them. You get what you want; they do, too. Is that so terrible?"

Canaris eyed Heydrich. "You didn't expect that, did you, Reinhard?"

Heydrich stroked his chin. "You know, Friedrich, you may be onto something. This way, more leave Germany sooner. What a brilliant plan!"

"I want no part of this, Reinhard. You take all the credit."

After our private conversation broke up, Erika Canaris sought to introduce me to their neighbor's niece, who often joined their musical interludes: Carla Bartheel. Carla had porcelain skin with exquisite features. Her lively hazel eyes, highlighted by thin brows, a perfect nose, and teeth that dazzled when she smiled, melted me. Her blond hair was pulled back and held in place by a tortoise-shell comb.

"You look familiar," I said, after being introduced.

"I'm insulted you don't recognize me. I was on the UFA movie lots the same time you were writing scores there."

"Why didn't you make yourself known to me?"

She made an exaggerated show of inspecting my face. Turned it this way and that. "What happened to the ring in your nose? Lilian Harvey? Remember?"

"Was I that unapproachable?"

"Lilian made sure everyone knew you were taken."

I frowned. "I didn't know it was that bad."

"Please. You loved it. You were a glamorous couple."

"The operative word is 'were.' Why didn't you reach out after she left Germany?"

Carla's eyes twinkled. "Don't think I didn't try. I looked for you, but you never returned to the studios. I was under contract for two more movies. Our paths never crossed." Then she added, "Until now."

She is enchanting.

"What happened after you made those movies?"

She looked away before answering. "I wasn't comfortable with talkies."

"Would I know your films?"

She shrugged. "My one claim to fame was an independent Austrian film with Conrad Veidt. It was the first partial talkie shown in Germany. That got me a tiny bit of notoriety. My last picture was in 1933." She studied me. "You resemble Conrad a little. Only better looking."

"You are not the first to say that. Thank you. What have you been doing since you stopped acting?"

"When I knew my acting days would soon be over, I spent every spare minute as an apprentice to August Sander. He's the greatest portrait photographer in Germany. He taught me enough to open my own studio. What about you, *Herr* Richard?" She made a point of looking at my uniform. "Are you still involved with music? Is that why you are here?" She smiled. Then she added sheepishly, "You did come a bit late."

Sassy and playful.

"I stopped writing movie scores to work on special projects for the Reich."

"Could you be more specific?"

I was unsure how much to say when Heydrich grabbed my arm. "Excuse me, *Fräulein*, I need to take this handsome man away for a few moments. I promise to return him when I am finished."

Carla winked. "*Herr* Heydrich, this one is interesting. Don't disappoint me."

*

A man with an angular face and an aquiline nose sculpted to a point waited in a far corner. "Friedrich, let me introduce you to my new protégé, Adolf Eichmann. He recently transferred into the Jewish Department of the *SD*. His job is to make life unbearable for Jewish business owners, so they leave Germany. I was telling him your idea about working with the Zionists."

He clicked his heels. "It is an honor, *Herr Obergruppenführer* Richard. Your notion of helping the Zionists is contrary to everything I have been doing. I must say, though, it has much appeal. But it could cause problems."

I was puzzled. The concept was meant to solve problems, not cause them. "How? If it's what you and they both want."

"If too many emigrate to Palestine," explained Eichmann, "it could create a Jewish State. That is the last thing Germany wants."

"That's a long time from happening," I said, "If ever."

I glimpsed Carla out of the corner of my eye.

"If you excuse me, *mein Herren*." I nodded to each goodbye, saying, "There's something about keeping a lady waiting."

Long strides brought me to Carla.

"Sorry about that," I said.

"I have met Heydrich here before. I don't like him. And the other man? They both have evil in their eyes. Why were you talking to them?"

"It wasn't by choice. What about mine?" I asked.

"Your eyes? They're filled with kindness."

"Are you always such a good judge of character?"

"It hasn't failed me yet," she answered.

"Will I be able to see you, again?"

"Are you asking?"

"I thought you could read minds, too."

"I can." Then she slipped her business card with her phone number into my hand.

Chapter 6

May 29, 1935

Hitler stood in my doorway. This was unusual; he never walked into anyone's office. His face was contorted in pain.

"It's Eva. Her sister called not a minute ago to tell me Eva tried to kill herself again." He let it all out in a rush. "Not a gun. Pills this time. She's safe in her parents' house. Resting."

I jumped up. "When do we leave for Munich?"

Hitler hung his head. "Now that I am *Führer*, I can't visit her."

"She *will* want to see you."

"In due time. Wherever I go, guards surround me. There would be no way to keep this quiet," he whispered. "Friedrich, would you . . . ?"

Eva's parents had no clue she had been sneaking around more than three years to see Hitler. Whenever she spent a weekend at the Obersalzberg, Eva told them she was on a photo shoot with her employer, Heinrich Hoffmann, Hitler's exclusive photographer. When Hitler did manage to see her, his driver dropped Eva a block or two away from her parents' house. This seedy, shadowy romance, without contact for long periods of time, had driven her to attempt suicide before.

"You needn't ask, Wolf. I'll go."

He smiled at hearing his moniker from the days before he was *Führer*, when I took care of his problems with young women.

"I'll tell Eva how much you care for her. I'll say something about how affairs of state forced you to remain in Berlin. That you will be by her side the first chance you get." I hoped this reassured him.

Hitler shook his head. "That's not enough. Tell her I will get her a place of her own. She can live there with her sister, Gretl. Not Ilse. That one works for a Jewish doctor."

Even in an emergency, always an anti-Semite!

"If you get her a place to live, how long before the outside world connects you two as a couple?"

"That can never happen," Hitler insisted. "Heinrich Hoffmann will either rent or buy something under his name. She works for him. No one will question it. Hoffmann should not mind doing this for me, given how much money he has made from my photos. If I must, I will reimburse him."

That would pose no problem for Hitler. The royalties from *Mein Kampf*—which was required reading throughout Germany—made him millions. When Hindenburg died, Hitler added the president's salary to his as chancellor. Not satisfied with the two salaries, Hitler copyrighted his own image and charged the Reich for its use on stamps and currency. Then, with a torrent of money coming in, he passed a law exempting himself from income taxes.

I readied myself to leave when Hitler stopped me.

"Make certain she knows I will be there as soon as I am able."

"That goes without saying, *mein Führer*."

"There is one more matter you need to attend to in Munich." His face colored.

"Does it have to do with Eva?"

"*Nein.* Friedrich, do you remember Maria Reiter?"

How could I forget? She was the sixteen-year-old he began an affair with a decade ago. Hitler unceremoniously dumped her when anonymous letters surfaced accusing him of statutory rape and Party Judge Walter Buch opened a case.

Like one other before and others after, Maria tried to commit suicide when Hitler ended their affair. I had to clean up the mess by having Maria sign an affidavit that there had been no sexual activity between her and Hitler—in order to end the matter before Buch. Later, when she was unhappily married, Hitler had his personal lawyer, Hans Frank, handle the divorce. Soon after, Geli Raubal, Hitler's half-niece and young lover, committed suicide. So, Hitler took up with Maria again until she pushed him to marry her. That was the end of Maria . . . or so I thought, until just now.

"Yes, Wolf. I remember Maria. Why bring her name up now?"

"She has been trying to contact me at the Chancellery."

"Did Eva find out?"

This was sounding too much like history repeating itself. The day Geli killed herself, she had helped Annie Winter, Hitler's housekeeper, straighten his room. Geli found a note in Hitler's coat pocket from Eva Braun. Convinced that Hitler was two-timing her, Geli shot herself that night.

Hitler shook his head. "I never took Maria's calls. Eva would have no way of knowing."

So that wasn't the reason Eva tried to commit suicide . . . this time.

"What do you want me to do about Maria?" I asked.

He handed me a piece of paper. "Here's her phone number. She lives in Munich. Call her after you see Eva. Take care of whatever Maria wants as long as you keep it away from Eva . . . and keep me out of it."

And then he was gone.

As I gathered my things, I promised myself not to let Hitler's sudden errands ruin my opportunity with Carla the way they had killed my relationships with Lilian and Marta. I reached for the telephone.

"I wondered when I would hear from you," Carla said.

"I'm calling now." We made small talk and agreed to meet in a couple of days.

*

The moment I arrived in Munich I went straight to the Braun apartment on *Hohenzollernstraße*. Eva's mother answered the door. A middle-aged housewife with three daughters, Franziska Braun had short, dark wavy hair. She was a former ski champion that remained trim into her early fifties. Franziska studied me up and down, stared long at the bouquet in my hand, and beamed. *Frau* Braun and her husband Fritz were always on the lookout for suitors for their beauties.

"May I help you?"

"I am Friedrich Richard. Heinrich Hoffmann asked me to deliver these to Eva."

"I don't know your name. Do you know Eva from the studio?" *Frau* Braun asked.

I know your daughter from her many visits to Hitler's Berchtesgaden retreat.

"I don't work there. As I said, I am a friend of *Herr* Hoffmann. If you tell Eva that Friedrich Richard is here, she will know."

When Eva's mother and I entered her room, Eva strained to see if Hitler lingered behind.

Her face fell when she saw that I was alone.

Ilse, her older sister, sat in the chair beside her bed.

"Look, Eva. Flowers." Franziska Braun showed them to Eva before leaving to find a vase.

I nodded to Ilse. "I heard how you saved her. Thank God you were there."

"This makes two times we were lucky." Ilse, the oldest, had strong features and looked most like their mother. "There can be no more."

Eva ignored Ilse and pouted. "He's not coming, is he?"

I shook my head. "You know he can't."

"After this?" said Ilse. "How could he not?"

Eva scowled. "It's been weeks since I've seen him. He never calls. He doesn't give a damn. In March, Adolf was on business in Munich and made no plans to meet me. I knew his schedule. I was desperate to see him. I waited three hours outside the Carlton Hotel. He emerged with flowers in his hand. I was such a fool. I thought: 'How sweet. Flowers for me.'"

Her nostrils flared as she relived the story.

"Do you know what he did? Marched right past me to Max Schmeling and his wife, Anny Ondra, who were sitting not far away. Oh, Adolf saw me, all right, but ignored me to keep up appearances. Then, of all things, he hands *her* the flowers."

Tears streamed down her cheeks.

"He treated me like a common rag woman."

"That is not what he thinks, Eva," I said. "You know that."

She dabbed her eyes dry and continued. "Later that day, we met for dinner—if you can call it that—at the *Vier Jahreszeiten* Hotel. We sat at different tables. Friedrich, he was cruel. We were close enough to talk, but I was forbidden to utter a single word to him in public."

Her pupils widened.

"Then, do you know what he did at the end of dinner? Hands me an envelope with money! Like I was an escort or something worse!"

Her eyes bulged in fury.

"Not a kind word in passing. Not even a note with the money. Why didn't he take me to *Herr* Hoffmann's house? At least we could have talked in private there. I'll tell you why he didn't. He doesn't give a damn!"

Poor Eva. She paid the price for loving a man who cared more about his sham image as the celibate bridegroom of Germany than the woman who loved him.

"Eva, he will visit you as soon as possible."

She crossed her arms, "Tell him not to bother. I don't want to see him."

I glanced at Ilse and then at the door; Ilse looked from me to Eva and excused herself.

I moved the chair closer to the bed and lowered my voice. "Eva, the *Führer* is making arrangements for you and your younger sister, Gretl, to have your own house. He will be able to see you away from prying neighbors or your parents."

She remained unmoved. "Tell him that . . ."

"*Herr* Hoffmann has already begun the search for a suitable house. Your Adolf asks for you to be patient and understanding."

This touched her. She grabbed my hand. "Is this true, Friedrich? Will he really do this for me?"

"He will, Eva."

"I knew Adolf loved me. I knew it," she squeezed my hand tighter. "Please thank him for me, Friedrich. Promise you won't forget."

"I promise."

On the way out, Eva's mother was fussing with the flowers. "Will you be visiting us again, *Herr* Richard?" Her smile was so broad, I thought her lips would crack.

"Perhaps, *Frau* Braun. Once Eva is better."

I left the Brauns' house, which took longer than I expected, to meet Maria Reiter at the restaurant Osteria Bavaria.

"Why here?" I asked after apologizing for being tardy.

"This is *his* favorite restaurant in Munich," she answered. "Did you know that? We came here a number of times."

The café was warm and cozy. Parquet floors. Arches that blended into walls painted to look like Italian frescoes of Mediterranean scenes. Roman gardens with armless statues. Given the décor, perhaps a different name for the café would have been more apt.

Did she know that he took Eva and Geli here, too?

"I never thought the food special," Maria continued, "but he loved it. That's why I asked to meet here. For the memories."

"Memories are nice, Maria, but why now? Are you interested in taking up with Wolf again?"

"Is that why he wouldn't take my calls? No. No. It's the very opposite. I want to get married again. To Georg Kubisch. Georg is in the *SS*. A *Hauptsturmführer*. He's currently posted here in Munich. Well, not exactly. He's a guard in Dachau. Before that, he worked in Himmler's office."

The words "guard in Dachau" sent chills up and down my spine. I started to say something, swallowed, and then said, "I am happy for you, Maria. What is holding you back?"

"You know that an *SS* man and his fiancé have to register and pass the test. I had no problem providing 'Proof of Aryan Ancestry.' But when Georg applied to the Berlin *SS* Office of Race and Settlement for marriage forms, he was told there was an issue with his evaluation. His superior reported that Georg 'lacked a strict, soldierly conception of his duties.' That he came across as 'somewhat of a dreamer.'" Maria grabbed my hands. "Oh, Friedrich. Can't you say something to Wolf? Please? I know he would want me to be happy. If only he knew about this, he would change things so Georg and I could marry."

"Maria, do you truly love this man?" I asked.

"He's not Wolf. I love Georg in a different way." She took a deep breath. "I know we can be happy."

"I'll see what I can do."

*

I left Munich knowing Eva would be all right—at least for the time being—and with a promise to Maria Reiter that I believed Hitler would honor. I reported to Hitler in his Chancellery office as soon as I returned to Berlin.

"Whom do you want to hear about first? Eva or Maria?" I asked.

"I spoke to Eva. You made her very happy when you told her about the house. But she's not the only one."

"You mean Gretl? The two of them . . ."

"No. The mother." He laughed. "Franziska thinks you are courting Eva."

"Oh, the flowers. She made no effort to hide that."

Hitler cleared his throat. "Enough about Eva. You accomplished what you had to. *Danke.* I know Eva won't be so foolish in the future. Now tell me about my *Mitzi.* Did she keep her figure?"

After I explained her dilemma, I said, "She is twenty-five now. Trim and still beautiful."

He turned his back on me, locked his hands behind his back, and gazed out his office window.

"I would have married her, you know . . ." His voice trailed off, then he was quick to add, ". . . if I would have married anyone. Those threatening letters appeared. Geli arrived on the scene . . ." He faced me. "Did Maria speak of me?"

"She said that no one will ever replace you, *mein Führer,* but this man makes her happy."

"That's all I need to know."

"Then you will call Himmler?" I asked.

Hitler shook his head. "*Nein.* I do not want to deal with Himmler on this matter. You understand. It is better if you call him."

"And tell him what? That the *Führer* wants this man Kubisch promoted?"

He nodded. "Himmler will not question this request."

"From me he will. Our history has been anything but cordial."

Hitler smiled for the first time since I arrived. "You are my liaison. No matter what he thinks, Himmler will not question you. I stay out of it, and everyone is happy."

I made the call. Word filtered back to Kubisch's commanding officer that the *SS* man had friends in high places. Very high places. The commanding officer withdrew the complaint from Kubisch's record. A new report was submitted to Himmler extolling *SS Hauptsturmführer* Kubish as a zealous, conscientious, punctual, and hard-working National Socialist.

A promotion followed.

With Himmler's approval, wedding plans for Maria and Georg were no longer on "hold."

*

Now that Hitler's present and past girlfriends' problems were resolved, I could concentrate on Carla Bartheel. We spent afternoons at cafés and strolled along the winding paths of the Tiergarten, that idyllic park in central Berlin. In time, we graduated to dinners.

"You've told me how much you enjoy photography. Portraits in your studio. But why the long, aimless walks around the city or hauling a heavy camera to the countryside?"

"Taking portraits pays the bills. As for my 'aimless walks,' can't you appreciate that when I wander around—as you put it—I am casting about for a unique face or someone in the act of performing everyday work?"

"Where is the art in images of ordinary people? What do you do with them?"

"Friedrich, for someone once in the arts, you lack a rather fundamental understanding of the power of images."

"Please enlighten me."

"Photographs not only capture an image at a given moment but contain a basket of emotions . . . both the subject's and the photographer's. When my images touch those who view them, I've succeeded. When they continue to think about what they saw even after they've walked away, then my work has changed that person. Do you know how gratifying that is?"

"You take this seriously, don't you?"

"How can you think otherwise? An artist is always an artist, just like a soldier is always a soldier, and a politician is . . ."

I held my hand up. "I get it. I do. Now that you've brought it up . . ."

"What?" Carla asked.

"You saw whom I talked with at the Canaris's house and my uniform, yet you have not asked about my politics or if I am a Party member."

"I'm not interested in politics or the Party. If it is important to you, I'll ask. Are you a Party member?"

I shook my head. "Never have been."

"Good."

Nothing else. No more questions. When she was ready to hear more, I would tell Carla my history . . . at least the parts I remembered.

We reached for our glasses and our fingers touched. Rather than pull away, hers lingered.

I slid my hand on top of hers. Neither of us spoke. We didn't have to.

That was the first night we spent together. Carla lived in a small flat on *Oranienburger Straße*. It was furnished with the bare necessities. Minimalist was apropos.

"Why live here?" I asked over morning coffee.

"This used to be the Jewish section. So many have left that there is a glut of apartments. Landlords were forced to lower the rents. That's when the artists came. And me."

"Don't forget the prostitutes we passed on the street last night."

She sipped her coffee. "Everyone needs a place to work and live." The morning light flattered Carla. Her skin was flawless.

Carla cleared her throat. "Friedrich, getting to know you has been wonderful. Last night couldn't have been better. But there is something I need to tell you."

"Finally, a secret." I smiled.

"This is not easy for me." Her lips trembled. "You need to know I have a brother in the Schönbrunn Psychiatric Hospital in Dachau. I am the only one he has. Usually, when I tell a gentleman about Ludwig—that's my brother's name—they stop coming around."

"I am not like other gentlemen, Carla. Having a family means more to me than you can know. Are your parents still with you?"

"They died long ago. I visit Ludwig whenever I can. He can't speak. He can only make guttural sounds. I want to believe there is recognition in his eyes when he sees me. He knows who I am. I'm sure of it. And he likes music. Maybe my parents knew he would, and that's why they gave him that name."

"Is that why you live here? Because of Ludwig?"

"The cheap rent lets me send extra money so Ludwig can get special care."

"Will he ever get better?" I asked.

She shook her head. "He can't. Soon after he was born, he had grand mal seizures. His damaged brain is beyond repair. He has the mind of a six-month old, at most. He wears a diaper. He can't feed himself. It is so sad . . . but I love him."

I stared out a window, wondering if there was a family that still longed for me after all these years. I turned back to Carla, still thinking of what I didn't know about my past.

When I didn't react, she said, "I knew I shouldn't have told you."

I shook off thoughts of my own issues. "On the contrary, I care for you even more, knowing how much you love and have sacrificed for your brother." We kissed.

"My thoughts did wander. I was thinking how to protect your brother."

Her brows arched. "I don't understand."

Hearing about Ludwig reminded me of the time I saved Kitty's niece. Early in the Nazi rule, Wilhelm Frick, the minister of the interior, introduced forced sterilization to ostensibly prevent future birth defects. When Kitty's niece, Mila, tripped and had an isolated seizure, the Nazi apparatus listed her for forced sterilization. I used the power of my position to save her. But then Frick, a product of the Thule Society and their Aryan racial theories, wrote laws to compel abortions of "inferior" human beings, those with chronic diseases as well as Negroes. How long would it be before they started to euthanize living "defective" people? I was chilled at the thought that, one day, Ludwig might be at risk.

"I wonder, Carla, is there a facility closer to Berlin? That way, you could check on him more frequently. Make sure he's safe. That's what I was thinking."

She rested her hand on mine. "How sweet that you worry about Ludwig. You don't even know him. Closer would be easier but he's not good with change. Ludwig is better off staying where he is."

"You know best," I said. "By the way, is your studio nearby? I would love to see it."

Carla's studio was located at street level, a few blocks from her apartment. Portraits of individuals and families were on display in the windows on either side of the entrance. They were exquisite in detail. Without knowing who they were, I could see that Carla captured their essence, making me want to learn more about each one. The studio was filled with tools of the trade: screens, chairs covered in elaborate fabrics, benches, and movable backdrops that gave the illusion of a parlor or a park setting. There were white umbrellas, different-sized reflectors, and lamps necessary to create various effects.

A camera was perched on a tripod. "A Leica. Impressive."

"I do my best work with it. And their changeable lenses are a photographer's dream." She pointed to a door. "The dark room is in there."

Off to the side, a cluster of chairs surrounded a coffee table that held magazines—arranged into neat rows—for those that might need to wait.

I reached for the topmost magazine, *Sonne ins Haus*. The cover was graced with the angelic face of a wide-eyed, beautiful child wearing a white bonnet, tied in a bow on the left side of her chin. There was a wisp of hair on her forehead, and a blond curl peeking out from the sunhat.

Carla smiled. "Do you know that magazine?"

"*The Sun in the Home* is not on my reading list. But this face," I pointed to the baby, "I've seen it before."

"Of course you have. It is on birthday and greeting cards everywhere."

Carla giggled.

"What's so funny?" I asked, puzzled.

"I took that picture right here in my studio."

"Impressive." I studied the baby's face. "What makes her so special?"

"Turn to the article inside." When I found it, she explained, "I entered a contest to find the perfect Aryan child. My entry won. I received a lot of money for it, including royalties on every birthday card sold."

"How special! I'm proud of you." I pointed to another picture of the infant. "She is beautiful."

"Beautiful, yes. Aryan, no."

"I don't understand."

"It was a joke. Don't you get it?" Carla asked.

"Forgive me. I don't."

"It was my personal dig at the stupidity of the Nazi racial theories. The baby's name is Hessy Levinsons. Hessy is a Jew! The Nazis picked her as the perfect Aryan child among the thousands of photos submitted. This epitomizes their insanity." Then she gasped. "Have I offended you? What I said about the Nazis?"

"Not in the slightest. My only concern is that you might get in trouble if they catch on."

"Why should I worry? They asked for baby pictures. They picked the one I sent. The Levinsons, on the other hand, were appalled when they found out. I am too much a lady to repeat what they said. The worst of it is that they can't take a chance to be seen walking or playing with the perfect Aryan child. Not as Jews. They are forced to keep Hessy in hiding. You don't know how much I regret that."

Chapter 7

1936

Enough time had passed that Querner's death was no longer at the forefront of anyone's mind. After careful research, I was ready to set my plan in motion to deal with Jüttner and settle the second half of my promise to avenge Max's murder.

I told Carla I needed to be away on business. I figured it might take as long as a week.

* * *

We met at a local café upon my return.

"Did you accomplish what you needed to do in Munich?"

My answer came in the shape of a flat, brown envelope.

She ran her hand across. "Nothing lumpy."

I smiled. "You sound disappointed. Were you expecting jewelry?"

She played the innocent as she lifted the flap. When she saw what was in it, she gushed, "This is the best present ever. How did you manage this? He looks wonderful."

It was a picture of her brother, Ludwig.

"Once I concluded my business, a driver took me to Schönbrunn Hospital. I wanted to make certain your brother was well-cared for. It was not easy arranging the photograph."

"Leave it to you to get it done."

"Do you like it?"

"Like it? I love it!" She threw her arms around my neck and kissed me long and hard. Still holding me, she asked, "Were you able to walk around? Whenever I go there, they have me sit in an isolated room with a few toys or I take him outside to a gated area with only a table and bench."

"The halls and nurses' stations were spotless. Everyone appeared well-fed. I poked my head into any number of rooms. All appeared in order."

She sat back. "Are you this good to everyone?"

"Not to everyone."

"Then I am a lucky girl. And did I ever mention that I am glad Lilian Harvey went to America?"

"I don't mean to break the mood, but she is back in Germany to make a movie."

Carla frowned. "Have you seen her?"

"For a few minutes after the Gestapo held her for questioning. The important thing is that I am here with you. I have no interest in being with anyone else."

She feigned pointing a dagger at me. "And you better keep it that way, buster."

I held my hands up in mock surrender, but not before motioning to the waitress to bring two fresh coffees. "What did you do while I was away?"

"I had a most interesting experience. A commission with General Beck. I am sure you helped. Thank you. The man was quite chatty."

It had become de rigueur for military personnel to have photographic portraits of themselves, especially with each promotion and change in uniform. Army Chief-of-Staff Colonel General Ludwig Beck had mentioned that he would like a photograph of himself that did not make him look stiff or wooden. Without Carla knowing, I arranged the commission to be offered to her. She would find it lucrative and as special liaison to the *Führer*, I might gain information that some men were only too happy to divulge to a beautiful photographer. If this proved fruitful with Beck, I would find other *Wehrmacht* leaders for her to photograph.

I acted as disinterested as possible, taking a sip of coffee. "Anything worth mentioning?"

"I usually close my ears whenever politics are brought up. But he put recent events in perspective that made them interesting."

"Such as?"

"He said the *Führer* was clever to support Italy in its war against Abyssinia. He mentioned something about the Stresa Agreement. I didn't follow that."

"When the Austrian Nazis attempted to take over Austria, it put a strain on our relations with Italy. Italy turned to England and France. The three countries formed an alliance—the Stresa Agreement—to isolate Germany from the west and south."

"That explains it," she said.

"Did Beck mention anything else?"

"That he was still peeved that Hitler disregarded the military leaders' advice and ordered troops to march into the Rhineland. General Beck was worried it would turn into a war. If it did, he said, we would have lost. Lucky for us it didn't happen." She paused. "Why all the questions? If I had known you were so interested in everything he said, I would have paid more attention. Better still, I would have asked you to be my assistant."

"Curiosity got the better of me. Sorry. Given all the conversation, did you manage to take *Herr* Beck's photograph?"

"I did. He has a fine chiseled face with somewhat sad eyes. I was able to capture both his apparent sensitivity along with the taut tension that wouldn't leave him. He was pleased."

*

Each day back from Munich, I searched the papers for mention of a fiery wreckage that took the life of Konrad Jüttner, the Dachau guard. I started to think of different reasons why it had not yet appeared when the phone shrieked.

"Friedrich. Come here. I want to show you something."

When I got to his office, Hitler was nowhere to be seen. I called out.

"*Mein Führer*, where are you?"

"*Kommen Sie hierher.*"

I found Hitler on his knees behind a console table, inspecting the back of a machine.

He stood and pointed to the large box dotted with numerous small gadgets. "Do you know what this is?"

I did. "It's a Hollerith machine."

Soon after Hitler became chancellor, we used Hollerith machines to collate the data from the 1933 census. International Business Machines, an American company, owned ninety percent of *Deutsche Hollerith-Maschinen Gesellschaft* or Dehomag.

"Their punch cards make our trains run on time," explained Hitler. "I've been in discussions with its leader, a fellow named Watson, to have his company solve other problems . . . like knowing where every camp inmate is at any given time. I've been promised these machines can tabulate and find each prisoner in seconds."

Hitler rubbed the top of the machine as if it were a child's mop of hair.

"I gave them a contract to install a Hollerith machine in every concentration camp and subcamp."

"When will they start delivery?" I asked.

"Not soon enough." Then he asked, with a familiar gleam in his eyes, "Is there news about the general staff?"

I must give him something.

"I have a contact who spoke with Chief-of-Staff Ludwig Beck. He has concerns about how swiftly you are moving."

Hitler snickered. "He's not the only one, Friedrich. Besides Chief-of-Staff Beck, I am shackled with Bloomberg as minister of war and Fritsch, the army commander-in-chief. Those three were happy to have me rebuild the army in violation of the Treaty of Versailles. Now they drag their feet when it comes to retaking lost territories."

"They don't want us forced into a war we cannot win."

Hitler smashed his fist into his palm. "Don't they understand the genius of my plan? I will not let them stand in my way as we move forward. Either they are with me, or they are not."

As he said this, his face contorted into a mask that made me shudder. There was no question in my mind that the generals would pay a price if they continued to disagree with Hitler's plans for Germany. The only question was, how steep would it be?

Finally! The following day a small piece buried on the paper's back page jumped out at me.

SS GUARD DIES IN FIRE

The article reported that a car registered to Konrad Jüttner had smashed into a tree, burst into flames, and that his body was burned beyond recognition. Jüttner's identity was confirmed by dental records.

I closed the paper and stared off. "Max," I said out loud, "now you can rest in peace."

Ten days later, a young *SS* man in a crisp uniform knocked on my office door. Ramrod straight, he gave me the Hitler salute. "Herr *Obergruppenführer*, I have been ordered to escort you to *Prinz-Albrecht-Straße*."

I plumbed his face for a clue as to what this might be about. It was blank. "Who dares order me to Gestapo Headquarters?"

"*Reichsführer* Himmler and *Gruppenführer* Heydrich."

I waved him off, as if shooing a fly. "Tell them I'm busy. If it is so important, they can come here."

"They said you would say that."

I snapped my fingers. "Come, now. There must be more to the message. Make it quick."

"What they have to say to you, *Obergruppenführer* Richard, must be said in person. They said it was for your own good."

I made the young man stand there while I thought this through. In the end, I decided not to second-guess myself.

The *SS* man brought me to Himmler's office. Himmler was seated at his desk made of dark wood. He had six buttons installed into the right edge of his desk to summon various aides.

His hand rested on two closed folders.

Himmler pointed to a chair in front of his desk. "Have a seat, Friedrich. For now, this is a friendly investigation."

At that moment, Heydrich slid through the door and leaned against the wall behind Himmler.

"What is this about?" I asked.

Heydrich stepped forward. "Some months back, Felix Querner went missing."

"Am I supposed to know who Felix Querner is?"

"Querner was a guard at Dachau. One of the best," Heydrich explained. "We found his car a short drive from where he lived. By Lake Walchensee. There was an empty booze bottle on the front seat. Everyone knew he drank too much. His car was parked next to a mooring. We found the boat miles away. Empty. Everything pointed to Querner falling overboard. It was too far out and too cold to swim back. We sent divers, but it was a waste. The lake is deepest there. We never did find his body. For the record, his death was listed as an accident."

"Why tell me this?"

Heydrich didn't answer. "Recently, another Dachau guard died. It was a stormy night. He apparently lost control. His car crashed into a tree and exploded. The body was badly burned."

"I saw something about that in the paper. A terrible way to die," I said.

Himmler added, "His name was Jüttner."

"Again, why . . . ?"

Heydrich interrupted. "Here is where it gets interesting, Friedrich. Jüttner's crash was staged. It was meant to look like an accident."

My mouth went dry. "How would you know this?"

"His gun was not on his body," Himmler answered. "After an exhaustive search, we found Jüttner's gun five hundred yards from the crash site. At the side of the road. In undergrowth. We asked ourselves: Why wasn't his gun in the car with him at the crash site? You are a clever fellow, Friedrich. Any ideas?"

I acted bemused. "I don't see the point of this or why you think they are connected to me."

"Here's one explanation," Heydrich said. "Someone stopped Jüttner. There was an altercation. The gun was thrown. Jüttner was killed near where we found the gun. Once we found it, we ordered an autopsy."

Heydrich's slender lips creased upward. "There was no smoke in his lungs. Jüttner was already dead before his car crashed and burned."

"Maybe he had a heart attack while driving? Stopped breathing before the crash."

"If that's the case, how would you explain Jüttner's broken neck?" Himmler asked.

"The impact of the tree," I answered. "I would think that obvious."

"That's one possibility. Another is that someone broke it for him."

Beads of sweat trickled down my back. "That's quite a story. Now if you don't mind . . ."

"Oh, but we're not finished, Friedrich," said Himmler. "Here comes the juicy part: Jüttner was paired with Felix Querner at Dachau."

Heydrich picked up the thread. "Think of it, Friedrich. We have one *SS* guard who liked to indulge, took out a boat, slipped into the water, and drowned. Another guard dies in a fiery crash made to look like an accident. The guards worked together at Dachau. That's quite a coincidence, wouldn't you say? Well, we don't believe in coincidences. That means Querner's death may also have been due to foul play. The question before us: who would want both dead?"

I turned to Himmler. "This is all very interesting, Heinrich. A tale worth telling around a campfire. Frankly," I hopped up to leave, "I have better things to do."

Heydrich cut me off at the door. "One more minute of your time. That's all we ask."

I tried to push past him; he held steadfast. There was little point in making a bigger scene.

I returned to the chair.

"We're not fools, Friedrich," Himmler said. "Imagine our surprise when we learned that Querner and Jüttner were involved in Max Klinghofer's death. Then what do we discover? That you live in Klinghofer's former house."

I had a coughing fit.

How far are they going to take this?

Heydrich poured me a glass of water; I took my time emptying it.

"It is no secret that my first job was in Max's nightclub after the war. We were friends until he died. Max did leave me his house. Where are you going with this?"

Himmler continued. "We found your car rental records. You were in Munich when Jüttner was murdered and also when Querner went missing."

"My missions for the *Führer* are not your concern. As a matter of fact, one of the *Führer's* assignments was not to embarrass you, Heinrich. It had to do with an inaccurate status report a commanding officer gave this guard. You do remember, don't you? I called specifically about the guard that wanted to marry someone once close to the *Führer*. The report had to be changed to save face. Otherwise, it would have fallen on you, Heinrich."

"Georg Kubish. I remember."

I don't know whom I loathed more: Himmler or Heydrich.

"You should," I said. "What you fail to realize is that I perform many missions for the *Führer* that nobody knows about. Often in Munich. Your arrogance . . ." I glared at Heydrich. "To presume that I was involved in the deaths of your guards is not only outrageous but an insult to me and the *Führer*!"

I stood to my full height of six-foot-seven. Straightened my uniform and stepped back to see both their faces at the same time.

"Let me remind you: I was next to Hitler before either of you were in the Party. No one is closer to the *Führer* than me. Out of respect for your positions, I listened to your insinuations. Did you bother to present a shred of evidence that linked me to either man? You couldn't, because there is none. From where I stand, you are leveling false accusations at me because you both envy my closeness to the *Führer*!"

I gave Heydrich a mighty shove out of the way of the door. I experienced more than a touch of *schadenfreude* when his head banged into the wall causing him to wince.

"No one is accusing you of anything, Friedrich," Himmler called after me.

*

Back in my office, I weighed what had just happened. Although there was no direct evidence against me, Himmler and Heydrich would not stop at my proclamation of innocence. My very closeness to Hitler would obligate them to investigate my background. They were sure to ferret out Friedrich Richard's military record. When they would learn, to their surprise, that Richard died at Pasewalk Hospital, they would go to Pasewalk to check the hospital files only to discover no record of Friedrich Richard having ever been there. That would perplex them even more. The potential fallout was explosive.

There was only one way to diffuse what they would surely discover.

*

"*Mein Führer*," I closed his office door, "I wouldn't barge in like this if it were not urgent."

He took off his reading glasses and pointed to the chair by his desk. "Tell me."

"Himmler and Heydrich just interrogated me. Informally. Just the same, they dared question me."

"It wasn't about changing that report on Kubisch, was it?"

Most often Hitler was two steps ahead when I thought I brought him new information. Not this time.

"Not Kubisch. It was about two guards that worked together at Dachau that died under mysterious circumstances. Because I knew an inmate they killed, Himmler and Heydrich are trying to link the guards' deaths to me."

"My top people don't have to like one another. In fact, I'm not distressed when they don't. But I can't have them turn against each other. I'll talk to them."

"I'd rather you didn't."

"Then what's your concern?" Hitler asked.

"That they will dig deeper."

"Deeper how?" asked Hitler.

"My army records. Then on to Pasewalk."

"But you took care of everything years ago. There's nothing for them to find."

"That is the problem, isn't it? When they don't find my hospital records, then they . . ."

". . . will come to me," Hitler finished my sentence.

Carla greeted me at her door. "Is this a bonus visit? I thought we were getting together this weekend."

"Truth be told, I had a rough day at the office and needed to get away. I could think of no place I'd rather be."

I stepped inside and looked about. "What are you doing? There is no place to sit."

Photographs were strewn all over. Like a beaming parent, she explained, "I took these pictures when I was fortunate enough to travel throughout Finland. I visited remote villages and stayed in hunting lodges. The indigenous people were only too happy to let me take their pictures. I am sorting them for a book. The tentative title is *Adventure on the Arctic Ocean Road*."

Carla learned her craft well. It was as if I could touch them and know what they were thinking. I particularly liked the ones of the northern fishermen.

"Can you give me a hand?"

For the next couple of hours, we sifted through scores of photographs, arranging them in two piles: those worthy to be in the book and those that were not.

"Why are you looking at me like that?" Carla asked.

"Can't I admire a talented artist?"

With the photographs sorted, there was room to sit next to each other. I held her face in my hands. Our lips touched, and the rest was glorious.

Chapter 8

"Friedrich!" To my surprise, I heard Kitty's voice. It was stretched thin. Like a dam wall strained to the limit. "Come to the salon as soon as you can. I am beside myself." Before I could ask about her problem, the call disconnected.

I hurried to Pension Schmidt. I found Kitty bawling alongside a young woman with swollen eyes and makeup streaked down her cheeks. The stranger appeared to be in her late twenties, not too tall, with a round face, greenish eyes, and chestnut-brown hair chopped unstylishly short. When she saw my black *SS* uniform, she sprang from the chair and began to pound me on the chest.

"You did this to my father! You did this!" she screamed. She had a slight French accent.

I grabbed her wrists. "Who are you? Why are you attacking me?"

Kitty looked up through bloodshot eyes. "Is it true, Friedrich? Is it true? Tell me!"

"Kitty, you need to calm down so I can make sense of this. And you, young lady," I let her go, "have some explaining to do."

"How can I calm down . . ." Kitty continued to cry, ". . . when you kept this from me?"

"Am I supposed to know who you are?" I asked the stranger. With her simple clothes, cropped haircut, and no makeup she could not be one of Kitty's girls.

"My name is Heidi Koch. But to you, I am Max Klinghofer's daughter. We just came from the rabbi who buried him."

Max's daughter! Rabbi?

Kitty turned into a tornado of rage. "Now I understand why the casket had to remain closed." Her chest heaved with each challenge. "Why didn't you tell me, Friedrich? Why lie about a heart attack? To protect me from the truth? That was not your choice to make. I find out, now? From Heidi, of all people!"

"Kitty. Painting you a picture of Max's mutilated body was too much for me to bear. I spared you the pain of how it happened and a memory you didn't need to have. If I had to do it over, I would keep how Max died from you, again. I swore to avenge his death for both of us."

There was no other way to explain it.

"And did you?" Heidi asked.

"Did I what?"

"Avenge my father's death?"

Part of me wanted to describe how I made the two brutes suffer, but these details would place them in danger. Instead, I wrote down two names along with dates. "Check the back pages of the *Deutsche Allgemeine Zeitung* on these days. Look for articles about the mysterious disappearance of Felix Querner and the fiery death of Konrad Jüttner."

Heidi's fierce face relaxed. "I'm sorry I hit you, Friedrich. I saw the uniform and . . ."

"No apologies necessary. Did you visit the grave after meeting the rabbi?"

"We did," Kitty answered.

"We left stones on the tombstone as remembrances," answered Heidi.

Guilt washed over me for not having visited the cemetery. I promised to go the first chance I got.

"Kitty told me how you brought him back from Munich and made all the arrangements. Thank you," Heidi said. "Maybe I can repay you one day."

"Max repaid me many times over when he was alive. He even left me his house, but it's yours if you want."

"I would like to see it one day. Nothing more," said Heidi.

"My turn. How come Max never mentioned a word to me about you?"

Kitty continued to hold Heidi's hand. "Heidi's mother worked for Max back in the days of the Kaiser. When nightclubs were literally underground. She was young; he was single. They had the typical boss/worker fling. She became pregnant and quietly returned to Aachen without telling Max why she left Berlin."

Heidi continued the story. "My mother remained in Aachen after I was born and worked in the family restaurant."

"Living in Aachen explains your accent," I said.

"We're close to France. Most people in Aachen are multilingual," explained Heidi.

"Knowing different languages is always useful. Question. Over the years, didn't you wonder who your father was?" I asked.

I do mine.

"Of course. Ever since I could remember. Whenever I asked, my mother's answer was always the same: a man she met a long time ago that didn't want children. She would never tell me his name. She knew I would try to find him, and she wanted to spare me being rejected."

"Honey, if Max had met you," said Kitty, "he would have adored you."

"Kitty, did you know about Heidi?" I asked.

Kitty nodded. "Sometime after she was born. When Max found out about Heidi, he had me send money every month to help care for her and her mother. Max paid for Heidi's schooling, birthday presents, and more."

"That sounds like Max," I said.

Heidi wiped away a tear. "I first discovered his name after my mother died. That's when I found letters from Kitty." Heidi pecked Kitty on the cheek. "You always sent a kind note with them along with your address. By the time we spoke, Max had died. Just when I thought I still had a parent I became an orphan a second time." Heidi turned to Kitty. "Why didn't he love me enough to reach out?"

"He said he was going to . . . more than once."

"But he never did."

"Max had his reasons," Kitty explained. "Mainly, he didn't want you to know you were part Jewish."

"That wouldn't have mattered to me," said Heidi.

"Given the world we live in, Max was both generous and prescient. Being part Jewish does matter in Germany these days. Be smart. Keep that to yourself," I explained.

We fell silent.

"Here we are, the three of us," I said, "grieving over a man we all loved. Now that you are here, what are your plans, Heidi?"

"I sold the restaurant after my mother passed. There's nothing for me in Aachen. I had to come to Berlin, if nothing else, to meet Kitty and learn more about my father. Going to the cemetery helped."

"You can stay with me," said Kitty. "There's a furnished room upstairs."

"It's comfortable," I said. "I stayed there when I worked for Kitty."

Heidi smiled.

"It is not what you think. I was a bouncer." Then it struck me. "Kitty. Heidi knows the restaurant business. Why not put her to work in the Nightingale? I am sure Marta can use the help."

*

I left Pension Schmidt, rounded a corner and stopped short: teams of workers were scrubbing anti-Semitic slurs from walls and signs. The next day, rules forbidding Jews to assemble in public were lifted. They could mingle freely on the streets.

Why this transformation? Hitler was forced to erase overt signs of racism in Germany—which meant anti-Semitism—in order to stage the 1936 Olympics. The prize was too great to forego. Apart from being a showpiece for the world to see the great strides Germany had made under his control, Hitler had a personal reason for Germany to hold the games.

"Imagine, Friedrich," he said when I met with him later, "every nation will follow the Olympic tradition and dip their flags to the leader of the host country. Me. Adolf Hitler . . ." He made a sweeping arc with his right hand, ". . . saluted by every nation as they march before me in *my* capital city."

For that reason alone, German Jews could breathe easier until the Olympic Games ended.

Chapter 9

My office in the Chancellery building was perched in a way I could see visitors come and go. More often than not, I paid no attention to the patter of boots on the stairs. But the angry stomping of leather striking the marble steps was hard to ignore. I glanced up to catch Heinrich Himmler and Reinhard Heydrich march past, trailed by a woman dressed in her Sunday best.

Their hurried pace left little doubt where they were headed.

In a matter of minutes, I was summoned to Hitler's office.

I found Himmler and Heydrich standing, arms folded, on either side of the woman who was seated opposite Hitler. She appeared to be in her forties. Her hair pulled tight in a bun. Simple dress. Pale lips pressed together, she trembled being so close to the *Führer*.

Hitler motioned me to stand next to him.

Himmler pointed an accusatory finger at me. "Is *this* your husband, *Frau* Richard?"

"No." Her answer was almost imperceptible.

Hitler cupped his ear with his hand. "*Lauter bitte.*"

"No." This time her voice was loud and clear.

"Are you certain?" challenged Himmler.

"My husband died in Pasewalk Hospital in 1918."

"There is no chance you are mistaken, *Frau* Richard?" Heydrich asked.

She looked neither left nor right. Only at Hitler.

"*Nein*. My husband was short. This man is a giant."

Himmler's glower thawed. "We are sorry to have put you through this after all these years, *Frau* Richard, but we had to be certain. Thank you for coming." He accompanied her to the door. "You have been of great service to the Reich. A driver will return you home."

When Himmler rejoined us, Heydrich said, "Do you see, *mein Führer*? *Frau* Richard confirms that her husband, Friedrich Richard, is dead."

"Yes, we all heard," Hitler said.

Himmler inched forward. "Reinhard and I are concerned for your safety. We are not satisfied how the deaths of two guards at Dachau were resolved. *Obergruppenführer* Richard was included in the investigation. Nothing conclusive came of it."

"I was informed," Hitler stifled a yawn. "But what does that have to do with this woman?"

Himmler's face reddened. "According to the Army records, Friedrich Zalman Richard died at Pasewalk Hospital in 1918. His widow just confirmed it. So, who is this man?" Again, he pointed at me. "We need to know."

Hitler, ever the actor, played to the farce. "I am surprised you ask, Heinrich. You've known Friedrich for years."

Himmler stamped his foot. "But Friedrich Richard is dead."

Hitler hoisted my hand. "I believe we can all agree that *this* Friedrich Richard is very much alive." Then he turned to me. "Tell us, for the record Friedrich, have you ever been married?"

"No, *mein Führer*."

"Did you know *Frau* Richard, who just left?"

"No, *mein Führer*."

Hitler wrapped concern around his next question. "Were you ever treated in Pasewalk Hospital?"

"No, *mein Führer*."

Huffing, Heydrich said, "But this Friedrich has the same middle name, *mein Führer*. Zalman. That Friedrich was a Jew. This Friedrich could be a Jew, too."

"I see." Hitler turned to me. "Friedrich, these *Herren* suggest you are of the Hebrew persuasion. Are you?"

"No, *mein Führer*."

Hitler turned to Himmler and Heydrich. "You've carried this charade long enough. Why don't you both admit you made an honest mistake? No one has been hurt by it."

The two remained steadfast.

I stepped away from Hitler, undid my belt, unfastened the front buttons to my trousers, and pulled down my pants. I hesitated and then hooked my thumbs on the rim of my underwear.

"For the record," I began to tug.

Himmler's hand shot up.

"That won't be necessary, Friedrich. We trust you are not a Jew." Himmler faced Hitler. "For the last time, *mein Führer*, for your own protection: Do you know who this man is?"

"Of course, I do . . . and so do you. Friedrich Richard." Hitler stood. *"Dann ist alles geklärt."*

"With respect, *mein Führer*, all is *not* settled," said Heydrich. *"Frau* Richard said he is not her husband. I accept that. Her husband died in Pasewalk. That confirms the military records. That *her* Friedrich Richard's medical chart is missing, well that is unusual, but I will accept that as well. Then there can only be one conclusion: there are two Friedrich Richards."

"It has taken you this long to arrive at the obvious conclusion?" Hitler said. "You should have realized that from the beginning."

"But there is no record of *this* Friedrich Richard anywhere in the Reich," Himmler said. "No registry of his birth. No induction into the army. No official *Ausweis*. How can someone exist in Germany without an identity card?"

Without answering, I slipped the identity card Hitler made me years ago from my wallet and held it to their faces.

"Here is my *Ausweis. Obergruppenführer, SS* Friedrich Zalman Richard."

Hitler shook his fist. "Do either of you think me fool enough to place myself, the *Führer* of Germany, in danger with an imposter?" His azure-blue eyes grew darker. "I demand that both of you apologize to Friedrich, now. If you are lucky—and he is munificent—he will forgive you. When he does, that will be the end of this foolishness . . . forever!"

Neither Himmler nor Heydrich could look me in the eye when they apologized. After they left, Hitler and I convulsed in laughter.

"Imagine their faces when they did not find Friedrich Zalman Richard's file at Pasewalk?" That drove us into more spasms of laughter.

"I hope this is the end of it," I said.

Hitler pretended to scowl. "I'm angry at myself. I should have told them your real name: Patient X."

With that, we roared louder.

*

How close did Himmler and Heydrich come to finding out the truth about me? Far too close for my taste. A second Friedrich Zalman Richard, without a history, would leave them forever unsatisfied.

With the H&H show shuttered for the time being, the third H—Hitler—asked, "You killed those two men to avenge that Jew friend of yours, didn't you?"

Lie or face the consequences of the truth?

"He was my friend," I ventured.

There was a heavy silence between us as I waited for his explosion. But when he gave a slight shrug, relief flooded through me.

"Max was your *Alter Kämpfer*. Loyalty trumps all."

"Even for a Jew, *mein Führer*?"

He arched his brows and turned away.

*

Hitler's parting words reminded me of a promise I had to keep.

Bitter memories bubbled up on the drive to the Weissensee section of Berlin. I turned onto *Herbert-Baum-Straße* and drove through the main entrance of the largest Jewish cemetery in Europe. It was divided into one hundred and twenty sections. I passed the wealthy, lionized in ornate mausoleums. Max was interred in a peripheral section . . . with other upper- and middle-class Jews.

Max's tombstone was simple. A six-pointed Star of David was chiseled into the gray, speckled granite, with an olive branch that extended beneath it. The dates of his birth and death were etched under his name that was carved in block letters. There were also Hebrew letters I did not understand.

I searched for a loose rock and placed it next to the ones Heidi and Kitty left in remembrance of a man we all loved.

I dropped to my knees and ran my fingers over each letter: M-a-x K-l-i-n-g-h-o-f-e-r. Then, as if Max knew I was there, the sun peeked out from the clouds and caused the granite to sparkle.

*

Anxious to see Carla, I was disappointed to find a note poking out from her door: she was developing pictures at her studio. When I got there, the door was unlocked. The red bulb above the dark room was lit. I knew enough not to enter.

I called out. "You should really keep your front door locked when you are here alone."

"Hello to you. If I did, how would you have gotten in? I wanted to process these pictures. Almost finished."

I thumbed through a magazine in the waiting area without seeing a thing. I was numb from all that happened, and the day wasn't over!

"Once again, I have to thank you," Carla said when she emerged from the darkroom. She pressed my hands for a flash, pecked me on the cheek, and then sat next to me.

"For what?"

"Another commission. Or have you forgotten?"

It was a momentary blank. Then I snapped my fingers. "Fritsch. I do remember. How did it go?"

"You'd think that the commander-in-chief of the Army might be filled with his own self-importance. But Fritsch isn't. He was easy to work with. But . . ."

"But what?"

"He did have some choice words about the present state of affairs."

"Meaning?"

"Fritsch was not happy that *Herr* Hitler disregarded his military advisors and took risks they advised against."

"I assume he referenced the Rhineland."

"Frankly, I didn't see the point he was trying to make. Nothing happened when we retook it. Hitler was right and the generals were wrong."

"Did he mention Hitler looking beyond Germany's borders?"

"No more than Beck did," answered Carla. "What impressed me about Fritsch and Beck was that they are cautious men who do not want to risk jeopardizing peace."

"That is reassuring," I said. "Did Fritsch happen to mention that he never married?"

"Is that your way of asking if he is homosexual?"

"Do you think he is? There have been rumors."

Carla shrugged. "All I know is that he did not seem interested in me. He may be that much of a gentleman. I don't know." Then she gave a wistful smile. "You know, Friedrich, I'm not stupid. You were in uniform when we met at the Canaris's house. You never did explain about the Reich projects you work on."

"It never came up again."

"I have discovered how close you are to Hitler. Is that why you can arrange portrait commissions of *Wehrmacht* leaders with me?"

"Can't a guy help the woman he cares about?" I answered. "Besides, portraits are your forte. There is something magical when you take them."

"All of this is not a coincidence. There is another reason, isn't there? And it has nothing to do with making it easier to pay my bills."

I opened both hands. "Whatever do you mean?"

"You probe me after each session trying to discover if the generals revealed state's secrets or something. Am I right?"

She took my hand.

"There's no need to say anything, Friedrich. I am sure you have your reasons. Nothing you have asked about is earthshaking or that confidential. So, as far as I am concerned, I am okay with whatever it is you are doing. What is important is that you are a good man. A kind man. When you went to see Ludwig in the sanitarium, I learned all I ever needed to know about you."

Chapter 10

"Don't you look dapper." Carla eyed me up and down in my black tuxedo.

"No one can hold a candle to you tonight." I admired everything about her. "You look absolutely smashing."

We were dressed to the nines for a state dinner to honor the upcoming Olympics. "I still do not understand the fuss. These quadrennial games last a few days and are forgotten until the next time." Carla wrapped an imported royal blue silk shawl around her shoulders that made her white gown even more striking.

"The simple answer? Bragging rights for the host country."

"But there's more to it this time, isn't there?" asked Carla.

I pecked her cheek. "Both beautiful and smart. The '36 Olympics were awarded to Germany before Hitler and the Nazis came to power. Yet no one understands their immense value better than Goebbels. Goebbels will make certain they are bigger and gaudier than they were four years ago in Los Angeles. Germany will do everything it can to win the most medals so that Goebbels can trumpet Aryan superiority to the world."

*

The evening's festivities were held in the Chancellery's recently renovated large reception hall/ballroom that spilled into the adjacent conservatory. Chandeliers dripped with crystal prisms that shimmered like stars on a clear night. Few knew that secret rooms known as the *Vorbunker* had been installed during the renovations with thick, oversized concrete walls which supported the ballroom. The *Vorbunker* was listed as the Reich Chancellery Air-Raid Shelter, large enough to accommodate Hitler, his guards, and servants.

Most Nazi top brass were on hand for the state dinner. Carla and I waited on the receiving line to pay respects to our host and hostess: Adolf Hitler and Emmy Göring. Emmy, the wife of the Luftwaffe's commander-in-chief, Hermann Göring, served at state functions as Germany's official first lady while Eva Braun remained a state secret.

I introduced Carla to the *Führer*, who, with an Austrian flourish, brought her hand to his lips. "Friedrich, where have you been keeping this beautiful woman? And such a talented actress." Hitler continued to hold Carla's hand and gaze. "I have enjoyed your movies, *Fräulein* Bartheel. Perhaps you will make them again. Germany needs stars like you."

Carla's cheeks turned rosy. "It is an honor to meet you in person, *mein Führer*."

We paid our respects to Emmy Göring before moving on to the honored guest of the evening—Hans von Tschammer und Osten, head of the German Olympic Committee—and his wife, Sophie Margarethe von Carlowitz.

I had not met Tschammer before. By way of greeting, he asked, "Why aren't you on our basketball team? With your height, you could be our center."

"First of all, I'm too old. More importantly, you haven't seen me play basketball."

We moved to the main ballroom where I grabbed Baccarat flutes of champagne. As Carla and I toasted each other, I felt a tap on my shoulder. It was Theodor von Lewald, the man Tschammer replaced as head of the German Olympic Committee.

"Excuse me, *Fräulein*, may I borrow your charming escort for a few minutes?"

"Go ahead," Carla said. "I want to speak to Emmy Göring. She didn't recognize me in the receiving line. We were actresses together, years ago."

I watched Carla sashay away before turning to Lewald. "What do you think of the evening so far?" I asked.

Rather than answer, he pointed to Avery Brundage, head of the American Olympic Committee, an avowed anti-Semite, and Charles Hitchcock Sherrill, also a member of the American Olympic Committee. The two were huddled in animated conversation in a far corner.

Lewald explained, "If it were not for Sherrill over there, Germany would have lost the games. They were about to move them to another country."

"At this late date? Could they do that?" I asked. "*Would* they do that?"

"Host countries must abide by Olympic rules," Lewald answered. "There can be no discrimination of any kind."

No discrimination meant German Jews could not appear to be excluded from the games.

"What if a country has no Jews capable of making the team?"

My question was academic. We had plenty of Jewish athletes that could qualify for the Olympics. Margaret Bergmann, for one. Bergmann won the British High Jump Championship two years ago and last year won the Württembergian Championships, missing the German record by 0.5 cm. It was only a matter of time before she broke the record. Lewald's mouth twisted in a wry smile. "Brundage evaluated our Olympic program two years ago. Hitler not only charmed him, but convinced Brundage that Jews were not Germans; therefore, they could not represent us in the Olympics. Brundage bought Hitler's explanation at face value. However, Sherrill knew the International Olympic Committee would not accept Brundage's report. He took it upon himself to meet Hitler in person. Of course, Hitler charmed Sherrill, too."

"That doesn't answer how Sherrill managed to keep the games here."

"He did it by pulling off a major miracle. He convinced the committee that if Germany had just one Jew on their team, the Olympics would stay in Berlin. That, dear Friedrich, is the reason for tonight's celebration."

"Then Margaret Bergmann is the obvious choice," I said.

Lewald shook his head. "Hitler would not have her. Both parents are Jewish and the last thing Hitler could stand was a Jew winning the gold medal. Instead, they picked the fencer, Helene

Mayer. She's perfect: blond-haired, blue-eyed, and only one-half Jew. It was her father. A doctor. And he's deceased."

This choice came as a surprise. "Mayer stayed in Los Angeles after the '32 Olympics to attend university. Your organization stripped her of membership in the German fencing club. Why would she come back?"

"She is willing to overlook what we did for the chance to compete again," explained Lewald. "Mayer won the gold in '28 but faltered in '32. She hasn't lived in the US long enough to represent them and wants one more chance to win a medal. With Mayer on our team, Germany gets to keep the games."

"Theodor, you worked hard to put these games together. What I don't understand is why you were removed as head of our Olympic Committee at this late date."

He took a long pull of his drink and gazed at nothing. I was about to repeat myself when he asked, "Do you want the truth or their bullshit line?"

"Always the truth."

"I was raised Christian, but my grandmother on my father's side was Jewish."

Chapter 11

Beginning in 1926, Hitler vacationed in Berchtesgaden. He stayed in hotels and enjoyed long walks on ancient trails in the Bavarian Alps. Not long after, he rented Haus Wachenfeld from the widow of industrialist *Kommerzienrat* Otto Winter, a businessman from Buxtehude. Haus Wachenfeld was perched in Obersalzberg, with majestic views of snow-capped mountains and fields of wildflowers. Once he became chancellor, Hitler converted the modest chalet into a country manor. A new railway station was built to make access easier. Offices were constructed, hotels renovated, and support services provided to ensure the comfort of guests. Hitler renamed the expanded house "Berghof" (Mountain Court) and spent as much time there as possible.

The Berghof was Eva Braun's domain. While excluded from Hitler's life everywhere else, she presided over lavish dinner parties wearing exquisite dresses Hitler bought for her. It was at the Berghof that a select group mingled and dined with Germany's ruler and "real" first lady . . . who was relegated to anonymity everywhere else.

On a weekend that Carla visited her brother, I was the lone guest with Eva and Hitler at the Berghof. We hiked the steep Alpine trails, picnicked in sun-drenched meadows, and sipped Alsatian wine while Hitler drank tea on the outdoor terrace. We indulged Hitler in his favorite pastime: watching movie after movie in the cavernous living room that converted into a large screening room.

When it was time to leave, Eva put a secret plan into effect.

"Let's stop at the Lambacher Hof for lunch," Eva suggested as we approached our car at the head of the entourage that accompanied Hitler everywhere. "Lake Chiemsee is magnificent this time of year."

The Lambacher Hof sat on the north shore of the lake, situated between *Gollenshausen* and *Seebruck*. We drove up to the white building with the peaked roof made colorful by red, yellow, white, and orange flowers that spilled from boxes attached to the balcony railing above the front door. Each window sported hand-carved wooden frames. Two painted murals stood out above them: an elegant carriage on the right side and an old-time covered wagon on the left, each pulled by a team of horses.

The patrons eating outside gawked when *SS* security piled out of their vehicles and scurried into a protective phalanx as the *Führer* marched past. Eva, relegated to playing the role of a dutiful secretary, lagged behind. Inside, the hostess nodded when she saw Eva and—without a word spoken—ushered us to a private alcove where two people were already seated . . . their faces obscured by the bright sunlight behind them . . . but I suspected who they might be.

Eva clapped in glee. "What a surprise! Look who's here! *Mutti* and *Vati*."

Mama and Papa!

Franziska and Fritz Braun rose, openmouthed, at the sight of the *Führer*.

Hitler turned to me in horror.

I whispered, "They are just as surprised as you are."

Hitler stepped forward and without greeting either, took Franziska's hand and kissed it. When he reached out to Fritz Braun, Fritz started to take Hitler's hand then jerked back into a Hitler salute.

Everyone's awkwardness was palpable.

I broke the ice. "It is so good to see you, again, *Frau* Braun. Remember me?"

"You are Herr Hoffmann's friend," she answered. I clicked my heels and bowed.

"You brought those beautiful flowers when Eva was so . . . so fatigued."

Eva beamed that she could introduce her parents to the *Führer*.

The Brauns, unsure what to do next, slid onto their seats. Eva and Hitler sat at opposite ends of the table. Hitler remained mute during those early minutes.

"*Mutti. Vati,*" Eva said to her parents, "the *Führer* and I met many times in Herr Hoffmann's studio."

Franziska, at the *Führer's* left, was mesmerized being so close to Germany's leader. She stared at me across from her and peeked at Hitler every so often.

For his part, Fritz Braun winced each time Hitler and Eva used the familiar "*Du*" to address each other. The more they spoke, the more he twisted his napkin until it was a mangled mess, all the while his ruddy cheeks grew redder.

Hitler smoothed his moustache. He brushed back his forelock. He blotted his lips with a linen napkin though no food had been served. If he made eye contact, it was only with Eva. Finally, food arrived: sauerbraten and Pilsner for everyone, and steamed vegetables for Hitler, who moved them around the plate without eating.

What little conversation there had been was replaced with chewing sounds, the clack of utensils on plates, supping drinks, and glasses clattering on the table.

With the dishes cleared, tea was served. Without asking if she wanted any, Hitler added spoonful after spoonful of sugar into Franziska's teacup. He stopped only after the tea spilled over the lip onto the saucer.

Franziska stared in bewilderment; Hitler managed a meek smile.

I sat thunderstruck at the scene as it unfolded. Here was one of the great orators of our time, a man comfortable speaking in front of thousands, transformed into a mush of nerves before a retired schoolteacher and his wife.

When Hitler could bear no more, he stood, bowed, mumbled something to the Brauns about pressing duties, and tugged on my sleeve. By the time I turned to join him, Hitler was halfway out the door, leaving Eva stranded to make her way back to Munich with her parents.

Outside, Hitler said, "Friedrich, I don't know what happened in there. My tongue swelled inside my mouth. I could barely talk."

*

"Did you hear me?" Carla poked my arm. "You need to listen when I talk. Our relationship is too new to ignore me."

No matter how I tried, I could not lose the image of Hitler heaping spoonful after spoonful of sugar into Franziska Braun's tea.

I snapped my head toward her. "Sorry. I was thinking of something."

"What I said was that I met with the minister of war. He sat for a portrait. Thank you, again."

"General Field Marshal Werner von Blomberg has a reputation for being quite stern. All business. How did you find him?"

"That's partially accurate," Carla said. "At the start, he appeared to have more starch in his body than in his shirts. I know the questions you tend to ask when I return from these commissions, so I probed him for his feelings about the Rhineland takeover. Unlike Beck who opposed it, Blomberg supported Hitler's decision despite the chance it might provoke a war, but he seems less enchanted with Hitler now."

It was Blomberg, in '34, who told Hitler to get rid of Röhm before Hindenburg died or the army would support von Papen, rather than Hitler, to be the next president. He then supported Hitler's early efforts to reverse Germany's losses under the Treaty of Versailles. His change of attitude was most interesting.

Carla had become a valuable resource. Although disinterested in politics, she steered conversations along the lines I suggested. She had no idea that Bernhard Weiss existed, let alone that I shared much of the information with him. As long as she believed that I wanted the information in my official capacity in the *SS*, she had the perfect defense if she fell under suspicion.

*

A week later, Carla and I were about to go out to dinner when the phone rang.

"Can you meet me tonight?" Kitty's voice was laced with concern.

"What's wrong, Kitty? Is there a problem in the salon?"

"It's the Nightingale. Some so-called patrons are getting out of hand. Marta doesn't know what to do about them."

"Marta could have called."

"She said not to bother you. But I have no one else to turn to."

When I was the Nightingale's bouncer, it was my job to deal with boisterous patrons.

"Isn't there a tough at the front door to keep everything in order?"

"He is afraid to cross them. They are policemen. Please meet us there, Friedrich."

"I have plans with Carla. I'll cancel them."

"No. Bring her. Meet me at the Nightingale in two hours."

Chapter 12

Two hours later, Marta met us in the entrance to the Nightingale. After I introduced Marta to Carla, Marta said, "Friedrich, I didn't want Kitty to bother you, but I *am* glad you're here. Ever since Max died, the local police have gotten more demanding. In the old days, they took their cut and protected us. Never hung around. Now they stay in the club after they collect, eat and drink every week without paying, and—this is recent—have the nerve to demand more money. Worse, they harass the staff. Especially Heidi."

"I thought Heidi was a chef?"

Marta shook her head. "She wanted out of the kitchen. She's been an immense help out front."

"Are those men here tonight?"

"They will be here later. They come once a week. Always drunk. We're their last stop, so they stay. At least you picked a good night. Leander is performing tonight. She plans to sing her latest hit."

Hearing Zarah Leander's name, Carla grew wide-eyed.

Zarah Leander was a leading film and cabaret star. In her new contract with my old studio, UFA, she demanded half her salary be paid in Swedish kroner and deposited directly in a Stockholm bank.

"Joseph Goebbels labeled her an 'Enemy of the State,'" I said as an aside to Carla, "because she refuses to attend Party functions. Goebbels once met her and asked if Zarah was a Jewish name. She gave it right back. Said it was no more Jewish than Joseph."

Heidi joined us dressed in a see-through black camisole, skimpy skirt, and black fishnet stockings; the latter I first saw worn a dozen years earlier by the dancers at New York's Cotton Club.

"Heidi, did you borrow that outfit from one of Kitty's girls?" I asked.

"Don't you like it?" She twirled around. "I'm a Berliner, now."

Carla poked me in the ribs before I could say that Max might not have approved of her dressing that way. Instead, we followed her to a table.

By the time the lights dimmed, the ne'er-do-well cops had not arrived. Marta introduced Zarah Leander, whose sultry sensuality, combined with a singing voice of operetta quality, made her a current darling of the German public. Merge Marlene Dietrich's looks with a better voice, and Greta Garbo's Swedish coolness, Zarah Leander would be that person.

Before Zarah sang her closing song, *"Davon geht die Welt nicht unter"* ("This is not the end of the world"), she announced, "This is dedicated to lyricist Bruno Balz, whose release from prison was arranged by composer Michael Jary. As a team, Jary and Balz have composed many songs I sing, especially those tonight. Bruno is a homosexual. To remain free, Bruno had to agree that his name could no longer appear in public. He also had to agree to enter what we call a *lavender* marriage to a woman. Even though he was forced underground, Bruno Balz continues to write. This is one of his greatest songs."

As Zarah began, there was a flash of light from the back. I turned to see three men standing in the shadows. After Zarah sang her last note, she received a standing ovation. When the applause died down and the lights rose, one called out, "Jary should get a pink badge and sent to Dachau. You should be arrested with the other queers."

Although not in uniform, they were the three cops Marta had described.

"The one who shouted is the leader," Marta explained. "He makes the weekly collection. The others tag along. This isn't the first time they've shouted at our performers. The guests know to ignore the blowhards."

The three sat at a back table. They guffawed at their own jokes, took good-natured jabs at each other's arms, and ate as if at a trough, all the while slurping beer after beer.

"Are they like this every time?"

"Worse," answered Marta. "Wait. It is only a matter of time."

It did not take long before one pinched a waitress. She performed an artful balancing act without dropping her tray of food.

Heidi neared their table. I was about to spring to her aid.

Kitty grabbed my arm. "Watch."

The leader yanked Heidi onto his lap. In a flash, she elbowed him in the gut; he yelped.

She bounded up, smacked the top of his head, and stormed off while the three roared.

"Heidi can handle herself," Marta stated. "Others can't. Trays get dropped, drinks spill. These pigs grab breasts. Sometimes worse. I'll pay their bribes, but I can't countenance this behavior any longer."

"Did you try talking to them?" asked Carla.

"You're sweet," answered Marta. "I can see why Friedrich likes you. Of course, I tried. More than once. But talking to them is like herding cats. Doesn't matter which direction the conversation goes, in the end, they do what they want." She looked at me. "It's good that you saw this, Friedrich. It must remind you of when you worked here."

Only Max knew that a drunk swung at me on my last evening as a bouncer. My brass-knuckled fist smashed into his trachea. He died on the spot. I had to flee Berlin. That was more than fifteen years ago, when the city was in the midst of a revolution and unexplained deaths were commonplace.

"When will they be here next?" I asked.

"Same time next week," answered Marta.

"That's all I need to know," I said.

"Whatever you do, will you avoid a ruckus in the club?"

I smirked. "You have to ask?"

At home, Carla asked, "How do you plan to make these men behave?"

"I can be persuasive when need be."

"That does not surprise me . . ." She kissed me and tugged my hand. ". . . as can I." Carla put the Nightingale out of my mind for the rest of the night.

*

Marta greeted me at the club entrance the following week.

"I thought you would be in uniform," she said.

I brushed my fingers against my shirt. "Avoids paperwork. Are they here?"

Heidi nodded toward them. "Nothing worse than usual. They pinched a waitress's ass. It was amusing to see martinis spill all over them, but not when they got angry afterwards."

I stepped toward them.

"Remember, there's three of them," she called out.

In a flash I was inches from the main guy. I waited. When he did look up, his words were slurred. "Whaddya want? Beat it, bean-pole." Then he took a better look. "Tree trunk would suit you better." He crossed his eyes to be funny; his friends rolled with laughter.

I glared at him. "You and your friends have had enough to drink. It is time to leave."

He hiked his thumb towards me. "This mountain of a jerk thinks he can tell us what to do." He flashed a shit-faced grin. "Should we teach him a lesson?"

I grabbed his thumb and twisted. He squealed. "The three of you have overstayed your welcome. Outside." I smacked the back of his head for good measure. "Now." By the time they tottered to their feet, I was out the side exit and at the rear of the darkened alleyway I knew so well.

The leader poked his head out the door. I called out. "Back here!"

The three advanced down the alley. Drunk as they were, they stalked as a synchronized unit.

I cocked my pistol. They stopped in their tracks. "Hands up. Now!"

They raised their hands, palms forward.

"Here is what we are going to do . . ."

"Before you go further, *mein Herr*," the leader stepped forward, hands still up, "we are Berlin Police."

The moment the other two inched closer, I jammed my gun against the leader's cheek. "Stay where you are or . . ." I jabbed harder and he yelped, "next time you see your friend, it will be in the morgue."

Rather than stop and wonder if I was crazy enough to shoot a cop, they fanned out in a wider arc. Though crocked, they knew to spread out.

I fired a shot alongside the leader's head; the bullet bounced harmlessly off the brick wall. "The next one won't be a warning. You two: step back."

The leader rubbed his ear from the pain caused by the close blast but made no effort to have them stand down.

The two stood fast.

Without another word, I kneed the leader in the groin. He collapsed, rolled on his side, writhing. I wagged the gun to hold the other thugs at bay. But when the leader reached for his holstered gun, I kicked his hand and stepped on his fingers. There was the crunch of bone.

"Here, let me get that for you."

I grabbed his gun and barked, "No more games. You two. Guns on the ground! One finger only."

They had seen enough and withdrew their pistols as instructed.

"Help your friend up and then the three of you hug the wall like it's your long-lost mother."

With my gun trained on their backs, I kicked their revolvers out of harm's way.

"What's this all about?" asked the leader. "I remember you from last week."

"For one thing, it's about your manners."

"What about them? You don't like us eating with our fingers?" said the leader.

The others cackled.

I switched gun hands and jabbed him in the kidney. His knees buckled. I caught him and pressed him back against the wall.

"You want to know what this is about? I understand bribes. It's the world we live in."

"Glad you see it our way." He lifted his head off the wall.

"I didn't say you could move." I grabbed him by the neck and scraped his cheek against the brick. I squeezed hard. His face darkened. "I see nothing your way!" I said through clenched teeth. I eased my grip and he staggered, gasping. His comrades moved to help him; I brandished the gun. "Don't even think about it. Back against the wall."

"I'm only going to say this once. Taking bribes does not give you the right to free food or drink. It certainly does not give you the right to put your hands on the staff. Do I make myself clear?"

The goon to the right turned his meaty face to me. "We don't know who you are, mister, but no one messes with Berlin policemen."

I slammed my gun across his cheek. His head bounced off the wall and he crumpled to the ground.

I shoved the leader hard; he smashed into the wall.

"No more," the leader said through clenched teeth. Blood gushed from his nose. "We get your message."

"Which is what?"

"Leave the merchandise alone."

"You're not as dumb as you look. Collect your money and leave. No more food or beer. If I ever hear that any of you stayed an extra second at the Nightingale or, worse, touched the help, that will be the last time you touch anyone again. Is that clear?"

They grunted their surrender.

I stepped back. "Get up," I ordered the one still on the ground. "You two turn around." When the three faced me, I said, "Before we part ways, *mein Herren*, give me your *Ausweis*."

"We need our IDs," protested the leader. "We can't give them up."

"You will . . . and you'll leave your guns where they are."

"How will we explain losing our service weapons?"

"Not my problem. But I promise this. If you don't honor our little contract, the president of the Berlin Police will wonder why your guns and *Ihre Ausweis Karten* mysteriously showed up at his door after you claimed to have lost them. Think of the explaining you will have to do. Is that understood?"

Eyes downcast, they all mumbled something inarticulate meant to be affirmative.

"One last thing: from now on your protection money is cut in half."

Chapter 13

As the Olympics neared, Joseph Goebbels let loose a storm of propaganda for what proved to be the greatest games ever held. A new airfield was inaugurated in Berlin. Seen from the air, it was shaped like an eagle in flight. A brand-new stadium that seated in excess of one hundred thousand was finished ahead of schedule.

Goebbels orchestrated the events' grandiose moments. For the first time in history, a chain of runners would carry the flame from Athens to the host city—Berlin—to light the Olympic torch in the new stadium. The moment the flame set the torch ablaze, the airship *Hindenburg*, would fly over the new Olympic Stadium to the thunderous cheers of one hundred and ten thousand people, while groundbreaking TV and radio broadcasts would be seen and heard around the world. Anti-Semitic posters had been papered over. Not a trace remained.

*

Carla returned from photographing Hermann Göring at his estate named for his deceased first wife. "Have you ever been to Carinhall? I tell you, Friedrich, I didn't know what to look at first. Renoirs. Monets. Van Goghs. Medieval carvings. It was as good as or better than any museum I've ever visited."

This art was not donated by patrons. It was bartered at deep discounts from Jews seeking safe passage out of Germany.

"Was Emmy there?" I asked.

"We spoke for a few minutes and then she left us alone. Göring wore a new white uniform. So many medals dangled from it, I thought he would topple over."

"Did Göring chat with you?"

"Chat?" Carla exclaimed. "The man would not stop talking. He will soon oversee three cabinet positions: economics, agriculture, *and* industry. Imagine. Hitler gave him a new title: Reich Plenipotentiary . . . with the power to cut through red tape. Göring needed to consolidate these departments to execute the Four-Year economic plan. And he still runs the Luftwaffe."

"The man's ego is as large as his girth," I said.

"Bigger than you might think," answered Carla. "Herr Göring said—more than once—that while Hitler was our leader, he, Hermann Göring, would be the one to save Germany."

*

Excitement for the upcoming Olympics was ubiquitous. Even people uninterested in sports jabbered about the Games. I could not wait to see Jesse Owens, the Negro track star from the United States, perform. I'd first heard of Owens after his historic performance in Michigan a few months back. There, Owens broke three world records in one day, and tied a fourth. Knowing that Hitler and the other Nazis disdained Black people, I was anxious to see Hitler's reaction to this great athlete and the other seventeen talented American-Negro Olympians accompanying him.

*

I received an unexpected call from Reinhard Heydrich.

"Friedrich, would you meet me at the shooting range at Wannsee? I need to discuss a delicate matter with you."

Heydrich was uncharacteristically cordial; my antennae perked up. "Can't we do this over the phone, Reinhard? I'm quite busy at the moment."

"If it were anything else, Friedrich, I would be only too happy to accommodate you. But not in this instance."

An hour later, I found Heydrich at the shooting range.

"Here." He handed me a pistol. "It's a new Walther autoloader with a lightweight slide."

"It has a nice feel to it." I raised the pistol and sighted down the barrel. "What's this about?"

"I'll explain in a moment. But first . . . follow me."

We marched to a barrier where he pointed to a target retracted on its side. He pulled out a stopwatch.

"That target is twenty-five meters from here. On the count of three, I will push a button and the target will become visible. You will have eight seconds to fire a string of six shots. You repeat this twice more. The only break between each string is the time needed to reset the target."

"That's a string of eighteen shots. Then what?"

"Then it gets tougher. You do the same thing, only this time you have six seconds to fire the string of six. After those three times, the time shortens to four seconds for each string and then to three seconds."

"Why am I doing this?"

"I will explain after you finish."

For the next half hour, I shot three strings of six shots in intervals of eight, six, four, and three seconds.

Heydrich retrieved the targets and shuffled through the stack, his eyes widening with each page. "You hit perfect targets in all the rounds except the last one, where you missed twice. That's thirty-four out of thirty-six hits. Good enough to make the team."

"What team?"

"Why, the Olympic team, of course. This qualifies you."

"I have no intention of taking anybody's place on the team. Those men have worked hard to get where they are."

"You don't understand. Our best marksmen are Cornelius van Oyen and Heinz Hax. Heinz won the silver in '32. After your little display, you are as good as either one. With practice, you could be better. Even win the gold. But that's not the point. Hax's gun backfired at practice yesterday. He scratched his cornea and is forced to wear a patch. The doctor said it could take weeks to heal. Even then, his vision might be blurred. If that happens, he can't compete. You can solve that potential predicament as an alternate."

I had never competed in anything; at least I had no such memory. Part of me wanted to say "yes."

"Give me a couple of days to think about it."

"Remember, Friedrich, this is not about you. It is for the glory of the Reich."

*

For years, I avoided stepping out of the shadows. I shunned the limelight to preserve the secrets of Pasewalk. But if I were front and center during the Olympics, someone might recognize me or my style of shooting. Who knows? It could be a start to learn about myself and a step closer to discovering my true identity. Did I dare do it?

I wrestled with this question for two days before I brought it to the only person who could understand my dilemma.

*

Hitler was eating a lunch of berries and cream when I showed up at his office.

"I am glad you had time to see me, *mein Führer.*"

He put his silver spoon down, patted his lips clean, and offered me a seat.

"There is always time for you, Friedrich. What is troubling you?"

How to start?

"Do you remember when we went to Berlin in 1920 to learn from the Kapp Putsch?"

"We didn't learn very well, did we? Our putsch also failed."

"I was referring to how I stayed behind in the hopes I would find a clue to my identity? To this day, I stare at buildings, look down alleyways, linger when I see children playing in a park, all in the hopes to jar a memory loose. I never stopped wanting to know who I am. Do I have relatives? Was I married? I may even have children. I wish I knew."

Hitler turned solemn. "What brought this on?"

"One of the members of the twenty-five-meter rapid fire pistol event injured his eye. Heydrich knew I shot well. He invited me to the pistol range without telling me why. He had me shoot at targets. It turns out I scored high." The more I spoke the more agitated Hitler became. I ended by saying, "Heydrich wants me on the team."

Hitler jumped to his feet. "You must never think of such a thing."

My body stiffened. "Wolf, this is something I want to do. Before you arrived at Pasewalk, I discovered I was an expert marksman."

Veins swelled on his forehead. He wagged his finger.

"I never want to hear the name Pasewalk mentioned again. That part of our past is finished. Done. Buried for all eternity."

I was crestfallen. My shoulders slumped as he spoke.

His face softened. "Friedrich. Think what could happen. The shooting range is at Wannsee. Not many spectators will be on hand. That is not so terrible. But if you win a medal? You will be on the platform in front of more than one hundred thousand, not to mention hundreds of cameras clicking your picture. Newspapers. Interviews. Magazine pictures. You will be asked about your history. Where were you born? Who was your father? Your mother? Do you have any brothers or sisters? What schools you went to? Where did you learn to shoot like that? Was it in the army? Nothing that you say can be verified. If you say the wrong thing, it comes back to not only bite you but me, too. Everything we have worked for will be ruined. We can't let that happen."

"I need a chance to prove myself."

"Friedrich, you *have* proven yourself. Countless times. The dozen or so men who lead this country know who you are, very well! What more recognition do you need?"

I struggled to corral my emotions. He was right.

Hitler patted my shoulder. "Friedrich. If the medal is that important, I will have a special one made for you. Out of gold."

*

The Games went forward with me as a spectator. As a special treat, Hitler permitted Eva to attend. But, of course, she could not sit by his side. The one hundred and ten thousand souls in the stadium had no idea that the pretty girl seated behind the *Führer* was the anonymous first lady of Germany.

I escorted Eva from the stadium after the last event when she drew me out of earshot to tell a story. "You were there when my father first learned about the *Führer* and me. *Vati* doesn't believe for a minute that *Herr* Hoffmann provided a house for Gretl and me to live in alone. He knows the *Führer* is behind it. And he knows it is not innocent." Eva giggled. "My father had the nerve to write the *Führer* a letter. He referred to him as His Excellency and complained about having 'extreme distress as a paterfamilias.' He ended the letter urging the *Führer* to 'please advise Eva to return to the bosom of the family.'"

I scratched my head. "How do *you* know what was in it? I doubt your father showed you the letter."

She flashed her pretty teeth. "He asked *Herr* Hoffmann to give it to the *Führer*. Hoffmann was naughty. He read it. When he saw what was in it, he gave it to me. I was horrified. I ripped it to pieces and threw it in the garbage. The *Führer* will never know my father wrote him a letter, let alone what it contained."

*

The Olympics delivered everything the Nazis sought. World attention. Kudos for a flawless extravaganza. Even acclaim for the most medals won: eighty-nine. The United States was a distant second with fifty-six.

Nevertheless, one person prevented the Nazis from portraying their victories as proof of Aryan racial superiority: Jesse Owens and his four gold medals exploded the Nazi myth of Aryan supremacy.

Chapter 14

The end of the Olympics marked the resumption of the Nazi mania to drive the Jews from Germany. The posters were back, and new pressures wielded.

The day after the foreign athletes left, Kitty called in a panic. "Marta was served papers that claim the Nightingale's ownership must be transferred out of Jewish hands to some man, an Aryan businessman I never heard of. I made calls; tried to explain that I own the Nightingale and am not Jewish. I couldn't get anyone to listen."

I instantly understood. As part of their program to force the Jews to leave, the Nazis were compelling Jewish owners of manufacturing businesses, publishing houses, banks, breweries, and department stores to sell their companies for a fraction of their worth.

"Now that the Olympics have ended," I told Kitty, "They are focused on Aryanizing smaller Jewish businesses. With majority ownership, the Nazis will use those receipts to help fund Göring's Four-Year Plan and squeeze more Jews out."

Kitty protested. "But I'm not Jewish. It's a mistake to take the Nightingale from me."

"Did you ever get papers of ownership after Max's will was read?"

"I assumed that the ownership would have been properly recorded when it passed to me."

"Any number of things could have happened. The lawyer may have forgotten, but I doubt that. My best guess is that local bank managers comb through lists of Jewish-owned businesses. When they come across one, they exert pressure for their cronies to get them on the cheap. The Dresdner Bank is one of the biggest culprits."

"I thought banks were above these types of shenanigans," Kitty said.

"Not when their major client is Himmler and the Nazi Party. The Dresdner Bank finances the acquisition of land and construction for the concentration camps. Putting pressure on Jewish-owned businesses is child's play for them. Let me look into it."

*

I wanted to help Kitty but given the overlapping bureaucracies, I was uncertain the best way to go about this. My first thought was to hire a lawyer. I ticked off names until I stopped and laughed. What was I doing? Minister of Interior Wilhelm Frick and I went back to 1920. If anyone could straighten this out, he could.

I made the call. Frick was out on some matter; I got one of his top deputies. "Vize-Minister Jäger. Speaking?"

"This is *Obergruppenführer* Richard, liaison to the *Führer.* There has been a mistake, Vize-Minister Jäger, that you need to correct immediately."

"What is the issue?"

"The ownership of the Nightingale Club is listed wrongly. It must be clarified. The previous owner, Max Klinghofer, is dead. Kitty Schmidt is the legal and rightful owner now. The records must reflect this."

"Are there papers that confirm this?" Jäger asked.

"Klinghofer's will transferred the club's ownership to *Frau* Schmidt upon his death . . . that event occurred two years ago. Some fool in the bowels of your department ordered the club's ownership transferred to an Aryan. Schmidt is German. She is an Aryan. The order is illegal and must be rescinded at once."

"Our records . . ." Jäger started to say.

"If your records were accurate, I would not have had to make this call."

I waited a beat. "Jäger? Are you there?"

"I am almost finished, *Obergruppenführer.*" Metal grated against metal; a file door closed. "There is no record of the club's ownership having been transferred to *Frau* Schmidt."

"Do I have to come down and find those papers myself, Jäger? Or better still, should I bother Minister Frick to have a nice little chat about the efficiencies of your office?"

"That will not be necessary, *Obergruppenführer* Richard," answered Jäger. "It will be done immediately, sir."

"In that case I will be certain to commend your work, Jäger, when I see the minister again."

*

The phone rang, disturbing our cocktail time at home. My glass was empty. "How about a refill?" Carla asked as I hopped up to take the call.

It was Gestapo Headquarters. An *SS* officer advised me that Lilian Harvey was being interrogated because she helped a homosexual choreographer, Jens Keith, escape to Switzerland. She refused to answer any questions. *Reichsführer* Himmler ordered that she be kept overnight . . . or longer.

"Did she ask that I be called?"

"*Nein.* This is a courtesy call. Your name is in her file."

After he told me his name, I said, "*Hauptscharführer* Bauer. This is a direct order: nothing is to happen to *Fräulein* Harvey until I get there. Is that clear?"

"*Jawohl!*"

I slammed the phone down.

Carla approached, two drinks in hand. "What was that about?"

"Lilian Harvey tipped off a choreographer the Gestapo was about to arrest. She's being held for questioning."

"Will they send her to a camp?" she asked, following me to my closet.

I shrugged into my uniform. "There is that chance."

Carla said, "I'm coming with you."

At Gestapo Headquarters, the clerk led us to an interrogation room in the basement.

Lilian threw up her hands in disgust as we entered. "I thought you were more of a man, Friedrich. How could you do this to me?"

"You've got it all wrong. I am here to help you."

"Spare me your holier-than-thou crap, Friedrich. I am sorry I ever stepped foot back in Germany. It is so much worse than when I left. How do you live with yourself? Half my friends have been forced to leave. The others walk in fear that they will be arrested and put in your camps for no reason."

"They are not my camps, Lilian."

"This is black and white, Friedrich: you are a Nazi. That makes every concentration camp yours. You may believe you are a good person. Innocent of wrongdoing. Here's a news bulletin: If you hang around Hitler and his goons, you are as guilty as they are." Then Lilian addressed Carla. "And you, honey, if you know what's good for you, you'll leave this jerk before he hurts you . . . like he did me."

I took Carla's arm. "Let's go. This was obviously a mistake."

Carla pulled away to face Lilian. "You don't know me, but I was on the set next to yours, at the studio, more than once. So many girls looked up to you. Admired you. Even wanted to be you. I was one. I'm sorry things turned out the way they did for you. Life is tough. But let me tell you this: You are wrong about this man. They were about to send you to a cell and then to the camps. That's why we're here. Friedrich made certain you would go free. And how do you thank him? By being a nasty, ungrateful bitch."

Lilian started to say something.

Carla stamped her foot. "Don't dare say anything." She grabbed my hand. "Now we can go."

As we headed for the stairs, Carla clutched her chest. She grew pale, her breathing shallow. She leaned into the wall. Her skin was moist to the touch.

"What's wrong?" I asked. "What can I do for you?"

"My heart races when I get excited. I got light-headed. That's all. It's happened before." She glanced at her purse. "Pills in the side pocket," she whispered.

She popped one under her tongue. I eased her onto the lone chair in the hallway. "Are you okay for me to leave to get water?"

After a few minutes, Carla felt better.

"Can you climb the stairs?" I asked.

She nodded. "Just don't let go."

It took time to navigate the stairs. Carla rested when we reached the first floor while I found *Hauptscharführer* Bauer.

"*Reichsführer* Himmler said to tell you *Fräulein* Harvey gets a pass this time, but she must be very careful whom she associates with in the future. They will watch her every move."

"When will she be released?"

"After papers are filled out."

Outside, Carla took a deep breath. "I feel better now. Thank you for your help."

"You got me worried. How come I didn't know about this condition before? How serious is it?"

"It hasn't happened for a long time. Certainly not while I've known you. It's another reason I left the film business. Too much stress."

"Is there anything I can do to help?" I asked.

"You are my best medicine. As long as we are together, I will be fine."

She kissed me and then asked, "What will happen to her?"

"Goebbels controls the career of every artist in Germany. If an actor or actress doesn't do what Goebbels wants, they are finished. Lilian is principled. Pig-headed even. As bright as her star was, the Nazis will make certain it fades to nothing. In time, she will be forgotten."

Chapter 15

"We received an invitation addressed to us as a couple for the first time," Carla announced with excitement. Against all convention, she had recently moved in with me. At first, Carla was reluctant to leave her flat. The reason she gave was that *Oranienburger Straße*—the former Jewish neighborhood— had evolved into the center of Berlin's art scene. Her real reason was that married couples lived together, single women lived with their families or on their own . . . until which time they got married. That was the German way.

I couldn't tell her the real reason I could not marry was that I had no memory of a past life and that maybe, somewhere, there was a wife waiting for me. Instead, I said, "Given my rank and position, no one would dare say anything or think ill of you."

That was the reassurance Carla needed to hear. She still had her studio nearby. As for me? When Carla moved in, I was happier than I had been in years.

I hung my jacket on the hall coat tree and pecked her on the cheek. "What invitation is that? Did the *Führer* ask you to photograph him?"

Carla put her hands on her hips. "And offend Heinrich Hoffmann? We both know that will never happen," she answered. "No, Erika Canaris invited us to dinner next Friday. What do you make of it?"

"They're the reason we met," I said. "It's a nice gesture on their part."

"Imagine if you never showed up that afternoon," Carla said. "We may never have found each other."

I pulled her into me; we kissed.

"What was that for?"

"For staying long enough for me to show up," I answered. "What if I got there later?"

"Truth be told, once I knew you were coming, I was prepared to wait as long as necessary."

"Is that so?"

Carla wrinkled her nose and gave one of her dazzling smiles. "And my intuition was right."

I sniffed this way and that. "My intuition tells me there is nothing on the stove that will burn. Am I right?"

"What did you have in mind?"

"Hors d'oeuvres."

Hand-in-hand, we scampered upstairs.

*

The following Friday, Erika Canaris greeted us at the door. "I am so pleased you could join us. Come in. Wilhelm is somewhere with his beloved dachshunds."

Admiral Canaris was in his study with one treasured dog on his lap and the other at his feet. A lit pipe smoldered in an astray. The admiral eased the one on his lap onto the floor and stood as we entered, kissed Carla on both cheeks, and then asked his wife, "Is there something Carla could help you with? I need a moment with Friedrich."

Two high-backed leather chairs were angled toward each other in front of a floor-to-ceiling bookcase. A cut-crystal decanter and two glasses rested on top of a small table that separated the chairs. A map of the world was inlaid into the table's surface. Canaris lifted the decanter and removed the handmade glass stopper. "Scotch?" He didn't wait for an answer. "This is known as a captain's decanter," he explained as he poured. "It has an extra wide base so it will not tip over on rough seas. I've taken it wherever I've lived since I first saw it in Gibraltar during the Great War."

We toasted each other. The aged scotch was smoky and burned as it slid down the back of my throat.

"Mind?" Canaris rattled a box of matches. I shook my head. He struck a match and puffed until orange-blue embers flared and crackled.

Admiral Canaris did not spend time with anyone without a reason. I didn't have to wait long to find out why I was alone with him. "I need your help," he said through a haze of smoke.

"Care to elaborate?" I asked.

"How well do you know Reinhard Heydrich?"

Is this a trap?

I sipped the scotch before answering. "We've had more than our fair share of run-ins. What is it that you want to know?"

"Some months ago, Heydrich came to see me about a 'sensitive matter.' Do you have any idea what it could have been?"

"I haven't a clue."

Canaris puffed on his pipe and then said, "The sensitive matter was you. He told me that according to army records, you died in Pasewalk Hospital."

I swallowed hard. "As you can see, I am very much alive."

Either Canaris didn't hear me or chose to ignore what I said.

"Imagine. When Heydrich went to Pasewalk Hospital, there were *no* records concerning a Friedrich Richard."

"What has this to do with me? He was after a different Friedrich Richard."

Canaris threw up his hands. "That's what I said. But Heydrich would have none of it. He pointed out that army records are never wrong. Not when it comes to listing the deaths of soldiers. He came to me only after he checked every other agency for another Friedrich Richard."

One of Canaris's dogs whimpered. He gave it a biscuit. He struck a match to relight his pipe except it was still lit. He smiled and extinguished the flame.

"What did Heydrich hope to gain by coming to you?" I asked.

"He wanted to know if there was a Friedrich Richard in our foreign intelligence files. I checked but knew there no such person in our services."

I stood. "If there's nothing else, the women must be wondering what happened to us." Canaris lifted the second dog onto his lap.

"You need to hear the rest." His tone was firm. More like a command.

I sank back into the chair, certain I did not want to hear what else Germany's spymaster was about to say.

"It's no secret that you've known the *Führer* since when? 1920? Possibly before that? No one has remained as close to him as you. That got me thinking that you two might share a secret. Maybe more than one."

He plumbed my face for a flicker of a response. I didn't twitch or blink.

Canaris continued. "Like most Germans, I am well aware that Hitler wrote in *Mein Kampf* how he was blinded in a gas attack. That his eyes turned to glowing coals. He was treated at Pasewalk Military Hospital. But his autobiography never mentioned the name of the doctor who treated him. Why is that Friedrich?"

"Perhaps an oversight."

Canaris reached for his pipe. "Or perhaps quite deliberate." The tobacco sparked. "I never gave it a thought before. But after Heydrich came to me, it seemed important. It occurred to me that if Friedrich Richard had once been at Pasewalk, it might have been when Hitler was there."

"Why would it matter?"

"Hear me out, Friedrich. Once I latch onto a notion, I follow it to a logical conclusion based on reasonable probabilities. This is no different. I took Heydrich's lead and went to Pasewalk Hospital. Sure enough, there was no medical record for Friedrich Richard."

"Why is that surprising? Heydrich already told you it was not there."

Canaris ignored me. "I dug deeper."

"The *Führer* was injured in Flanders. In Belgium. Why would they transport him hundreds of miles from the front when there were qualified hospitals closer to the battlefield? He could have been at any one of them."

Canaris put his pipe down. He motioned me closer.

"What is crucial in my little tale is that as long as I was at Pasewalk, I decided to see if there were records of Hitler's treatment by an eye doctor there. There weren't . . . there was no record of any treatment of Corporal Hitler by any doctor, but you knew that already, didn't you?"

By now, I'd clenched my hands so hard I thought I would break a finger.

Canaris continued. "What everyone forgets is that hospital commandants keep separate intake records. Do you know what I found in the commandant's file at Pasewalk?"

Droplets of sweat wobbled on my upper lip. I ran my sleeve across my mouth. "What?"

"A report that Adolf Hitler was a psychopath suffering from hysterical blindness. The commandant's notes contained a psychiatrist's report on Hitler's sanity." Then added, "Or should I say, lack thereof?"

"Was the psychiatrist identified?"

"Not by name."

"Did you find Friedrich Richard's intake record?"

I was lightheaded that our long-kept secrets were about to be exposed.

"It was there . . . but I dismissed it as not being you. The man wasn't nearly as tall or broad. And that poor chap committed suicide. You're here." His eyes crinkled with warmth. "A dead Friedrich's treatment record doesn't interest me. Hitler treated in a mental ward by a psychiatrist does."

"I don't suppose you would part with that document any time soon. Would you?"

Canaris stroked his dogs. "I intend to keep it safe. Unseen by anyone."

"What good is it safe? Is it an insurance policy?" I asked.

"It's more than that, Friedrich. There will be a time to bring it out. Expose him for what he is. But not now." He placed the dogs on the floor. "Now it's time to see the ladies."

We joined Carla and Erika. Dinner consisted of *Hasenpfeffer*— German stew made from marinated rabbit braised with onions— plus boiled potatoes and sautéed cabbage.

Sated, we sat around the fireplace sipping a fine cognac.

"Friedrich," Erika said, "your secret is out."

I was startled. *Her too?* But she put me at ease when she continued, "I understand from Carla that you play the piano. Would you do us the honors?"

Carla grabbed my hand. "Please? You've only talked about it. We would *all* like to hear you play."

I stuttered. "It's been a while since I played in front of anyone."

"We're not just anyone," said Erika, "we're friends. Don't disappoint us."

Canaris smiled. "Give it a go, son."

I did. I played one of my favorite pieces: *"Die Moritat von Mackie Messer"* from *Die Dreigroschenoper.* Carla, Erika, and—to our surprise—Wilhelm, joined in singing the opening stanza.

"It's a shame Kurt Weill and Bertolt Brecht were forced to leave Germany," Canaris said. "Politicians should not be concerned about artists. If anything, artists should be given special consideration for the contributions they make."

"They had no choice but to leave," Carla said. "Weill is a Jew and Brecht has Communist leanings. If they stayed, who knows what would have happened to them?"

"Regardless," said Erika, "'Mack the Knife' and *The Threepenny Opera* will surely live on."

I agreed: "Mack the Knife" and *The Threepenny Opera* would live on. But if I were to tell good old Wolf about the document Canaris cleverly uncovered, I could not say the same for the admiral. He would immediately be arrested. And then? Everyone has their breaking point. Canaris would talk and Hitler would get hold of the last existing document revealing his mental condition.

That is why Canaris's secret had to be protected and I had to trust that one day, written proof of Hitler's mental instability would surface at the right time.

Until then, Canaris and I had an unspoken bond; a bond to protect each other.

PART II

PART II

Chapter 16

November 5, 1937

After all these years, it had become clear that Hitler was an unbalanced gambler relying on instinct and intuition. He had no interest in hammering out the details of any program. He also had no interest in assembling a competent bureaucracy to implement his grand strategies.

For example, he assigned Hermann Göring, a man without appropriate credentials, to mastermind and oversee Germany's Four-Year Plan for economic development. To no one's surprise, Göring's fiscal policies were failing as the country slid back into economic despair. Without additional resources, it was impossible to create the jobs and products Germany needed for expansion.

Fighting amongst military leaders over limited resources took center stage. Admiral Raeder, head of the navy, complained that the air force and army would not release enough steel and raw supplies to rebuild his service.

Something had to be done to resolve these issues.

*

On November 5, 1937, an extraordinary event occurred. It started simply enough. The heads of the army, navy, and air force requested a meeting with Hitler to mediate their disputes. By the time it ended, Hitler laid out a reckless plan to invade Germany's neighbors.

The meeting was scheduled for 4:00 p.m. in the Chancellery building. Hitler and I arrived before the others.

"Friedrich, it is important that you understand what is about to happen," Hitler explained. "Until now, the military has been risk-averse. They have counseled against my efforts to reclaim lands taken from us after the war. The world understood that the

Saar Basin should never have been stripped away from us. It is German land populated by Germans, and the nearly unanimous plebiscite proved this. And yet, my military advisers balked against doing what was right. Then the Rhineland. Again, the generals opposed me. They feared the worst. Yet I knew we would march into the Rhineland without opposition." Hitler's face colored. "This time, when Germany marches forward, my generals *will* be behind me. They *must* be behind me."

"Is this about Austria?"

Everyone knew Hitler wanted to create a union between Germany and the country where he was born and raised, although there was no historical basis for it.

"That's the starting point," whispered Hitler.

"Starting point for what?"

"You will learn in due time." His eyes darkened. "No other country has bothered to rebuild their arsenals as we have. No other country has made the improvements in weaponry that we have. We have the best-trained soldiers in the world, Friedrich. I did this so our generals would be prepared when they take the field. So far, however, the only things they take are seats around conference tables. That is about to change."

"Why are you telling me this? *Mein Führer?*" He did not answer.

I clapped to get his attention. "*Mein Führer?*"

Hitler snapped out of his trance. "Today the generals will cheer me, Friedrich. You wait and see."

At that moment, the door opened. Hitler's key military chiefs filed in: Werner von Blomberg (minister of war), Werner von Fritsch (commander-in-chief of the army), Erich Raeder (commander-in-chief of the navy), Hermann Göring (commander-in-chief of the air force), and Friedrich Hossbach, Hitler's military adjutant. When Konstantin von Neurath (foreign minister) trailed behind the others, the military men appeared confused.

Without preamble, Hitler stood. "In any other country, what I am about to say would be said in front of a full cabinet. But this subject is too important to spread across a wider circle. Each of you has been selected because you hold a key post in Germany's future." Ever the actor, Hitler paused for effect. His tone was somber.

"In the event of my death, consider the matters I set before you today, as my last will and testament for Germany."

He addressed Göring—his named successor—directly. "Is that clear, Hermann?"

"Yes, *Mein Führer.*"

"*Mein Herren,* when we combine the number of pure Germans living in the Fatherland with those in neighboring countries, the German racial community totals more than eighty-five million. We do not have enough food or land to preserve our racial purity and way of life." He pounded his palm with a closed fist. "These needs give us the right to expand our territory. Unlike England, our expansion cannot come from acquiring colonies beyond Europe. We must annex Austria and Czechoslovakia in order to expand."

Hitler's language and tone were clear and decisive. "Expansion," he said, "has to occur no later than 1943. Sooner, if possible."

Blomberg, Fritsch, and Neurath squirmed in their seats. They made no effort to hide their discomfort as Hitler outlined Germany's future.

Admiral Raeder and Göring, on the other hand, hung on Hitler's every word, nodding their approval.

Hitler continued. "Germany's expansion will be nothing new. Throughout history, strong countries have overwhelmed weak ones."

Fritsch nudged Blomberg under the table to say something.

"*Mein Führer.*" Hitler scowled at Blomberg for interrupting. "This meeting was called to discuss how best to allocate raw materials. The Reich's future was not on the agenda."

Hitler slammed the table. "The Reich's future is now on the agenda! Protecting the purity of the German people requires giving them room to live and includes seizing needed raw materials. Field Marshal Blomberg, Germany will use whatever force is necessary to take what we need from whoever possesses it. It is no more complicated than that. Sitting here, the only questions are, 'When?' and "How?'"

Fritsch, the army commander-in-chief, interjected, "Your timing makes us vulnerable to defeat. England's navy is superior to ours, *mein Führer*. France's army is larger and stronger."

Again, Hitler slammed the table. "England's strength lies in its alliances with other countries. They cannot stand alone. As for France, their political turmoil makes them weak. Neither will stop us. Germany is Europe's colossus."

"France has an alliance to protect Czechoslovakia," Foreign Minister Neurath said. "England will rally to France. We will face another world war."

"On the contrary," Hitler said, "if allies do not have the courage of their convictions, alliances mean nothing. The point to consider is that our rearmament is nearly completed, while the rest of the world only begins to rearm. Until now, time has been our friend. It will soon be our enemy. We must not wait until the others catch up!"

Blomberg knew better than to argue with Hitler. He turned to Göring. "Hermann, if your economic programs delivered half of what you claimed they would, there would be no need to contemplate a course that jeopardizes our country's future."

Göring turned red. His eyes bulged. While I never cared for the man, I didn't want him to have a stroke. I slid a glass of water across the table to him.

The generals bickered for hours, while Hitler remained stone-faced. His blue eyes darted from one to another without reacting to what was being said.

Finally, after he had enough, Hitler put the coda on the meeting.

"*Mein Herren*. Let me put your minds at ease. As long as Mussolini lives, we have nothing to worry about from Italy. As for Czechoslovakia," he explained, "England is the key. As long as the British remain neutral, we can attack without interference. France will never go it alone."

*

Back in his office, Hitler plopped onto a couch and wiped sweat dripping down the sides of his face. I sat opposite him.

"Give me your assessment, Friedrich? How did it go?"

I was numb from what had just happened. How best to answer?

"Raeder and Hermann supported you. They were never in doubt. But did you really think the war minister, the foreign minister, and army chief would welcome the invasion of two countries at the risk of a full-fledged war?"

Hitler sneered. "What do they know? I've proven them wrong before. The so-called 'victors' have lost their will to fight."

I swallowed hard to keep down the bitter taste of rising bile. "Wolf?"

"You used to call me that all the time, years ago. It reminds me when everything was simpler, when we knew what we had to do to gain power." Hitler's eyes seemed to gaze into the past.

"You have that power now. Why jeopardize everything by risking war?"

Hitler's gaze turned to a glare directed at me without answering. Then he pushed off the couch and circled to his desk. He made a show of fumbling through a stack of papers, his eyes fixed on nothing. He lifted one paper and brought it close, pretending to read it.

His message was clear: Germany was on a path to war.

Chapter 17

I stood in front of my house, key in hand, staring at the door. I remembered leaving Hitler and the Chancellery building but how I reached home was a haze. I kept trying . . . but the key didn't want to work.

The door cracked open.

"I thought I heard you." Carla's smile vanished when she saw my face. She reached for my hand. "What's wrong, Friedrich? Are you ill?"

I brushed past her and headed for the bar. I poured a generous amount of my favorite scotch—Auchentoshan Single Malt—downed it, and poured another. Auchentoshan was meant to be sipped. Not guzzled. I didn't care.

Carla approached gingerly. "If you're not going to tell me what's wrong, at least ask how my trip to Munich was?"

I downed the second glass of scotch before glancing at her. Expressionless.

She folded her arms over her chest. "My brother is the same. As always. I can't tell if he recognizes me. No matter. It makes me feel better to see him."

I refilled the glass.

"I promised my parents I would never abandon him. I love him."

With the glass in one hand and the bottle of scotch in the other, I headed for the kitchen, stopped, and turned. "Sorry. I am not going to be very good company tonight."

"Oh! I hadn't noticed." Carla wheeled around and stomped off.

*

I planted myself on a kitchen chair and didn't move until I had sucked down the last drop of Auchentoshan. While I sat there, I thought of nothing and everything. My overwhelming thought was that Hitler was prepared to start a war. Possibly another Great War. Even in my inebriated state, I realized it wasn't about *Lebensraum* or food or for any other reason he conjured up to explain the invasion of our neighbors. In Hitler's mind, conquering Europe would enshrine him in history. Austria and Czechoslovakia were the first steps.

Then my mind drifted to 1918 when I woke up in Charité Hospital after being in a coma for a week. The pain. The broken bones. The morphine stupor. The war had cost me everything, including my memory. I reflected about my days in the Freikorps, the fighting in the Berlin streets, retaking the Bavarian government from the Reds, the Beer Hall Putsch. I fought for a cause I believed worthy at the time. No longer. My old friend Wolf was about to open the gates of hell . . . and take everyone through them.

I tipped my glass back. It was bone dry. Same for the bottle. I stumbled to the cabinet and grabbed my last fifth of scotch. I plopped back on my chair and poured two fingers. I swirled the liquid. Ripples of amber lapped over the edge and onto the table. I emptied the glass.

How did it come to this?

Still holding my glass, I pushed back from the table and tried to stand, but my legs gave way. I tumbled to the floor, smashing my head against the wall, the glass shattering. A jagged piece sliced deep into my palm.

I felt nothing. I lay bleeding.

Sometime later, I awoke.

On the floor.

Screaming.

Congealed blood all around.

A familiar coppery, sickening smell. I was on my side, legs tucked up.

Cowering.

Bombs exploding.

Nostrils singed with smoke.

I called out. "Retreat! Retreat! French on the right."

Someone shook me.

Screamed at me. "Wake up! Wake up!"

I opened my eyes.

"You're hurt," she said, clad in white, "let me dress your wound."

"Anna, I remember. I remember. Our orders were to go forward. We advanced too easily. The French trenches were empty. It was a trap. They caught us in a pincer move. Word came to retreat. I started to run. A shrill whistle. The brightest light. Explosion. The last thing I remember . . . flying through the air."

"Friedrich, wake up! You're dreaming."

Arms lifted me to a sitting position.

"Is the doctor coming soon?" I asked, still believing I was in the hospital.

"Friedrich, open your eyes. It's me. Carla."

"Carla? What are you doing here?"

Worry was etched across her face. "Who is Anna?"

"Why are you in the hospital?" I asked again.

"Friedrich. You're home. In the kitchen. You drank a bottle of scotch. From the looks of it, more. You fell and cut yourself. Look."

My hand was wrapped in a towel.

"I stopped the bleeding. I didn't feel any glass shards, but you need to go to the hospital."

I peeled the blood-soaked towel back. A gash across my palm was open but the bleeding had stopped. "Pour alcohol on it. There's iodine upstairs. Bandage it tight. The last thing I want is to go to a hospital."

"I'm no nurse but you need stitches," Carla firmly said.

"Have you seen the other scars on my body? This is nothing. I'll be okay." Carla started to protest.

I shook my head.

"Then promise me if it starts to bleed again, you'll go." I nodded.

Carla made a pot of coffee before cleaning up the mess. When the last splinter of glass was scooped into a dustpan and all was in order, she eased across from me.

"Are you able to tell me what this is all about?"

"I had a bad dream."

"I've been with you awhile now, Friedrich. You don't toss, turn, mumble, or say anything when you sleep. This was different. It was like you were transported someplace. If it was a dream, it was very real. You said things that frightened me."

"What did I say?"

"Something about the French Fourth Army on the right flank. Bombs bursting. Retreat. You mentioned Reims Cathedral. General Ludendorff. Flanders. What was all of that about?"

Pain shot through me. I winced until it passed. Then, as if it were yesterday, I said, "The Second Battle of the Marne. General Ludendorff wanted us to be a diversion so he could send the main divisions through Flanders and surprise the enemy." I smacked the table with my damaged hand. "Ouch!"

"Why did you do that? It had to hurt!"

I managed a stupid grin. "I forgot. You don't understand how momentous this is. I have waited years to remember something about my past. When I was a soldier."

"How could anyone forget fighting in the war?"

I was bombarded by images of Hitler. War. Scotch. Hitting my head. Blood. Curled like a fetus. Blood's metallic smell. Carla's white robe.

Whatever the trigger, something had jolted me back to the Second Battle of the Marne. Dr. Forster always said it would happen this way; that a memory would show its face when I least expected it . . . or for no particular reason. Well, it just did.

I struggled to remember more.

Carla tugged on my good hand.

"Friedrich. Where are you? I am losing you. What are you thinking about?"

I studied her angelic face. "If I told you, you wouldn't believe me."

"Try me," she urged.

I took a deep breath knowing this was a make-or-break moment.

"I was in battle. So many terrifying images. The explosion. It all happened."

"You were there, Friedrich. They did happen."

Still holding her hand, I said, "That's just it, Carla, until this moment, I had no memory of the war. The nurses and doctors who put me back together told me I had been wounded in the Second Battle of the Marne. That I had been in a division of the German Third Army. We were attacking the French Fourth."

She covered her mouth with her free hand and spoke through the web of her fingers. "I don't understand."

"An enemy shell exploded near me. I had a broken arm. Broken leg. Broken ribs. Broken jaw. My face was ripped apart. Burns all over. I was in a coma for a week. They weren't sure I would wake up. When I did, I couldn't remember what happened. Carla, do you understand? I couldn't remember anything!"

She stroked my cheek; inspected my face. "You were lucky. You had great care. In my photographic work, I see soldiers missing parts of their face. They wear prostheses fashioned out of tin and painted to look real. But they are never right."

"I was at Charité Hospital. I had the best plastic surgeon in all of Europe: Dr. Jacques Joseph."

I placed Carla's hand to my cheek. The love in her eyes gave me strength to continue. "It took dozens of surgeries and months for my body to heal. But . . ." I touched my skull with my bandaged hand, "my memory never came back. It's been twenty years, Carla. This dream or vision or whatever it was, was my first memory of anything that happened before I woke up in Charité Hospital. It was amazing. It means so much to me."

I held my breath. Either Carla would rally with compassion . . . or withdraw.

"You poor man. I can't imagine how you lived all this time, not knowing anything about your past. Wait a second!" She made a queer face. "Your recognition disc would have had your name, identification number, regimental history, and where you were from. All soldiers wore them around their necks."

"How do you know these things?"

"Remember? I've been creating a twenty-year photographic retrospective of soldiers wounded in the war. It's gaining interest, too. But that's not the point. Is Friedrich Richard your real name?"

I shook my head. "At Charité I was known as Patient X. After my wounds healed, Dr. Joseph had me transferred to Pasewalk Hospital. A psychiatrist there tried to help me."

"But he couldn't. Right?"

"Nothing worked. Not only did I lose my history, but I also lost what family I might have had. Friends, too."

"I feel terrible for you. It must have been awful being so alone like that."

"Except for the soldier I befriended in the bed next to mine."

"Are you still in contact?"

I managed a fractured smile. "The funny thing is, Carla, you know him. It was Adolf Hitler."

"The *Führer*? That explains . . ."

"Let me finish. We went our separate ways when the war ended. Germany was in ruins. Fighting everywhere. Soup kitchens. Bread lines. Then—the reason is not important why—we reunited in Munich. Hitler had become a polished, inspirational speaker by then. He gave people hope that better days would come. It was easy to attach my star to his."

"They *were* better days." Carla lowered her eyes and repeated *sotto voce*, "Then."

"You're right. The better days have turned into times of terror. And then yesterday. The meeting was scheduled to talk about shortages of materials and how to get more steel to build ships. Instead, Hitler crossed the line. He announced we would soon invade Austria and Czechoslovakia."

"Whatever for? They are not our enemies," she said.

"He's not sane, Carla."

"Crazy people do not run countries, Friedrich."

"If that were only true," I said. "He rationalized invading those two countries for their land and food. He expects one million Austrians and two million Czechs to die in the process, which would leave more food for Germans."

"Friedrich. There is no way Hitler meant that!" said Carla. "Who talks that way?"

"There's more. After invading these countries Hitler wants his military leaders to create twelve new army divisions from these two countries."

Her eyes crinkled trying to make sense of what this implied.

"Don't you get it?" My voice pitched higher. "If we already conquered Austria and Czechoslovakia, why would we need more soldiers?"

"We wouldn't . . ." Carla hesitated, ". . . unless . . . unless he is planning something else."

"Yes!" I cried out. "An even greater war! Hitler wants to rule the European continent. That means an incalculable number of deaths because our weapons are more destructive than twenty-plus years ago. Then there are the Balkans."

"Don't tell me. Is there no end?"

"Not before Germany takes over the southern Balkans. He has no regards for the Slavs or the Russians. Hitler sees those people as subhuman races. He intends to make them slaves."

"Friedrich, you're scaring me."

I huffed. "You should be scared. The world should be scared."

"Shh. You're shouting. I'm right here."

I needed to catch my breath.

"You said the generals were at that meeting; didn't they try to convince him otherwise?" Carla asked.

"Oh, they tried. While they understand the concept of *Lebensraum*, the need for more living space, they told Hitler the timing wasn't right. That England and France were too powerful. But that's not what they really meant. They were making up excuses. The last thing military men want is war."

"Couldn't they have been more forceful?"

"Blomberg did have a fight with Göring. I admit I enjoyed when they went at it. But tragically, Carla, Hitler will do what he pleases."

Carla grew quiet. She started to say something and stopped.

"My hand and head both hurt. Would you mind getting me a Bayer, please?"

After I took the aspirin, Carla said, "Here's what troubles me. Given all that you've said, why do you stay with Hitler? Nothing is holding us here. We can take my brother and move to another country." Then she added, "You do understand I can't leave him behind?"

"Of course, I do. As for leaving Hitler and Germany, I tried the night of the Reichstag Fire. Hitler hadn't been in office thirty days. I saw his obsession with power. How determined he was to get rid of the Jews. I wanted no part of it."

"Why didn't you leave? What kept you here?"

"The loving answer is that I needed to meet you." She grew flush. "The real answer has to do with Bernhard Weiss."

"Isn't he the one Goebbels made fun of in cartoons?"

"The same. The night of the Reichstag Fire, the order went out for Weiss's arrest. I grabbed him and helped him cross the border into Prague."

"You saved a Jew?"

"Does that surprise you?"

She slid her chair closer. "I would expect nothing less. But if you were so against Hitler, and already in Prague, what made you come back?"

"Weiss and I feared the same bleak future for Germany. We understood that news from Germany would be censored. He asked me to return to Berlin to record events as they unfolded. But more than that, he realized that I more than anyone else would be in a position to blunt what was coming."

Her eyes widened and her lips parted, absorbing what Weiss asked of me. "That was brazen, to ask an *Obergruppenführer* to assume such a role."

"I suppose he saw something in me that I didn't see in myself. Over time, I have stopped thugs from beating up an old Jew.

Saved Kitty's niece from being sterilized. Made headway easing oppressive laws on Jewish civil servants. They were isolated events that only helped a few. But after yesterday? The magnitude of it! I feel helpless. I can't see how to stop Hitler from plunging us into war."

"Then shoot him!" shrieked Carla. "You are with him almost every day. Kill the snake before it strikes."

I grabbed my head. The aspirin helped the pain in my hand, but not the pounding in my brain.

I looked up at her. "No matter how terrible he's become, he's always supported me. Trusted me. I can't."

"There is no place for loyalty to the Devil."

Tears trickled down my cheeks. "Truth be told, I have thought about it. But removing Hitler means Göring, Himmler, Heydrich, and Goebbels all remain. Any one of them would step into Hitler's shoes. Nothing would change."

A blanket of silence covered us.

After what seemed like an eternity, Carla said, "This is too incomprehensible to absorb."

Then a kernel of an idea formed in my mind. "There may be a way out of this after all. I need to think it through, but it may be the answer."

"Tell me."

I shook my head. "You have your brother to think about. The less you know the better."

"At least, let me meet Bernhard Weiss. He has had such an impact on you. We could take a weekend and go to Prague."

"Thankfully, he's in London now."

Her concern turned into a glorious smile. "Well, guess what, *Obergruppenführer* Richard? A gallery in London has expressed interest in showing my photos. There's been talk that it might be this summer."

Chapter 18

I left Charité Hospital late the next morning with sixteen stitches in my hand. The phone jangled as I entered my office.

"Friedrich. It's Heidi. I need your help."

"Have those cops gotten out of hand, again?"

"Nothing like that. I don't know what you did to get them to behave, but they have been perfect gentlemen since your little talk. I'm calling about something else. Is it possible for you to come to the club now?"

If Heidi's voice had not been edged with concern, I would have said, "No." My bandaged hand throbbed. My head ached. I was spent thinking about Hitler's plans to plunge us into war. The last thing I wanted to do was drag myself to the Nightingale.

"No trouble at all," I said. "I'll be there in a couple of minutes."

I found Heidi at the bar. Though empty of patrons, Heidi said, "Not here." But first, she slipped behind the bar and reached for a bottle of scotch.

I waved my bandaged hand. "Not for me. I had a date with a bottle last night. This is the result."

She winced. "Does it hurt?"

"Only when I think about it."

I followed Heidi into Max's old office. It was unchanged since my days as a bouncer.

How many times had I come to Max in this room to have him save my neck?

Heidi took Max's seat; I sat in the chair I had parked myself in countless times before. "Is Kitty coming?"

Heidi shook her head. "This has nothing to do with Kitty. It's about me. I want more."

"If you are not being compensated enough, it *does* have to do with Kitty. I will put in a word for you."

"Friedrich. I don't need help when it comes to money or position." She pursed her lips, looked away, and then met my eyes. "How should I best explain this? Living in Aachen, I was removed from the day-to-day horrors I now see in Berlin. People were nice to each other there, not like here. More to the point, even though I never knew I was part Jewish, we welcomed the Jews. Their history in Aachen dates back to the Roman empire."

"These are rough times for everyone in Germany. Where are you going with this, Heidi?"

"That's just it, Friedrich. I want to do something useful. Help people. I don't want to wiggle my ass showing patrons to their tables while keeping a smile plastered on my face until my cheeks hurt. You know people. Can you find me a more meaningful position?"

When she finished, Heidi's jaw was clamped tight and the muscles in her face pulsed.

"You're serious, aren't you?"

"This took a lot of courage especially since Kitty has been so generous. They don't need me here. They never did. Marta ran the Nightingale before I ever showed up. Kitty offered me a job because of Max."

"But you *are* Max's daughter."

"Which is why you should help me."

Her strong jaw melted into an impish smile. I knew the look. She could not know it, but her father made the same face. There would be no deterring her until she got what she wanted.

"How many languages do you speak?"

"Besides German, French, Dutch, and English. I understand Italian, but don't speak it very well."

"Give me a few days. I will find the right thing for you."

*

I never raised a child but could appreciate the trials and tribulations they put parents through. Helping Heidi was not the issue. Keeping her out of danger from the Nazis was. But first things first: I had to run this past Kitty . . . or she would never forgive me for not consulting her.

*

"What was I supposed to do?" Kitty said when I told her about Heidi. "She knew how to cook, and an extra pair of hands is always needed in a kitchen. When she wanted to be part of the action, we moved her to the front. I know she doesn't belong there. But these are rough times, Friedrich."

She poured two coffees.

"Someone with Heidi's ambition needs challenges. The trouble these days is that whatever she ends up doing will shine an unwanted spotlight on her. Any query into her past will bite her," I said.

"That doesn't leave many options for her in Germany. Not these days." Then, as if describing a ho-hum day, she said, "Heidi could always have a job here."

"Did you really say that? Max's daughter in a brothel?"

Kitty, the businesswoman, had blurted it out before thinking; we both knew it was absurd. "Speaking of which, I took your advice, Friedrich."

"Refresh my memory."

"About no longer using Jews to run money to England or Holland. So . . . I did it myself."

"You did what? Do you realize what would have happened had you been stopped?"

"A quick turnaround. Amsterdam. Deposited the funds. No problem any step of the way."

"Kitty! You were lucky. Smuggling money out of Germany is a serious crime. It's not worth it. Promise you'll never do it again."

Kitty leaned forward. Her ample bosoms half-exposed. A diamond pendant drew my eye to her cleavage. "Who's going to stop me, Friedrich? Don't you worry. I can take care of myself."

What to do with a young woman whose only prior experiences were as a chef and club hostess? Then it came to me: I could kill two birds with one stone.

"Thank you for taking the time to see me." *Abwehr* operations were in the Army Headquarters Compound on *Bendlerstraße*.

Admiral Canaris closed the door behind me, lit his pipe, and said, "I am glad you called. There is something I wish to discuss with you, too."

"Is Erika putting another musical soirée together?" I asked.

Canaris cracked a rare smile. "Not to my knowledge." He pointed his pipe stem at me. "You, first. What's on your mind?"

"One way of looking at it: I need a favor."

"And the other?"

"I'm doing you a favor. Either way, you benefit," I explained.

"Seems I can't lose." Puffs of smoke curled upward. "I like the odds."

I described how I knew Heidi Koch, what her father—Max Klinghofer—meant to me, and that she wanted a challenging job.

"The *coup de grâce* is that she speaks four languages fluently . . . and understands a fifth."

"Multilingual agents are hard to find."

"A spy? No. She's like a niece to me. I don't want her in harm's way. My thought was to put her linguistic talents to effective use inside *Abwehr* headquarters. Is that a possibility?"

Canaris relit his pipe. "I should have no problem finding something here for her. Have her see me tomorrow morning."

"There is one more thing," I added. "I don't want her to come to the attention of the Gestapo. Not for any reason. They killed her father at Dachau. I want to make certain she is left alone."

Canaris's thin smile vanished. "Is she a Jew?"

"A *mischling*. Heidi has her mother's last name: Koch. She was raised Catholic. She only recently found out she was part Jewish. Is that a problem?"

"I'm not a big fan of their tribe, but people are people. I would never turn someone away for how they were born or what they believed in. There's no problem," he said as he retrieved papers from his desk drawer. He handed them to me. "Your name is mentioned."

It was the memo of the November 5 meeting between Hitler and the heads of the armed services. Given Canaris's long reach, I was not surprised he had a copy.

"According to Hossbach's notes, you were present. There is no mention that you spoke. What was your perception of what happened?"

"I was both horrified and terrified for Germany."

Without comment, Canaris produced another report. "Have you seen this? Chief of Staff Ludwig Beck sent the *Führer* his analysis. He was not there but based his memo on Hossbach's minutes."

"That was meant only for the *Führer's* eyes."

Canaris shrugged. "I have my sources. Beck agrees with Blomberg and Fritsch. It is preposterous to annex Austria and Czechoslovakia for food. Beck offered a number of suggestions to solve our food shortages as well as identifying the shortcomings of Göring's Four-Year Plan."

Before saying anything else, I reached for pen and paper. In clear letters, I wrote:

Is it safe to talk here?

He nodded.

Unchecked, I said, "Yes, I came to find a position for Heidi. More importantly, I needed to be certain of your reaction to the November 5 meeting. Along with our conversation about Pasewalk, I hoped to find steps to avoid the disaster Hitler is certain to create."

Canaris tapped the cold ashes into a glass ashtray with a polished silver rim. He opened the Cherrywood humidor and repacked the bowl. After tamping down the few shards that stuck out like blades of wild grass, he struck a match. The random pieces curled and vaporized. Swirls of smoke spiraled above his head.

"Agreed. We must find those steps and the people to take them with us." Then, unexpectedly, Canaris said, "I know about you and Bernhard Weiss."

My mouth slowly opened.

"Come now. Don't be surprised. I have agents abroad. Many in England. How could I explain failing to keep tabs on such a prominent former citizen . . . so passionately an anti-Nazi? We both know we can rely on Weiss."

It didn't escape me that Canaris used "we."

Canaris continued. "There will come a day, sooner than later, when we will need Weiss's help, and others like him."

"Others? What others?"

"Chief of the general staff Beck, for one. Then there is Hans Oster, my right-hand man in the *Abwehr*. Oster does his best to hire recruits to the *Abwehr* that have strong feelings against the regime. Recruits like Werner Schrader. Do you happen to know him?"

"Only that years back he was one of the leaders of the veterans' organization from the Great War—*Der Stahlhelm*—the Steel Helmets. He squawked when his group was incorporated into the Brown Shirts. He lost his standing after that. When we came to power, he was tossed into a concentration camp. I wondered what happened to him."

"If you can believe it, he escaped from the concentration camp and rejoined the *Wehrmacht* as a captain. He kept a low profile until he came to someone's attention from his past. He was about to be rearrested when I snatched him in time and stationed him in Vienna. He is one of my best at espionage."

"Are there others like him?" I asked.

"Hans Gisevius, for one."

"I know Hans from when I worked with Frick in the Ministry of the Interior."

"Now he works with the Berlin Police," Canaris explained. "A name that might surprise you is Hjalmar Schacht."

"Head of the Reichsbank? That is a name! More than anyone else, he guided Germany out of the Great Depression."

"Hossbach's memorandum incensed Schacht. He is convinced Hitler's policies are wrong for Germany," Canaris explained.

Hearing about other prominent Germans who felt the same reinforced my resolve. "Does that include the *Anschluss* with Austria? They have raw materials Germany does need."

Canaris drew on his pipe, orange embers flared. "Forget Austria. Italy is the only country that might care about them. To insure that won't happen, Hitler has been romancing Il Duce ever since those Austrian Nazis bungled their attempted coup four years ago. Our line in the sand must be Czechoslovakia."

"I agree. At first, Hitler will claim that the Sudetenland Germans should be reunited with Germany the way other German-speaking territories already have been. Then, when every European leader, plus Roosevelt and Stalin, give a sigh of relief that all Hitler wanted was that fraction of land, Hitler will waltz in and take the whole country. Wilhelm. How do we stop this? We both know that, in the end, military leaders fight wars."

"Friedrich. You more than most know that is not true. Beck, Blomberg, and Fritsch are all against Hitler's proposed aggression. Many others think the same way. What has been missing is someone to coordinate the various segments in the *Abwehr*, the Foreign Service, the Wehrmacht, and those influential citizens against the regime."

"You're talking insurrection, Wilhelm."

"Isn't that what we've been talking about this whole time?"

"I never framed it that way. I just knew Hitler had to be stopped."

"Are you certain now?"

"I am."

Canaris stuck out his hand. "Good. Because we can't move forward without eyes and ears in the *Führer's* inner circle. Welcome to the rebellion, Friedrich Richard."

Chapter 19

By the time I left Canaris, I wanted nothing more than a quiet evening with Carla.

It was an Arctic-cold November night. I came home to find a roaring fireplace. I stood in front of the hearth, leaning in to get warm.

"I'll put tea up," she said.

"Brandy is quicker."

She frowned.

I gave in. "Tea it is."

I changed into warmer clothes and returned to find a cup of steaming hot tea waiting on an antique sideboard.

"What's all this?" I asked. Photos covered every part of the dining table.

"Given my series about soldiers twenty years after the war, it seemed logical to visit cemeteries where our soldiers are buried. What do you think of them?"

"Is that where you went a few days ago? I thought you visited Ludwig."

"Forgive me. I prefer an air of secrecy about projects until I know they will amount to something. This worked."

I pointed to one picture. "Where is this?"

"It's the Langemarck German War Cemetery in western Flanders."

"Why Belgium?"

It was near the Second Battle of Ypres . . . where Hitler was exposed to a gas attack. As a result, Germany was changed forever.

"Soldiers were buried where they fell during the war. It was too costly to ship them home," Carla explained.

I held the photos by their edges. They depicted rows and rows of flat granite grave markers in various lights taken from different angles. Far and closeup.

"How many are buried here?"

"Forty-five thousand all together. It's quite remarkable, don't you think?" Carla said.

"I'm not sure 'remarkable' is an apt description," I answered. "These are stark. Powerful. Beautiful in their simplicity. Their symmetry." I pulled one closer. "There's a Jewish star on that headstone."

"Twelve thousand German Jewish soldiers died in the Great War. Their graves are intermixed with everyone else's."

"It was one army then," I said.

"I am glad you feel that way because you and I are going on a little trip this weekend. For me, it's business. For you, well, I'll let you decide for yourself."

"Apparently, I have little say in this. Do you mind if I ask where we're going?"

"Belgium. I got to thinking that if you visited the cemetery where soldiers from the Second Battle of the Marne are buried, it might jar more memories."

"Where is this place? How would I know what I'm looking at?"

"The *Loupoigne* Franco-German Cemetery. Half the buried there are French, the other half are German. Four-hundred seventy-eight to be exact."

I shook my head. "You're asking me to travel to a cemetery in Belgium in order to read names of dead soldiers . . . hoping something might register?"

"What are you afraid of?"

"I'm not afraid of anything. It will probably turn out to be a huge waste of time. More than one hundred thousand Germans lost their lives in that battle. Why start at such a small cemetery?"

"We have to start somewhere. This is manageable. Humor me. If nothing else, we take a short trip and I get some work done."

*

I cleared my schedule. A few days later, Carla and I found ourselves fifty kilometers south of Brussels on Rue de Presbytère. The cemetery was simple. The mowed grass field was punctuated by row after row of crosses rimmed by stands of trees. Could I picture a pitched battle here? Not at all.

"Let's walk through the rows," said Carla. "Maybe a name will be familiar."

I let go of her hand. "Let me do this myself. Besides, you can't take pictures if I'm hanging on to you."

"Are you sure you'll be all right?"

"There is no one here but us two. You'll know if I'm not."

I broke away from Carla and read the name on each cross out loud. None registered.

Halfway through the third row, I stopped. Inched closer. "Eberhard Zinnmacher."

I know that name.

Carla was on the other side of the cemetery. I called out. She ran back.

I pointed to Zinnmacher's name etched on the cross. "I remember that name."

Carla almost jumped on top of me. "This is so exciting. Are you sure?"

I knelt and ran my fingers across Zinnmacher's name.

"I used to call him Ebbe. You know how they say opposites attract? Well, I was the tallest one in the regiment, and he was the shortest. Somehow, we became sidekicks." I squinted, as if it would bring the memory into sharper focus. "I'm trying to picture him. All I see is the top of his head. He had blondish-brown hair and green eyes. He was thin. Wiry. He used to give me some of his food because I was so big and hungry all the time."

"Do you remember what he called you?"

I struggled to find a clue, a syllable, a letter that might lead to my identity. "Nothing comes to mind."

"Do you remember anything else?"

"Only that when he removed his helmet to wipe his brow, he took a bullet in his head. He was dead before he hit the ground."

"I'm sorry, Friedrich."

I stood. Carla grabbed my hand and we ambled past the rest of the markers; no other jarred a memory.

Only Zinnmacher's.

"Friedrich. Let's try to locate Ebbe's family. He might have sent a letter home telling them about his tall friend."

I stopped and pulled Carla into me.

"Maybe I don't want to know." My lips brushed her hair. "I must have fought alongside many of these men. I made it. They didn't."

I stepped back. Our gazes locked on each other.

"I know who I am now. I have you. We have each other. That's enough."

Chapter 20

December 22, 1937

Thousands lined the streets of Munich to say farewell to Erich Ludendorff, the former first quartermaster general of the German army. Four soldiers marched in front of the cortège, each holding a red velvet pillow that displayed the scores of medals Ludendorff earned during his long military career. I was one of the generals that marched alongside the wooden hearse pulled by four majestic black horses. The coffin, draped in the black, white, and red of the imperial army, rested on the open wagon. Behind us, Hitler marched alone. Hermann Göring followed him . . . and then came the funeral cavalcade that consisted of goose-stepping regiments from every branch of the German military. A horse-drawn cannon brought up the rear.

We turned down *Ludwigstraße* and entered *Odeonsplatz* whose grandeur was modelled after the *Loggia dei Lanzi* in Florence. The plaza ended in the *Feldherrnhalle*, site of the battle of the Beer Hall Putsch led by Hitler and Ludendorff in 1923. It was now a monument to honor the fallen Nazis of that failed coup. Ironically, it was Ludendorff's incompetence that let the ruling triumvirate of Bavaria—Kahr, Seisser, and Lossow—leave the *Bürgerbraükeller*. Once free, they rallied the police to crush the coup. Hitler never forgave Ludendorff. Eleven years later, Kahr was murdered with pickaxes during the Night of the Long Knives.

The funeral procession halted at the monument. The coffin was carried onto a pier built at the foot of granite steps flanked by two great lions. Hitler, aided by soldiers, placed a large wreath bearing the *Führer's* name across a velvet sash on the coffin.

In a voice that only those near Hitler could hear, he said, "In the name of the united German people and in deep gratitude, I deposit this wreath before you." Hitler then retreated to the front of the long line of military men without offering other words of praise.

It was General Blomberg who marched to the microphone to deliver the nation's tribute, after which the casket was placed in a hearse for burial in Tutzing, a simple Bavarian village twenty-five miles south of Munich.

As crowds dispersed, Hitler stood with Himmler and Heydrich. A short distance from them, I observed General Blomberg intercept Göring. I had no idea what they were saying, but as Blomberg talked Göring nodded. Blomberg seemed to be in distress. They came to some sort of understanding because Göring placed his meaty paw on Blomberg's sleeve to Blomberg's relief. The mini drama over, I turned to ask Hitler if he would join the funeral cortège to the internment at Ludendorff's grave site, but he was no longer there. His quiet exit was my answer.

Göring approached Himmler, Heydrich, and me with an ear-to-ear grin.

"One of our problems is about to be solved," said Göring, his voice pitched high with excitement. "Blomberg apologized for the way he attacked me at the November 5 meeting. He said he was under pressure and asked that I forgive him."

"What kind of pressure?" Himmler asked.

Göring chuckled. "You remember that his wife died some years back. It seems that our upstanding general went to the *Oberhof* in Thuringian Forest. When the hotel manager noticed him eating alone each night, he asked if our war minister might like some company. He introduced Blomberg to a 'woman of the people.' The man has fallen in love and wants to marry her."

"How does this solve a problem?" Himmler asked.

"For starters, Blomberg's new love is only twenty-five. Her mother runs a massage parlor."

"Massage parlor?" gasped Himmler.

"Did the daughter ever work for her?" asked Heydrich, sensing where this was going.

"Blomberg was too fragile to ask," answered Göring. "What he did say was that there was a younger man vying for his *Fräulein*'s attention. He asked if I could make the fellow disappear."

"Do you want me to arrest the beau and send him to one of the camps?" asked Heydrich. "That's the easiest way."

"No need to be barbaric, Reinhard," Göring answered. "We're civilized. Remember? I will offer the lad money and a job in Argentina. My South American friends relish working with Germans. As for the wedding, Blomberg asked me to serve as best man. It needs to be soon: the future *Frau* Blomberg is with child. Blomberg's actions are a disgrace to the Officer Corps. When this comes to light, we will replace him with a war minister who knows how to work with us."

We all knew Göring coveted Blomberg's position as minister of war.

"The *Fräulein*'s name is Erna Gruhn." Göring drew a card from his jacket and wrote down the girl's name. "See what you can find out about her and her mother. There must be more to this."

"You said this solved one problem. What's the other?" I asked.

"Fritsch," answered Göring. "If we manage to get rid of Blomberg, Fritsch, as commander-in-chief of the army, would succeed as war minister. We can't have that! Fritsch must *also* be removed. The question is: how best to accomplish this?"

Himmler turned to Heydrich. "Reinhard. Do you remember that file on Fritsch from two years ago? The one that claimed he was a homosexual that Hitler thought was rubbish? How hard would it be to reconstruct it?"

Heydrich gave a guileful smile. "*Herr Reichsführer*, this is one time you will be pleased someone refused to follow a command. When Hitler ordered the Fritsch file destroyed, I thought better of obeying. I placed it in a safe. It will be on your desk tomorrow."

"Lucky for us you did. If memory serves me, the original was not strong enough," Göring said. "Reinhard, find ways to enhance the old stuff."

I absorbed the scene in silence. It was clear Göring wanted Blomberg's job . . . which meant both Blomberg and Fritsch had to go. Himmler, who desired the *SS* to become a fourth and separate branch of the armed services over Blomberg's and Fritsch's objections, also wanted them out of the way. And Hitler? Before the November 5 conference, I would have said "No." But now it was different. Since November 5, they were both in his way.

My conclusion: Blomberg had already placed one foot into his professional coffin. While it had to play out, I doubted he could remain war minister. This made it paramount to save Fritsch. If he were removed, both top military men that opposed Hitler on November 5 would be gone.

*

I left the others and drove to the bucolic cemetery in Tutzing. As I entered the town, I passed a park dedicated to Johannes Brahms, who spent a prolific summer at this shore resort perched on the Starnberger See, where he completed his Strings Quartet Opus 51 and wrote his Haydn Variations.

I paid my condolences to Ludendorff's wife, Mathilde. I made an excuse for Hitler's absence before I joined the honor guard of soldiers and villagers gathered to pay a last tribute to a man many considered one of the great military leaders in German history.

Three volleys were fired as the casket was lowered into the grave.

I stood ramrod straight, saluting, until the last shovelful of dirt was heaped onto General Erich Ludendorff's casket.

*

There are many reasons to remember General Ludendorff.

None will forget his bravery that day in 1923 when our ragtag band of revolutionaries met resistance in the *Odeonsplatz*. When shots rang out, most of us dropped to the pavement. But not Ludendorff. He marched into a hail of bullets and miraculously emerged unscathed. But I remember General Ludendorff for a more salient reason. "Prescient" might be a better word. The day after Hindenburg appointed Hitler chancellor—January 31, 1933—Ludendorff sent a telegram to President Hindenburg:

> Hitler is not who you think . . . I prophesy that this evil man will plunge our Reich into the abyss and will inflict immeasurable woe on our nation. Future generations will curse you in your grave.

Hitler knew about this telegram. That is why he limited his homage to bestowing a wreath and nothing more.

Hitler never forgot.

Chapter 21

December 25, 1937

Simultaneously being a member of Hitler's inner circle while working behind the scenes to stop his march toward war caused me many sleepless nights. Christmas dinner provided a reprieve.

Carla slid into the dining room as I set the last plate. "Seven?" She gave me a queer look. "We're only five. Why seven place settings?"

I put on my innocent look. "I guess in the excitement of the holiday, I forgot to tell you I invited two more. Hope you don't mind."

"I had all to do to cook for Heidi, Kitty, and Marta. Five was challenge enough. Two more? I didn't prepare enough. May I ask, at least, who else is coming?"

"Consider extra guests my Christmas present to you."

Carla rolled her eyes. "Men! A Christmas present is perfume. A scarf. I should be so lucky as to get a piece of jewelry. How are additional guests any sort of present?"

I started to offer a weak excuse, but she stopped me. "No time. I need to get back to my kitchen and figure out how to feed two more. You need to finish setting the table. *All* of our guests will be here soon."

I finished laying out the flatware and stepped back to admire the circular *Adventskranz*. The Advent wreath was made from evergreens and rested in the middle of the table. Fragrant pine-cones and berries, along with violet and rose-colored dried flow-ers, filled its center, with four fresh candles posted on the rim. A white candle stood tall in the center. Knowing our guests would soon arrive, I lit all five.

A cabinet slammed shut.

"I didn't mean to make you angry," I called out. "I should have told you. I was wrong."

Carla appeared at the doorway with something behind her back. "I'm not angry. Just surprised." She handed me a wrapped gift. It was no more than six inches long and narrower in width. "This is for you."

The little boy in me came out. "May I open it now?"

I ripped the paper off. Carla had framed the black-and-white photo found in my boot when they carried me into Charité Hospital twenty years ago. Commonsense said it was of a husband and wife standing behind their children: a boy and a girl. Though perhaps an early teen at most, the boy was taller than the father. The girl was younger and shined with innocence. I always presumed the boy was me standing with the family I could not remember. But there was no way to be certain. Today's date was engraved into the frame, along with Carla's initials.

I swept Carla into my arms and kissed her while eyeing the picture behind her back. "What a wonderful gift."

"You told me you could never be sure who those people were."

"The story I always told anyone who asked about it was that an army buddy carried it throughout the war. He gave it to me when he was mortally wounded and asked that if I ever found his family, to say that he loved them." Then I added, "Going to that cemetery in Belgium didn't change that. Any one of those buried there could have given it to me."

"It's a good story, but I'm not sure you believe it. I don't. If you ask me, that's you and your family. Regardless, I duplicated it and sharpened the features. Keep it on your desk. Maybe looking at it every day will jar more memories back. Good memories. Not like the ones you had when I found you bleeding in the kitchen that day."

The doorbell rang.

"Perfect timing. Is that my surprise?" she asked.

"Fifty-fifty. Heidi, Marta, and Kitty arranged to come together." I knew it wasn't them. I opened the door and stepped aside.

"It's Ludwig!" Carla cried. "I can't believe you did this!" She darted to hug her brother.

Before Carla met me, she spent every Christmas holiday with her brother. This year, she remained in Berlin so we could celebrate together. But I knew how important it was for her to be with her brother, to keep family traditions alive. All it took to become a hero was a phone call to the hospital administrator to arrange for one of the staff nurses to care for Ludwig, and also arrange their transportation.

Ludwig was bone thin. Maybe five-foot-eight, pale, with hair cropped close to his scalp to easily inspect for lice. Ludwig's right hand curled back on itself like a talon. It was useless. He was so severely pigeon-toed that when he walked, he was in danger of toppling with each step.

His mouth was always open, displaying crooked, yellowed teeth. Ludwig could only make guttural sounds. No words. He was unable to dress or feed himself. In his early thirties, he needed a diaper. But when Carla rushed to hug him fiercely, there was a spark of recognition in his eyes. An understanding that he was loved.

I turned to the nurse. "Inge, thank you for doing this."

"Ludwig is such a pleasure, *Herr* Richard. This means a lot to him." She smiled. "He looks forward to seeing his sister every year for Christmas dinner."

Carla helped Inge guide Ludwig to the festive table. "When are the others coming?" she asked over her shoulder.

As if on cue, the doorbell rang; it was Heidi, Marta, and Kitty. I hung their coats on the hall coat tree; Carla introduced Inge and Ludwig.

I clapped my hands to draw everyone's attention. "Tonight is special. We celebrate a traditional Christmas dinner together with Ludwig and Inge. We also celebrate Heidi and her new job." I motioned with an empty hand. "*Prost.*"

"Cheers," echoed the others.

Blotches of red appeared on Heidi's neck and face. "Thank you, Friedrich, but there is no need to make a fuss."

"On the contrary. Working for Admiral Canaris is quite special. Now, who is hungry?"

Heidi handed Carla a plate with a homemade desert. "Here is the dessert I promised."

"Your *Stollen* looks scrumptious," Carla said. "What's your secret recipe?"

"Besides flour, dried fruits, nuts, and lots of spices, I add a touch of zest to the powdered sugar on top . . . that was my mother's secret ingredient."

Dinner consisted of goose with an apple and sausage stuffing, red cabbage, and potato dumplings. When Inge cut Ludwig's food into small pieces, Carla moved closer. "Let me do that," said Carla. "It has been so long since I fed Ludwig."

While Ludwig never spoke, he would break out in his version of song, singing the same notes over and over again. To my trained ear, he had surprisingly good pitch. Ludwig didn't chew the way adults did; he chomped up and down like a child. Crumbs trickled onto the napkin inserted under his chin in an effort to keep his shirt clean. Even so, he made a mess.

"Marta," I said, "how are things at the Nightingale?"

"The crowd is rougher these days, but business is good. My main problem is that every so often, one of my employees doesn't show up for work. I screen the new people as best I can, so nothing in their past will draw the Gestapo's attention . . . but they are forever making new laws to arrest more people." She shrugged. "It is the way of the world these days."

"Himmler and Heydrich reign by terror. There's not much I can do about that. But if you lose a key employee—for any reason—call me as soon as you can."

Marta added, "I want to thank you and Carla for inviting me tonight. It means a lot to me."

Carla reached for Marta's hand. "Friedrich often says how much you and Max helped him in those early years. You never forget people who were kind to you."

Carla always knew what to say.

I cleared my throat. "Kitty, you've been rather quiet. Is everything all right?"

"I can't help but think how many wonderful holidays you, Max, and I shared in this house together. God, I miss him."

"We all do," I said.

"I wish I knew him," Heidi said.

"You would have loved him, Heidi," Kitty said. "You have that same fire in your eyes. We are lucky to have you here with us now."

Heidi kissed Kitty on the cheek. "I'm the lucky one. I lost my mother and then the father I never knew. Now you are all my new family. Thank you."

When the meal dishes were cleared, Carla served Heidi's *Stollen*. Dessert was a hit . . . especially with Ludwig, who appeared to crave treats.

I kept everyone's mug filled with *Glühwein* . . . mulled wine.

"Is this *your* mother's recipe, Friedrich?" Heidi savored the warm brew. I was momentarily nonplussed.

"No," Carla quickly jumped in, "it's my mother's."

When we had our fill of holiday sweets, we moved nearer the fireplace, *Glühwein* in hand.

"How is it working for Admiral Canaris?" I asked Heidi.

"He told me not to talk about my job." She failed to hide a smirk that broadened into a grin. "He also told me you would pump me for information."

I feigned outrage.

Heidi giggled. "I'm only teasing, Friedrich. Admiral Canaris has me doing basic secretarial work. Filing memos and the like. Occasionally, he asks me to translate a courier's message or the transcript of a phone call in French. Most have to do with the unions preparing a nationwide strike there."

"France's Premier Blum reduced their work week and raised wages," I explained to the others. "With their inflationary spiral, most French are no better off than they were in the depths of the

Depression. They can't compete with our German workers who work fifty to sixty hours a week."

"Admiral Canaris has many eyes monitoring what happens there," Heidi explained. "He says it affects our foreign policies. Is he right, Friedrich?"

"The world is shrinking. Anything that happens in one country often impacts another." I could not add that this internal French crisis gave Hitler the confidence to plan an *Anschluss* (union) with Austria.

"Carla, if you don't mind, may I borrow Friedrich?" asked Kitty. "There is something we need to discuss."

Kitty and I excused ourselves and made our way to the den.

"Is there a problem?" I asked after I closed the door. I moved two nail-head club chairs with ball-and-claw feet close together.

"It's getting rougher to move money out of Germany. Of late, I pay stationmasters to warn me at the border. Twice there was about to be a raid. They gave me time to take my bag off the train and remain in the loo until the train pulled out. Then last week I was on my way to Brussels. Without warning, Gestapo agents swarmed onto every train car at the same time. There was no way to escape."

"You must have done something right. You're here and not in a Gestapo cell."

"I did what every damsel in distress knows to do: faint. I fell right onto this *SS* man's shoes. I added a bit of thrashing for effect."

"I would have liked to have seen that performance."

"I deserved an award. I never feel sorry for *SS* men, but this one became so flummoxed, he didn't know what to do first. He ran. Got me water. Then reached into my dress for a fan I deliberately had peek out from my bosom. He did not hesitate to take it to stir the air until I revived."

"Clever placement! Then what?"

"What do you think? He got out of there as fast as he could. Never bothered to check my bags."

"You were lucky, Kitty."

"That's why we're talking. I don't want to chance that again." She gave me one of her classic smiles.

"Amsterdam is probably the best place I could go these days. If I hire a heavy, that will draw unwanted attention. I would feel safe traveling with an *Obergruppenführer.* Give some thought to taking a day trip with me. Ok?"

"I will."

*

Ludwig and Inge stayed the night. In the morning, after we said our good-byes, Carla could not stop thanking me.

"He requires a good deal of attention, but he was a joy to have," I said.

"I wish everyone accepted a handicapped person as easily as you do."

"You're forgetting my handicap. You just can't see it."

"Nice try. You're sweet, Friedrich, admit it. I did receive another sort of present, today. Remember I told you a gallery was interested in giving me a show? I didn't get too excited because it was so far away and, well, anything could happen. But it's real, Friedrich. My agent contacted me. The gallery asked me to resize some of my photos and add more pieces to the collection. It's going to happen! Have you been to London before?"

"Only to Southampton, where the cruise ships dock. I never made it to London."

"There is so much to see there. It will be special to share it with you."

"Congratulations. I am happy for you."

"For us."

"London means I have something special to share with you. Actually, not something . . . someone. You will meet my dear friend, Bernhard Weiss."

Chapter 22

January 12, 1938

Every January 12, Hermann Göring threw himself a grand birthday party at his Carinhall estate. Why not? He loved parties, and those invited knew he loved presents even more. This birthday was no exception. Hitler gave him a superb painting of a hunting scene by the multi-talented Austrian, Hans Makart. I was lucky enough to procure an early German Wheellock hunting carbine that was a meter long and dated to 1520. The lock was decorated with a deer hunting scene and the stock sported high-art inlays of boar hunting. Göring promised to cherish it.

This year's event was marred by a scheduling conflict: Blomberg's wedding. Hitler, unaware of Göring's machinations following Ludendorff's funeral or of the bride's pedigree, willingly consented to be a witness at the ceremony.

*

It was two weeks after the Ludendorff funeral that Heydrich presented his "findings" to Göring and me in Himmler's office. These "findings" concerned Werner von Blomberg's upcoming marriage to Erna Gruhn.

"The mother's 'massage parlor' is a whorehouse. She has been convicted twice of prostitution. Blomberg's soon-to-be wife followed in her mother's footsteps," Himmler reported. "Like mother like daughter."

Heydrich then drew a thick file from his briefcase and read from the first page. "Erna Gruhn has been arrested for prostitution, participating in nude orgies, and selling pornographic pictures of herself taken by a Jewish photographer, no less."

He handed a stack of glossy photos to Göring, who lingered over them before passing them to the rest of us.

Heydrich continued. "She was granted parole only months before being introduced to Blomberg."

"Which charge did she serve time for?" I asked.

"Larceny. She stole a gold watch from a customer."

"Blomberg would never let any of his officers marry beneath their station. Of all people, how could he marry this woman?" I asked.

"Come now, Friedrich." Göring reached to gander at Erna's pictures again. "We all know that love is blind, and lust conquers all. Isn't that right, Heinrich?"

Most of Hitler's inner circle knew Himmler was having an affair with his secretary, Hedwig Potthast.

Himmler glared at Göring. "I am not the one marrying a whore."

Göring rubbed his fleshy hands together. "The *Führer* must not get wind of this. If he did, he would force Blomberg to cancel the wedding. That would ruin it for us."

"Us" meant him and Himmler.

"Agreed," said Himmler, the color returning to his face. "The moment the wedding is over, the new *Frau* Blomberg's file will find its way into the hands of the police. It will move up the chain of command until it reaches the *Führer's* desk. I can almost hear his explosion now."

*

The wedding was small. Blomberg's adult children attended, as did the bride's mother. The bride was radiant, with a bouquet of flowers adorning her hair. When introduced, Hitler—in his best Viennese manner—kissed the soon-to-be *Frau* Blomberg's hand.

Göring and Hitler—as best man and witness respectively—took center stage with the bride and groom as the ceremony began. It was followed by a celebratory dinner. Seated at the place of honor next to the bride, Hitler shared an animated conversation with her. One thing never changed: Hitler loved beautiful women. But it was easy to predict his reaction when he found out whose hand he had been kissing.

*

A few days later, *Frau* Blomberg's police file, replete with pornographic pictures, reached the desk of Berlin Police Chief Helldorff. He brought the file to General Wilhelm Keitel. Keitel worked under Blomberg. His son, Karl-Heinz, was engaged to marry Blomberg's daughter.

"We have no choice. We must bring this to Göring," Keitel told Helldorff, who reported the conversation to Göring.

*

January 24, 1938

I was with Hitler when Göring put on a performance worthy of a Hollywood Oscar. Tears streamed down the man's florid face in a hastily called conference in Hitler's office.

"*Mein Führer. Mein Führer.*" Göring's massive chest heaved with sorrow. "It's our Blomberg. You cannot believe what he has done!"

Hitler jumped up in alarm. "Did something happen to him? Is he safe?"

"Worse," cried Göring. "Much worse. He married a whore! And if that weren't bad enough, her pimp was a Jew!"

Hitler's eyes bulged. Veins pulsed in his temple. He paced, muttering to himself. Then he wheeled around.

"No officer of mine can marry such a person. Bring him to me." Then Hitler wiped his mouth, "And to think, my lips touched her hand."

By the time Blomberg arrived at the Chancellery, Hitler was apoplectic.

"How could you marry such a woman? Why didn't you tell me?" demanded the *Führer.*

Blomberg turned to Göring. "You reassured me the *Führer* approved. How could you do this to me?"

Göring rolled his eyes and Blomberg knew he had been both duped and betrayed.

"Werner: have the marriage annulled. There is still time to rectify this," said a calmer Hitler.

Göring grew distressed as Hitler spoke. But I knew Hitler said what he needed to in order to persuade Blomberg to get rid of the woman without a scandal. No matter what Blomberg did, Blomberg was history.

"That is not an option. I love my wife," said Blomberg.

"Then you leave me no choice but to ask for your resignation," Hitler said. "We will keep this under wraps, for now. The announcement based on reasons of health will be made once everything is sorted out."

Chapter 23

January 25, 1938

The following morning, Hitler and I pored over a list of potential Blomberg replacements when Göring and Himmler appeared at the *Führer's* door. Their faces were flushed from climbing the stairs. Sweat dripped from Göring's chin. He wasted no time to deliver their message.

"Now that we are rid of Blomberg, Fritsch needs to be removed," said Göring.

"Removed?" Hitler's surprise was genuine. "Blomberg went so far as to suggest that Fritsch replace him as war minister. Fritsch is at the top of our list."

Himmler cleared his throat. "*Mein Führer*. Paragraph 175 is quite explicit: sex between men is illegal. Unnatural. A homosexual cannot lead the armed forces. Think of the scandal. We brought you Fritsch's file from two years ago. Fritsch must go."

"*Mein Fuhrer*, this is old news," I blurted. "The last time these charges were brought, you dismissed them out of hand. You said they were nonsense."

Göring huffed. "Friedrich, you know the file has been *enhanced* with new information." Then Göring turned to Hitler. "We have a firsthand witness to corroborate Fritsch's disreputable liaisons." Göring tapped his chest. "Believe me, this pains me as much as you, *mein Führer*. But facts are facts." Göring nodded at me. "Don't you agree, Friedrich?"

I wanted to shout that any enhanced evidence was bogus. That it was all lies. But the die was cast. Göring would get Blomberg's job and Himmler's *SS* would become a full-fledged fourth military branch. It was too dangerous to go any further.

I gestured at Göring. "I forgot."

Himmler opened his leather briefcase. "Here is the new evidence Heydrich collected, *mein Führer*. The facts are irrefutable."

Hitler tossed the file on his desk without bothering to look at it.

"Hermann, can these charges be substantiated?"

Göring clicked his heels together. "Fritsch's guilt is proven beyond a doubt, *mein Führer.*"

Hitler swiveled. We were almost toe-to-toe. His clear blue eyes locked on mine as he validated their claim. "You say you have an eyewitness?"

"We can produce him tomorrow, *mein Führer*," Göring answered.

*

At home I went straight to the bar.

Carla took one look. "Is it that bad?"

"Worse." I hoisted the crystal decanter. "Care for one?"

"If you insist. Someone has to save you from drinking alone." I poured a stiff one and handed it to her.

"Cheers," she said. "Tell me what's going on?"

I studied Carla's face. She was exquisite even with her wrinkled brow of concern. "You know I love you," I said.

"I haven't heard that in some time." She threw me a kiss. "You've been under a tremendous amount of strain these last couple of months." She grabbed my hand and we eased onto the couch.

"It is going to get worse. Suffice it to say that by the end of tomorrow, our vaunted *Führer* will be one step closer to controlling the *Wehrmacht*. It will be harder than ever to rein him in."

"Can the outcome be changed?" Carla asked.

"I wish I had an answer."

Carla lifted her glass. "To finding answers."

I touched hers with mine. "Sooner, rather than later."

*

January 26, 1938

I trudged into Hitler's office in the Chancellery Wednesday morning knowing Fritsch was about to be ambushed. I should have realized he was doomed the moment Blomberg got himself in trouble.

Hitler's private phone rang. He listened and then replaced the receiver. "They are here, Friedrich."

I trailed Hitler into the hallway as Fritsch, with Göring at his elbow, mounted the Chancellery stairs. When they got to the first landing, Hitler signaled a Gestapo man waiting in the shadows of the library doorway. Moments later, he and another Gestapo goon hauled a pale-faced man out of the library. Bright light streamed through the hall windows. Otto Schmidt, a petty criminal, squinted. His jaw dropped and knees buckled when he saw the *Führer*. If not for the Gestapo men holding his elbows, Schmidt would have crumpled to the floor.

Himmler found Schmidt incarcerated in the *Börgermoor* concentration camp in *Emsland*.

A wisp of a man with weaselly features, Schmidt—a month previous—began a seven-year sentence for blackmailing prominent homosexuals. His *modus operandi*: introduce prominent men seeking illicit liaisons to young studs in Schmidt's stable of boys-for-hire. For this, Schmidt charged a small fee. He made the real money afterwards, extorting his clients with threats of exposure. Though barely thirty, Schmidt had been in and out of prison most of his life.

Göring looked from Schmidt to Fritsch and then back to Schmidt. He bellowed. His voice echoed off the marble walls. "Is this the man you witnessed having sex with another man in the Wannsee railroad station four years ago?"

"It is, *Herr* Göring," Schmidt said in a pinched voice, stealing a peek at Hitler. "They were downstairs, in the station toilet. They were . . ."

"What did you witness them doing?" Göring demanded.

Schmidt looked at Hitler, wary to say more.

"Don't be afraid," Göring said in a softer tone.

Schmidt steeled himself, glared at Fritsch, and said, "That old tart made Bavarian Joe strap a studded collar around his neck. Then he made him prance like a dog before . . ."

"Before what?" Göring shouted. "Say it!"

Schmidt shuddered, pulled his arms tight to his side, as if about to be struck, and said, "The boy put his mouth over Fritsch's wrinkled cock."

All eyes shot to Hitler. But Hitler said nothing. Instead, he stood arms folded, rocking back and forth, heel-to-toe.

Fritsch, on the other hand, turned pasty white. Beads of sweat dotted his forehead. The general opened his mouth to say something. Nothing came out. Wide-eyed, he looked from Göring to Hitler to Schmidt.

"This man . . ." Fritsch swallowed hard. He tripped over the words. "This man . . . is . . . mistaken." Fritsch, his shoulders hunched from the weight of the accusation, focused on Hitler. Finally, he found his voice, though weaker than expected from a man falsely accused. "I have never seen this man in my entire life, *mein Führer*. Believe me. I am not a homosexual."

Hitler glared at Fritsch, unmoved by the general's denial.

Göring went for the kill. He nudged Fritsch one step higher. "Look at the accused one more time, *Herr* Schmidt." Again, Göring pointed to Fritsch. "Are you absolutely certain this is the man?"

"He is the one, Your Excellency. He offered me money to never talk about it." A lecherous grin spread across Schmidt's narrow face. "A handsome sum it was."

"*Mein Führer. Everything* this man says is a *total* lie." Fritsch's color returned. He stood taller. With passion, he said, "You are the leader of Germany, *mein Führer*. This man is beneath you. He is beneath all of us."

Hitler moved to the edge of the top step and spoke in a cold, measured tone.

"Colonel General. This man Schmidt has no reason to lie. Under no circumstances can you continue to lead the army. You must resign."

Fritsch was dumbstruck. Mouth agape.

A pained silence filled the stairwell until Fritsch collected his wits. "Resign? Resign? I am the commander-in-chief of the army. I refuse." He pointed at Schmidt. "This man is a sewer rat. I *demand* the right to defend myself in a court of honor. This is madness. Sheer madness."

*

The next night, January 27, Canaris asked that I meet at his house along with Ludwig Beck, the army chief-of-staff who was now "technically" acting as commander-in-chief due to Fritsch's dismissal. I knew Beck to be a brilliant tactician who opposed Hitler's plans to move on Austria and Czechoslovakia. I also knew that once he read Hossbach's notes of the November 5 conference, Beck would write a blistering memo objecting to the invasion of Czechoslovakia. Still, I did not know if it was wise to lift my mask to him. On the other hand, considering the present state of affairs, I had no choice. To successfully block Hitler's path to war, the circle of collaborators had to be broadened.

"I do not understand," Beck began after our perfunctory greetings, "why Fritsch has not asked his fellow officers to stand by him?"

"I had a few words with him," Canaris explained. "Fritsch knows that Göring and Himmler—with a boost from Heydrich—are behind this. Fritsch believes they duped Hitler into believing these falsehoods about him. Fritsch is certain the charges will be set aside once Hitler learns the truth."

"Is he that naïve?" I asked.

"In a word, yes," Canaris snorted. "Whether the claims are true or not doesn't matter anymore. Göring's, Himmler's, and Heydrich's motives no longer matter. The *Führer* made it clear: he will not tolerate opposition to his plans for Germany's conquests. Dismissing Fritsch serves Hitler's overall purpose. We three understand that."

Then Canaris added, "You realize, Ludwig, that Hitler has declared war on the army. First Blomberg. Now Fritsch. How long do you think it will take before Göring becomes minister of war and the *SS* becomes a fighting branch of the armed forces? And the clock is ticking. Before long, we will march on Austria and Czechoslovakia."

"None of that is lost on me, Wilhelm," Beck replied. "I see it as clearly as we all do. But the army must remain apolitical. We're here to defend the country, not take it over. Remember, we each pledged our personal loyalty to Hitler."

I waded in. "I am sorry to tell you, General, not only is your loyalty misplaced but so is the entire military's. Name another country in the world where the army does not pledge to protect its nation? Its people? You have sworn an allegiance to a single man. One human being. Nothing else!"

"Hitler gave us no choice, Friedrich."

"General, you had a choice . . . you made the wrong one. I know. I have made wrong choices, too. Long before yours . . . which is why I am at this meeting. We must make amends. If Fritsch goes, the army loses independence from the Nazi Party. Germany will be left in the hands of people without scruples or morals. Can you look me in the eye and tell me that freedom for the German people is not the army's concern?"

Beck clasped his hands together. "Friedrich. Wilhelm. I'm on your side. The military leaders will not allow Fritsch to be crucified."

Canaris tamped-down the pipe tobacco, struck a match, and coaxed the shreds to life. "Fritsch must have his name cleared and reinstated to his post. We all agree. But we face a bigger crisis than saving Fritsch. You understand, Ludwig, don't you?"

Beck squeezed his lips tight. "Let's not dance around the issue. You're asking if German military leaders would support a rebellion? There have been rumblings. Without mentioning names, there are those in favor of rising up against Hitler that would surprise you. Until now, we didn't have a clear cause to rally behind. If Fritsch isn't reinstated, this could be the trigger we need."

"When it comes to rallying the troops around Fritsch, you need a plan." Canaris puffed away. "There is a faction in the *Abwehr* that wants the military to take Himmler and Heydrich down. Their thinking has merit: decapitate the Gestapo and the *SS*. This makes Hitler vulnerable. Then the country can regain its sanity."

Their bluntness amazed me.

Beck held nothing back. "We know your people want us to get rid of Himmler and Heydrich. As odious as those two are, that will not happen. The army cannot be drawn into internal problems."

"How can you make that distinction?" I challenged. "There are two sources that cause Germans' misery: Hitler is one and the Siamese twins of horror—Himmler and Heydrich—the other. Choke off either head and the other withers. To be safe, do all three. If you want to ensure success, add Göring and the poisonous Goebbels. Those five men have a stranglehold on Germany."

Beck shook his head. "Don't ask the military to start a revolution that nullifies the vote of ninety percent of Germans. That is in stark contrast to the army defending one of its own who has been humiliated on false charges for political purposes. Disparaging a senior officer like Fritsch denigrates the entire military. Let's hope the military tribunal is clearheaded enough to toss out the charges."

"How can that satisfy you?" Canaris asked. "The main characters will still be in power to do their damage."

"Fritsch reinstated gives me time to rally the military leadership. Hitler is going to march into Austria with or without our approval. When that happens, he will have drawn the proverbial line in the sand: Czechoslovakia. There is no way the army will allow him to invade a sovereign, democratic state that has not attacked us. It goes against all German principles . . . not to mention it would be an unmitigated disaster."

I challenged Beck. "You expect too much. Hitler and Göring will not let Fritsch have a military tribunal. They plan to get Fritsch in front of the *Volksgerichtshof*, the People's Court, run by

Roland Freisler. His court is an apparatus of the Party, not the country. You know what that means."

The ever-solemn Beck smiled. "I anticipated that. That's why I've already contacted Franz Gürtner. As minister of justice, he agreed that the law is clear: Fritsch can only be tried by a military tribunal."

"Since when does Hitler adhere to the law?" Canaris asked.

"He has no choice. The minister of justice supports Fritsch on this," Beck answered. "In fact, the trial is set for March 11."

"Do you know who the senior judge will be?" I asked Beck.

"Fritsch can only be judged by military officers of his rank or higher. By the time the trial comes around, my best guess is that Göring will be the senior judge. Certainly, Admiral Raeder will be included. A colonel general from the army branch would be a third."

I threw up my hands. "Who cares who the others are? With Göring and Raeder presiding, how can Fritsch get a fair trial?"

"There's your challenge, Friedrich," said Canaris. "You have five weeks to get the facts and put holes in the prosecution's case."

"Me?"

"Yes," answered Canaris. "There is no one else."

Before I could protest, Beck asked, "Where will you start?"

I thought for a moment. There was one logical starting point.

"By finding the rent-boy that Schmidt claimed had sex with Fritsch," I explained. "I am going to prove that Schmidt is lying."

"It would help if you had a name," Beck said.

"I do, in a way: Bavarian Joe, the name was in Heydrich's file," I answered. "Him aside, we need to approach this from three angles. I will help ferret out evidence to clear Fritsch. Ludwig, you need to identify those military leaders that will go against Hitler now. You can't wait for the tribunal. In this way, you will be ready whenever Fritsch asks for your support."

"And me?" asked Canaris.

"The circle of dissidents in the *Abwehr*. What can we expect from them?"

"Finally, someone with a plan!" said Canaris. He tapped tobacco from his pipe into an ashtray. "I'll get their ringleader here tomorrow night."

I turned to Beck. "Are you good with this, Ludwig?"

"I will get the military support you need."

Without thinking, I thrust my hand out. Beck placed his on top of mine. Canaris on top of his.

"One for all and all for one," I said.

"For the Fatherland," said Beck.

We sat back.

"You know, gentlemen, there were four Musketeers, not three, as most believe," said Canaris.

"Athos, Porthos, and Aramis were the original three," Beck said.

"But the man who told the story was D'Artagnan. He officially became a Musketeer deeper into the book," Canaris said.

"Who is *our* D'Artagnan?" I asked.

"Hans Oster. He will be the one here tomorrow."

Chapter 24

I left Canaris's house exhausted. When I got home, Carla was sitting on the couch, an aperitif in hand. Music filled the room. As I leaned to kiss her, I stumbled and grabbed the back of the settee to stop from falling. My head began to pound. The hairs on the back of my neck bristled. Somehow, I wound up next to her.

"What's wrong, Friedrich? You look like you've seen a ghost."

I pointed to the new record player—an Odeon-Favorit 107W—that Carla and I bought for Christmas. It was housed in a high-polished, wooden case. "That music."

"What about it?"

"I've heard it before."

She poked me in the ribs. "You have, silly. The Heroic Polonaise by Chopin."

"A-flat major," I muttered.

"Of course, you know it. It's very famous."

I tried to put words to what was rattling in my head. "Every time I've heard it, it reminded me of something. I never knew what. You know, like a whispered memory that fades before you can catch it. But . . . this time was different."

"Friedrich, darling. You're scaring me. How is it different? What do you remember?"

As I moved closer to the record player, an image—clear as day—popped in my mind. It was as sharp as a memory could be. I whipped around.

"It was 1910. Frankfurt. My father took me to the Hoch Konservatorium to hear a special concert by the winners of the Anton Rubinstein Competition that had been held in St. Petersburg earlier that year. The Rubinstein was just the most famous music competition in the whole world back then. Alfred Hoehn, who had won for piano, gave a technically perfect performance. Hoehn was followed by the man who had received honorable mention at the competition. That man was thin. Small. He had the same last name as the man who founded the competition, but his first name was Arthur. They were not related."

"Oh, Friedrich. You're remembering!"

I clutched Carla to my chest, not wanting to let go for fear I would lose the memory.

I continued, whispering into her ear. "My father took me backstage before the performance. I stood not ten feet from Arthur Rubinstein. He wore black tails that draped over the piano bench." I looked into Carla's face. "It was an incredible sight. Rubinstein practiced his piece on an wooden table. There was a thin strip of mirror the length of a piano's fall board, perched upright. He focused on the mirror to study his finger placement while he played on imaginary keys. It was amazing. His eyes were vibrant. Alert. They danced across the mirror as his fingers moved in a blur. Rubinstein heard every note in his head. Right then and there, I made up my mind to practice the piano harder than ever before."

Carla led me back to the couch. "I am so happy for you," she said. "And then what happened?"

"And then . . . and then . . . that's all I remember."

"Think, Friedrich. Did you live in Frankfurt or near Frankfurt? Is that why your father took you to the concert?"

"I don't know."

"Can you picture what your father looked like? What was he wearing? What were you wearing?"

I struggled to picture either the boy or man . . . but could see neither.

"Think hard, Friedrich. Are you certain it was you and your father?"

"I can see Rubinstein as if he were sitting in the room with us right now. I can hear the thumping of his fingers on that wooden table. I can hear the Polonaise like I have never heard it before." I turned to her. "It was me, Carla. I'm sure of it. And my father."

She took my hands. "When you are alone in your office, from time to time, glance at the copy of the photograph of your family that I made for you. Perhaps it will jog a memory."

"I will."

*

The next morning, I awoke determined to find the evidence to exonerate Fritsch. The only lead I had, *a nom de passage*—Bavarian Joe—was uttered by an unreliable criminal regarding an alleged event several years ago. Given the recent roundup of homosexuals, the odds of finding "Bavarian Joe" were small. However, after gentle questioning of closeted gay men I knew, I discovered that homosexual clubs still existed in and around Berlin though they were banned when the Nazis came to power. The few that existed were tucked behind ongoing businesses or in lofts at the end of dark alleyways. Passwords were often necessary to gain access.

I began to make the rounds. Whenever I gained entrance to a club, I asked if anyone knew Bavarian Joe. I got the same answer everywhere: no one knew him.

It was time to make a call.

*

"I thought you forgot about me," Bernhard Weiss said when he answered the phone.

"Things have been hectic these last few days. Göring and Himmler have resurrected a false Paragraph 175 charge against Werner von Fritsch. Have you heard anything concerning these allegations? They aren't public yet."

"Nothing from my sources," Weiss answered.

I described the scene with Schmidt standing at the top of the Chancellery stairs.

"Schmidt claimed to be an eyewitness to a homosexual tryst between Fritsch and a young boy-for-hire that goes by the name

Bavarian Joe. I've tried every which way to locate him but keep coming up with dead ends. I don't even have his real name."

"Are you sure he is alive?"

"I can't be sure of anything."

"If he were ever arrested, his name would be in the police files. When I headed the police, we cross-referenced pimps with their prostitutes and street names. Let me make some calls."

*

While waiting for Weiss to perform his magic, Canaris and I met in Lt. Colonel Hans Oster's office.

After we greeted each other, Oster said, "I have made the Fritsch case my own."

Oster was fifty years old. A veteran of the Great War, his promising military career had been derailed because of an affair with the wife of a fellow officer. Canaris not only gave him a second chance but rescued him from civil service anonymity. In the process, he arranged for Oster's rank to be restored. The two men shared a common distaste for the Nazis that was heightened after the Röhm Putsch.

"Can you be more specific?" I asked.

He glanced at Canaris, who nodded.

"I have access to intelligence information that our resisters will need," Oster began. "I am able to provide false papers and camouflage certain activities as *Abwehr* missions. Wilhelm has given his blessing to coordinate resistance cells through this office."

"This is admirable, Hans. But why take these risks?"

Oster explained. "If you are asking if I hate Hitler that much, I do. Since I have been at the *Abwehr*, I have gathered names of like-minded Germans, waiting for the right time to strike. Fritsch appears to be that catalyst."

"What's Fritsch to you?" I asked.

Oster reminisced. "Years back, I served under Fritsch." He turned to Canaris. "I bet you didn't know that."

"Of course, I did," answered Canaris, "or I would not have been doing my job."

"There is nothing I wouldn't do for him," Oster said. "I've already reached out to General Witzleben, who commands the Berlin military district. Unfortunately, he is in the hospital at the moment. Know this: If we are to move against Hitler and the *SS* leaders, Witzleben is the lynchpin. We must have troops behind us. The Berlin garrison is the obvious choice. Otherwise, we will be forced to go to each commander of the other military districts in the outer provinces to get the troops we need."

"Troops and information," Canaris said. "Without one, we can't have the other. Speaking of which, what news do you have from Schrader?"

"You mentioned him once before," I said. "Is he still in Vienna?"

"He keeps me one step ahead of everyone else there," answered Oster. "Schrader doesn't look like much. He's older. Out of shape. Still has that cherubic choir boy face. But he has a steel trap mind when it comes to remembering details. His files on Nazi crimes are extensive. He's the sort that can be in a room and no one remembers him ever being there. He's on board with whatever movement we manage to organize. Of late, I rely on him more and more to catalogue Nazi misdeeds."

*

Weiss did not disappoint. Two days later I learned that Bavarian Joe was born Joseph Weingärtner. Weiss even had the address of his favorite haunt.

Kasino der jungen Löwen, located between *Nollendorfplatz* and *Wittenbergplatz* in the Schönberg district of Berlin, was a favorite hangout of well-to-do men looking for "young lions." When the Nazis banned homosexuality, the club owner bought the building behind it. The original *Kasino* became a legitimate restaurant. Access to the "new" club was through the rear kitchen wall.

"May I help you?" asked a rather tall, emaciated waiter sporting an ill-fitting tuxedo. He had sunken cheeks, wore red lipstick, dark eye shadow, and enough pancake to be in the Follies. He looked me up and down, and then stared with dreamy eyes.

"Scrumptious."

"Excuse me?" I said.

"Sorry. Sometimes I can't help myself. Are you a free man?"

"What are you talking about?"

"You are certainly not a sword. No matter." He pointed with his left hand to a nondescript door at the rear of the kitchen with a slit at eye level. "Knock once. Wait a second, then knock twice. Say, 'Horst sent me.'"

I had gained entrée to a handful of clubs. Most were seedy. Not this one. The interior of the *Kasino der jungen Löwen* was wood-paneled with hand-carved appliqués of naked men in intimate poses. Red-velvet walls separated curved leather banquettes meant for privacy. Pink backlighting cast rosy shadows anywhere one looked.

"First time?" asked a muscular man wearing tight black pants and a leather vest that exposed his hairy chest. He jerked his thumb over his shoulder. "If you don't see what you want at the bar, you'll find it in here."

He handed me a booklet. "What's this?" The cover page was titled, *Je t'aime*.

"It describes what each stoke at the bar prefers to do. Name your pleasure, we can provide it."

I took out fifty Reichsmark and waved it in front of his nose. "This is for you, if you give me what I want."

He stuttered. "Don't get me wrong, *mein Herr*, it's just that . . ." His eyes drifted left. Two brutes came out of nowhere to pin back my arms. *Herr* Leather-Vest's tone changed. His voice deepened. More cutting. "Who the fuck are you?" And not-so-gently patted me down.

When he found the under-arm holster, he removed my gun. After making certain no bullet was chambered, he shoved it into his waist.

As he reached for my wallet and *Ausweis,* I struggled to free my arms, but the bouncers held tight. I hissed. "You are making a mistake."

"I doubt it, *mein Herr.* Let's find out who you are." When Leather-Vest read my ID, the smirk evaporated from his face.

"Let him go," he ordered.

I shrugged them off and grabbed back my wallet and ID. Then extended my hand. "Gun, please."

He handed me my Sauer 38H. "Sorry, *Herr Obergruppenführer.* I pray this visit is for pleasure. Not business."

"If I wanted to cause trouble, I would have worn my uniform and come with a backup squad."

"Forgive me," the man pleaded.

"Let's start again." This time I pulled out one hundred Reichsmark and waved it under his nose. "I am looking for Joseph Weingärtner. Do you know him?"

Before Leather-Vest could respond, the man on the right behind me answered, "You mean *Bayern Seppl?* Bavarian Joe? That's what he goes by."

I turned to him. "Do *you* know him?"

"Will he be sent to a camp?"

"Nothing of the sort. I need to ask him a question, get my answer, and he will never see me again." Then I added, "For that matter, neither will any of you."

"Do I get the bill if I tell you where to find him?"

Leather-Vest punched his arm. "He asked me first."

The third guy added, "Hey, I'm here. I know where he is, too."

"Stop bickering," I handed fifty Reichsmark to each. Without a word, Leather-Vest pointed to the bar at the rear. "Second stool on the right. Next to the wall. Wearing a lavender silk shirt."

Weingärtner's head was buried in a drink. His sleeves were rolled up. Needle marks in both arms. He could not have been more than twenty-one. Twenty-two at the most.

"Joseph?"

He continued to stare into his drink. Carla had printed a picture of Fritsch for me. I shoved it in front of Bavarian Joe's face. "Do you know this man?"

He didn't bother to look up. "Who wants to know?"

I tossed two hundred Reichsmarks on the bar top. "Professor von Liebig wants to know."

That turned his head. "Is that your name?"

I stabbed the picture embossed on the front of a one hundred Reichsmark. "Professor Justus von Liebig."

Weingärtner's eyes went from the money to the black-and-white picture of Fritsch then back to the money.

"Do you know him?" My finger pressed the top of Fritsch's picture.

Head down, he said, "I've been with many men, *mein Herr*. Maybe yes. Maybe no."

"The Wannsee Station. A little more than four years ago. It was arranged by Otto Schmidt. Try to remember."

"That slimy turd? I hate that man. He tells me one price and then gives me half of what he promised."

Having seen the man in person, that did not surprise me. "Look at this picture again. Please."

He brought it closer and tilted it into the light. After a few seconds, he placed it on the bar top and pointed to Fritsch's uniform.

"The guy I did in the station had retired from the military. Is this man *still* in the army?"

I nodded, holding my breath.

"Then this isn't the guy." Joseph handed back the picture and turned to his drink.

"Are you certain? You have no idea how much is riding on your answer. Look again."

"I don't have to. The man I did was old and creepy. He was crippled. He had been out of the army for years. I wanted to get it over with right there on the platform, but he insisted we have privacy. We used the toilet in the underground station. It took forever to go down the steps. He used a cane. The man disgusted me."

I could not wait to tell Canaris, Oster, and Beck. "Can you remember anything else that distinguished him?"

Weingärtner glanced at the money. "There was something distinctive about him."

"A scar? A tattoo? Try to remember?"

"Nothing like that. It was a while ago." Then he snapped his fingers. "Horses. That's it. He loved horses. He was in the cavalry. A horse threw him and messed up his leg. He'd been on pension ever since." Weingärtner looked up. "Is that good enough to earn another one of those Professor Liebigs?"

I handed him a third. "You earned it." Then I asked, "How does Schmidt fit into all of this?"

"He runs a stable of young boys. Most of the time, he arranges the meets. Takes a cut of what they pay us. Sometimes steals a bit more. Claims he has extra expenses. I hate the fucker, but he gets us business. Last time I saw him was before Christmas."

"That's when he was arrested."

"Good. It's one thing to take money for sex. But Schmidt's more interested in what happens after. That's when he blackmails the poor sots. That captain we're talking about. That's right. I remember now. He was a captain. Well, Schmidt followed him to his home. When he confronted him, Schmidt told the old boy he would ruin his reputation and career unless he went straight to the bank and paid Schmidt not to squeal. It usually worked. This guy was no different, and once they paid Schmidt, he went after them again and again. Schmidt only backed off when the marks threatened to go to the police."

I tossed one more Liebig onto the bar.

"What's that for?"

"For saving a man's career."

*

Armed with the good news, I met Oster and Beck at Canaris's house. Beck was late. We started without him.

"I found Bavarian Joe," I began. "Fritsch was not the man he did in the Wannsee Station. It was some retired cavalry captain. We will be able to prove Fritsch's innocence and get his post back. Then we will have breathing space to thwart Hitler's war plans." I turned to Oster. "Did you find support from the district commanders?"

"Most provincial commanders are with us, but not all. The ones ready to join us have two caveats: the first is that the military leadership must be all-in if the commanders commit their men to overthrow Hitler," Oster explained.

The doorbell chimed as Canaris picked up the thread. "Their other stipulation is that the leadership must originate from the top. That means Berlin. At this moment, that is impossible. Witzleben is still sick. For all intents and purposes, the Berlin military is leaderless. But I think . . ." he stopped in midsentence.

A grim-faced Beck entered the study. "*Mein Herren*, I'm afraid it is all over."

"What's all over?" asked Oster.

"Moments before I left," Beck answered, "I got word that Fritsch resigned. It changes everything. There is no one for the army to rally behind. It's over."

"Doesn't he know what we're ready to do on his behalf? Bring him here. We'll convince him to rethink this. We can get him his post back," I said.

"Fritsch is a man of honor," explained Beck. "He took the high road. He would rather fight his battle in court than cause a military insurrection that might ignite a revolution."

This was a body blow to our plans, but not a knockout. After I explained to Beck that Weingärtner had been found, I said, "This is all the more reason to assemble the evidence to exonerate Fritsch and expose Himmler's and Heydrich's attack on the army. Then we will see what the General Staff is prepared to do."

*

"How did it go today?" Carla knew about Fritsch and what I hoped to uncover.

"There could be a glimmer of light. Bavarian Joe said the man he met had been a career cavalry man who had been injured. I found the names of a dozen men about the right age. Each retired after an injury. I need to find where they live. It will take some doing. My intuition tells me I'm on the right track."

Carla fixed two scotches. We sat on the couch and clinked glasses.

"I've done a bit of investigating myself," she said.

"For a new photography project?"

She flipped the hair off her face. "Not exactly. I tracked down Eberhard Zinnmacher's family. They live in a small village outside of Nuremberg. In the same house they raised Ebbe."

I felt a sudden chill. "What were you hoping to find?"

"One of us had to see if Ebbe wrote letters home before, you know . . . and might have mentioned his friends' names."

"You disturbed them after all these years? How did they take it?"

"After I told them that my friend fought with their son at Marne, they invited me inside."

"Did they have any letters?"

"Only one. It turns out that Ebbe was an ersatz soldier. A substitute. He was conscripted to replace men aging out. I learned that his family comes from a long line of toymakers that specialize in tin soldiers. Ebbe learned the trade. They thought working with metal would keep him out of the army . . . but it didn't."

"How old was Ebbe?"

"It was on the grave marker: eighteen. He was their only child. Imagine how heartbroken they must have been when they received the news? They still are. He had been gone only a few months. I read the letter. It was mostly about how scared he was and how awful it was to sleep in the trenches. He described the piercing whistle dropping bombs made. He did mention that one soldier was especially kind to him. A gentle giant. But no name. That had to be you."

"It could have been anyone."

She patted the couch; I sat next to her. "I had to do it. You understand. I hoped it would open a door. In the end, it closed a lead."

I put my arm around her. "I'm glad you did. But to be honest, it is a bit of a relief to still be Friedrich Richard."

PART III

PART III

Chapter 25

February 4, 1938

I plowed through the reports on my desk so I could get back to my covert project when Hitler called me to his office.

"*Guten Morgen*," I said.

"And good morning to you." Hitler jumped to greet me. When he rounded his desk, he grabbed both my hands. "Come, Friedrich. I have much to tell you before my meeting this afternoon."

"I wasn't aware of a meeting scheduled for later today."

"It is for the full cabinet plus certain military leaders. No need for you to be there."

Good!

We settled into chairs parked on either side of a small table. There was a silver tray with a pot of tea, porcelain China cups, and a plate of his favorite snack: *Apfelkuchen gefült mit Nüssen und Rosinen*. Apple cake filled with nuts and raisins.

"Isn't it joyous, Friedrich? Fritsch resigned yesterday. I will finally have my way." Then he said, "Today I will announce that Fritsch and Blomberg have stepped down for health reasons. With both men out of the picture, I now control the officer corps . . . or I will as soon as I remove the remaining malignancies, as we did in the Röhm Putsch."

My stomach flipped. I thought I had seen the last of the ruthless assaults on our own people. "How bad will the bloodshed be?"

Hitler's eyes twinkled. "Now, now, Friedrich. No one is going to die . . . assuming they obey orders."

"And if they don't?"

"That won't happen. To begin with, I am abolishing the position of war minister."

"Göring wants that position."

"Of course, he does. But that is not what *I* want."

"If not Göring, then who?"

Hitler thrust his thumb into his chest. "*Ich*. There will be *no* war minister. *I* am taking personal command of the entire armed forces. The *Wehrmachtsamt*—War Office—will be replaced by the *Oberkommando der Wehrmacht*. The High Command will be known as the OKW for short. I don't need to be bothered with the day-to-day operations. Wilhelm Keitel will have those responsibilities. But . . . from now on, the armed forces will report to me and no one else!"

Keitel was a "yes" man. For that reason, most referred to him as "Lakeiel" . . . which is a play on the German word *Lakai* or lackey.

"Keitel is a man you can count on," I managed to say. "And who will replace Fritsch as commander-in-chief of the army?"

Hitler sipped his tea and took a bite from his apple cake. He chewed slowly. Then, with a mischievous grin, murmured, "Walther von Brauchitsch will be the new commander-in-chief."

Deep furrows appeared on my forehead. "Everyone knows Brauchitsch has wife problems. The last I heard he intended to resign from the army. How did you convince him to stay on?"

Brauchitsch had the deportment of an aristocratic soldier. He was cultivated, well-groomed, and yet an introvert who could barely cope with Hitler, cowering whenever the *Führer* made demands of him.

"I gave Brauchitsch eighty thousand Reichsmark to pay his wife off for a divorce. Now he is free to marry his true love. Did you ever meet Charlotte Rüffer? I don't blame him for wanting her."

I didn't know her.

Hitler sipped his tea and then explained, "Brauchitsch is mine. He will make certain that the army is no longer independent from the Party but will align with us."

"That still leaves Göring."

"Hermann has enough power. More importantly, I do not want anyone between me and the armed forces." Hitler tipped his teacup toward me. "Not even you, *Friedrichchen*."

"You must have tossed Göring a bone?"

"You know I did. I elevated Göring to field marshal. With Blomberg gone, he will be the highest-ranking military man— except me, of course—but without control over any service branch other than the *Luftwaffe*. How perfect is that?" Then he burst out laughing at his own cleverness.

"Brilliant, *mein Führer*." The sad truth? It was brilliant. Then I added, "Make certain you give him a new medal to pin on his chest. That will go a long way to making him happy."

"It is already made," Hitler said.

Of course it was.

Hitler took another bite of cake.

"There's more. Later today, I will announce that thirteen other generals have 'retired.' Some are aristocrats that still yearn to restore the Kaiser. Others do not support the Party or endorse our goals. There will never be dissidence at the top of the army again."

"Those are radical changes."

"Not radical enough! I will also transfer forty-four top ranking officers that don't agree with me—but are not dangerous—to distant posts."

"You will have absolute control of the military," I said.

"Oh, but I didn't stop there, Friedrich. Remember how Neurath agreed with Blomberg and Fritsch at that November 5 meeting? It was only a matter of time before I removed him, too. Today is that day. Unlike the others, I must elevate him since, as our foreign minister, he is known and liked around the world. Neurath will become the president of the newly created Secret Cabinet Council."

"Without power?" I knew the answer before asking.

"Naturally," Hitler answered. "With Neurath in a new position, Joachim von Ribbentrop will be recalled from Britain to become my new foreign minister. Herbert von Dirksen, the ambassador to Tokyo, will replace Ribbentrop in London. Then I recalled Ulrich von Hassell from Rome. I need someone in Rome who supports our goals and can work with Mussolini. The Italians don't like von Hassell."

Hitler's *coup d'état* left me breathless. "Anyone else?"

Hitler held up one finger.

"Can you picture Franz von Papen's face when I told him he would no longer serve as ambassador to Austria? He protested, of course. He reminded me of our links to the past, thinking that would change my mind. I asked him to recall how lucky he was to be alive given that Himmler and Heydrich wanted to finish him off during the Röhm Putsch. Hearing that, his indignation vanished."

Papen owed his life to Hitler. I was ordered to spend three days in Papen's house during the Röhm Putsch. My presence prevented Heydrich from sending a death squad to kill him. Had that radical step to kill the vice-chancellor been taken, the army was prepared for President Hindenburg to declare martial law and force Hitler out of office. The Röhm Putsch was not as much about the wanton killings of those that threatened Hitler but something he had to do to remain in power.

"How did Papen take it?"

"After making a fuss, not badly. He will remain in his post until the end of next week's meeting with Austria's Schuschnigg. Then I will appoint Franz ambassador to Turkey. It is a demotion, but he will accept it because he likes having an official position."

This was the first I heard of a meeting with Austria's chancellor. "Are we traveling to Vienna?"

"No. Schuschnigg must come to me. To Berchtesgaden. His government is tottering. He's lost the will of the people. The time to strike is now."

*

My head was spinning. In a coup of his own making, Hitler surgically rid himself of all opposition from the corps of military officers and diplomats that balked at his plans for war, while outflanking Göring and Himmler's personal ambitions. In deft strokes, the former corporal, twenty years out

of the military, was now in sole command of the most powerful military machine in the world. Just as astounding, all of
this accomplished in just three months since the November 5
meeting . . . without firing a shot!

Chapter 26

There was no time to brood. To thwart Hitler's revolution, we had to win a victory for Colonel General Fritsch in court. Given that Göring would preside, the evidence of Fritsch's innocence had to be overwhelming. In the process, we hoped to discredit Himmler and Heydrich and to unite the generals behind regime change.

While Hitler announced his coup to his cabinet, I was en route to meet Joseph Weingärtner at the station where he and the cavalry captain had rendezvoused. I wanted to feel those stairs under my feet and stand where Schmidt claimed to hide when he observed the two emerge from the toilet.

I parked my car and found Joseph waiting on the platform. He sported a yellow shirt that peeked out from a brown beaver coat a size too big for him. His Persian wool hat was dyed to match the coat. The outfit detracted from his rakish good looks.

Snow started to fall.

Joseph pointed to railroad tracks. "Those are new."

"How do you mean?"

"Back then, they were converting the trains from steam to electric. There was construction all around as new lines were laid on the western side of the building. It was easy to remain in the shadows and not be seen."

We covered the length of the station, walked down the stairs to the toilet, and then climbed back to the platform.

"Where was Schmidt standing?"

"Behind there." Joseph pointed to a steel support column.

"Did you know he would be waiting?"

Joseph nodded. "Schmidt knew the layout of stations like the back of his hand. He arranged the appointments and knew where we would be. He followed the marks to their front door to shake them down. Schmidt always carried a small camera. I was never sure there was film in it, but if they protested, he would wave it in front of their faces."

Then Joseph mimicked Schmidt's weasely voice. "'You don't want me to make public what's in this camera, do you?' Schmidt bragged how scared they all were. The man disgusted me."

"I appreciate your help, Joseph."

His face softened into a fragile smile. "It's nice to hear my name spoken. I rarely hear it."

"If you want to be called Joseph, make people use it," I said. "Don't kowtow to others. Keep your dignity."

He gave a mock salute. "I'll bear that in mind." He turned to leave.

"One last question, Joseph. Why here? Why come to Wannsee?"

Joseph rocked from side-to-side. "The old man paid extra to come here. He wanted to be close to where he lived but far enough away not to be recognized. He knew about the construction. My guess is that he had been here with others."

"Do you happen to remember where the old man lives?"

"Lichterfelde."

"That should help us find him." I handed Joseph another Liebig.

He balked. "You gave me plenty last time."

"Not enough, as far as I am concerned. You earned it."

Two rough-looking young men stood at the end of the platform, shooting furtive looks our way. One poked the other and nodded as Joseph stuffed the bill into his pocket.

Joseph turned to leave.

I called out. "Should Colonel General Fritsch's lawyer ask, would you be willing to be a witness at the trial?"

The blood drained from his face. "Are you trying to get me killed? The moment I'm identified as a homosexual, they'll send me to a camp. That's what happens, you know. No one will ever hear from me again."

I waved my hands. "Slow down. If it should come to that, I can protect you. I am not saying that you will be called. I am only asking if you would be willing." I had already arranged with Canaris that Joseph would be issued a false *Ausweis* and the means to get him out of the country. "Do you have relatives anywhere you could visit?"

"Visit? I want to leave Germany forever. If I testify for your man Fritsch, I want to be sent to Palestine. I have relatives there. I want proper papers and enough money to live until I get settled. Germany is no place for a gay man, and certainly not a gay Jew. Can you arrange that?"

"Yes, Joseph. I can. The trial is a month away. Until then, don't talk to anyone about this. Keep your head down and your mouth shut."

Joseph gave a broader smile. "You mean, act normal."

"That's exactly what I mean. Do you want a ride back?"

He shook his head. "The train is fine. I have an appointment a couple of stops from here."

I watched Joseph saunter down the platform. It didn't take long before the two toughs angled his way. As they neared, they separated, one making a wide sweep behind Joseph, the other sliding to his right.

They did little to hide their intent.

I pulled out my gun and edged closer.

The one who first saw the hundred Reichsmark drew a butcher's cleaver from a leather sheaf on his belt. When he raised it to threaten Joseph, I fired. The cleaver flew from his hand and clattered to the track below.

The thug yelped.

I charged.

The hooligans bolted to the street below.

"That was some shot!" Joseph said as I neared. "But I could have handled myself."

I shrugged. "You were about to be chopped by something that looked like a guillotine."

"They wouldn't have hurt me. They wanted the money you gave me. We're easy marks. It's happened before, it will happen again."

"That's no way to live. It's time to get you out of Germany."

Disbelief was written across his face. "I've been promised things before."

"If your wish is to get to the Holy Land, Joseph, I will make sure you do."

And then, without warning, Joseph Weingärtner hugged me.

*

February 5, 1938

The next morning, I was about to leave for the Lichterfelde section of Berlin to find Weingärtner's cavalry officer when my phone buzzed. Every instinct said to ignore the call.

It was Hitler. "We must speak."

"I was about to step out. Can it wait?"

"It's about yesterday's meeting."

I found Hitler having his morning snack.

"Were they shocked?" I asked as he chewed on an *Apfelstrudel*

"They reacted the only way they could. They understood the value of centralizing the army's command under my leadership. They approved my changes without question."

"Brauchitsch and Keitel?"

"Not a peep," answered Hitler.

"Neurath and the other diplomats?"

"The same."

"And Göring?"

Hitler shook his head. "No more questions, Friedrich. It's over. I've won." He sipped his tea. When he replaced the cup, he said, "That's not the reason I wanted to see you. These last few weeks have been exhausting. Come with me to Berchtesgaden, Friedrich. To the Berghof. I need the mountain air to revive me. You need a break, too."

Hitler was pale. There was no question that the drama of the past weeks had taken its toll on him. I was bone-tired myself, but I did not want to interrupt my investigation.

"Tomorrow is Sunday, *mein Führer*. How long did you anticipate staying at the Berghof?" I asked.

"Through the following weekend. Remember? Schuschnigg will be there."

"You're not wasting any time, are you?"

"Papen set this meeting up weeks before I gained control the army. Ever since the November 5 meeting, taking Austria was never in doubt. The timing of Schuschnigg's visit could not have been better planned. I want you by my side as I spell out the *Anschluss* to Schuschnigg." Then he added, "Besides, you don't want to miss Franz von Papen's last hurrah."

Fritsch's military tribunal was scheduled for March 11, a little over a month away. Ten days at the Berghof would put my investigation in a hole. But I had no choice.

"Would it be all right if Carla accompanied me, *mein Führer*?"

"Eva is left alone too much. A new friend would do her good." Then he asked with a quirky look, "But can I trust her? Your Carla?"

I stuttered. "What do you mean?"

"You know what I mean, Friedrich. She's a woman. Women have their own ideas. The last woman you brought to Berchtesgaden filled Eva with all sorts of crazy notions. The next thing I knew, I had to spend more time with Eva. Treat her better. Give her expensive gifts. Call more often. Do you remember, Friedrich? Trude Mohr?"

The last time I heard Trude Mohr's name was from Joseph Goebbels's lips when he told me she was the one that accused Max Klinghofer of being a communist sympathizer. The thought of her made my blood boil.

"Whatever happened to good old Trude?" I growled. "I lost track of her career."

"I can see you are still agitated that she turned your friend in to Goebbels."

"You never told me you knew."

"You know the virtue I admire most is loyalty. That's why I understood about those two guards. As for Trude, she married an *SS* man. As chance would have it, her present job is to monitor the social services for the employees of the Hermann Göring Works. I will never forget how she tried to convince Eva that I was using her. I punished Trude for that, you know."

"How?"

"She had an ego, that one," said Hitler. "It galled her that she had a high Party number. She petitioned for a lower one. For its status. After all, she had been the leader of the *Bund deutscher Mädel.* When her application got to me, I denied it." Hitler put his hand on my shoulder. "I did it for you as well. To this day, she doesn't know why she was turned down."

Not for me. It was for your own petty revenge.

"I don't know what to say."

"There is nothing to say. I only ask that you don't bring Carla if she is anything like that Mohr woman. I will not have her under the same roof as Eva if she is."

"You needn't worry. Carla is the opposite. She and Eva share a passion for photography. The two will have much to keep them busy."

". . . and out of trouble!" added Hitler.

Chapter 27

I loped down the Chancellery steps, concerned about the Fritsch case. That Trude Mohr paid something for what she did to Max made the day sweeter. I smiled while picturing Carla's reaction to Hitler's invitation to the Berghof.

It was crisp and cold outside. The sun shone brightly. I shielded my eyes from the glare.

As I turned toward my car, I heard my name called.

"Entschuldigen Sie, Herr Richard, aber darf ich Ihnen eine Frage stellen?"

A man in his mid-twenties, sporting a belted, Logan-green, double-breasted trench coat, gray pin-striped pants, and a gray fedora, leaned against the building. A Capstan cigarette dangled from the side of his mouth. While his German was perfect, the charm and clothing were British.

"I speak English," I said.

"Either language works," the stranger said.

"Who are you? Why do you want to talk to me?"

"My name is Ian Colvin. I'm a journalist with the *News Chronicle* here in Berlin. Don't confuse me with my father, Ian *Duncan* Colvin, who is also a journalist. That's not the point. My middle name is Goodhope. Catchy, don't you think? Given the times we live in?"

"Slow down, *Herr* Colvin. You're talking gibberish. What can I do for you?"

I knew of Colvin. He had a reputation as a pit bull of a journalist.

He grabbed my elbow and we tucked into a doorway around the corner. "Let's talk here."

I rubbed my hands together, blowing warm air on them. "Will this take long?"

"I've heard of you, Friedrich. You're known to be close to Hitler and yet you are never in the limelight."

I shrugged.

"You are different than the other top officials. Goebbels. Göring. Even Himmler."

"You're wasting my time, *Herr* Colvin. I'm a nobody." I turned to leave.

"Wait. I am about to submit my story as to what happened yesterday. Before I did, I wanted to give you a chance to verify some facts."

"Speak to Dr. Goebbels. He is the one to answer your questions."

"If I wanted to speak to him, I would have, Friedrich. Did you have a chance to read what the *New York Times* said this morning about yesterday's shuffle of military men?"

I shook my head.

"I've got the teletype right here. They said, and I quote, 'Hitler Assumes Control of the Army.' Then two lines below, 'London Hears Hitler Feared Coup by Army and Arrested von Fritsch.' The subtitle reads, 'Chancellor Is Said to Have Acted After Group of Generals Protested Policy in Spain and Link to Italy.' End quote. What do you have to say about these headlines?"

"The *New York Times* can write whatever it pleases."

"But is what they are saying true, Friedrich? My sources say General Fritsch was not arrested. Can you confirm this?"

I hunched my shoulders. Arched my brows.

"That's what I thought," said Colvin. "And changing military leaders had nothing to do with Spain or Italy? The *Times* got that wrong, too, didn't they?"

"Ask Dr. Goebbels."

"I am asking you."

I clamped my lips tight.

Colvin cleared his throat. "You know what I think? I say everything in the *New York Times* story is balderdash. I say yesterday was significant for other reasons. Now that Hitler controls the army, the military leaders have lost their chance to have a formal face-off against the Nazi Party. Hitler brilliantly rendered them powerless."

"Do you expect me to react, *Herr* Colvin?"

"I'm past you reacting, Friedrich. Just listen."

"Are you that sure of yourself?"

"Got to be in this business." Colvin continued. "Whether you know it or not, Hitler's coup has solidified the British European policy. Make no mistake, it is one of caution and compromise. This opens the door to Austria, doesn't it? Hitler knows Britain will not make war against him."

"These are things I know nothing about."

"Your silence speaks volumes, my friend. I'm sure you would set me straight if I were wrong. Thanks. That's all I needed to know."

"On the contrary, *Herr* Colvin, I've said nothing. I am standing in the cold out of respect for you as a journalist. So, if you are finished, I need to go home. Where it is warm."

"Hear me out. Our Foreign Secretary Anthony Eden sees through Hitler. Unfortunately, my sources tell me Eden will be replaced in two weeks' time by Halifax. Halifax told your vaunted leader last November that Britain would not lift a finger if Germany tried to subsume Austria. In a way, Chamberlain is getting rid of anyone who objects to his way of thinking, the same as the little corporal did."

"It's getting colder by the minute, *Herr* Colvin. And so are your theories."

"I know more than you think, Friedrich."

"What do you think you know, Colvin?"

"For one, I met with the former mayor of Leipzig when he came to England."

Last June, England was one of many countries Carl Goerdeler visited in an effort to drum up support against Hitler. He was dismissed by everyone as a lone operative without authority. Many felt he spouted treason.

"What else, *Herr* Colvin?"

"I know that Beck tried to rally the military leaders behind Fritsch. That should tell you something about me."

"I must go, *Herr* Colvin."

"Before you do, a last question: have you seen the beard of a Jew before?"

I stood thunderstruck, in disbelief that he uttered the code Bernhard Weiss and I agreed to use when it was urgent to contact each other. Before I could question Colvin, he strode away.

*

I dashed into the Hotel Adlon and found an empty phone booth.

"What can you tell me about Ian Colvin?" I asked when the call went through.

"I first met Colvin in Berlin when he covered the story about that monarchist, Ewald Kleist-Schmenzin. Remember him? The chap who refused to fly the Nazi flag when Hitler first became chancellor?"

"He was brave, if nothing else. Colvin got my attention when he mentioned that he was aware of what Beck was doing."

"Ian Colvin knows the right people. Especially here in England," said Bernhard. "He's the real deal. When the time comes, you will be glad he is on our side."

"What you're telling me, Bernhard, is that I can trust him."

"What I'm telling you is that you should enlist him in the cause."

*

Despite Bernhard's reassurances, I found the encounter with Colvin unnerving. I slipped the key in the front door. Rather than unlock it, I retraced my steps to the street and then looked each way to be certain I hadn't been followed. Of late, I had a sense of being watched . . . but there was never anyone there.

Inside, Carla said, "I thought I heard you at the door."

"Sorry. I needed to check something before I came in."

We embraced. I held her longer than usual.

"What was that for?" she asked when I finally let go.

"Does there have to be a reason to hold you close to me?"

She flashed her infectious smile. "Do you feel guilty about something?"

"Let's sit for a moment."

"Why all the mystery?"

On the couch, my knee pressed against her thigh. "It's a mystery you will like. How does a vacation sound to you?" I asked.

She sniffed. "Did you stop for a drink? You are acting very strange."

I frowned. "Why must I have had a drink to ask you on a trip?" Then I smiled. "Am I that neglectful of you? That's terrible."

She jabbed my arm. "Only kidding."

"Many a truth is said in jest," I said. "This is how I am going to make it up to you. We have been invited to join the *Führer* in his alpine home in the Obersalzberg."

"The Berghof? I have heard it's magnificent."

"We can leave tomorrow."

She grew concerned. "Will there be other guests? What should I bring to wear? I want to make you proud of me."

I swept Carla into my arms. "Everything you do makes me proud. As for what to wear, bring what to hike in and clothes for formal dinners. We'll be there for about ten days."

"Will we watch movies in his theater? I can't wait."

"Movies and more. I will need to attend meetings at the end of the week. Guests from Austria are expected."

"What am I supposed to do while you're busy?"

That's when I told Carla about Eva Braun.

"And be certain to pack your cameras."

* * *

With the renovations recently completed, Hitler's Berghof mountain retreat was stately. Majestic. We were ushered into the Great Hall with its wide-beamed, coffered ceiling. A magnificent fireplace dominated the massive room that was divided into sections. There was a seating area in the right corner with plush chairs draped in cranberry-colored fabric around an inlaid table with four place settings. A polished teapot sat in the middle of the table next to freshly baked biscuits that filled the air with a welcoming aroma.

When we entered, Hitler and Eva Braun were peering through the expansive, mullioned windows that overlooked *Untersberg* Mountain in the Bavarian Alps. Austria was to the left. They turned at the sound of our heels clacking against the polished marble floor.

Hitler bowed.

"Welcome to the Berghof, *Fräulein* Bartheel. It is a pleasure to see you again."

He brought Carla's hand to his lips and edged back. "May I present *Fräulein* Eva Braun?" Eva kissed Carla on both cheeks. "I understand you are a professional photographer."

Carla blushed. "I do my best."

"I am an amateur photographer, myself. I work for the *Führer's* photographer: *Herr* Hoffmann."

Eva glanced over her shoulder at the enormous windows. She grabbed Carla's hand. "Come. Get your camera. This is the golden hour when the sun is low and doesn't cast shadows. We can get unbelievable pictures. I want to hear all about your photography."

Chapter 28

Carla and I made the most of our time at the Berghof. We skied, snowshoed, and took a horse-drawn sleigh ride buried under layers of thick blankets. When we were not together, Carla spent time with Eva. They had endless talks about photography. Given the two were the same size, Eva and Carla reverted to giggling girls playing dress-up, fooling with each other's hair, and having a grand time.

Thankfully, without drama.

*

"Did you know that Eva has champagne every afternoon? I'm not used to all the drinking," Carla said after the first days.

"She told the *Führer* how much she appreciates your company. Tell me," I asked, "does she seem happy to you?"

"We did do a lot of talking. She's happiest when the *Führer* is here. She doesn't see much of him anyplace else and accepts that she is limited to being mistress of Berghof while the rest of Germany doesn't know she exists."

"Not that long ago, she sang a different tune," I said.

"Eva unconditionally loves the *Führer*. It helps that he showers her with gifts. He gives her everything she wants." Then Carla took my hand. "Eva told me how you were by her side both times she tried to take her life. She may not have told you, but she appreciates it."

"I did what any human being would do."

"One thing Eva said struck me. That Hitler is the smartest man she ever met. Is the *Führer that* smart?"

My face puckered as if I had eaten sour candy. "If you are asking if I agree with her, let's just say that Adolf Hitler is a genius . . . wrapped in a chrysalis of insanity."

"You mean genius as to how he got to this point, and insane for what he plans to do next?"

I kissed her cheek. "You are savvier than most world leaders. That is exactly what I mean. Now, do you want to know about tonight's movie?"

"I pray it is not *Micky Maus* or *Schneewittchen*. I am tired of those silly animations," Carla said.

I feigned shock. "You don't like *Mickey Mouse* or *Snow White and the Seven Dwarfs*? In the *Führer's* mind, *Schneewittchen* is about the days when life was simpler and purer."

"And *King Kong*? How many times do we have to watch that over-sized gorilla climb the Empire State Building? Don't tell me Hitler identifies with Kong?"

"Alone. Ostracized. Misunderstood. That theme embodies his persona."

"Kong is an ape."

"Kong is a conqueror. King of his jungle." I shrugged. "But in the end, he didn't make it, did he?"

"Hitler must gloss over that part," Carla said. "With all this, you still haven't told me what film we are seeing tonight."

"*Viva Villa!* with Wallace Beery. The *Führer* relates to the son's need to succeed and Villa's father/son conflict. Not to forget that Pancho Villa was viewed as the liberator of his people."

"Who came to a tragic ending," added Carla.

*

February 12, 1938

Although I knew the Austrian chancellor was expected sometime that day, I thought Carla and I had time to take advantage of the fresh powder that had coated the ski slopes at Rossfeld overnight. I was on my way to check the equipment when Hitler pulled me over.

"Papen met Schuschnigg and the Austrian entourage at the border." Hitler pulled out his gold pocket watch, a gift from *Frau* Elsa Bruckmann, an early Party supporter. His nickname, "Wolf," was engraved inside. "They will be here shortly."

There goes skiing!

As it turned out, the cars that transported Franz von Papen and Chancellor Kurt Schuschnigg could not make the steep ice-covered inclines to the Berghof. Reconnaissance cars, known as half-tracks with wheels in the front and continuous tracks in the rear, were sent to fetch them.

Schuschnigg was whisked into Hitler's study the moment he arrived. Papen, along with Hitler's newly appointed foreign minister, Joachim von Ribbentrop, conferenced with Guido Schmidt, Schuschnigg's foreign minister and two Austrian aides in a separate room.

Our military men—General Wilhelm Keitel and the heads of the local army and air force—were positioned in a third room, ready to intimidate if called upon.

Schuschnigg bowed to Hitler. "This room has a wonderful view. It undoubtedly has been the scene of many a decisive conference, *Herr Reichskanzler.*"

"We did not get together to speak of the fine view or the weather."

Political civility had just been crushed. Schuschnigg rallied to address his main concern: Austria's independence.

"*Herr Reichskanzler*, thank you for giving me the opportunity for this meeting. I would like to assure you that we take the treaty between our two countries, which we signed in July 1936, very seriously, and that we are most anxious to remove all remaining misunderstandings and difficulties. We have done everything to prove that we intend to follow a policy friendly toward Germany in accordance with our mutual agreement."

Hitler scoffed. "On the contrary, Austria has done everything to avoid a friendly policy. For instance, you have remained a member of the League of Nations even though the Reich withdrew from the League. How is that a friendly policy?"

Schuschnigg objected. "Germany left the League long ago. Nobody asked us to do the same."

"It should have been self-evident that you leave the League. The whole history of Austria is one uninterrupted act of high treason," Hitler said, growing more agitated by the minute. "You must know how offended I am that Austria fortifies its borders with us. It is fool's play. Such defenses will never stop let alone delay me for half an hour. I can walk into Austria anytime I want. Perhaps, one morning, soon, you will wake up to find we have arrived and occupied Vienna. Unless you act *at once*, not even I will be able to stop the *SS* or my army's revenge. Blood will be shed. I would very much like to save Austria from such a fate," then added, "if possible."

Schuschnigg held his ground. "I know you can invade Austria, *Herr Reichskanzler.* If that were to happen, surely blood will spill. Such a step means war. Rest assured we are not alone in this world."

"*Herr* Schuschnigg, do not think for one moment that any country on earth will thwart my decisions. Italy? I see eye-to-eye with Mussolini. And if you are counting on England, they will not move one finger for Austria."

*

During the two hours they "talked," Hitler remained with hands folded on his lap, both feet planted on the floor, his blue eyes locked on Schuschnigg. Schuschnigg, on the other hand, continued to fidget. More than once, his eyes darted to the terrace outside. Schuschnigg was a smoker. Knowing Hitler disdained smokers, Schuschnigg suffered in silence. Hitler, knowing Schuschnigg needed a smoke, played on his discomfort.

Finally, Schuschnigg asked, "What exactly are your wishes?"

"That, *Herr* Schuschnigg, we can discuss this afternoon." Hitler rose abruptly. "Now it is time for lunch."

As the two leaders walked to the dining room, one thing was clear: the Austrian chancellor was outmatched. And Hitler had not yet made his demands.

*

The Austrians, the *Führer*, Ribbentrop, the German generals, and I met around a large table filled with German cheeses, *Käsespätzle*, a variety of wursts, *Kartoffelpuffer*, *Rouladen*, *Schnitzel*, *Sauerbraten*, assorted berries, yogurt, and beer. The *Führer's* favorite, *Apfelstrudel*, would be served for dessert, but only after Hitler served a meal-long discourse on his own greatness.

"The German people love me. For instance, I will build skyscrapers greater than any in America." Hitler's narcissism reached new heights. "I have accomplished everything I set out to do . . . which makes me the greatest German that ever lived."

Hitler continued to hammer on in that same vein.

Schuschnigg was not accorded the courtesy to address the attendees.

Instead, with unprecedented rudeness to the leader of a sovereign nation, he was forced to sit and listen without comment. The moment coffee and tea were served along with the *Apfelstrudel*, Hitler stood and abruptly left the room without a word.

As soon as Hitler left, Papen announced, "*Herr* Chancellor. The *Führer* wants you to understand that Austria will no longer remain a sovereign state. Its foreign policy, mutual to German-Austrian interest, will be turned over to the *Führer*. In addition, you must immediately lift the ban on the Nazi Party in Austria and release all Nazi agitators held in Austrian jails. Arthur Seyss-Inquart, the lawyer who represents the Austrian Nationalist Socialists, must be appointed minister of the interior in charge of all police. In that capacity, he will implement these new protocols."

Schuschnigg turned white. His hand started to shake.

"Franz," I said, "perhaps Chancellor Schuschnigg would like a breath of fresh air?"

Before Papen answered, Schuschnigg plucked a cigarette from his gold case and sprang from his chair.

"Thank you for this kindness, *Herr* Richard," he said over his shoulder as he struck a match.

When he returned, Schuschnigg's cheeks were ruddy from the cold. Ribbentrop announced, "Now that you are back, *Herr* Schuschnigg, we propose that the German and Austrian economies be merged with one currency and a combined customs union."

One could not help but marvel at the way Hitler orchestrated each minute of this meeting. He calculated how long it would take Papen and Ribbentrop to make these demands, the time needed to negotiate the points, and the ideal moment to reappear to seal the deal. By the time Papen and Ribbentrop finished, the thirty-eight-year-old Schuschnigg was horror-stricken. Austria's independence was about to be crushed.

*

Still shaken from Papen's and Ribbentrop's demands, the Austrian chancellor was guided to Hitler's study where the *Führer* waited behind his desk. Hitler thrust a sheaf of papers toward the young chancellor.

"Here is the document, *Herr* Schuschnigg. Not one word can be changed."

Schuschnigg scanned it. "*Herr Reichskanzler*, this document has no value. It calls for Seyss-Inquart to be appointed to the cabinet. Only the president of Austria—President Miklas—has the constitutional right to appoint someone to the cabinet. Likewise, he is the only one who can grant amnesty for your compatriots in jail. My signature would only signify my willingness to recommend these protocols to the president."

"Then what good is your signature?" Hitler shouted. "You must guarantee that this document will be approved by your president."

"What you demand is impossible!" cried Schuschnigg.

Without another word, Hitler stomped toward the adjoining room and flung open the door.

"General Keitel!" Hitler shouted, though there was no need to shout.

Next, we heard the cadence of military steps that presumably belonged to Wilhelm Keitel, the newly installed head of Germany's armed forces, the OKW. We heard him give the Hitler salute at which point Hitler closed the door behind himself, leaving Schuschnigg to wonder what was being said.

Schuschnigg and I strained to hear what Hitler said to Keitel. Though we heard nothing more than incoherent mumbling, the implication was clear: if Schuschnigg did not come around—and soon—the German military would march into Austria.

At that moment, Papen appeared in the study through a different door. "*Herr* Schuschnigg, don't be obstinate. You can't win. Think of your countrymen. You don't want war with us."

Message delivered. Papen left.

Hitler returned.

"For the first time in my life, *Herr* Schuschnigg, I have changed my mind. You will have until February 15—three days from now—to have President Miklas sign this document."

Schuschnigg cowered. "Given the day's events, are you going to arrest us?"

"If I had wanted to arrest you, we would not have wasted the day with meaningless talk. You may not believe me, but I want to spare Austria the bloodshed that will come at the hands of my *Wehrmacht* if you do not cooperate. Three days, *Herr* Schuschnigg. Three days."

Schuschnigg bowed his head. "There is much I have to do."

"It has been a long day, *Herr* Schuschnigg." A chameleon when he wanted, Hitler donned the face of a perfect host. "The hour is late. You and your people are welcome to stay until morning."

"Thank you for your hospitality," Schuschnigg managed to say, "but I need to return to Austria as soon as possible."

"Of course. Papen will escort you. But first . . . sign the document."

*

The Austrians left at 11 p.m. after signing what became known as the "Berchtesgaden Protocols." When Papen returned from accompanying Schuschnigg and his delegation to Salzburg, he took me aside. "If I had not spoken in the car, not a word would have been uttered during the entire trip."

"I can only imagine how defeated and demoralized Schuschnigg felt. What *did* you say to him?" I asked.

"The only thing I could say: the truth," answered Papen.

"Whose truth?"

Papen looked around making certain no one was in range. "I said that now you have some idea, *Herr Bundeskanzler*, how difficult it is to deal with such an unstable person."

More than unstable, Franz. A psychopathic narcissist . . . and getting worse!

*

February 13, 1938

Carla went on to Munich to visit her brother. I returned to Berlin to resume investigating Fritsch's defense only to be ordered to meet with General Keitel in his apartment. I was surprised to find Admiral Canaris there.

"We have orders to put pressure on the Austrian government today through Tuesday, the fifteenth," Keitel said. "The *Führer* asked that once we craft our plan, Friedrich is to report back to him for final approval."

I glanced at Canaris who kept a steady bead on Keitel.

"Here is what I am thinking," Keitel continued. "Once we get the *Führer's* approval, we fly warplanes over every part of Austria. Planes invading their air space sends a stern message that we mean business. We announce troop maneuvers near the Austrian border. Tanks and heavy artillery will clog the roads headed toward Austria. All furloughs will be cancelled until further notice. The military attaché will be recalled from Vienna to make it appear that we are preparing for war. And keep in mind, while Papen was at the meeting with Schuschnigg, he is no longer the ambassador to Austria. Leaving that office vacant even for a few days sends its own message. The sum total of these actions will force the Austrians to sign the Berchtesgaden Protocols."

Spymaster Canaris replied, "My agents will spread rumors that reinforce a military buildup and troop movement. In addition, we will increase radio chatter between Berlin and Munich about an invasion. We know the Austrians intercept these radio transmissions. These will be forty-eight hours the Austrians will never forget."

"Wilhelm," said Keitel, shifting in his seat, "the *Führer* wants you to stir the pot in the Sudetenland, too."

Czechoslovakia, so soon?

"We haven't gone into Austria," Canaris said, his voice almost a snarl. "How can the *Führer* think about Czechoslovakia? That is too much at one time."

Keitel shook his head. "Those are the orders. Three and a half million Germans are forced to live in a mongrel-of-a-country, cobbled together with slices taken from Poland and Hungary as well as from us. For the time being, only make noise where the Sudeten Germans live."

"Does *Herr* Hitler want war?" Canaris snapped back, "Because if he does, he will find it in Czechoslovakia."

"Maybe you're forgetting the *Führer* heads the military. Blomberg and Fritsch are gone. With Brauchitsch and me, the *Führer* gets what he wants. Do I have to spell it out any clearer?"

Canaris bit his lip and shot a furtive look my way. I was about to say something when he said, "I will find a way to make the *Führer* happy. But Austria takes precedence." Then he added, "Especially if we intend to avoid bloodshed."

"No one wants blood spilled, Admiral. The whole point of pretending to show force is to coerce Austria into handing over the keys to the country without loss of life."

"Let's make certain it plays out that way," said Canaris.

Keitel slapped his knee. "Now that we have it settled, Friedrich, explain our plans to the *Führer*. Get us the green light. There's not a moment to waste to ensure the Austrians sign the Protocols by Wednesday."

I returned minutes later with a thumbs up. "The *Führer* approves. He said for us to give the plan a name."

There was a pregnant pause before Canaris said, "Operation Otto. After the crown prince of Austria-Hungary."

Chapter 29

It had become apparent that only the officer corps could stop Hitler. It was our hope that when they learned the details of how Fritsch had been railroaded by the *SS* at the trial, they would unite to overthrow Hitler. This would only happen if we could document the injustice to Fritsch, and that depended on finding the retired cavalry officer . . . unless we relied on Weingärtner alone, and that seemed unwise.

Time was running out.

I studied the list that Canaris's people assembled. There were twelve men who had to retire after being injured in the cavalry. I was prepared to track each down . . . when one address jumped out. It was in Lichterfelde—the community Joseph had mentioned. If this was the captain Joseph met, my search would be over before it hardly began.

Lichterfelde was in southwest Berlin, the closest part of the city to Wannsee.

"Is the captain home?" I asked when a maid opened the door at *Ferdinandstraße*, 20.

"That's strange," she replied. "Four weeks ago, two men came asking for him, too."

"Why is that strange? Doesn't the captain have visitors?"

"I expect he does."

"Don't you work every day?" I asked.

"I do . . . but the captain doesn't live here."

My heart sank. "Do you know where I can find him?"

She pointed to the next house. "He lives at number 21. The army has the wrong number for the captain's house. He has tried to correct it many times but nothing ever changed."

"You appear to be fond of the captain."

"He's a dear old man. He hasn't been well." She tapped her chest. "His heart. Those other men got him so excited. They almost did him in."

"You said there were two of them. Four weeks ago. Do you know who they were?" I asked.

"Gestapo."

That means Himmler, Heydrich, and Göring knew the truth weeks before they staged that scene between Colonel General Fritsch and Otto Schmidt in front of Hitler.

Then the maid added, "Please be gentle. He's a good man."

My pulse raced. "The last thing I want is for anything to happen to the captain." I stepped away and then turned back. "You've been an enormous help."

There was a brass knocker attached to a lion's head at number 21. I banged three times. A nurse, in a traditional light blue dress covered by a pinafore apron and wearing a mobcap, answered.

When she saw my black uniform, she stiffened. "The captain is still shaking from the last time you people were here. He cannot have visitors."

"I am not 'those' people," I said.

"Please go. Come back when the captain feels better."

"I can't. I must see him now."

The nurse narrowed the door opening. "My captain's life depends on him *not* getting excited. Your cohorts rattled him to his core last time. He still hasn't recovered."

I looked about. "You don't need neighbors seeing me standing at your door. May I at least come in and tell you why I need to see him?"

"After what happened four weeks ago, who they see here really doesn't matter."

She moved to close the door; I pushed my way in. "I mean no harm."

Inside, I explained that this was about a case of mistaken identity. Only the captain could help clarify the mix-up and save the career of a very important military leader. I ended by saying, "I will be brief."

Arms folded, she frowned.

"Maybe this will convince you." I showed her both my *Ausweis* and the card with my name and information. The other SS men would not have identified themselves to her.

"If my intentions were anything but honorable, I would not have identified myself."

She knew she had no choice, but there was still fight in her eyes. The nurse wagged her finger. "I warn you. Do not get him excited. He won't survive another visit like the last one." Then added, "You have to wait here. It will take a bit of time. The captain is too proud to use a wheelchair."

The *Rittmeister* hobbled into the dark, musty salon. Long retired, he wore a dark suit that was a world too large for him. A colorful ascot attempted to hide his shriveled, stringy neck that hung out of his starched white shirt; he wore a monocle in his left eye. Cane in hand, he shuffled one foot in front of the other, his leather shoes scraping the floor with each step. He was round-shouldered and so bent over that I feared he would snap like a dry twig as the nurse helped ease him into a chair.

But the man had fire left in him. He didn't wait for a question. "I told your people when they came before, *Obergruppenführer* Richard, that I don't apologize for anything. They were uncivilized." His eyes met mine. "And, I might add, quite disrespectful."

"Who was here, *Rittmeister*?"

"Two Gestapo agents. Are you going to take me away, too?"

"I don't know anything about those men. I'm sorry if they caused you trouble. I'm here because Otto Schmidt accused General Werner von Fritsch, who was the army chief-of-staff, of meeting Bavarian Joe for a . . . a rendezvous . . . four years ago at the Wannsee station. Could that meeting have been with you?"

"It was me," he said in a clear voice. Then the Captain's weathered face wrinkled in disgust. "The very image of that man, Schmidt, makes me sick to my stomach."

"Did he ask for money?"

Rather than answer, the captain called his nurse. "I'll be back," he reassured me. The routine was reversed. She helped him out of the chair; I watched him shuffle away. In time he returned with a bundle of wrapped papers.

"These receipts show how much I paid Schmidt. He extorted twenty-five hundred Reichsmark from me. The bank statements confirm withdrawals in the same amounts. My only satisfaction was that the bank was closed at that hour, and he was irritated that he had to return the following day." He pointed with a quaking finger. "You can see Schmidt's signature at the bottom of the receipt. I thought I was done with him. Then, a few weeks later, he returned. Asked for more. I gave it to him. I had my good name to protect."

"And then?"

"He kept coming. Finally, I said 'Enough. This is the last of it. The next time I go to the police.'"

"And . . . was there a next time?"

His thin, blue lips arched in a crescent that revealed yellowed, overlapping teeth. "That was the last I saw of Schmidt or heard his name until the Gestapo showed up a month ago. Asked similar questions. They took me to the basement at 8 *Prinz-Albrecht-Straße*. Interrogated me like I was a common criminal. The nerve of them."

"But they didn't arrest you?" Then I muttered, "How unusual."

He shook his head. "They did warn me not to talk to anyone about this."

"Then why are you talking to me, now?"

"Damn the Gestapo if I can help the man Otto Schmidt falsely accused. Especially if he is a fellow officer."

"I wish there were more like you," I said. "Thank you."

"What did you say that soldier's name was again?" the captain asked.

"Fritsch. Colonel General Werner von Fritsch. Commander-in-chief of the army."

"My first name is Achim. His is Werner. How can we be confused?" the captain asked with a spark of playfulness in his eye.

I smiled back. "It is hard to imagine."

I stood to leave. "I appreciate your openness. You have been most generous with your time, *Rittmeister* Frisch."

"Ah," said Achim von Frisch, his brows raised, "perhaps it was the similarity of our last names that led to the confusion."

I grinned from ear-to-ear. "Now why didn't I think of that?"

Carla had not yet returned from Munich when I settled in with a glass of scotch to review the receipts *Rittmeister* Frisch gave me. They confirmed Otto Schmidt blackmailed *him* . . . not Werner von Fritsch. I was about to call General Fritsch's lawyer—Rüdiger von der Goltz—when I heard a metallic click at the front door. I put the receiver down.

A draft of frigid air whooshed into the room. I heard the rustle of a coat and the clatter of shoes tossed to the floor.

"How did you find your brother?" I called out.

Carla's face was drawn with dark rings under her eyes. She pointed to my glass. "I need one of those. It has been a very long day."

"Bad flight?" I poured her a drink.

"Nothing like that." She plopped on the couch and sighed. "It's my brother. When I got there, Ludwig didn't look right. There was pain in his eyes. There was a new attendant. I asked if anything was wrong with him. She shrugged and turned away. But I know my brother."

"What was the problem?"

"I didn't see it at first. I lifted his shirt. Pressed different areas. Nothing was red or swollen or appeared to bother him, but I smelled something foul. When I raised his trousers, his right leg was infected. Yellow pus oozed from it. Ludwig rarely runs a fever. His forehead was slightly warm. For him, that was serious. If you hadn't suggested I stop on the way back from the Berghof, who knows what would have happened?"

She tipped her glass to me.

"How did they treat the infection?"

"Cleaned the wound and gave him a new drug: Prontosil. By the time I left, his fever was down and as best I could tell, he was not in pain. I'll check his progress every day and return next week to see for myself." She sipped her drink. "Friedrich. How could they let this happen?"

"The *Führer* put Germany on war footing. Resources have been reallocated for the military buildup. It is sad . . . but the neglect that happened to your brother may become commonplace."

"People like my brother deserve to be treated humanely. The old Germany, the Germany before the new Reich, knew how to take care of its citizens. *All* of its citizens."

"This new Germany has different values."

Carla's eyes watered. "How can you stand it? Friedrich? Are you trying to convince yourself that staying is a good idea . . . because you don't have the strength to leave?"

I took her hand. "I hate everything about them. More than you can imagine. I stay for one reason: to change things. You need to trust that I am working on it."

"I do trust you, Friedrich." She wiped away tears. "Promise me that the weak will not be left behind. Promise your new Germany will take care of my brother."

"I will protect Ludwig at any cost."

Chapter 30

Carla and I talked all night and late into the early morning. When I awoke, I planned to meet with Rüdiger von der Goltz, Fritsch's lawyer, and brief him on *Rittmeister* Frisch and the physical evidence that proved it was the cavalry captain and not Werner von Fritsch who met Bavarian Joe. Moreover, Goltz would learn of the Gestapo's interview of the old captain weeks before the scene in the Chancellery, and the fact that Himmler and Heydrich knew the charges against the Colonel General were false when they staged the Schmidt-Fritsch confrontation before Hitler.

With this body of evidence, Goltz would build a case that would crush Heydrich, Himmler, and Göring in court and, in the process, bring the army's boots down on Hitler.

First, I needed to speak with Bernhard Weiss. Weiss had promised to tap into his connections on what the Berlin Police had on the "Fritsch Affair."

*

"My sources tell me that Josef Meisinger constructed the original report on Fritsch four years ago. He heads the Reich's Central Office for the Repression of Homosexuality. In fact, *Herr* Meisinger met with Otto Schmidt to prep him for the military tribunal."

"Will they call Schmidt at the trial?" I asked.

"Without him, there is no evidence. You should know that they threatened to kill Schmidt if he did not cooperate at the trial. They spent hours browbeating the so-called 'facts' of the case into him. Schmidt is cunning, but not the brightest. Meisinger will review everything one more time with him before the trial. Schmidt will perform like a trained parrot."

"Why does that not surprise me?" I said.

Weiss coughed before saying. "One of my men gained access to Schmidt's list of clients in the police files. Two names jumped out: Walter Funk, Reich minister of economics and Gottfried von Cramm, this year's Wimbledon runner-up. Cramm has won the French Open twice."

"Funk proves Hitler is two-faced. Funk remains in the cabinet without concern about his homosexuality. For that matter, Hitler never cared about Röhm's predilections, either. That putsch business was about getting the army off his back because the Brown Shirts were getting too powerful, not that their leaders were gay. But Cramm? He is venerated in Germany as one of our greatest tennis players in history. They wouldn't dare touch him."

"He's on tour now. The minute he returns to Germany, I suspect they will grab him. People are hardened to the pink roundup."

"And risk the bad publicity?"

"Arresting Cramm will add to Schmidt's credibility when he testifies against the colonel general. It will prove that another big-fish client of Schmidt's has been brought to justice."

"Speaking of which, I am on my way to bring everything I discovered about the *Rittmeister* to Fritsch's lawyer: Rüdiger von der Goltz. Do you know Goltz?"

"Like Colvin, father and son have the same name. I knew Goltz's father." Then Bernhard added, "It would be good to update Ian Colvin. He went out of his way to meet you at the Chancellery steps. As we discussed before, Colvin is well-connected. The day will come when he proves invaluable."

*

I found Fritsch's lawyer in his office.

"Wilhelm Canaris said to expect you." Goltz rested his hand on the stack of papers in front of him. "Will this take long?"

"If this is an inconvenient time," I began, "I could come back."

"Forgive me for not sounding enthused. This mound of paperwork aside, I'm asked to defend what appears to be an impossible case."

"But Fritsch is innocent."

"What does that have to do with anything these days? They have an eyewitness, and the president of the tribunal wants my client's head. And I . . . I am supposed to win the case by saying, 'But gentlemen, he's innocent. He didn't do it.'"

"You'll feel differently in a few minutes. I promise."

Seated in front of his broad mahogany desk, I told Goltz about Joseph Weingärtner and *Rittmeister* Frisch.

When I finished, Goltz beamed with confidence. "With these two witnesses, the receipts signed by Schmidt, and the bank records, I can't lose!"

*

Ian Colvin was next. We agreed to meet for coffee in an out-of-the-way café.

"Nice to see you, old chap. Have a seat," Colvin said. "What brings us together?"

"A mutual friend."

"Canaris called to say you checked me out."

"I called our friend in London after you gave me the code. He said I can trust you."

"I was wondering how long that would take."

Colvin took a Capstan cigarette from a pack lying on the table. The ashtray was already half-filled. "Mind?" He flicked open a silver-plated lighter.

As he extinguished the flame, I asked, "Are you planning to cover the Fritsch trial?"

"Not unless you tell me otherwise. It's a kangaroo court. The poor bloke doesn't stand a chance."

"What if I told you that he is being railroaded?"

"No shock there."

"And what if I told you that the Gestapo knew all along that Fritsch wasn't a homosexual and that the man involved was Captain Achim von Frisch. F-R-I-S-C-H. No 'T.' Cavalry. Much older. Wears a monocle. Uses a cane. Not our Fritsch at all."

"And this will come out at the trial?" asked Colvin.

"Among other things."

"What other things?"

"That depends on you," I said.

Colvin poked at the center of a smoke ring. "Why me?"

"Do you know Rüdiger von der Goltz? He is representing Fritsch."

"Must be the son. The father is too old to try this case."

"You're right." I edged closer, but not before checking that no one paid us any mind. "Under the right circumstances, this trial could turn on its head to reveal Reinhard Heydrich and Heinrich Himmler for what they are. If played right, the Gestapo's evil ways would end up on trial."

I liked Colvin because he didn't come back with rapid-fire questions and a journalist's need for quick answers. He digested all this implied.

After his cigarette burned down, he said, "Turning the trial on its heels to implicate the Gestapo is a tall order. If Goltz manages it, then what?"

"Canaris and I have a plan. There are others with us. That's all I can tell you now." I sat back. "Ian, cover the trial."

Colvin ground out the stub. "Journalists are banned from the trial."

"I will make certain you are allowed into Fritsch's trial as an aid to the defense. That guarantees you the exclusive story."

"I can't ask for more than that," said Colvin.

"You could. But for now, that's all you are getting."

Chapter 31

Keitel and Canaris had forty-eight hours to create the illusion of an imminent invasion of Austria. Simulated troop movements and convoys of military vehicles clogged the roads to Austria. German planes pierced Austrian airspace. Troop furloughs were canceled. False radio reports were broadcast.

"Does Schuschnigg believe we will attack?" I asked the day of the deadline.

Canaris had found time to meet with me for a few minutes in his office. Before answering, Canaris cycled through the ritual I had come to expect: fill a pipe bowl with tobacco, tamp it down, and puff until the embers glowed a proper yellow-orange.

With a curl of gray smoke spiraling upward, he answered, "Schuschnigg is no fool. He sees through our bluster. He *does* believe we will march into Austria, but not in the immediate future. Until that happens, he intends to change Hitler's terms to retain some modicum of power." Canaris concluded. "Unsigned, the Protocols have already caused unintended consequences."

"A run on the banks?" I asked.

He nodded. "That was expected. What no one anticipated was a run on Nazi uniforms. Not a shred of brown material can be found in all of Austria. We had to procure bolts of brown cloth from Egypt."

"Heaven forbid Nazi-wannabes didn't have their uniforms," I said.

"Brown cloth is one thing," said Canaris, "but music! That is an entirely different matter. I don't have to ask. I know you appreciate Arturo Toscanini's brilliance."

"I saw his last performance at the Bayreuth Festival in '31. When Hitler took over in '33, The Maestro refused to return. That's when he moved his performances to Austria."

At that moment, I realized the obvious.

"Salzburg."

Canaris nodded. "Toscanini has already canceled his appearance at the festival there this coming summer. He was to conduct five Wagnerian operas."

"Hitler mentioned more than once how he looked forward to attending them."

"Oh, but Toscanini didn't stop there." Canaris pointed to a headline in the *New York Times* on his desk:

MAESTRO REFUSES TO PLAY IN AUSTRIA.

"Let me read you what Toscanini said:

'I think of those poor young men who are going off fooled or forced to get themselves killed, not for their country, but for delinquents named Mussolini, Hitler, and Stalin.'

Canaris glanced up to gauge my response before he continued to read. "Toscanini also announced he will perform in Tel Aviv this April, in spite of being warned that his presence there might incite an Arab attack."

When Canaris laid the paper down, I said, "Toscanini is making a powerful statement, Wilhelm. He will only perform where people are free."

"I knew this would affect you," said Canaris.

"In so many ways, Wilhelm. The maestro's lesson is clear: to stop Hitler, we must find our own Toscaninis in the officer corps."

*

As February wound down and we focused on invading Austria, Schuschnigg made speech after speech, reminding his people of their rich history. The more Schuschnigg spoke, the more his popularity rose.

Berlin grew concerned.

*

My own concern was not with the events unfolding in Austria, but being certain that Fritsch's defense was rock-solid. The witnesses—Weingärtner and Frisch—would make a liar out of Otto Schmidt. Captain Frisch would testify that the Gestapo interviewed him, *and* that Göring *et al.* knew the truth before they put on their big show in front of Hitler at the Chancellery. The trial would not only reveal the Nazi plot to remove military leaders opposed to Germany's plans for aggression but would also be the catalyst for the officer corps to revolt.

*

Carla visited her brother in Munich which afforded me the luxury of an evening by the fire, a generous helping of scotch, and cracking the cover of Scottish author A. J. Cronin's latest novel, the worldwide bestseller, *The Citadel*.

I was jarred awake. For a moment, I didn't know where I was. Book on the floor. Fire reduced to embers. Only then did I recognize the piercing ring of the phone.

"Friedrich, it's been a total nightmare. My poor brother. I don't know how he will survive."

"Carla, slow down. I am not fully awake. Start from the beginning."

"It's awful. Ludwig was being transported to the hospital as I arrived. The infection spread to his bones. Osteomyelitis. They needed to operate at once or he would have died. Friedrich, they amputated his leg." She sobbed. "It was awful. I wish you were here."

"It was obviously a matter of life or death. They did the right thing. What I don't understand is that he was getting better."

"He was. Until they ran out of the medicine. How could this happen?"

"I will find out who's responsible. More importantly, how is Ludwig now?"

"Still groggy from the anesthesia. They're giving him morphine. I need to be here."

"Of course you do. Do you want me to fly down? I could be there tomorrow."

"As of now, everything is under control. If I need you, I promise to call."

*

March 5, 1938

I arrived at my office anxious to inquire about the medicine shortage at Schönbrunn Psychiatric Hospital when I found Reinhard Heydrich sitting in my chair.

"Aren't you the early bird," I said.

He held the picture Carla sharpened and framed for me, which I kept on my desk, in his hand. Heydrich pointed to the boy in the photograph. "Is that you?"

I shook my head. "A dying soldier gave it to me. Asked me to find his family and tell them he loved them."

"Then what is it doing here?"

"I never found them. I keep it on my desk as a reminder."

"Of what?"

"Of him. Of the war. Of loved ones lost."

Despite my answer, Heydrich studied my features in an attempt to match them to the boy's.

I rounded the desk toward my chair. "I am sure you have more important things to do than ask about people you don't know. What brings you here?"

He replaced the photo as he stood. "You're right. As the *Führer's* liaison to the Wehrmacht, what have you been hearing?"

"Could you be more specific?" I scooted to the edge of the seat, revolted by the residual warmth from Heydrich's body heat.

"While the officer corps gave no support to Blomberg, we are hearing noise about Fritsch being framed on false charges," Heydrich said.

"Should that surprise you? Schmidt is a pig."

"That doesn't mean the charges are false," answered Heydrich. "As it turns out, we have found a way to corroborate Schmidt."

"It's hard to prove something that doesn't exist."

"Does the name Manasse Herbst mean anything to you?"

I nodded. "I know the name from when I worked at the UFA studio. He was in a long-running operetta before we came to power."

"Apparently he gave more noteworthy private performances. Today, we arrested Gottfried von Cramm at his parents' estate. Herbst is his Jew-lover."

I shuffled through reports on my desk without looking at Heydrich, "Other than the fact that Cramm is the greatest tennis player Germany ever produced, why does this interest me?"

"Isn't it obvious?" he said.

I looked up and glared. "Nothing is obvious when you talk in riddles."

"Let me elucidate," smirked Heydrich. "Cramm was on Otto Schmidt's list of clients. That 'pig,' as you call Schmidt, procured rent-boys for Germany's greatest tennis player. This will validate Schmidt's testimony regarding Werner von Fritsch. He was on that same list."

Leave it to Bernhard to get the inside scoop.

I was not concerned in the least. This "corroboration" would not save Schmidt after Weingärtner and the old cavalry officer testified.

"Then you won't have a problem proving this at the trial, will you?" I said.

Heydrich gloated. "It will be like taking candy from a baby."

That's what you think!

*

Later that day, Hitler granted me a few minutes.

"Something disturbing has happened, *mein Führer*." He motioned for me to explain. "Carla's brother lives in the Schönbrunn Psychiatric Hospital. He had a leg infection that was on the mend until they ran out of medicine. Without the medicine, the infection worsened with a vengeance. They had to remove his leg. My concern, *mein Führer*: How could a hospital run out of a critical medicine?"

Hitler looked up from reading a report.

"All medicines used in asylums have been diverted to the *Bundeswehr* hospital centers for military use because of what may happen in Austria. There is no need to waste them on marginal human beings who are unworthy to live and nothing but a burden to the state."

"What if these medicines are a matter of life or death?"

"What better life to save than a soldier's?" answered Hitler. Then he said, "Do you remember when you returned to Pasewalk Hospital to, ah, deal with our medical records?"

"Why?"

"Do you remember Dr. Ferdinand Sauerbruch?"

"Sauerbruch was in the operating room when they put me back together at Charité Hospital. He recognized me when I returned to Pasewalk to take care of 'matters.'"

"Lucky for Carla's brother, he remembered *Obergruppenführer* Richard. Thank Sauerbruch for saving Ludwig's life."

"I don't understand."

"Sauerbruch is now at the *Reichsforschungsrat*. One of the many things he does at the Research Council is to oversee medical care in asylums. Once we stopped sending them medicines, all extraordinary treatments ceased for the useless eaters. Knowing Ludwig was compromised, an aide took it upon herself to reach out to Dr. Sauerbruch. She mentioned your name. Something about meeting you for a Christmas dinner."

Inge, you are a saint!

Hitler continued. "Sauerbruch recognized your name. When he called my office to ask what he should do, I ordered him to save Ludwig's life."

"Thank you, Wolf. Carla will be forever grateful."

I shuddered at how pleased this made him. A man of contradictions, Hitler was all the more dangerous for his calculated brutality sprinkled with acts of extreme loyalty. But I wasn't taken in by an act of kindness. Guilt had no role in stopping his march to war.

Chapter 32

March 8, 1938

Hitler did not seem to mind that Schuschnigg dragged his feet implementing the Berchtesgaden Protocols as long as there was some progress forward. The *Führer's* tolerance was short-lived when it was learned that Schuschnigg scheduled a plebiscite for Sunday, March 13. The referendum asked a simple yes-or-no question: Do Austrians want Austria to remain free and independent? Schuschnigg's intent was to have the Austrian people vote before Hitler could act . . . and thereby forestall an invasion.

Hitler called an emergency meeting.

"That petty pedestrian Austrian thinks he can outwit me," Hitler said once Göring, Himmler, Goebbels, and I were assembled.

"An overwhelming 'Yes' vote would make it impossible to justify invading Austria. World opinion would be against us," I said.

"I thought you were on our side," growled Göring.

"I am just stating the obvious," I explained.

"Obvious or not," said Göring, "if Schuschnigg thinks this will deter us from our mission, he is sadly mistaken."

"The man is desperate," Himmler said. "According to Seyss-Inquart, when Schuschnigg announced the plebiscite, he wore a Tyrolean *Tracht* hoping to unite his people against us. He ended his speech with the Tyrolean battle cry: *Mander, es isch Zeit!*"

I couldn't help but think that shouting, "Men, the time has come!" was not very stirring. "He lost his people's support long ago," Göring said. "Wearing *Lederhosen* will not make for a successful plebiscite. They haven't had an election in eight years. There is no registry of voters. There is little to worry about."

"On the contrary," Goebbels cautioned. "This gives Schuschnigg the perfect opportunity to railroad the vote and gain the victory he seeks. It's nothing we haven't done in the past. The issue is not to let *him* do it."

Hitler held up his hand. "There will be no plebiscite." He turned to Himmler and Göring. "Are the men ready?"

I didn't understand.

Himmler answered. "We are." Then he explained. "Heydrich and I have trained twenty thousand men in secret for this moment."

"When did you start preparing to invade Austria?" I asked.

"January," answered Göring.

Before Blomberg and Fritsch were dismissed?
Before Hitler took command of the Wehrmacht?
Twenty thousand SS men?
Herr Himmler got his wish!

A demonic smile crept across Hitler's face.

"Schuschnigg made the mistake of a lifetime when he announced a plebiscite. Bring Keitel and the other military leaders here tomorrow. We invade Austria in two days."

*

As our meeting broke up, Hitler turned to Göring. "Hermann, postpone Fritsch's trial. The moment I leave Germany to enter Austria, you become acting *Führer*. Colonel-General Brauchitsch must join me in Austria. There will be no senior officers left to sit as judges for the tribunal."

"*Mein Führer*, there are reports that we will not meet resistance. Is military intervention even necessary?" Göring asked.

"Hermann, regardless of how we are received, we cannot chance that the plebiscite will go against us. Better to attack now than risk being sorry later." Then he added, "One way or another, we will take control of Austria."

PART IV

PART IV

Chapter 33

March 9, 1938

By the following afternoon, *SS* men, police units, and reconnaissance squadrons attached to the Eighth Army, numbering more than one hundred thousand men, were poised at the Austrian border. *Luftwaffe* transport aircraft were readied to ferry additional troops. Bombers were placed on high alert while Goebbels printed thirteen million pamphlets to be dropped over Austria.

Hitler instructed Arthur Seyss-Inquart, his hand-picked member of the Austrian cabinet, to demand that Schuschnigg cancel the plebiscite or face a full-scale invasion.

"It is our right to hold a plebiscite in the way we set forth," Schuschnigg answered.

When Schuschnigg's response reached Hitler, the die was cast. A determined *Führer* issued his final order to Seyss-Inquart: "Close the customs offices between Austria and Germany. Stop all rail and highway travel. Issue an order to postpone the plebiscite by noon, Friday, or Austria will suffer the consequences."

*

Friday, March 11, 1938

One indispensable step remained before there could be an invasion: Hitler had to be certain that Italy would not mass its troops at the border—as it had in 1934—to protect Austria from the German attack.

"Friedrich, this is as far as we can go without Mussolini's approval. Please help me draft a letter to Il Duce," Hitler said.

"Perhaps list the benefits to Italy from Germany forming a union with Austria. They are logical and undeniable."

Hitler shook his head. "No. I will tell him that Austria and Czechoslovakia developed a relationship that poses a serious threat to the Reich."

"He didn't buy that four years ago when he positioned his troops on the Austro-Italian border after Chancellor Dollfuss was assassinated. We had all to do to get Mussolini to back down."

"I have worked hard to make certain that does not happen this time," Hitler said. "I was the only European leader to support his invasion of Ethiopia. Remember? We sent arms and munitions to him. Last fall, we entertained Mussolini in grand style. You were there. You saw his response when we showed him our weapon factories. Friedrich, I have been wooing Mussolini for three years! Still . . ." his gaze drifted, ". . . if Il Duce says, 'No,' we cannot invade."

*

The letter was completed a little after noon. Hitler appointed Prince Philipp of Hesse, a close friend of Hermann Göring and a Party member since 1930, to fly to Rome to hand-deliver the letter to Il Duce. The prince frequently acted as a liaison between Hitler and Mussolini. It helped that Prince Philipp was highly regarded in Italy . . . along with the added prestige from his marriage to Princess Mafalda, daughter of the king of Italy.

*

While Hitler waited for Mussolini's response, he turned his attention toward the looming plebiscite. Would Schuschnigg cancel?

At 2:45 p.m., Friday afternoon, Hitler's phone rang. Göring answered. He mouthed, "It's Seyss-Inquart."

"Is there any news?" Göring asked Seyss-Inquart louder than necessary.

We were riveted to Göring's every move. He nodded, muttered words, grinned, and then, when we were convinced that

Schuschnigg would not capitulate, Göring stuck his thumb up as he returned the telephone to its cradle. "Schuschnigg canceled the plebiscite."

A cheer erupted and then evaporated as quickly when Hitler said, "I have had enough. We must bring it to a head. Call Seyss-Inquart back. Tell him that he and Schuschnigg must resign from the cabinet. Once they do, President Miklas must appoint Seyss-Inquart as the new chancellor. As chancellor, Seyss-Inquart will declare an emergency and request German troops to restore order for the new Austrian government."

Chapter 34

It had been a long, draining day. At 10:30 p.m., Prince Philipp called from Rome. An anxious, pale Hitler listened without comment. As the seconds ticked by, the tension etched in Hitler's face melted away. Color returned to his cheeks. The corners of his mouth turned upward. His eyes filled with joy. His palpable excitement gave way to what could only be described as ecstasy.

On its face value, the call gave Hitler the permission he wanted to march into Austria without any hesitancy about what Mussolini might do. Nothing would stop the *Anschluss* now. But I believe the call will be so potentially important to the future that I include its verbatim transcription taken by a stenographer as the men spoke.

Prince Philipp: I have just come back from the Palazzo Venezia. The Duce accepted the whole thing in a very friendly manner.

Hitler: Then please tell Mussolini that I shall never forget him for this . . . *Never, never, never, never,* whatever happens . . . As soon as the Austrian affair has been settled, I shall be ready to go with him through thick and thin, no matter what.

Prince Philipp: Yes, my *Führer.*

Hitler: Listen. I shall make any agreement—I am no longer in fear of the terrible position which would have existed militarily in case we had gotten into a conflict. You may tell him that I do thank him ever so much I will *never, never* forget him. I will *never* forget him.

Prince Philipp: Yes, my *Führer.*

Hitler: I will *never* forget it, whatever may happen. If he should ever need any help or be in any danger, he

can be sure that I shall stick with him whatever happens, even if the whole world is against him.
Prince Philipp: Yes, my *Führer*.

Hitler replaced the receiver, stared at me in wonderment, and then did a little jig, shuffling his feet and pumping his arms. It was a moment . . . then he caught himself.

"Now we can proceed without any outside interference," said Hitler. "Aren't you going to say something, Friedrich? Isn't this wonderful?" I watched how, in a twinkling, Hitler transformed from a worried leader to a little boy who was just told he would get the new toy he dared covet for so long. I didn't know if I was in shock by his audacity and disregard for the implications of what he was about to undertake or repulsed by his glee. This was the man whose food I cut into small pieces, whom I led to the WC when he was blind and could not navigate the hospital halls. This was a man who still cried for his mother. And this was a man who was hell-bent on replacing God as head of his own religion based on terror and fear and dictatorial domination.

All I could manage was a weak smile.

Hitler did not wait for my answer. Instead, he picked up the phone. Still glowing, he issued the order that would make him master of his birthplace. "Keitel, send the troops across the border!"

*

Much later that evening I called Ian Colvin from a secure phone.

"Ian, sorry for the late call, but you need to know that the Fritsch proceedings have been adjourned."

"Austria, obviously. The fireworks have already begun."

"What have you heard?"

"A short while ago, William Shirer, the American journalist, called from the airport. We go back awhile. Shirer is the European broadcast chief for Edward R. Murrow and CBS. Once your boys stormed into Vienna, they shut down the radio station. Shirer had no way of reporting what was going on there. Murrow told him to get back to London. Jews escaping Austria took every available seat on the direct flight so Shirer had to fly through Berlin."

My right foot bobbed up and down, a nervous metronome marking the seconds until he came to the main point. "What did he see?"

"Shirer reported that the Austrians have taken to the streets, delirious with joy. He said they shouted, 'One people, One empire, One leader!'"

"*Sieg Heil! Heil Hitler! Ein Volk, ein Reich, ein Führer*," I blurted in German.

"That's it. Those are the words."

"What about the police?" I asked.

"What about them?"

"Did they try to stop the people from demonstrating against their own government?"

"It was the opposite. Shirer said that many police wore swastika armbands. Everything points to the Austrians giving their outright support to this *Anschluss*." Then he lowered his voice. "Shirer also reported that a pogrom has started against the Jews. It erupted the moment the Germans marched in. Bricks thrown through shop windows. Men, women, and children beaten on the streets. Graffiti against the Jews everywhere. I tell you, Friedrich, they are handing Hitler the country."

"You mean Schuschnigg is?"

"No. The Austrian people are. Schuschnigg wouldn't abandon his people. They arrested him. Can you believe it? His own people arrested him."

I was speechless.

Colvin asked, "Friedrich, are you still there?"

"Sorry. That is a lot to absorb."

"Give me a call when the trial is back on, ok?"

Chapter 35

Saturday, March 12, 1938

Hitler and I flew to Munich early that morning. I dashed to Schönbrunn Psychiatric Hospital to see how Carla was managing with Ludwig while Hitler visited Eva for a few minutes in the house she shared with Gretl, her younger sister. Hitler and I agreed to meet at his apartment at No 16 *Prinzregentenplatz* before leaving for Austria.

Hitler's excitement was palpable as he slipped into his military jacket. This entry into Austria would be his first time since he snuck across the border in 1931 to visit his niece–cum–lover's Austrian grave following her suicide in the same Munich apartment in which we now stood.

"Friedrich, we will soon be in Vienna. You do not seem very excited or pleased with the *Anschluss*." He adjusted the buttons on his tunic.

I was never much of an actor. Carla and Ludwig. Fritsch. The upcoming military tribunal. The conspiracy. Edging closer to war. I had much on my mind and no time to sit in a car and parade through Austria next to Adolf Hitler.

"Carla has her hands full with her brother. She needs me to be with her."

"This is our moment, Friedrich. Yours and mine. It is a milestone in the journey we began together nearly twenty years ago. You, as much as anyone, have made this glorious moment possible." When I didn't say anything, Hitler grabbed my arms and shook me. "More than any of them—Göring, Goebbels, Himmler, or Heydrich—*you* earned the right to be next to me when I enter my homeland. We *must* share this together."

He left me no alternative: I would ride into Austria with him.

Hitler marched in front of a mirror to check that his uniform was perfect. He strapped his patent-leather belt on, fixed the shoulder strap, and stepped away.

Then, as if talking to himself, he said, "I hope she listens."

"Who, *mein Führer*? Carla? If I can't be there, she will manage without me."

"I am talking about Eva. She wants to join with us, but I can't let that happen. I will be in the spotlight like never before. Thousands of cameras upon me. Riding in an open car. It is out of the question."

What about the danger? "Troops on the march. Tanks rolling over roads. Fighter planes crisscrossing the skies. She could not have been serious."

Hitler grimaced. "When have you known Eva to make a joke about something she wants to do? Danger aside, I cannot have her follow through on this silly idea."

*

It was 4 p.m. when Hitler and I crossed the narrow iron bridge pitched above the Inn River that connected Simbach, Germany to Braunau am Inn, Austria . . . Hitler's birthplace. Our heavily armored cavalcade lingered only long enough for Hitler to view the house in which he was born. Linz, the next town on the schedule, meant more to him. It was there that he grew up as a boy.

But the drive to Linz took twice as long as planned as wildly cheering crowds choked the road. Women were the most excited. They strained security's ability to hold them back.

We stopped at the outskirts of Linz after nightfall, where Hitler pointed to a small structure at *Michaelsbergstraße, 16*.

"I lived in that house, Friedrich. It's too dark to see now, but the view of the mountain from the back window is forever imprinted in my brain. I would stare at it for hours, dreaming of making my way in the world. You've heard me say my father was a tyrant. My mother, on the other hand, was a saint. She showered me with all the love a mother could." Then, as quickly as it appeared, his reverie vanished. "Enough of the past."

Any lingering question of the Austrian people's reaction to Hitler and the German invasion was dispelled the moment we turned down Linz's main thoroughfare. Although it was after 8 p.m., tens of thousands lined the streets. Church bells pealed. The *Führer* saluted the throngs wearing his widest grin. Having surrendered his citizenship to avoid deportation to Austria after the failed Beer Hall Putsch and banned from returning to Austria since 1924, this was Hitler's moment of triumph.

Although exhausted from the day's stresses, Hitler did not hurry to our hotel. He squeezed every drop of adulation from the crowd. When our cavalcade reached the town square at *Franz Josef Platz*—having been renamed *Adolf Hitler Platz*—Hitler was forced to abandon his car to make his way on foot to Linz's town hall. Inside, he climbed the stairs and emerged onto the balcony as tears streamed down his face.

He began with his famous slogan that Austrians were shouting in the streets. "*Ein Volk, ein Reich, ein Führer*! We are one people, one empire, one leader!"

Deafening cheers erupted from the crowd that filled every available space in the plaza. "*Ein Volk, ein Reich, ein Führer*!" they shouted back.

Hitler raised his arms in triumph. As he spoke, the crowd quieted. "If it was Providence that once called me from this city to the leadership of the Reich, then it must also have given me the mission to restore my homeland to the Reich . . . You must look on the German soldiers who are marching into Austria at this time, as fighting men ready to sacrifice themselves for the unity of the whole German nation, for the might of the Reich, for its greatness and majesty, for now and evermore. *Deutschland, Sieg Heil!*"

The crowd roared back. *Heil. Sieg Heil,* over and over again.

Hitler shouted in my ear. "Friedrich, change the plans. We are not going to Vienna now. Tonight, we stay in Linz. With my people."

Changing plans for an entire entourage took some doing. I commandeered the Hotel Weinzinger perched on the Danube, reserved its lone telephone for Hitler's exclusive use, and ensured that he could view the Pöstlingberg Mountain from his room as he had from the rear window of his boyhood apartment.

That night, with little fanfare, Hitler culminated the *Anschluss* by signing a paper that incorporated Austria as a province of the German Reich.

From that moment on, Austria lost both its autonomy and its name: it would henceforth be called *Ostmark*.

Chapter 36

Sunday, March 13, 1938

"Come, Friedrich. Visit my parents' grave with me." It was a short ride to the Leonding Cemetery. When we stopped, Hitler pointed, "There. Over there."

The driver retrieved a magnificent wreath of white lilies from the car and handed it to Hitler. Black-uniformed bodyguards remained alert near their vehicles.

I kept a step behind, as Hitler approached the grey granite tombstone resting under an expansive tree. A black, oblong marble disc was inlaid into the stone marker. Etched into it, in gold lettering, were his parents' names—Klara Hitler and Alois Hitler—and the dates of their deaths. A ceramic picture of Alois was inserted above his name on the disc, while a smaller picture of Klara was embedded in the stone below it. The tombstone narrowed as it rose, topped by a large, granite cross.

Hitler stood, hands folded, head down, mumbling words . . . remembered, perhaps, from when he attended church as a boy. He laid the wreath down, leaned, and kissed his mother's name, stroking her ceramic image with a lover's touch.

Rising, he walked over to me. "Nothing and no one can replace a mother, Friedrich." He wept without shame.

I offered him a handkerchief; he dabbed his face and blew his nose. When he was more composed, he recited the poem he claimed to have written and dedicated to his mother years ago, and for whom he turned Mother's Day into a national holiday as soon as he became chancellor.

When your mother has grown older,
When her dear, faithful eyes
No longer see life as they once did . . .

He lost control; his body shook.
. . . The hour will come when,
weeping, you must accompany her on
her final walk.

He mumbled through the rest of the poem. Here stood the most important figure in the world, grieving as if his beloved mother died only days earlier rather than decades ago.

Then, as if a sudden north wind swept away his emotional detritus, Hitler stiffened, turned, and said, "No matter what summit I achieve for Germany, no matter how many countries we conquer, my one failing will always be that I could not save my mother when she needed me most."

"Wolf, your mother had incurable cancer."

He glared at me, his eyes burning coals. "Had I been the man then that I am now, I would have found a way to save her."

*

Monday, March 14, 1938

Hitler's handmade G-4 Mercedes could aptly be described as leviathan. It had an open carriage that comfortably sat seven. The car was painted a shiny gray with gloss-black fenders and running boards. Due to its enormous weight, the car needed six tires on three axles, each fitted with a separate hydraulic brake.

A convoy of cars—front, side, and rear—was to escort us from Linz to Vienna. Soon after the caravan set off, Hitler ordered his driver to stop.

Brakes screeched. Cars skidded.

We were in front of *Landstraße, 12*, a Baroque-styled house. A portly man with gray, wavy hair and a moustache in need of a trim, stood at a large window. He peered out at the motorcade.

Hitler battled sun glare and waved to him.

The man waved back.

Hitler glowed.

"That is Dr. Eduard Bloch. My mother's doctor." Then, for the second time that day, tears streamed down his face. When he composed himself, he said, "I am glad he is alive. Look," Hitler pointed to a post on the front step, "he still hangs out his shingle."

Then he shocked me.

"This man is an *Edeljude*—a noble Jew. If all Jews were like him, Friedrich, there would be no Jewish question."

"You talked fondly of him in P . . ." I caught myself from uttering Pasewalk in public.

"Friedrich?"

Hitler didn't seem to notice my near slip. "Yes, *mein Führer*."

"Once the tumult of our entry dies down, arrange for a Gestapo man to stop by this house. Have him tell Dr. Bloch . . ." Hitler stopped. "Better yet, you do it now. I will leave a car for you so we can meet on the road to Vienna afterwards. Go to Dr. Bloch. Tell him that no matter what happens to the other Jews in Austria, he and his family will be protected. Tell him that he can continue to practice medicine, even if the others of his race cannot. And then . . ." Hitler stared off, lost in nostalgia.

"*Mein Führer?*"

He cranked his head back toward me. "Ask him to give back the painting I once gave him. Also, the postcards I sent from Vienna." He chuckled. "You know, I made them look antique by drying them near a fire. One was of a Capuchin monk lifting a glass of champagne. I wished him Happy New Year on it: *Prosit Neujahr.*"

"Why ask for them back after all these years?"

"Tell Dr. Bloch you are taking them for safekeeping. Nothing else is to be touched. Is that understood?"

*

Dr. Bloch remained at the window as Hitler drove away. I knocked on the door. I banged louder over the din of the departing motorcade. The door opened and we locked eyes.

He knew military insignia. "Welcome, *Obergruppenführer*. What may I do for you?"

"I have a message from the *Führer*. May I come in?"

Rather than invite me into his salon, he ushered me to his doctor's office off the hallway. The office was well-lit, with large, floor-to-ceiling windows. There were medical instruments galore, an eye chart in the corner, and a patient's chair that folded down with stirrups to position women for exams. Dr. Bloch sat at his weathered oak desk that had a roll-down top. I sat in the green-cushioned chair next to it. There was a small, faded, rectangular area rug under his chair that had seen better days. It was not lost on me that a young Adolf sat in this same chair during one of his adolescent visits.

"Dr. Bloch, German laws will apply in Austria now, but the *Führer* wants you to know that you and your family will be protected no matter what happens to people of your race. He also wants you to know that while no other Jewish doctor will be allowed to practice medicine after today, you may continue without interference."

"Please thank the *Führer* for me." Bloch's tone was flat. "Is that all?"

"There is one more thing." I shifted in the chair. "He asks that you give me the painting and signed postcards he sent from Vienna before the Great War. Do you still have them?"

Without a word, he plodded to the wall and removed a watercolor landscape whose composition reminded me of a Cezanne with its stand of trees, a field of tall grasses, and a sloping mountain in the background. Then he retrieved two postcards tucked in the bottom drawer of his desk.

I took the painting and cards from him. "Are there any more?"

He shook his head. "Why does he want them?"

"For safekeeping."

"I see," was all he said.

I stood to leave when I asked, "Can you tell me about Hitler when he was a boy?"

The doctor settled back into his desk chair. A faraway look entered his eyes. "As a youth, he was quiet, well-mannered, and neatly dressed. He would sit patiently in the waiting room until it was his turn to be seen. As did every fourteen- or fifteen-year-old boy in Austria, he bowed as a sign of respect. Always polite. Always thanked me at the end of the visit."

The doctor paused, casting through memories for another.

"Like many youngsters in Linz, he wore short *lederhosen* and a green woolen hat with a feather. As a youth, Adolf was tall and pale. He looked older than his age." Bloch sighed. "Adolf inherited his mother's eyes. They were large and melancholic. Full of thought. To know Adolf was to know a boy who lived within himself. What dreams he dreamed? I do not pretend to know."

"We were in a hospital together at the end of the war," I said. "From the time I met him, he never stopped talking about his mother."

Bloch nodded. "It was always about his mother. But Adolf was not a mother's boy . . . not in the usual sense. Yet I never witnessed a closer attachment between mother and son. They had a mutual love for each other. When she died," Bloch bowed his head, "he was the saddest boy I had ever seen. He loved her that much."

Then Bloch's stare turned hollow. Foreboding.

"Hitler's mother was a pious woman. A kind woman. *Sie würde sich im Grabe herumdrehen, wenn sie wüsste, was aus ihm geworden ist.* She would turn around in her grave if she knew what became of him." Then, for the first time, Bloch turned animated. He covered his mouth with his hand. His eyes widened. "I'm sorry. I should not have said that."

I reached out and touched his hand. "In the *Führer's* mind, you can do no wrong, Dr. Bloch. As for me, I understand."

*

I left *Landstraße, 12,* with Hitler's reclaimed painting and postcards . . . and much to think about. Dr. Bloch was every bit the compassionate, kind, caring man that Hitler said he was. There was little doubt that Bloch served as a father figure to a vulnerable young man who hated his own brutish father. What made little sense were the critics who attributed Hitler's virulent anti-Semitism to the doctor's failure to cure his mother. Nothing could be further from the truth.

Bloch did not perform the surgery on Klara Hitler. She was left with open wounds that would not heal. Bloch tried to help her, but his antiquated treatment made her worse. Klara Hitler died a painful death. However, in Hitler's eyes, Bloch did the best he could . . . and he was forever grateful to the doctor for that.

The enigma remained: Where did Hitler's virulent anti-Semitism come from?

Chapter 37

March 14, 1938

After catching up with Hitler's caravan, we rode into Austria's capital together. Cardinal Innitzer, Archbishop of Vienna, ordered all Catholic churches to ring their bells in honor of the self-exiled native son that now returned as the nation's dictator.

Swastika banners flew from church steeples. Stalwartly Catholic Austria unreservedly placed itself at his feet.

Flowers and flags adorned windows and light posts.

It was a hero's welcome in what became known as the *Blumenkrieg*. The Flower War.

"The people want to hear you speak," I said.

Hitler's lids were slits. "When did you ever know me to be too tired to make a speech? I can't manage one tonight."

"They have been waiting hours to see you. At least show your face," I said.

Though wracked with fatigue, Hitler slogged his way to the Imperial Hotel balcony, waved to the exuberant crowd below, and then made haste to his room.

The following day, feeling refreshed and rejuvenated, Hitler addressed a quarter-million people that filled the *Heldenplatz*.

Hitler shouted in a strong, clear voice, "What is now known as *Ostmark*, the former Austria, will serve as a buffer between Germany and Russia. Let history record that my homeland has become part of Germany forevermore."

*

Not all Austrians shared in the joy of their prodigal's return. The lives of the one hundred and seventy thousand Austrian Jews turned into a living hell.

A pogrom was unleashed. Windows were smashed. Jews were beaten. Jewelry, rugs, and valuable artworks were taken while the owners stood by, too frightened to lift a finger in protest. Those foolish enough to dare were carted off. Throughout the city, Jews of all ages were forced to get down on their hands and knees to scrub anti-German plebiscite graffiti off the sidewalks in front of their neighbors.

I couldn't live with myself if I did not try to stop this.

*

Heydrich had commandeered a desk in the town hall. When I found him, I demanded, "Reinhard, end this violence against the Jews."

He threw up his lank arms. "What are we to do? Now that we've taken over Austria, we have more Jews than when we started five years ago in Germany."

What will appeal to him?

"Reinhard, I appreciate your delicate dilemma. Consider that most perpetrators are local police who either are committing these acts or looking the other way when they occur. Since you control their police now, it reflects on *you*. Without a systematic program, without rules that you enforce, this mayhem will damage your career."

Here I was, trying to convince the cold-hearted, ruthless, anti-Semitic Reinhard Heydrich to put the brakes on a pogrom that had spontaneously erupted against the Jews in Austria. Either he would lash out at me for meddling or take my words to heart. It hung in the balance.

"You're right, Friedrich. I can't let a bunch of wild animals continue this lawlessness." As he said these words, I let out a stream of air. Heydrich continued. "Any Nazi who does not obey my orders will be arrested. That should cool their heels."

As unlikely as it seems, Heydrich ended the pogrom. Then he wrote an article that appeared in the Party newspaper, *Völkischer*

Beobachter, and denied that it was the Nazis. He laid the blame on Communists dressed in Nazi uniforms.

*

With calm being restored I had my first opportunity to call Carla. "How is your brother?"

"The wound is healing. He is less agitated. I don't see that hurt in his eyes anymore."

"Have they put him in a wheelchair yet?"

"He's still too weak. They are trying to build his upper body strength, but he doesn't seem to understand what's happening."

"Let's pray he catches on. If he needs special treatment, we'll get it for him."

"Friedrich, I can't thank you enough for what you are doing for me and Ludwig."

"I'm doing this for Ludwig. For you, I have other plans."

"Oh, what sort of plans are you considering?" There was a playful inflection in her voice.

"The kind that involves a ring. That is, if you are interested?"

She screamed so loud I thought I was stabbed in the ear.

"Is that a proposal? Are we getting married?"

"It's time, don't you think?"

"Oh, my dear. Yes. Yes. Yes."

I hung up knowing I had just made the best decision in my life.

*

Hitler ignored the chaos and mayhem in the streets. What he couldn't ignore was a phone call from Eva Braun. He slammed down the telephone and brushed back the forelock that had fallen onto his forehead.

He was apoplectic.

"Friedrich, Eva ignored my warning about danger. She and her mother are in Vienna at this moment."

"You were explicit that she could not come," I said.

"Regardless, she wanted to share in our triumph."

He wrote their hotel address on a piece of paper. "I pray they are there and not out doing mischief."

An adjutant appeared at the door.

"The cardinal is here to see you, *mein Führer*."

Cardinal Innitzer represented the Austrian prelates, all of whom were prepared to pledge their unanimous support and blessing to Hitler . . . the foe of the godless Bolsheviks.

"Show His Eminence in." Hitler turned back to me. "Find those two and deal with them before they cause a scandal we can't contain."

*

I found Eva and her mother, Franziska, in their hotel restaurant, which was not far from the Imperial. Half-eaten dishes were being cleared away as I approached. Their faces lit up when they saw me.

"Eva, the *Führer* is furious that you are here."

Eva puckered her lips in innocence. "I don't know why. We are perfectly safe. In fact, when we arrived, the Austrians cheered us." She smiled demurely as she sipped her coffee.

My pulse quickened. "Did you say anything about knowing the *Führer*?"

"Never," Eva scowled. "I know better than to do that."

"They cheered because we are Germans," Franziska explained.

"You realize you took an awfully big chance coming here. Luckily for all of us there was no fighting."

Eva waved her hand. "The *Führer* worries too much. If we thought there would be trouble, we never would have come. Right, *Mutti*?"

"Friedrich, it was supposed to be a short ride," Franziska explained. "We planned on surprising him at Braunau am Inn, but he wasn't there. Then we went to Linz. He wasn't there either. Then we said: why not go to Vienna? We had no extra clothes with us. No toiletries. We had to ask the hotel porter to get us toothbrushes. The *Dummkopf* brought only one. Can you imagine? We had to share it."

They cackled. I saw no humor in it.

"The *Führer* insists you both return to Munich as soon as possible. If you want, Eva, you can fly back with me and the *Führer*." I turned to Franziska. "I am sorry, *Frau* Braun, there is only room for one more on the plane."

Eva turned to her mother. "*Mutti?*"

"Go ahead. The driver will take me back to Munich." Then Franziska clapped. "Wait until your papa hears about this adventure!"

That two women enjoyed themselves amidst the chaos brought smiles to the other patrons' faces.

The waiter brought the check; Eva handed it to me. "Do you mind, Friedrich? We don't have any money."

I not only paid the lunch fare but settled their hotel account. Before heading back to the Imperial Hotel with Eva, I made certain Franziska's driver knew to avoid parts of town that still had anti-Jewish violence.

*

The plane ride back to Berlin gave me time to think. Hitler's professed timetable for *Lebensraum* that would expand Germany's living space in five to eight years had absorbed Austria in a mere four months since that fated November 5 meeting. With that pace, how long would it take Hitler to destroy Czechoslovakia? I promised myself it would not come to that. The Fritsch trial had been rescheduled for March 17, three days away. Chief-of-Staff Colonel General Beck and Admiral Canaris were in the wings ready to pounce once Fritsch was acquitted. *Alles in ordnung.*

Everything was in order.

Chapter 38

Carla remained in Munich to monitor Ludwig's healing. I needed to liaison with Canaris, Oster, and Beck in Berlin about plans for the insurrection that would follow the trial. But first I had to introduce Rüdiger von der Goltz, the defense attorney, to his witnesses: Bavarian Joe and *Rittmeister* Frisch.

*

The *Kasino der jungen Löwen* had a new password: *Katzenmutter* (Mother Cat). Seemed apropos for the "Young Lion's Casino."

The same man guarded the door. "What took so long for you to return?" asked Hairy Chest. His black leather vest was replaced with one made from leopard skin. He leaped forward until we were toe-to-toe. The stink of cabbage was on his breath. He held up a brightly painted index finger. "I have something special for you," he said. "Wait here."

Two minutes later, he returned with a white envelope. "Bavarian Joe left this note for you."

"Where can I find him?"

"Read the note. It's all there."

"Did you read it?"

"Of course, I did." His hand swept through the air. "We have to look out for each other. No one else will."

"Then tell me what it says."

"It says that he changed his mind."

"Why?" I asked.

"Isn't it obvious? Too dangerous."

"I promised to protect him."

"Listen here, *Herr Obergruppenführer*. Oh, yes, I remember everything about everyone who walks through that door. Joseph Weingärtner is a homosexual Jew in Berlin. Fifty thousand homosexuals have already been arrested. How could he take the chance to testify in a court? The man you are so concerned about is a general. Nothing is going to happen to him other than a slap on the wrist."

I reached for my wallet.

He put his hand on my arm. "No amount of money is going to help. Joseph is long gone. One of those Zionist organizations was only too happy to help him reach the Promised Land. Joe is not coming back . . . for any reason."

I was crushed. Our bullet-proof case to clear Fritsch's name was just dealt a severe blow. We still had the old captain. In so many ways, he was more important to the case. I asked to use the phone. I called Rüdiger von der Goltz using a code for a moment such as this.

"Rüdiger, remember the cousin I wanted to introduce you to? It turns out he's on holiday. He left a message that it would be all right to visit his uncle tomorrow. Meet me there at nine."

The following morning, Goltz met me in front of *Rittmeister* Frisch's house at *Ferdinandstraße*, 21, in East Lichterfelde. I rang the bell. No one answered. I rang again. Nothing. I banged on the door. I looked at Goltz.

"No one is there," announced a voice from my right.

It was the housekeeper from number 20.

"Where did they go?" I asked.

"It was so sad. The old man died. All that excitement. His heart couldn't take it."

"When did this happen?"

"A day or two after you left," she replied.

"Is there a next of kin? Someone to look after his estate?" Goltz asked.

She shook her head. "Not a soul." A distant bell rang out. "*Das ist meine Frau.* She calls me. Sorry I could not be of more help."

We stood frozen in front of *Rittmeister* Frisch's house.

Goltz spoke first. "This is a disaster. What are we going to do?"

"Are you forgetting you have every receipt signed by Schmidt for payments Frisch gave him? And you have Frisch's bank statements that verify the withdrawals. What else do you need?"

"A witness! Pieces of paper are not enough. They must be identified and verified by a live body. Otherwise, the court will not accept them in evidence."

The trial was set for the following morning. I called an emergency meeting with Beck, Oster, and Goltz at Canaris's house.

"If Weingärtner is in Palestine, it would take little effort to throw a black hood over his head and secret him back here," said Canaris. "At least we would have one witness."

"We could never pull it off in time. Even if we could, the moment he left the tribunal, the Gestapo would grab him, pin a pink badge on his chest, and send him to a concentration camp to rot until he dies . . . or worse," I said. "We have to find another way."

"Why do we need any verdict from this kangaroo court? Can't the officer corps see the injustice for what it is?" Oster asked Beck. "We all know Fritsch is being railroaded by the Gestapo."

Beck shook his head. "The officers need *proof.* A verdict for Fritsch will coalesce the military leaders against the Gestapo."

Canaris rapped the table with his pipe bowl. "Gentlemen. Gentlemen. You are off point. We should be helping Rüdiger plan how best to navigate what will happen tomorrow without our witnesses. Stop bemoaning what we don't have."

I agreed. "Rüdiger, you might be able to salvage this if you twist this around. Make it less about Fritsch and more about the heinous crimes, lies, and deceit Himmler, Heydrich, and the Gestapo foisted on the German people."

Rüdiger, who had been uneasy while I spoke, became exasperated. "While you are at it, why don't you think of something challenging for me to attempt?" Goltz grimaced. "I'm about to go up against five biased judges without a single witness, and you expect me not only to gain a verdict for Fritsch, but also to condemn the Gestapo for its nationwide sins at the same time?"

*

"What are you doing here?" I found Ian Colvin waiting in front of my house.

"The trial is tomorrow. You never called. What was I supposed to do? I've been waiting for two hours."

Colvin was hatless. His coat was too thin for the time of year.

"You must be freezing."

"Nothing brandy wouldn't fix."

Inside, I poured two snifters of Hennessy XO brandy left from Max's time.

Colvin raised the glass. "I should come here more often. XO is not in a journalist's budget."

We touched glasses.

"About tomorrow," I said. "Let's sit down."

"I sense a problem."

"You knew before those journalists were *verboten*. I thought I could get around that. But no matter how I tried, I could not get you approved as my assistant. Your name is too well known."

The last thing we need is to read about tomorrow's disaster in the papers.

Colvin shook his head. "I knew getting a scoop like this was too good to be true."

"I'm sorry to disappoint you, Ian. Truly, I am. Be patient. A story will break your way."

Chapter 39

March 17, 1938

The trial was situated in cavernous chambers once known as the *Preußisches Herrenhaus*. The Prussian State Council held its meetings there until the building was rededicated by the Nazis in 1933 and affiliated with the Reich Aviation Ministry. Translation: Hermann Göring had offices here. Of particular interest was that the original building on this site was owned by the Bartholdy family until 1851. It is where their son, Felix Mendelssohn Bartholdy, composed his music for *A Midsummer Night's Dream*.

Mendelssohn was born a Jew.

The five judges sat at a crescent-shaped table pitched on an elevated stage. Göring presided and sat in the center. Admiral Raeder sat to his right and Colonel General Walther Brauchitsch, commander-in-chief of the army, to his left. Two Supreme Court judges bookended the panel. A stenographer sat at a small table on the far right.

Fritsch and Goltz sat at a solid oak table in front of the judges. Otto Schmidt slouched against a side wall, handcuffed, and shackled, with a guard at each elbow. I was the only spectator.

Göring was resplendent in a new white uniform. More medals dangled from his chest than usual.

He banged his gavel.

"This tribunal will come to order. Let the record reflect that *Herr* Fritsch is a former military officer who exercised his right to this military tribunal to prove his innocence. He is accused of being a homosexual by that man."—Göring turned to the stenographer. "Let the record show that the chief judge pointed to Otto Schmidt."—Göring continued. "*Herr* Schmidt will tell the court, in his own words, how the former army chief-of-staff violated Paragraph 175 of the German Criminal Code established on May 15, 1871 that makes homosexual acts between males a crime."

Göring glanced at the stenographer to make certain she captured every word. When she nodded, he continued.

Then Göring addressed Fritsch. "You are entitled to this, and we have honored your wish, though frankly . . ." he glanced at the men to his left and then the right, "the evidence seems clear enough."

Goltz jumped up. "My client is entitled to a fair trial. That's the purpose of this tribunal. Your remarks are prejudicial and make a mockery of these proceedings."

Göring looked down from the bench. "My dear counselor, I only state the truth. We will now hear the evidence of his violation of Paragraph 175." He motioned to the guards. "Bring the witness forward."

The gendarmes guided the manacled Schmidt to a chair in front of the tribunal. "For the record, *Herr* Schmidt, state your name, date of birth, and present address," ordered Göring.

"My name is Otto Schmidt. I was born in Berlin on August 16, 1906. I presently reside in Emsland."

"Can you be more specific?" asked Göring. "Where exactly in Emsland do you reside?"

Schmidt squirmed. "In Börgermoor concentration camp."

"Tell the court why you are there."

The man grinned. There were gaping holes where teeth should have been. "Blackmailing rich men that like cock."

Admiral Raeder looked away.

Brauchitsch paled.

Göring banged the gavel. "I will have you respect this court in the way you speak. Otherwise, it will be a long time before you see the light of day again."

"Forgive me, your worship, it's just that the laws against what's natural to some are antiquated. Don't get me wrong. I make my living because of them. But men having sex with men goes back to ancient times. To Biblical times, as far as I know. Wherever you look in Germany these days you find it, especially in the military."

Göring slammed the gavel down. "I will have none of that, *Herr* Schmidt!"

"Sorry, your worship."

Göring continued. "Were you offered anything in exchange for your testimony here today?"

Schmidt shifted positions in the chair. "I was promised nothing. I do hope I will get some consideration. Right now, I'm serving seven years and a loss of civil rights for ten years."

"State your crimes."

"This time? Fourteen cases of extortion."

"I see. Now *Herr* Schmidt, on November 22, 1933, did you arrange for one Joseph Weingärtner, also known as Bavarian Joe, to rendezvous with Colonel General Fritsch?"

"I did."

"And where did this liaison take place?"

"In the toilet at the Wannsee train station."

"Why there?"

"Men try to hide what they are. They believe what they do in such places will not be witnessed by anyone they know. It gives them a sense of security."

"In this case, you knew," said Göring.

"Yes, your worship. It is part of my job to linger about. Make sure the rent-boys get paid. After, I follow the unsuspecting blokes to their home. Most times, I pretend to be a detective. Threaten to arrest them. Expose their 'predilection' for young swords."

"On this particular occasion, what happened when you accosted Colonel General Fritsch?"

"I object," Goltz was on his feet. "You are assuming a fact not in evidence."

"What fact?" Göring, who considered himself a consummate actor, appeared perplexed.

"That the person he 'accosted' was my client, the colonel general."

"That's absurd," Göring returned. "We all know Schmidt says it was Fritsch. Overruled!" Göring turned back to Schmidt.

"Answer the question. What happened when you accosted the colonel general?"

"I identified myself as a policeman. I told him he should be ashamed of himself. I also waved a camera at him. They all assume I have pictures. There's never any film in it." Schmidt snickered. "The man almost fainted from fright. I had all to do not to laugh in his face."

"But you respected his rank, didn't you?"

Schmidt saluted. "Of course, I did."

"Then what happened?" asked Göring.

"I went through my usual song and dance that if he didn't want anyone to know about his perversion, I could make it all disappear . . . for a price."

"Did Colonel General Fritsch protest? Did he say it wasn't him? That you were mistaken?"

Schmidt shook his head. "None of that, your worship. He asked how much. I told him I needed five hundred Reichsmark on the spot. He left me standing there, went into his house, but came up short. I pointed to the bank across the street. He said it was closed. That I had to come back the next day."

"And did you?"

"What? Come back the next day? Of course. Had to get my money. When I tried to leave, the bloke asked me to sign a receipt for the money he gave me."

"Did you sign a receipt?"

"It was the only way I could get paid."

"Do you see this man in court? The man who paid you?" Göring asked.

"I do."

"Can you point him out?"

He pointed to Werner von Fritsch, who did not flinch or show any emotion.

"Are you certain this is the man?" Göring asked.

"Without a doubt."

Göring turned to the other judges. "Does anyone have a question for *Herr* Schmidt?"

"*Herr* Schmidt," began Admiral Raeder, "from that time you first asked Colonel General Fritsch for money, when was the last time you saw him?"

"I saw him every time I went back to collect more money."

"How many times was that?"

Schmidt reached to stroke his chin, but the chains limited him. He made a sour face and then said, "Four more times. Five, if you count when I returned after that first time."

"Let's call it five times altogether," Raeder said. "When did you see the colonel general after the last time you collected money from him?"

"That would be this morning, your worship."

Schmidt was coached not mention the scene in front of Adolf Hitler in the Reich Chancellery.

Göring knew Schmidt was lying and kept his head down, making a show of fussing with papers.

Brauchitsch asked, "And you are absolutely certain this is the man you witnessed coming from the toilet after having sex with this Bavarian Joe at the Wannsee station?"

Schmidt made the sign of the cross. "I swear on my mother's grave."

Göring's head shot up, plastered with a smirk. "*Herr* Schmidt. There is no need to exaggerate. Isn't your mother still alive?"

"She is, your worship. But if she were dead, I would swear on her sainted soul that this is the truth . . . with all my heart."

Göring peered down at Rüdiger von der Goltz. "Let's take a short recess before you query the witness. I expect you will make it brief, counselor. No sense wasting the court's time."

Chapter 40

I hated watching the destruction of an innocent man. I wanted to offer encouragement to Goltz and Fritsch as they marched up the center aisle to lunch to presumably talk strategy, but I couldn't. The judges had to believe I was there on Hitler's behalf.

*

"How is the tribunal going thus far?" asked Bernhard Weiss when I reached him by phone in a nearby hotel.

"Otto Schmidt has stuck to his story that incriminates Fritsch. Both of our star witnesses are no longer available since we last spoke. The cavalry captain's weak heart gave out and Joseph Weingärtner found his Jewish soul and fled to Palestine."

"I am sorry to hear about Frisch and you can't blame Weingärtner for running, can you?" said Weiss.

"Of course not," I said. "Weingärtner owed Fritsch nothing. He was more than decent to go as far as he did. None of that matters now. But it puts an end to Beck's plan."

"Friedrich. When I headed the police, I learned that no case is over until the last witness is called."

"You have more faith than I do, Bernhard."

*

Goltz did not have the aristocratic bearing of his war-hero father. But he did look every bit the lawyer he was, from his three-piece tweed suit with a white pocket square to the gold chain stretched across his plump belly. He looked soft; but his first question wasn't.

"*Herr* Schmidt," Goltz began, "how many times have you been arrested?"

Schmidt counted on his fingers. "Eight, maybe nine times."

"Review for the court what those offenses were?"

Schmidt did not hesitate. "Pimping. Blackmail. Extortion. Thieving. Embezzlement. Fraud. That covers most of them."

"What about telling the truth?"

"What about it?" asked Schmidt.

"How do you expect us to believe anything you say with a history like that?"

Göring slammed the gavel. "Move on, Goltz. This is getting us nowhere."

"*Herr* Schmidt," said Goltz, "describe the man you claim your Bavarian Joe had sex with."

"Why? Why? He's right there." Schmidt pointed at Fritsch without looking his way. "See for yourself."

"Tell the court what the man looked like at the train station." As he said this, Goltz blocked Schmidt's view of Fritsch. He raised his arms to appear wider.

Schmidt looked to Göring for guidance. Göring looked away. Schmidt turned back, craned for a better view, but each time he did, Goltz moved into his sightline.

Thwarted, Schmidt made an exaggerated show of straining to remember details about Fritsch. "He was of medium height. Average in weight. I remember he did wear a monocle. And he used a cane. A cane with a silver knob."

Goltz stepped aside and pointed to Fritsch. "As you can see, my client does not wear a monocle and he has no use for a cane. His military bearing gives him a distinguished appearance that his hard to forget. The man Schmidt described is not Colonel General Fritsch."

Göring bounced off the platform and strutted within two feet of Fritsch. "There is an indentation around the left eye. Do you, sir, use a monocle?"

Fritsch pursed his lips. "From time to time, I do."

Göring winked at the other judges as he lumbered back to his chair. After he plopped down, he said, "Continue, *Herr* Goltz. But not much longer, I hope. As you just witnessed, *Herr* Schmidt has described your client down to the minutest detail."

"There are many who use monocles, Field Marshal Göring. That proves nothing. With respect to this man's testimony, my client does not use a cane."

"The monocle proves Schmidt is telling the truth. The cane might have been used as a prop. A costume, if you will, so as not to be recognized. Continue your questions or we shall make our ruling now."

Goltz flipped to the next page of his notes. "*Herr* Schmidt, you say that you followed the man who had sex in the toilet to his home. Is that correct?"

"Yes."

"And where was the home of this man?"

"East Lichterfelde."

"Would it surprise you to learn that my client, Colonel General Fritsch, has never lived in East Lichterfelde? In fact, he has not been to that part of Berlin in more than twenty years."

"I could be mistaken," Schmidt said. "It was dark. I don't know every part of Berlin."

"Mistaken? I see. But according to your story, you went to his home repeatedly, each time to collect money. In fact, how many times did you return there to ask for more money?"

"I don't remember."

"Let me remind you. You told us five times in total. You collected money each time. Now, are we to believe that you got the address wrong every single time?" Schmidt turned slack-jawed. He looked to Göring to explain the discrepancy.

"None of this is relevant," Göring said. "We will note that the witness got the address wrong, *Herr* Goltz. Is there anything else you wish to ask Schmidt?"

"I request a recess. I need the evening to prepare additional questions to cross examine this witness."

"*Herr* Schmidt must be returned to his camp. What more could you possibly ask?"

"Field Marshal Göring, would you deny me the right to question this witness further? After all, we are talking about the career of one of Germany's most important generals."

Göring looked to Raeder and Brauchitsch for support, but neither would shut Goltz down.

Grudgingly, Göring turned back to Goltz. "No matter how many witnesses you call, this trial ends tomorrow. Is that clear?"

"Understood, Field Marshal Göring."

Göring brought his gavel down. "This court is adjourned until 10 a.m. tomorrow."

*

I headed for *Friedenau Stubenrauchstraße* to do an errand that was very much on my mind. "Are you Johann Schlueter?" I asked. His shop was located in the only coach house that remained on the street.

"What can I do for you?" Schlueter, trim yet pasty-looking from working indoors, was draped in a smudged smock that covered most of his shirt and pants. Jeweler's loupes protruded from his eyes like twin telescopes. The man was bent from being hunched all day, designing and crafting jewelry.

"I expect to be married soon and would like a wedding band made of interlocking branches that end in two joined hearts. Can you make that?"

"When it comes to silver and gold, I can do anything." Schlueter removed his magnifying lenses and studied my face to the point that I broke eye contact. "I need to ask how you came up with that design?"

"When I thought about a wedding band, the image came to mind. I don't know why or where I got it from," I answered, "but I would like to have it made for my intended."

"Who referred you to me?"

"No one in particular. Others you may have designed jewelry for might have mentioned your name in passing."

Schlueter eyed me up and down. "You don't look familiar, but I feel I have met you before."

"You have me confused with someone else, *mein Herr*. I have never been on this street before today."

Schlueter eased onto his chair.

"I once had a customer about your size. It was years ago when I apprenticed at Wilkens & Danger in Bremen. The war had just started. He was a young man. Too young if you ask me. Wanted to get married before he went off to fight."

"*Herr* Schlueter. I am not the only one this tall in Germany and I cannot recall ever being in Bremen."

"But you are the only man who ever asked for the same design twice."

Those words took my breath away. I grabbed onto his workbench to steady myself. My mouth turned dry.

"*Mein Herr*, what's wrong? Can I get you some water?"

"Yes. *Wasser*, please."

After my breathing returned to normal, I said, "You said a man my size came to you years ago and asked for the same design? Do you remember his name?"

Schlueter shook his head. "I remember jewelry. Stones. Settings. Most faces. Not names."

"Would a record of that purchase still exist?"

"Years after I left, their shop burned down. Everything was lost."

I handed him a card with my name and number. "*Herr* Schlueter. If you remember anything else about that man, please call me. It could be very important." I turned to leave.

"What about the ring?"

"You've given me much to think about. I'll be back."

A young man. Too young if you ask me.

I left Schlueter in a daze. Was it possible I had been married before I left for war?

My thoughts turned to Carla. Should I tell her? What could I tell her? I had until tomorrow, when she would return from being with her brother, to decide.

Chapter 41

Still upset, I almost missed the note lying on the foyer floor when I opened the door. It was from Goltz.

Meet me at the Hotel
Adlon R v d G

*

Goltz sat alone nursing a brandy.

"I got here as soon as I found your note. Have you been waiting long?"

Goltz held the glass to the light. The amber liquor shimmered like liquid gold. "Friedrich, did you ever think about the shape of a brandy snifter? It's quite specific." He rotated it so that light passed through like a prism. "It's Rubenesque. It gives hope to overweight, middle-aged men that they are drinking from an ample bosom. Like their mother's teat." He brought the glass to his lips and took another swallow.

"You act like you have given up on the trial," I said. "Where's your fight?"

He dove into his glass. "The trial was lost before it started. No witnesses. And a biased tribunal, to top it off."

I grabbed his shoulder. "Get a hold of yourself, man. There is still tomorrow."

"What about tomorrow?" Goltz slurred.

"Tell them about *Rittmeister* Frisch. How Schmidt blackmailed him. You have the signed receipts in Schmidt's own hand. Prove it is his signature. Then there are the bank statements in the same amount as the payments from Achim von Frisch's account. Present that and the court will have no choice but to acquit the colonel general."

Goltz motioned for the bartender to refill his glass; I waved him off. "You've had enough. You need to clear your head. Granted, this is no longer an open-and-shut case. But you have ammunition, damn it. Use it! Beat those bastards!"

*

When I got to the *Preußisches Herrenhaus* the next morning, Goltz's exhibits were lined up on the table in front of him. Fritsch stared off into the distance.

Göring, Raeder, Brauchitsch, and the two civil judges marched into the chambers, chortling at something. When their eyes alighted on Fritsch, they turned solemn and looked away.

I was no lawyer, but this was a hanging tribunal.

Göring banged his gavel. "This court is now in session. *Herr* Goltz, call your first witness."

"I recall *Herr* Schmidt to the stand."

Unlike the day before, Schmidt's shackles had been removed and he was dressed in a respectable, though ill-fitting, blue suit.

Göring reminded Schmidt that he was still under oath.

Goltz handed Schmidt five pieces of paper.

"Do you recognize these?"

Schmidt thumbed through them. He brought them closer. His lips moved as his read. He turned each over, their backsides blank.

"They appear to be receipts of some kind," Schmidt answered after a long while.

"Do you know for what service?"

Schmidt scratched his head. "I have not the foggiest."

He tried to hand them back; Goltz would not take them.

"Look once more, *Herr* Schmidt. In particular, study the signature at the bottom."

"Looks like chicken scratch, if you ask me."

Göring chuckled. Schmidt beamed at Göring's reaction.

Goltz remained unfazed. "Isn't that your signature, *Herr* Schmidt? Didn't you sign each of those receipts for the money you extorted from the man Bavarian Joe met in the toilet at Wannsee Station?"

Schmidt was quick to answer. "No."

Goltz turned to Göring. "I ask that the court give *Herr* Schmidt pen and paper and instruct him to write his name a number of times as if he were signing a letter or document. I am prepared to bring a handwriting expert into court to compare Schmidt's signature with the receipts. When he does, the court will see they are one and the same."

"I see no relevance for this exercise, *Herr* Goltz. *Herr* Schmidt has testified that he does not recognize the signature. That puts an end to this line of questioning. Move on."

"May I approach the judges, Field Marshal?" Goltz asked.

"Be quick about it," answered Göring.

"I was prepared to offer a witness that would have sworn, under oath, that he was the one who Bavarian Joe met during the night in question. Schmidt extorted money from this witness for his silence. This same man provided these receipts for the money he gave Schmidt. I want the opportunity to prove to the court that the signature on each receipt *is* Schmidt's."

"Why are you wasting the court's time? Surely, if such a person exists, it would change the complexion of this trial. Why haven't you presented your witness before now, *Herr* Goltz?"

"Because he died two weeks ago, Field Marshal Göring. If I could bring him back from the dead, I would. His testimony would prove that Colonel General Fritsch is innocent."

"Perhaps you got these receipts from your client," Raeder suggested.

"I did *not*," Goltz protested.

"*Ach so.*" Göring became interested in the question. "Then from whom did you get these receipts?"

Goltz glanced my way.

I averted his eyes, silently cajoling him to turn back.

If you point to me, our entire conspiracy is over!

Benignly, Goltz revolved back toward Göring. "I'm not at liberty to say."

I exhaled. My hands were clasped so tightly, I had to pry them apart.

Göring steepled his sausage-thick fingers. "If you won't say where you got them, there is no point attempting to prove Schmidt signed those receipts."

"The evidence is compelling, Field Marshal Göring. The court *must* hear it," argued Goltz.

"You cannot introduce pieces of paper that cannot be identified. But I want to be fair, *Herr* Goltz. Produce this Bavarian Joe. The court is willing to hear his testimony. We will not send him to the camps . . . where, of course, he deserves to be."

"If I could produce him, I would, Field Marshal. The boy fled to Palestine, unwilling to testify in this court."

"A Jew, no less." Göring stared at Fritsch. "The commander-in-chief having sex with a Jew in a toilet. This is the most disgusting thing I have ever heard! Call your next witness, Goltz. Be quick about it."

Göring and everyone else in the courtroom presumed Colonel General Fritsch would be the next witness.

Goltz had no next witness. There was no point to putting his client on the stand when he had no way to buttress his bare denial.

And then . . . the back door creaked open.

Rittmeister Frisch's nurse stepped into the courtroom. She wore a white uniform. Her gray hair was pulled straight back and clipped tight under a starched nurse's cap. She walked tall and straight toward Goltz.

Behind her, out of sight from the others, Heidi peeked into the chambers from the hallway.

I mouthed, "Thank you."

Goltz turned to Göring with a grin. "I do have one more witness, Field Marshal. I ask for one hour to confer with the *Fräulein*."

Forty-five minutes later, Achim von Frisch's nurse swore to tell the truth.

Chapter 42

"Please state your name."

"Sabine Stark."

"And what is your profession?"

"I am a trained, full nurse."

"How long have you been a nurse, *Fräulein* Stark?"

"I finished my training right before the war broke out. I was part of the German Red Cross caring for wounded soldiers. I remained with the Red Cross after the war but left their motherhouse system to join the Professional Organization of German Nurses."

"Please tell the court why you left the Red Cross."

Göring interjected. "This is all well and good, *Herr* Goltz. The court stipulates that *Fräulein* Stark is a competent nurse. Now get on with your questions. We are losing patience."

"Can you tell the court, *Fräulein*, where you worked last?"

"I was the private nurse for *Rittmeister* Achim von Frisch," she answered.

"Please repeat his name and spell it slowly."

"Achim von Frisch. A_c_h_i_m von F_r_i_s_c_h. Achim von Frisch."

"There is no letter *T* in Frisch. Is that correct?" Goltz asked.

"That is correct," *Fräulein* Stark answered.

Goltz took a moment to enjoy the wide-eyed murmuring among the judges. "Where did *Rittmeister* Achim von Frisch live?"

"*Ferdinandstraße*, 21, in *Berlin-Lichterfelde*."

"You say *Lichterfelde*?"

"Yes."

"And where did you live when you cared for *Rittmeister* Frisch without a *T*?"

"In the house with him."

"So, is it fair to say you knew much about his private life? What he did, for instance? Where he went? Things like that."

"I was by his side morning, noon, and some nights."

"Why not every night, *Fräulein* Stark? You lived in the house with him."

Her parchment-like white skin reddened. "The *Rittmeister* liked his boys. He went after them at night. Often to homosexual clubs. Occasionally, I went with him."

"You mean *Rittmeister* Frisch was a homosexual?" asked Goltz.

"Yes."

"Did you see him with other men?"

"Yes."

"Did any ever come to the house?"

"The *Rittmeister* would never allow that. He would find discreet places to meet them."

"Such as the Wannsee Station?"

"He had been there more than once to meet young men."

"How do you know that?"

"He told me. In later years, he had difficulty meeting men in places like that. *Rittmeister* walked with a limp. He needed a cane."

Goltz then asked, "The court is interested in November 1933. Do you have any knowledge of the *Rittmeister* traveling to the Wannsee Station the night of November 22, 1933?"

"I do."

Göring interjected. "How could you possibly remember one night more than four years ago, *Fräulein*?"

"Because when *Rittmeister* Frisch came home that night, his bath was delayed because a man met him at the door," she replied, unfazed by Göring peering down at her.

"Do you remember who that was?" Goltz asked.

"Yes." She pointed to Otto Schmidt. "It was that man."

"Let the record show that the witness identified Otto Schmidt."

Göring jumped in again. "Why do you remember *Herr* Schmidt so clearly? Could you be mistaken?"

"Not at all. He asked *Rittmeister* Frisch for money to keep silent about what happened at the train station. The *Rittmeister* didn't have enough cash on hand to satisfy him. *Herr* Schmidt asked the *Rittmeister* to get more from the bank across the street, but it was closed. *Herr* Schmidt returned the following day, but

Rittmeister Frisch would not hand him the money until *Herr* Schmidt signed a receipt. The *Rittmeister* was very proper about his recordkeeping."

"And did *Herr* Schmidt sign the receipt for the *Rittmeister?*" asked Goltz.

"Yes. Each time he gave him money, *Herr* Schmidt signed a receipt."

"You say, 'each time.' Did this happen more than once?"

"Yes."

Goltz raised his brows. "How many times?"

"Four more after the first time."

Goltz handed her the receipts that had been resting on the defense table. "Are these those receipts?"

She shuffled through them. "Oh, yes. I recognize them."

"How can you be certain these are the receipts?"

"Because I kept *Rittmeister* Frisch's files. I placed these receipts in the miscellaneous file."

"Did you see *Herr* Schmidt actually write them?"

"He never had pen or paper with him. I gave him both and watched him sign his name to the amount of money the *Rittmeister* gave him each time."

"And is that *Herr* Schmidt's signature on each receipt?"

"It was the day he wrote them."

"Do you know how I came into possession of these documents?"

"Yes. I provided them."

Goltz turned and lifted a second batch of documents from the defense table. "I would like to submit these bank statements into evidence, Field Marshal."

Göring glanced at them. "Proceed."

"Can you tell the court, *Fräulein* Stark, what these are?" Goltz asked.

"They are bank statements."

"I have circled certain numbers. Can you tell the court what they represent?"

"They are the withdrawals that correspond to the amounts given *Herr* Schmidt each time he came for money."

"*Fräulein* Stark. Did the Gestapo visit *Rittmeister* Frisch regarding Otto Schmidt's testimony?"

"Yes. Two Gestapo agents came to the house on January 15. They questioned *Rittmeister* Frisch about *Herr* Schmidt."

"Did the Gestapo learn about these bank statements prior to this trial?"

"Yes. I showed them to the agents. Then they took *Rittmeister* Frisch to Gestapo headquarters for more questioning. I was worried. He was so fragile. I didn't think he would survive their interrogation. But he did."

"Did he return that night?" Goltz asked.

"He returned the next day. Then, a few days ago, Rittmeister Frisch died. His heart gave out."

She started to weep.

Goltz waited for her to compose herself before saying, "Thank you for coming here, today, *Fräulein*. No further questions, Field Marshal."

"I have one," said Admiral Raeder. "The defense counselor appeared surprised when you walked into to the courtroom. Why is that?"

Not a good question for me. I hope Canaris and Heidi thought to have her manicure me out.

She blew her nose before answering. "When *Rittmeister* Frisch died, his nephews—he had two of them—wasted little time selling the house. When they did, they asked me to leave on short notice. Luckily, I found another position with a wonderful family in Alstadt Spandau. *Herr* Goltz couldn't locate me until I sent my change of address to the police."

I was grateful no one recognized that she avoided answering the question and was allowed to leave.

"Field Marshal Göring," Goltz stood. "I recall Otto Schmidt to the stand."

As Schmidt moved toward the witness chair, Goltz gave a faint nod that meant he was about to launch an attack on the SS, Göring, and Hitler.

Goltz turned to Schmidt. "*Herr* Schmidt. When, exactly, were you brought here from Börgermoor concentration camp?"

Schmidt fidgeted before answering. "Two days before the trial started."

"That would make it four days ago. Is that correct?"

"If you say so."

"And at that time, did anyone from the Gestapo or someone representing this court, review the case against Colonel General Fritsch with you?"

"They assigned an *SS* man to refresh my memory."

"And did they review the story you told here at that time?"

"No review was necessary. I don't forget my rent-boys or my johns."

"Thank you for that," Goltz said. "And did they show you a picture of my client?" He pointed to Werner von Fritsch.

"Yes. He's the one."

"And why are you so sure?"

"Because his name was on the photograph that they showed me."

Goltz, who had the habit of taking a few steps to the left or right as he asked questions, wheeled around. "Excuse me? Could you repeat what you just said?"

"They wanted to make certain I remembered who the old wanker at the Wannsee Station was. So, they showed me your chap's photograph with his name written across the bottom. I knew that the man with Bavarian Joe was named Frisch. This man was named Fritsch. They didn't want me to make a mistake."

"And did you?"

"Did I what?"

"Make a mistake?"

"No. That's him right there."

"Are you saying that *Rittmeister* Frisch and Colonel General Fritsch are the same person?"

Schmidt hunched his shoulders. "They could be."

"*Herr* Schmidt. Is that what the Gestapo told you?"

His voice quavered. "I don't remember what they said."

"What did they promise you?"

Schmidt turned to Göring. "Your lordship, I've been telling the truth. Haven't I?"

Göring's face was as bloodred as a summer's setting sun.

"Don't ask me questions," Göring pointed to Goltz. "Answer his."

The other judges grew animated as they whispered among themselves.

"I will repeat the question," said Goltz. "Did the Gestapo promise you anything for identifying my client as the man Bavarian Joe met at that train station four years ago?"

If eyes could talk, Schmidt's screamed for help. None was forthcoming from Göring or the other judges. Set adrift, Schmidt buried his face in his dirty fingers and sobbed. "They told me if I didn't identify Colonel General Fritsch, they would execute me the moment I returned to the camp."

"How did the Gestapo know about *Rittmeister* Frisch?"

"The Gestapo had seen the cavalry captain's name on a list of clients I supplied when I was arrested two years ago," wheezed Schmidt. "When they brought me back, they asked if I could be mistaken? They told me that *Rittmeister* Frisch was really Colonel General Fritsch. I told them, 'No.' I gave them the *Rittmeister's* address."

Schmidt wiped his eyes in his sleeve. His mouth was partially covered when he said, "The nurse was telling the truth."

"Excuse me, *Herr* Schmidt. Could you repeat what you just said? Louder?"

In a clearer voice, Schmidt said, "The nurse was telling the truth."

"That means you made up the entire story about the colonel general being at the Wannsee Station. Is that correct?"

Schmidt nodded. "It was the cavalry captain." He pointed to Fritsch. "Not him."

Goltz glanced at Göring. "*Herr* Schmidt, do you recall being taken to the Reich Chancellery by . . ."

This was the moment to implicate Göring and Hitler in this horrific charade. I held my breath.

A sheet-white Göring shouted, "Stop, Goltz!"

Göring turned his back on the court and gathered the other judges for a whispered conversation. All nodded. When their heads separated, Göring swung back around to the court and announced, "*Herr* Goltz, it is the judgment of this tribunal that Colonel General Fritsch has been abused and defamed by this piece of human garbage who calls himself Schmidt. We will not listen to another word from him. As to the colonel general, it is our pleasure to acknowledge him as a man of honor. We are delighted to enter judgment for him. Case closed!"

With a tap of his gavel, Göring fled the room.

*

The following evening, our group met at Canaris's home to discuss measures to recruit the officer corps to launch a coup.

"This trial has given you all the ammunition you need to muster the military leaders," Oster said to Beck.

Before Beck could answer, Canaris said, "That would have been true before Austria. Every agent I have around the world now says the same thing: Hitler is riding a crest of unparalleled popularity. World leaders praise his actions in unifying the German-speaking people of the Saar region, the Rhineland, and now Austria, under one flag. His foreign popularity is dwarfed by his idolization at home. The man is viewed here as godlike."

"Unfortunately, Wilhelm is right," Beck said. "The military leaders are furious that Hitler usurped the *Wehrmacht's* leadership. But his success in Austria puts him beyond their reach."

"What if he invades Czechoslovakia?" Oster insisted. "He'll do it by using the Sudeten Germans as an excuse."

"That is another story," Beck said. "No matter how he tries to justify it, we will not let him start another Great War."

"Then continue to enlist sympathetic colleagues," I urged. "Czechoslovakia is around the corner."

"Hitler has yet to say anything to the military," Beck countered.

"Why should he bother? Do you think he cares what you and the others think?" Canaris answered.

*

I had one stop to make before heading home.

"Admiral Canaris said you would be working late." I found Heidi at her desk in the *Abwehr*.

"You can imagine the amount of chatter throughout Europe after Austria. I have stacks of intercepted messages to translate," she explained, partially hidden behind a stack of communiqués.

"I won't hold you up, but I want to ask how you found Frisch's nurse and got her to testify?"

"Finding her was not that hard. Admiral Canaris cut through the red tape and found her address change."

"How much convincing did she require to get her testimony?"

"As you would expect, she feared the Gestapo. Remember, they had already come to the house and threatened her. She was told never to talk about it to anyone."

"How *did* you convince her?"

"I knew the captain was an elegant gentleman. A *bon vivant*. Kitty had regaled me about my father's early years and the club he owned that catered to homosexuals and transvestites before Hitler came to power: *Club Sei Dir Selbst*."

"*Club Be Yourself*. I worked there when I wasn't needed at the Nightingale."

"As soon as I mentioned the Club, Sabine's face lit up. She had accompanied the captain there many times. She knew my father. That's when she warmed to the idea that she would help. That, and I told her I had a high-ranking friend who would ensure her safety if she kept his name out of the trial."

"Heidi. You *are* Max's daughter."

Chapter 43

I had twenty-four hours to digest the encounter at the jeweler's shop before Carla returned from Munich. My mind continued to roil with questions as the front door clicked open.

Had I been married? Did I have children? If I had children, how old would they be? The jeweler said the ring was purchased as the war started. More than twenty years ago. . . closer to twenty-five.

"Hello, stranger," Carla said.

We kissed; I held her tight.

She purred. "Maybe I should go away more often."

I grabbed her hand. "Come. Sit. Tell me about Ludwig."

"He is the sweetest boy ever, Friedrich! Everyone expected him to be limited to a wheelchair, but he would have none of it. You should see him hop around like a kangaroo. His appetite has returned. His color is back. Everything has healed. There is life back in his eyes. The staff is taking extra special care of him. That's because of you."

"Thank Dr. Ferdinand Sauerbruch. He's in charge of hospitals. He put in a good word for Ludwig."

"He did more than that: he saved Ludwig's life."

I poured myself a scotch. "Care for one?"

"Sure," answered Carla. "It will help."

"Help with what?"

"Did you forget about getting married?"

"How could I forget?" I handed her a glass. "There's something I need to discuss with you, too."

Carla toasted. "To us."

"I . . ."

Carla cut me off. "Whatever you have to say, can wait. It can't be more important than what I have to tell you."

"I'm not so . . ."

"Hear me out," said Carla. "This is not going to be easy."

Back on the couch, I tipped my glass toward her. "Your show."

"I did whatever I could to help Ludwig each day, but Ludwig takes long naps. That gave me a chance to go to the *SS* headquarters on *Brienner Straße*."

"I'm familiar with the Brown House. Why go there?"

"Why do you think? To fill out a marriage application! When you asked me to marry you, it was the happiest moment of my life."

Then her smile evaporated.

"Why the sour face?"

"The *SS* marriage application requires that the bride and groom fill out their family histories going back multiple generations."

"Where are you going with this? It's been that way for a while."

Carla pouted. "Your personal history starts and stops with you. It means we can't get married."

I scoffed. "That is nothing to worry about. Are you forgetting my relationship with the *Führer*? When his former driver and pal, Emil Maurice, went through the necessary background check to get married, he discovered a lone great-grandfather was Jewish. Himmler denied the application and was about to eject not only Maurice but his brothers from the *SS*, when Hitler overruled him."

"Maybe Hitler would do the same for you. But think of the risk not only to you, but to Hitler. You have already had a confrontation with Himmler and Heydrich about your past—in front of the *Führer*, no less—a past they can't find. Hitler squelched that episode. If we apply for a marriage license, it opens a door you were barely able to close. We can't take that risk."

"You've given this a lot of thought. How does it translate to us?" I asked.

"There will always be an 'us.' I love you more than ever. It's just that we can't be married. We'll still be together. Are you okay with that?"

I sipped the scotch.

Carla's eyes puddled. "Say something."

"Like what?"

"Like you love me and want to be with me forever."

"You know I do."

"Then say it."

I put the glass down, wrapped my arms around her and held her close. I kissed the top of her head. "I love you," I whispered.

"I needed to hear that," she said into my shirt.

She pushed away, but I pulled her back. My arms locked around her. "There's something I have tell you."

Her body stiffened. "Whatever it is, can't you look me in the face?"

"I need to hold you close." When Carla didn't say anything, I continued. "I went to a jeweler yesterday. I asked him to design a wedding ring. I wanted to surprise you."

She looked up. Cautiously. "It can still be a surprise. I know how to pretend."

"The surprise was on me."

Hearing that, she pushed away, arched her brows and asked, "What sort of surprise are we talking about?"

"The jeweler said I had been there before."

"Should I be jealous? Did you buy jewelry there for another girlfriend?" She covered her ears. "Do I even want to hear this?"

I gently pulled down her hands.

"The design I asked him to make was identical to one a young man my size brought to him in the first years of the war."

"There are other men as big as you in Germany."

"I said the same thing. He couldn't remember the customer's name. He worked in Bremen back then. I have no recollection of any of this. What if it was me and it was meant to be a wedding ring, too? What should we do?"

"You could go to Bremen and wear a placard that asks if anyone recognizes you?"

"Be serious. Once I found out, I was tortured as to whether or not to say something."

"Why?"

"Isn't it obvious? I don't want to lose you."

"You have nothing to worry about. Look at it this way. Even if you had been married, no one waits twenty-plus years to see if a long-lost husband will turn up. They would have found your identification disk on the battlefield, pronounced you dead, and ended the marriage. That's not so unusual a story."

Carla took my hand.

"I want you to know that this changes nothing for me. I love you as you are, broken package and all." She laughed. "Anyway, between what I told you and you told me, we must stay just as we are."

What did I do to deserve this woman?

I clutched Carla so close that when we kissed, our teeth smashed together. We both laughed as we felt around to make certain no damage was done.

"Gentler this time," she said.

That night, I was gentler than I had ever been.

Chapter 44

March 28, 1938

I entered Hitler's office to find him staring at an updated map of Europe pinned on the wall. He had a rubber-tipped, wooden pointer in his hand.

"Ah, Friedrich. Perfect timing. Our guest will soon be here. Look at this." He tapped the western tongue of Czechoslovakia that penetrated into Germany. "See how Czechoslovakia is shaped like a dagger? It points to Germany's heart."

"With Silesia and Saxony to the north, rather than see the western part of Czechoslovakia as an incursion into Germany, I see it for what it is: a head caught between the jaws of a powerful lion," I replied.

"And the Sudetenland is the tip of the tongue, closest to us." Hitler clapped in glee. "Why didn't I see it that way before?"

"*Mein Führer*, I was with you when we marched into Austria, and you reassured the Czech government that no German soldiers would go near their border. You told them that Austria was a family affair, having nothing to do with them. That is why they did not intervene."

Hitler shook his head. "That was then. The Czechs maltreat the Sudeten Germans. It's getting worse. Our policy is to protect our racial German comrades."

As Hitler finished speaking, Konrad Henlein, the leader of the Sudetenland Germans, was announced. Ordinary in every sense, Henlein had a retreating hairline and wore plain, wire-rimmed glasses. While he did not appear frail, he was by no means a physical specimen. Yet, he was hailed there and in Germany for urging athletic fitness for the three and a half million German-speaking Sudetenlanders as a way to express their superiority over their Slovak "rulers."

Greetings and introductions were brief before Hitler issued Henlein his marching orders.

"As the rightful leader, you are now my governor of the Sudeten Germans. As such, the Sudeten German Party needs to make demands that the Czech government cannot possibly fulfill. Avoid working with their government. Remain in constant opposition. The outside world must believe that the only solution for the Sudeten Germans requires them to split off from the rest of the country . . . and that you need Germany's help to achieve it."

Henlein gave the Hitler salute and left.

When the door closed, I said, "With Mussolini's approval, Austria was yours for the taking. That will not be the case with Czechoslovakia, *mein Führer*. The Czech army is powerful. They have treaties with France and Russia. And England is pledged to support its ally, France. Your designs on Czechoslovakia could have our old enemies at our throats."

Hitler slid into his favorite club chair; he pointed to the one across from his. "Czechoslovakia is not the same as Austria," he agreed. "And you are right about the French and Russians being sympathetic to a partner. But keep in mind there is no treaty between the English and Czechs. I do not believe that England will intervene. Without England, France will remain quiet."

"But, *mein Führer* . . ."

"I considered all of this," he broke in. "No, Friedrich. The Czechs will be conquered without opposition."

*

Hitler moved with lightning speed. The program he'd announced four months ago on November 5 was in full throttle. Blomberg and Fritsch were gone. More than a dozen lesser generals dismissed. Scores of officers transferred. The Foreign Service rejiggered. Austria was no longer a separate country. And Czechoslovakia was at the precipice.

At my request, Oster, Beck, and I met at Canaris's house.

Canaris turned to Beck at the start. "What we discussed in the past is no longer hypothetical. Can we count on enough military leaders to take a stand against a future war?"

"Most of the officer corps believes Czechoslovakia will be Armageddon," Beck answered. "But the major issue remains. Most professional soldiers are torn between their oath to Hitler, who is the acknowledged leader of our country, or what they believe is best for Germany. While some see them as one and the same, others separate the two. Should it come down to fighting, soldiers will fight. That's what they do. But they also know we will lose a full-scale war against the same allies. No soldier wants to put our country through that again."

"And I presume that the military still won't challenge Himmler, Heydrich, and the Gestapo." Oster remained vexed that the military needed more ammunition than the Fritsch trial supplied to rally the officers that waffled when it came to taking down this odious regime. "So, what do you propose instead?"

Beck offered a considered answer. "Foreign opposition to Hitler's expansions has faded. We need the wartime Allies to issue a statement that if Germany invades a sovereign, democratic state without cause, they will come to its aid. If the military leaders on the fence see foreign support on the side of right, they will join our opposition."

"Let's call it for what it is," I said. "We need England. If Hitler believes the British will fight, he will stand down."

Oster scoffed. "You are asking the near-impossible. What German diplomat is capable of gaining the British's attention?"

All eyes focused on Canaris, who lit a fresh bowl of tobacco. "It may take some doing, but I know someone the British may respect enough to grant an audience. It will take time to set the parts in motion. And there will only be one opportunity."

"Time is what we don't have," Oster said.

"No shot has been fired," said Canaris. "We must do this right. Otherwise, it will fail. And if we fail, we may find ourselves in a maelstrom of horrors the likes of which the world has never seen."

Chapter 45

April 20, 1938

"It's Hitler's birthday," I said.

Carla looked up from a cluster of photographs spread over the dining table. Her right eye held a magnifying loupe that resembled a monstrous monocle. "Am I supposed to cheer?" She waggled her finger in the air. "Happy birthday, *mein Führer.*"

"Could you be any more sarcastic?"

"I'm being good," Carla said. "You don't know how sarcastic I can be."

"Well, you are going to have to hold your tongue. He asked that we join him when ten thousand men selected from thirty German and Austrian army units parade down *Unter den Linden* tomorrow at noon."

"Can't I be sick?" asked Carla. "Come to think of it, I am." She let loose a full-throated cough. "I am certain to be sicker tomorrow."

"Consider taking medicine now so you can make it," I teased. "At least you can skip Goebbels's toast to Hitler's birthday that will be broadcast to most of the world at midnight. I need to listen."

"Are you a schoolboy? Will you be quizzed tomorrow?"

"You are in rare form," I said.

"I'm sorry," Carla explained. "I received a phone call from Inge this morning that Ludwig is running a low-grade fever. They are giving him medicine. They said it was not that serious, but I worry. He is so vulnerable to infections."

"Do you want me to make any calls?"

She shook her head. "Listen to your Goebbels. I will call Schönbrunn tomorrow to make certain Ludwig is getting better. Expect that phone call to take all day."

I knew when to pick my battles. This was not one. "Understood."

At midnight, I turned on the radio. Goebbels's high-pitched, squeaky voice sliced through the airwaves like a violin out of tune.

> *Unser Führer*, Adolf Hitler exhibits a genius in statesmanship and military science as already witnessed by his historic courage that is blessed by the hand of the Almighty. Adolf Hitler is a conqueror of men's hearts, protector of world peace and above all, the savior and redeemer of Germany. *Alles Gute zum Geburtstag.* Happy birthday, dear *Führer*. Heil Hitler.

I envied Carla for not listening to this drivel. Tributes that followed Goebbels's toast included the ringing of the Braunau chimes and songs sung by National Socialist Youth organizations.

The following day, I made my apologies for Carla's absence. I loathed every moment I stood at attention as Hitler saluted the thousands that marched by to honor him. Out of the corner of my eye, I saw Ian Colvin off to the side. He motioned to meet after the parade. "Do you realize what just happened?" Colvin said two hours later, as we walked on *Wilhelmplatz* with the Chancellery building to our backs.

"Of course. Hitler has bamboozled the world leaders that he clamors for peace while he puts on a military display the likes of which have not been seen since the Great War."

"That's not the half of it," Colvin said. "This was more than a display of a rejuvenated *Wehrmacht*. What I witnessed was a Germany equipped for a new type of war. A war of sweeping flanking movements. Lightning attacks. Mechanized German armaments. The evidence is right there for the world to see."

"You saw all that standing on the sidelines?"

Colvin put his arm on mine. "For me, Friedrich, this was more than a celebration of Hitler's birthday. This military display was a declaration that war is just around the corner."

After checking that no one paid us any mind, we spent a few more minutes discussing who in England could get the British government to warn Hitler off.

Colvin offered little encouragement. "Right now, Parliament is tripping over itself between the desire to be an island apart from what is going on in Europe, quelling the Arab insurrection in Palestine, and dealing with India's desire for independence. The British powers are too preoccupied with their own problems to care that Hitler wants to gather disenfranchised German-speaking people back into Germany. Besides, Chamberlain believes the Treaty of Versailles was unfair to the Germans. He has no problem looking the other way if Hitler makes much-needed minor corrections."

"A correction is one thing. Invading a new democracy that has no connection to Germany is quite another matter. England will rue the day it sat on its hands and did nothing," I snarled.

Colvin tapped me on the chest. "Simmer down, old chap. I'm on your side, remember? I am working on the right channels. I need more time. Tell Canaris and your people to be patient."

*

April 24, 1938

A month after he left Hitler, Henlein succeeded in rousing the German-speaking Sudetenlanders to protest. As civil unrest accelerated, the Sudeten German Party convened their annual meeting in Karlsbad. There, Henlein presented the Czech government with eight demands. Known as the Karlsbad Eight, Henlein issued two requirements the Czechs could not fulfil. The first was for the recognition for the Sudeten Germans to become a legal entity within the Czech state. The other was to grant freedom for the German Sudetenlanders to accept and profess adherence to German ideology.

Czechoslovakia was a patchwork quilt of ethnicities cobbled together from the Czechs' long-term struggle with the Austrians and the Slovaks' resistance to assimilate with their Hungarian rulers. Throw in a slice of Germany and a strip of Poland and we have the new country of Czechoslovakia as created by the Treaty of Versailles. If the Czechs granted autonomy to the German element in their country, those of Polish and Hungarian descent would demand the same. Other ethnic groups would insist on similar rights. It would rip the country asunder.

To add to Henlein's local pressure, Joseph Goebbels poured his brand of verbal gasoline onto the fires with Henlein's false claims that the Czechs perpetrated atrocities upon the German-speaking Sudetenlanders. As the fire grew hotter, Goebbels added more fuel.

Chapter 46

Heidi called, frantic.

"What do you mean Kitty is missing? Meet me at the birdbath."

In recent times, we created code names for places that were safe to meet and where conversations could not be overheard. The "zoo" was the Tiergarten, Berlin's inner-city park. The "oasis" was the lobby of the Hotel Aldon. The "birdbath" was the Nightingale Cabaret which Marta checked regularly for listening devices. On my way to meet Heidi, I swung past Pension Schmidt in case one of the women had heard from Kitty.

None had.

I tore through the Nightingale's front door. Heidi and Marta waited at the bar.

"Any word?" I asked.

Both pale, they shook their heads.

'When was the last time you heard from Kitty?"

"I told her not to do it," Marta said, her eyes moist. "Kitty insisted she had to make one more run to the bank in Amsterdam."

We moved to a table.

"Kitty has managed to get to Amsterdam more than a couple of times despite increased restrictions," Heidi said. "She's been challenged but believes she can talk her way out of any situation."

"I had a feeling about this time," Marta said. "I told her, but she scoffed. Said I was a worrywart."

"I've told her, too," I said.

Heidi blanched. "The Gestapo must have her. You have to do something, Friedrich."

"I can't call them and say, 'By the way, I understand you arrested Kitty Schmidt today. All a mistake. Let her go.'"

A fog of silence drifted over us as we parsed through options. Then I jumped up. "Meet me here tomorrow night at midnight.

Knowing Reinhard Heydrich the way I do, I have an idea that just might work."

*

The following night, Marta, Heidi, and I met at the Nightingale. When I told Carla why I needed to be there, she insisted on coming.

The Junghans mahogany clock above the bar struck twelve. Each chime reinforced Kitty's absence.

Heidi's eyes were raw from crying. She blew her nose. "You said you could free Kitty. Where is she?"

"I said I had an idea. Have faith. If everything falls into place, Kitty will be here shortly." I turned to Marta. "Break out your best champagne and six glasses."

Carla's eyes narrowed. "This is no time for a party, Friedrich. Can't you see these girls are worried sick? I am, too."

As she said this, the door swung open. Two figures stood in the shadows.

Marta and Heidi cried out as one, "Kitty!" and bolted toward the door.

Kitty stepped into the light. Her escort fell behind.

Marta and Heidi froze. Kitty had a black eye, swollen cheek, and a split lip.

"Excuse how I look," Kitty said with a pained smile. "I didn't have time to put on my face."

Heidi and Marta clasped Kitty's hands and helped her to the table.

The man accompanying her turned to me. "Your idea was brilliant, Friedrich. Heydrich saw the possibilities in a flash." He patted his own face to highlight Kitty's injuries. "Too bad I couldn't get there before his goons . . ."

Kitty managed a crooked smile. "You got there just in time."

Once Kitty settled into her seat, Heidi said, "Marta, this is my boss: Admiral Canaris."

"Heidi tells me how much she enjoys working for you," Marta said.

"We are lucky to have her," he answered, then turned to kiss Carla. "I thought you might be here. How are your aunt and uncle? I haven't seen much of them lately."

"They find it safer to keep to themselves these days."

"That's wise," Admiral Canaris said.

"*Now*, I will get that champagne," Marta said.

Minutes later, glasses in hand, we toasted Kitty's return and Admiral Canaris for saving her.

"They were mere hours away from sending her to Lichtenburg concentration camp in Saxony," said Canaris. "The commandant is Eicke's protégé from Dachau."

Hearing "Dachau," we all shared a similar thought.

Marta raised her glass. "To Max," she said.

"To Max," the rest of us cho7used.

After we toasted, Kitty said, "Friedrich, your friend, Heydrich, interrogated me after they brought me to Gestapo Headquarters from the Dutch border."

My pulse quickened. "Did he . . .?"

"He wouldn't dare. Some goon did his dirty work. Heydrich badgered me for names of clients he could extort in the future. No way I would inform. Then he asked where I squirreled my money away over the years. I laughed in his face."

Heidi asked, "Admiral, how did you convince Heydrich to let Kitty go?"

He put his hand on my arm as he explained, "I told Heydrich that our intelligence services—his and mine—could use Kitty's bordello as a listening post. What better place to learn the secrets of influential political figures and foreign dignitaries than at Pension Schmidt?"

"Heydrich saw the potential the moment the admiral suggested it," Kitty added. "After all, *that* beast has sullied my establishment more times than I care to count."

Canaris continued. "The plan is simple. Each bedroom will be wired with a hidden microphone connected to a control chamber in the basement. And wait until you hear about the girls that will . . ."

"Admiral Canaris," Carla broke in. "Did Heydrich think to question how you knew Kitty was at Gestapo Headquarters?"

"Never an issue. He knows my reach. More to the point, once the germ of the idea took hold, Heydrich recognized that he could check on Nazi officers with loose lips during pillow talk in addition to influential Berliners and the occasional diplomat. Especially if we go to war. Now let me tell you about . . ."

"You make it sound so simple," Carla said.

"When it benefits the Nazis, everything becomes simple," Canaris answered. "As expected, Heydrich had caveats. Aside from listening devices, Pension Schmidt will become *Salon Kitty*. The *coup de grâce* is that the Gestapo will recruit twenty women to be both prostitutes and spies. Imagine that! The *SS* will train them how to extract information from special clients while they are . . ." he raised a brow, ". . . as they say, *in flagrante delicto*."

"How will he find these 'special' women?" Marta asked, her tone playful. "If the price is right, I might apply." Marta stood and performed a pirouette. We clapped; she bowed. "Do I pass?"

Kitty answered, "You would be perfect . . . but the Nightingale can't spare you."

"If you can believe it, Heydrich plans to ask every Gestapo department to screen for intelligent women who are multilingual and patriotic Germans," Canaris explained. "They must also be 'man-crazy.' That's how he described it: 'man-crazy.' To guarantee enough candidates, Heydrich issued a directive for the *Sittenpolizei*—the vice squad—to round up the most attractive prostitutes in Berlin to be screened as agents."

"How do you feel about this?" Marta asked Kitty.

"About Heydrich's Gestapo training girls to work in my brothel or me losing control of Pension Schmidt?"

"Either. Both."

"I will do anything to stay out of the camps."

"Kitty, I have a delicate question," Carla began after the hoopla settled down. "Would you be willing to come to my studio tomorrow? You know I'm a photographer. My show in London will be a twenty-year retrospective that depicts the horrors of war seen through soldiers maimed and mutilated in the Great War. My newest project is to take close-up pictures of how the Nazis mutilate and injure their own citizens. I started when my brother lost his leg because medicine was withheld due to his handicap. I would like to photograph your bruises. Close up. No one will be able to identify you."

"If you can make art of it," said Kitty, "why not?"

"More a statement, than art," answered Carla.

Marta refilled the glasses.

Though the club was empty, Canaris lowered his voice. "There will be more trouble for the Jews this week. Tuesday, a decree will be issued that forces Jews to list all assets above five thousand Reichsmarks. Money. Stocks. Furniture. Life insurance policies. Jewelry. Paintings. Anything of value. When assets of Austrian Jews are included, this could amount to seven billion Reichsmarks."

"Haven't we suffered enough?" Heidi asked.

The "we" was not lost on anyone at the table.

"Hitler doesn't have enough money to fund the military," Canaris explained. "Göring's Four-Year Plan is failing. As soon as the Nazis get these lists, the Jews' assets will be *Aryanized*. In addition to grabbing their money, this is meant to force the remaining Jews to leave Germany."

"But who will take the Jews?" asked Kitty.

*

"It was worse than I could have imagined," Carla said after photographing Kitty the following day.

I handed her a scotch. "How bad?"

She downed the drink. She held her glass out for a refill. "Bring the bottle."

I started to ask a question and decided it was better to wait. After the third drink, Carla was ready to talk about it.

"At first, Kitty was reluctant. I thought she was modest. I drew the shades so no one could look in, and then pushed white screens together as a barrier for privacy. I busied myself to give her time to get comfortable. Finally, she emerged in a fancy red Japanese silk robe she had brought with her. I set up the lights, adjusted the screens, and started with her eye, then her swollen cheek and then her lip that had crusted over. Finished, I stepped back. I was about to say, 'I realize how difficult and painful this was for you' when she offered, 'There's more.'"

"I knew from the way she walked that the damage was not limited to her face," I said.

Carla nodded. "I felt her pain. Her loss of dignity. It was difficult for Kitty to slip the robe off her shoulders. I offered to help, but she didn't want any. When she finally managed, I was horrified. They used lamp cord wire with a heavy plug at the end. After I photographed the welts, she dropped the robe even lower. There were huge purplish-blue hematomas on her flanks."

"Kidney punches. They do that so they are not visible when a prisoner is dressed."

"She's urinating blood. How can they do that to a woman? To anyone?"

I pictured Max Klinghofer's face beaten to a bloody pulp. His legs splayed in inhuman directions. "There is no answer."

Chapter 47

May 2, 1938

"Friedrich," it was Hitler on the phone, "I leave for Rome this afternoon. It is critical we meet beforehand." More and more, I gritted my teeth with his every intrusion. What I once found easier to tolerate grew thinner by the day.

As I neared the *Führer's* office, a repulsive mass of blubber rolled toward me. Dr. Theodor Morell, known as *Dr. Kurfürstendamm* for the street where his private practice was located, was darkly complected. He needed thick glasses, and sprouted more hair on his fingers, ears, and nostrils than on his balding head. This quack—Hitler's personal "physician"—kept the *Führer* pumped full of "medicines." Hitler, who constantly believed he was dying, kept Morell nearby at all times.

"He's as good as new, Friedrich," Morell said. Then added, "At least he will be when his Vitamultin injection does its magic."

Morell mixed Vitamultin powder—which came in thin, gold-foiled packets—with water, and injected the admixture to give Hitler his daily "boost." I once snatched a packet and had it analyzed: it was methamphetamine. Coupled with infusions of biologicals obtained from bull testicles, animal intestines, high doses of vitamins, male and female hormones, all mixed with dextrose, this mixture made Hitler a living test tube of bizarre remedies. While Hitler believed these treatments fortified him and kept him strong, those around him became more concerned as Morell's treatments and influence grew.

"Will you travel to Rome with him?" I asked Morell.

"You know he won't travel without me. Will you be joining us, Friedrich?"

"If I'm asked."

And with that, the repulsive man waddled away.

I had not been in favor of the trip.

*

The previous week, the German ambassador to Italy advised Hitler that the Italians believed the "German-Czech problem will come to a head very swiftly, but that Italy will cause no difficulties to the solution which Germany deems most suitable." I was present when Hitler received the report.

"After that report from the ambassador, why take valuable time to go to Italy when you have much to do in Berlin?" I had asked. "You know Italian protocol dictates you spend most of your time with King Emmanuel III rather than with Mussolini."

"Friedrich," Hitler had replied, "it is a good thing you are not a politician or a tactician. You are not good at either. Loyalty is your strength. For that, I'm grateful." He clasped his hands as a teacher about to give a lecture. "We need Italy to draw French forces to Africa as well as to protect the French-Italian border. In that way, the French will be less inclined to honor their pact with Czechoslovakia."

Hitler would not cancel his Italian trip.

*

When I entered his office, Hitler held a clutch of papers.

"There you are," he said, seated in his favorite club chair.

"Feeling better after your doctor's visit?" I asked.

"Don't be like that, Friedrich. I know you despise Morell, but he is a genius. Eva's mother swears by him. When Eva told me how Morell cured Franziska when other doctors had failed, I asked him to help me with my stomach cramps and eczema. Morell was the only one who knew what he was doing."

"I am not the only one concerned, *mein Führer*. Göring calls Morell *Herr Reich Injection Master*."

"The Vitamultin makes me alert. Without it, I would be drowsy all day." Hitler sighed. "Regardless of what anyone thinks, Morell is my savior. Now come here. I need to discuss these papers with you." He handed me the folio. "Take your time. Read with care."

The top page was official-looking. After some moments, I looked up. It was his Last Will and Testament.

"Go on. Read to the end," he said.

I slipped onto a chair, fascinated at his bequests. It stated that upon his death, the first people notified should be Martin Bormann, his secretary, and his longtime adjutant, Julius Schaub. Party Treasurer Franz X. Schwarz was named executor of the estate.

Hitler was to be buried alongside the *Blutzeuge*, the blood martyrs who died in the November 9, 1923, putsch. In '35, the sarcophagi of these first sixteen to die for the Nazi cause were moved and interred in the *Ehrentempel*. Eight were buried in each of two limestone temples. These monuments were built on the *Königsplatz* in Munich and crowned with steel and concrete roofs that sported inlaid glass mosaics.

"Why today?" I questioned.

"You saw Dr. Morell leave? Who knows how long I have?" Again, he pointed to the document. "Please. Finish."

The next item dealt with the belongings of his half-niece, Geli Raubal. Hitler kept her bedroom in his Munich apartment on *Prinzregentenplatz*, 16, exactly as it was the day she shot herself in September 1931. That he had kept her room and her things as a shrine all these years was known only to a few. The will directed that its furnishings and what remained of Geli's belongings be given to her mother, Angela Raubal, Hitler's half-sister.

The rest of the Will dispersed his vast wealth. There was no mention of the amount of the estate, although I knew that it was enormous given his untaxed income from book royalties and copyrighted photos. Most of Hitler's fortune went to the Nazi Party with directions that the Party pay monthly and annual stipends to Eva Braun; Angela Raubal; Alois and Paula Hitler, Hitler's brother and sister; loyal servants; Anni Winter; Julius Schaub . . . plus others.

"*Mein Führer*, you always think you are about to die. Is there something you are not telling me this time?"

"I have a fistula in my throat. I'm afraid it's cancer. Morell tells me not to worry." Hitler rolled his eyes. "I never believe him when he tells me it's nothing. I know I won't live a long life, Friedrich. Please witness as I sign this."

He initialed each page and signed the bottom of the last. Hitler gave me the pen and pointed to a blank line titled, *Zeuge*. "There. Sign as my witness." Then he added, "Schwarz will come by later this morning and place the Will in the Party safe. Now, I can go to Italy with peace of mind that my affairs are in order."

I wished him a successful trip and rose to leave.

"There is one more matter I need to discuss with you. It's about the Jews."

I sat down. "What about them?"

"Imagine. With every law we have passed, with every barrier we've erected, perhaps one hundred thousand Jews left Germany at most. Five years later and four hundred thousand still remain." His face purpled. "With Austria, we picked up close to two hundred thousand more. Added together, there are more Jews in Greater Germany than when we started. He smacked his fist into his open palm. "Can you imagine what will happen when we take over Czechoslovakia? More than three hundred fifty thousand more Jews!"

Then, like quicksilver, Hitler became the face of calm. He wrested the corner of a vanilla-colored printed card from under a stack of papers on the side table.

"Are you aware that the American president—Roosevelt— has convened a conference six weeks from now in Évian, France?"

"To what purpose?"

He handed me the details. Thirty-two countries were invited. Germany was not among them. The conference would discuss the plight of "political refugees." Roosevelt did not refer to Jews by name. He didn't have to. There was little doubt the conference's agenda was to provide asylum for the descendants of

Moses that the Nazis were adamant to push out of Germany . . . and now Austria.

"We have to hope that this conference will do more than pay lip service to the problem," I said after I finished reading it.

"Maybe there is something we can do to help them accomplish that." Hitler slid behind his desk, poured water from a crystal carafe, pushed back his forelock, and put pen to paper. Finished, he handed me a one-page statement.

> I can only hope and expect that the world, which has such deep sympathy for these criminals, will at least be generous enough to convert this sympathy into practical aid. We, on our part, are ready to put all these criminals at the disposal of these countries, for all I care. Even on luxury ships.

"Do you have to call the Jews criminals?" I asked.

"What would you like me to call them? Fellow Germans? Worthy people? Never. Friedrich, don't let your tender heart mislead you. None of the attending countries will take them. Their only purpose is to criticize us. Given that Roosevelt and the others cannot comprehend I want their conference to succeed, I am sending you to the conference to make certain my point is known."

"How? Germany is not invited."

"There will be credentialed journalists. I'll see to it that Goebbels issues you a set."

"Will you really let the Jews go, Wolf?" I knew he would not make it easy for them, no matter how badly he wanted them to leave Germany.

"Only after they repay what they have stolen."

"That is an impossible barrier to overcome."

Hitler shrugged. "Nothing is ever impossible, Friedrich. But a conference about taking Jews in can only be considered a farce."

At that moment, I recalled Kitty's words: *Who will take the Jews?*

Hitler knew the answer. "In the end, no one will take them."

Chapter 48

"It's a new recipe." Carla held out an oval-shaped plate. "Pheasant schnitzel." There were also sides of peas and carrots and warm potato salad.

I uncorked a chilled bottle of Riesling produced at Castle *Reinhartshausen*. Max's house had a bone-dry, stone wine cellar with close to eight hundred vintage wines kept cool year-round.

Heidi, a former chef, was first to try the pheasant. The flavors challenged her senses. "What am I tasting that makes this so wonderful? It's more than the bacon. What ingredient am I missing?"

"Hungarian paprika," answered Carla.

Dinner was a success. We sipped coffee as Kitty regaled us with stories of the candidates interviewing for the bordello at *SS* Headquarters.

"I told them that *Prinz-Albrecht-Straße* was no place to make women feel comfortable and sexy," said Kitty. "I suggested they reserve a suite of rooms in one of the hotels while they renovate Pension Schmidt. It will put the women more at ease during interviews. Once they are selected, what better place to train them than in a hotel room?"

"Did many apply?" Heidi asked.

"They had about forty candidates. No one had a clue what to do until I got there."

"So, how are they?" I asked.

"Are you asking if they are beautiful or are they talented enough to be spies?" Kitty asked.

"Both," I answered with a wink and a smile.

"As long as I am next to you, ask all the questions you want, Friedrich," Carla said. "The only urge you can satisfy is your curiosity."

We all laughed.

Kitty confirmed the obvious. "As far as looks, they are all beautiful. As for skills needed to interrogate clients, I left that to the Gestapo."

"Knowing Heydrich," I said, "he will probably give each a final test to see if they pass."

"So far Heydrich has stayed away from this part of the project. He's more interested in renovating the townhouse with eavesdropping equipment. I will say this: give me a couple of months and I am sure I will have plenty of stories to tell."

*

May 30, 1938

Monday morning, I looked up from my desk to glimpse General Keitel, chief of the OKW, and commander-in-chief Colonel General Brauchitsch sail toward Hitler's office. Seconds later the telephone dinged; I was summoned to Hitler's office.

When I got there, Keitel said, "*Mein Führer*, here is the latest revision for *Fall Grün*." *Fall Grün*—Case Green—was the code name for the 1937 plan to invade Czechoslovakia. Hitler's eyes grew darker and darker as he read the report out loud. When he finished, he barked at Keitel and Brauchitsch.

"This document talks about war on two fronts. There will *not* be two fronts. We conquer the Czechs first and then turn westward to support the regiments holding off the French. Is that understood!" Then his voice softened. "*Mein Herren*. This is no longer about the Sudetenland. Change the opening of this document to read: it is my unalterable decision to smash Czechoslovakia, so they no longer exist as a country no later than September 28."

He walked toward us until we stood in a tight circle.

"No one else knows this date other than we four, plus Göring, Goebbels, Himmler, and Heydrich." Then he shook each of our hands to seal the secret date.

*

June 13–18, 1938

Pandemonium reigned in the streets as *SS* men went on the attack throughout the city. Nine thousand Berliners were arrested.

I charged into Heydrich's office in *Prinz-Albrecht-Straße* as two *SS* men reported on the mass arrests.

"What is the meaning of this?" I demanded. "The city is in chaos!"

"I am doing what we should have done long ago: arresting the anti-social *Arbeitsscheu*. We can no longer tolerate those who are 'work shy.' Every citizen must contribute to the Reich."

"What will you do with them?"

"How could you ask? They will be sent to concentration camps to learn the meaning of work."

"Why so many Jews?"

"You know how they are," he answered with a tilt of his head

"What I do know is that first the Jews are not allowed to work. Now you arrest them for not working. To make matters worse, you throw them into concentration camps. This makes no sense!"

Heydrich shrugged.

Until now, the Jews had been bullied, intimidated in the streets, randomly beaten, had rocks thrown through their store fronts, suffered repressive laws, humiliated in front of neighbors, had their assets Aryanized . . . but never mass arrests.

There was only one person who could stop this madness.

*

Hitler was at his desk having tea and afternoon cakes.

"*Mein Führer*," I said, "What is the meaning of today's raids?"

He sipped his tea without answering.

"Why?" I asked.

He lowered the teacup. "To put pressure on them."

"Haven't we put enough pressure on them already?"

He took another sip. "Not them," he answered.

"Then who?"

"The countries sending delegates to next month's conference in Évian. I want them to have fresh images of what will happen to the Jews in Germany if these countries do not remove their bars to immigration. The future of German and Austrian Jews is in their hands."

"Couldn't you have issued a declaration about what would happen if they don't open their doors?"

Hitler took a bite of his favorite apple strudel. "When I least expect it, Friedrich, you surprise me. You, of all people, should know that messages don't work. I told the world what I was going to do in speeches as early as 1921. Then, again, in 1922. And every year since. I could not have been clearer in *Mein Kampf* or in our laws and regulations. Each year we increase the pressure on the Jews to leave. Though it disgusts me, we even work alongside the Zionists to help send Jews to Palestine. But the leaders of the so-called civilized countries continue to keep the Jews bottled up here . . . with no thought of taking in more."

"You could have waited. The conference is weeks away."

"What would be the point? The purpose is to make certain the delegates to the Évian conference understand that if they continue to fail to deal with our Jewish problem, we will!"

PART V

PART V

Chapter 49

July 6—July 15, 1938

"I've been to nice places," Carla said, "but nothing compared to this." I basked in Carla's wonderment as she absorbed the hotel's stunning cream façade punctuated by a sea of chocolate brown balconies. From a distance, the Hotel Royal looked like a box of truffles. Tucked on forty-seven acres of magnificence at the southern end of *Genfersee*—Lac Léman in French and Lake Geneva in English—the Hotel Royal was the site of the Évian Conference to begin the following day.

We entered the majestic lobby trailed by a uniformed bellman with our luggage. A multi-tiered, brilliant-lit crystal chandelier illuminated the vaulted lobby. To our right, a white marble circular staircase, accentuated by an elaborate black wrought iron railing, spiraled to the second- floor lounge and restaurants.

Once we were in our suite, I asked Carla, "Will you be okay while I am at the meetings?"

Carla stepped onto the balcony that overlooked the shimmering lake. She whirled around.

"Are you serious? There is so much to do here. I already know I never want to leave."

She ticked off taking pictures and strolling in the rose garden, the azalea garden, and the rhododendron garden; there were centurion trees that begged to be photographed; a fifteen--minute walk to the ancient town loaded with boutiques; and boat rides on the largest fresh-water lake in Europe. If these were not enough, there were mineral baths, deep-tissue massages, and horseback riding.

Carla threw her arms around me. "Thank you for bringing me. I needed this diversion. And Friedrich, you need this, too!"

Carla unbuttoned my shirt.

"Are you doing what I think you are doing?"

"When was the last time we made love in the afternoon?"

"Ask me that question in a couple of hours."

*

July 6, 1938

"How do I look?" I slipped a summer-weight, gray tweed suit jacket over my white shirt, the outfit completed by a blue-and-red-striped tie.

"Will any female journalists be there? Because if they are, tell them they are in trouble if they look at you too long," Carla warned.

"Not to worry. No one holds a candle to you." Partially covered by a robe, Carla leafed through a magazine in bed.

"If you reveal any more, I will be late for the conference," I said.

She turned the page and smiled without looking up. "That's the idea."

*

I was one of two journalists Goebbels documented to represent the Nazi newspaper *Völkischer Beobachter*. The other was a flag-waving, goose-stepping flunky that had finished university three or four years earlier. I let him know that he would be the one to submit articles to the *Völkischer Beobachter*, while I was on a fact-finding mission for the *Führer*.

After presenting my credentials, I explored the conference site. The hotel ballroom was divided into three sections. The most prominent section featured tables connected in a u-shape with a seat for each head of the thirty-two invited countries. The rest of each delegation clustered in chairs behind their respective leader. The remainder of the room was divided with journalists to one side and representatives from thirty-nine Jewish/non-Jewish Relief Organizations to the other.

I spotted an empty seat and excused myself as I shuffled past correspondents from Canada, the United States, and Australia, nicking a toe-tip or two along the way.

"Is this seat taken?" I asked a woman next to the empty seat. She wore a dark gray suit with a cream-colored, collared blouse. *The Nation* was printed on her badge. I recognized her name.

"You're their editor, Freda Kirchwey."

She smiled and then glanced at my lapel identification. The moment my name and the name of my newspaper—the *Völkischer Beobachter*—registered, she moved her pocketbook onto the empty seat. "I know who I am, and this seat is taken."

The same thing happened twice more. Forced to stand, I leaned against the back wall.

When most seats were occupied, a man in his late sixties rose. He wore a dark suit, a white shirt with gold cufflinks, blue tie, and a white square that peeked from his jacket pocket.

Myron C. Taylor had multiple, successful careers. The most recent: retired CEO of U.S. Steel. A friend of Roosevelt's, Taylor was elected president of Évian Conference in a preliminary session by the delegation heads before the official program began. He stood adjusting his wire-rimmed glasses, glanced at his notes, and then tapped the microphone to gain attention. The sea of murmurs quieted.

"It is my honor, as president, to call this Évian Conference to order. On behalf of the directors, I wish to express our gratitude to President Franklin Delano Roosevelt for his desire to devise a 'practical solution' to forced emigration that afflicts significant numbers of political refugees in Europe. It is the president's hope, and ours, that a general 'collaboration' of all parties will produce 'successful results.' Let me put minds at ease: no country is expected to receive a greater number of emigrants than is permitted by its existing legislation."

I could not credit what I just heard. How could this end well?

Taylor called his co-chairmen to make introductory remarks.

Senator Henri Bérenger, the chief French representative, welcomed the delegates and expressed his optimism that the conference would come to a consensus on reasonable and effective measures to resolve the refugee crisis. He was followed by his British counterpart, Lord Winterton, with a similar message. Following the co-chairmen, delegates from The Netherlands, Belgium, Australia, Canada, Argentina, and Brazil extended their greetings. Each expressed sympathy for the plight of present and future European refugees while making it clear that their respective country's immigration rules precluded helping them find a new home.

By the time Taylor rose to speak again, I knew Hitler's prediction was right: nothing positive would result from this conference. And this was the first of ten days!

Taylor motioned for quiet. "This refugee problem could not come at a worse time. The worldwide depression has caused massive unemployment. Strife abounds in many countries, while their ability to feed and care for their own people poses a greater challenge each day. These factors, and more, weigh on all of us as we search for answers to the growing refugee problem. A major goal of this conference will be to create an intergovernmental body that will continue to work on solutions to these problems long after the conference ends."

In other words: you will do nothing now except appoint a committee that will do nothing later.

It was time for lunch. Based on the morning's messages, two fingers of scotch seemed mighty appealing at the moment. Most strikingly, Taylor did not mention the word "Jew" once.

Why? Everyone in the room knew the conference was meant to deal with the hundreds of thousands of German and Austrian Jews being forced from their homeland with nowhere to go.

While I waited for the crowd to pass through the ballroom doors to the lunch area, a hotel security guard approached.

"Monsieur, President Taylor wishes to speak with you. Please follow me."

He turned before I could question him. I followed the guard to a small conference room. Myron Taylor sat in a high-backed chair at the head of a polished, oblong table made from some exotic wood. When he saw me, he extinguished his cigarette.

"Have a seat, *Herr* Richard," Taylor said in a tone just shy of a command. I could have pushed back, but it was his conference and I wanted to hear why he had summoned me. "Why are you here?" asked Taylor.

I fingered my **Journalist** badge. "To report on the conference, of course."

"Let's not mince words, *Herr* Richard. We double-checked. No one with your name is on the staff of the *Völkischer Beobachter*. My sense is that you are here to cause trouble. Sabotage the conference. Perhaps spy for your *Führer*."

"Assume the latter is true. What would be so terrible? The *Führer* has half-a-million reasons to want this conference to succeed. I am to report back to him once it ends." Then I added, "If we are not mincing words, Mr. Taylor, from what I heard this morning, he will be greatly disappointed."

"On the contrary," said Taylor, "the fact that so many are gathered here means the conference is already a success."

I scoffed. "We both know that if these countries do not change their quotas to take in more refugees, this conference will not only be a failure but will validate Hitler's belief that the rest of the world does not care about the Jews any more than Germany does. What struck me this morning was how you went out of your way not to mention the Jews by name. Why not?"

He blanched. "My hands were tied."

"How? You chair the conference."

"President Roosevelt is faced with a hostile Congress and immigration laws that, for now, are immutable. His political priorities must be in tune with what the American people and what his constituents are willing to accept. FDR's charge to me was simple: preside over a conference without making it a 'Jewish' problem . . . and without taking pro-active stances. America, *Herr* Richard, is an isolationist nation that does not want to become involved in European affairs. Especially after the Great War. The best America can do is maximize existing quotas for immigrants leaving Germany and Austria. To date, those quotas have gone unfilled. Beyond that, we cannot do more."

"Where is America's humanitarianism? What happened to the beacon of light that cries out:

Give me your tired, your poor,
Your huddled masses yearning to breathe free, The wretched refuse of your teeming shore.
Send these, the homeless, tempest-tost to me, I lift my lamp beside the golden door!

Taylor turned owl-eyed. "You know the Emma Lazarus poem?"

"By heart! For years I worked on a ship that sailed from Germany to New York. I fell in love with Lady Liberty. I visited Bedloe's Island, more than once. It inspired me to memorize the words to *The New Colossus*."

"And what did you learn from the time you spent in America? From your visits to the Statue of Liberty?"

"I learned the truth. That America is not willing to take in anyone's huddled masses."

Rather than get righteous or pompous—or both—by defending America's self-image, he answered, "We can't house or feed our own. Able-bodied Americans cannot find work after years of searching. Admitting large numbers of refugees would cause turmoil. Resentment. Possibly civil unrest. This Évian Conference, *Herr* Richard, is the best we can do."

"What is crazy, Mr. Taylor, is while the Nazis do not want the Jews, these people are, by and large, educated and industrious. They would be a boon to any country that would have them."

Taylor left me at the table without another word.

*

"How was the first day's meeting?" Carla asked.

"I'd rather hear about your day. Did you take a lot of pictures?"

"Enough that I'll be in the darkroom for days. Tomorrow is a spa day. I've scheduled a facial, a Swedish massage, manicure, and a pedicure. There is something to be said for being spoiled. I could get used to this."

"I am glad one of us is having a good time."

"You could enjoy yourself, too. They have massages for couples. Think of that. Lying side-by-side while the kinks and stresses are worked away. Afterwards, we could snuggle in our plush robes, have a glass of warm brandy, and take a nap. Who knows where that will lead?"

"Nothing would please me more . . . but I am here on a mission."

She burrowed into me, batted her long lashes, and said, "Surely, you will find time for me."

"That *is* my other mission: not to disappoint you," I said.

"That was the right answer."

*

The days droned on. Speakers referred to the Évian Conference as a beacon of light. But no words like "take more in," "change the quotas," "responsibility to fellow humans," "humanitarian cause," or "morally right" were uttered.

At one break, I approached a woman who appeared to be about forty. She wore a simple white blouse under a time-worn dark suit and plain, squared-off black shoes. Her chestnut hair was parted in the center and pulled back in a tight bun that covered her ears like a brown helmet. She was an observer from Palestine.

"What do you think of the conference so far?" I asked.

Trim, her back straight, she shrugged. "It is difficult to sit all day and hear they would all like to take in refugees but can't. It is one of the most terrible experiences of my life. I can only repeat what a colleague said. 'The world seems to be divided into two parts: those places where Jews cannot live and those places where Jews cannot enter.'"

I looked at her name tag as I extended my hand. "Here's hoping for enlightenment."

Golda Meir replied, "From your lips to God's ears."

*

I returned to my seat as the Canadian delegate, Humphrey Hume Wrong, addressed the conferees. "Canada has much sympathy for the impossible situation in which the refugees find themselves, but Canada can do no more than it is already doing. Certain classes of agriculturalists are welcome in Canada. Everyone else is out of luck."

When he mentioned agriculturists, there was a whisper of agreement by South American delegates.

T. W. White, Australia's minister for trade and customs, spoke next. How could Australia, as large as it was, not have room for new settlers? White talked about the years of steady migration from England to Australia and that, as a young country, there was a need for manpower. All encouraging signs.

"However," White continued, "undue privileges cannot be given to one particular class of non-British subjects without injustice to others. We have no real racial problem, and we are not desirous of importing one." Before he took his seat, he added, "I hope the conference will find a solution to this tragic world problem."

So much for Australia.

Senator Henri Bérenger spoke next. As chairman of France's Foreign Affairs Committee and co-chair of the Évian conference, he stated, "France has reached the extreme point of saturation as regards to admission of refugees."

*

Our last night in Évian-les-Bains would be special; I arranged dinner at the romantic seventeenth-century former farmhouse *La Verniaz*. Thousands of aromatic flowers surrounded the terrace, meant to transport diners to a surreal place. They worked.

Carla reached for my hand. "Leave it to you to find the perfect spot."

I raised a glass. "Enhanced by your exquisite beauty. To Carla."

"Listen to you," she gushed. "You have my permission to be like this whenever the mood strikes."

After cocktails were served, Carla asked, "Given that you need to report to Hitler, what are you going to tell him about this conference?"

"I would much rather hear about your horseback riding, sailing lessons, and where else you took photographs."

"I've described everything I've done this week multiple times. You, on the other hand, have barely mentioned your days. Tell me what you've learned from this experience."

"You really want to know? With hundreds of thousands of Jewish refugees in need of a new home, here is the shorthand version. Two nations stated they reached their saturation point for Jewish refugees. Four nations said they would only accept experienced agricultural workers . . . something Jews are not known to be. One would only accept immigrants that have been baptized. Nicaragua, Costa Rica, Honduras, and Panama declared intellectuals and merchants to be undesirable new citizens. That is code for 'never taking in Jews.' Argentina said it has already accommodated enough immigrants from Central Europe. One nation said, point blank, that the influx of Jews would arouse anti-Semitic feelings."

"Are you telling me no country would change their quotas to let in more Jews?"

"One. The Dominican Republic. They would take in up to one hundred thousand Jewish farmers . . . along with a steep price tag."

"You mean they want to be paid to take in refugees?" Carla asked.

"Now can you understand the reason for my mood all week?"

"I understand the words, but I can't comprehend that none will lift a finger to help." Then she added, "Has anyone noted that Évian spelled backwards is naïve? That about sums up the conference, don't you think?"

"It's worse than that, clever girl," I said. "This conference just empowered Hitler to do whatever it takes to rid Germany of Jews."

"How terrible for the world," Carla said.

"How terrible for the Jews," I answered.

*

I dreaded giving Hitler my report on the Évian Conference. When I got to his office, he handed me an article that had already appeared in the *Völkischer Beobachter,* submitted by Goebbels's eager-to-please young journalist.

No One Wants to Have Them
Fruitless Debates at the Jew-Conference in Évian
Évian-les-Bains, France
In accordance with their democratic ideology and
political tendencies, the official statements made
by the representatives of the United States, France
and—to a lesser degree—England, made noises of
moral outrage over the liquidation of the Jewish
problem in Germany. At the same time, however,
England and France were so reserved when it came
to declaring readiness to accept more emigrants, that
the representatives of other states, who did not wish
to speak out at all at the outset, found the courage to
express one after the other their reluctance to permit
new Jewish emigration.
Völkischer Beobachter, North German edition, 13
July, 1938

Hitler asked, "Does this article reflect what happened in Évian, or is Goebbels spinning stories?"

"The conference participants expressed sympathy for the plight of the Jews, but no country altered their quotas."

Hitler poured himself tea. "Would you care for some?" I shook my head. "See? No one wants the usurious Marxist Hebrews. The Évian Conference validated they are a plague on humanity."

"What will you do now?" I asked.

"About the vermin? This conference has left me no choice. Purge them one way or another."

Chapter 50

I made an overdue call.

"I wondered when I would hear from you," said Bernhard Weiss. "The papers . . ." he stopped to cough.

"Are you all right?" I asked, when his coughing eased.

He slurped water before answering. "My wife wants me to see a doctor. I assured her it was dust mites. Nothing more. What I tried to say before I rudely interrupted myself was that our statesmen are breathing sighs of relief now that the Évian Conference has ended. England was never willing to admit large numbers of Jewish refugees. The *other* countries' refusals have given the Brits cover."

"It was sobering to witness this firsthand. Jewish observers did not help themselves by insisting that German Jews should only go to Palestine."

Weiss's reply was smothered by another cough.

"You should listen to your wife. See the doctor."

"Friedrich, you nag the way she does."

"That's what friends do, Bernhard. I called to remind you that Carla and I will be in London in a few weeks."

"I haven't forgotten. I am anxious to meet her."

Then I related Kitty's arrest by the Gestapo and how Canaris secured her release by convincing Heydrich to rewire Pension Schmidt to record what patrons said in private.

Rather than chuckle and toss out a clever remark, Bernhard said, "I have contacts that would be interested in knowing this. The Brits are quite resourceful when it comes to intrigue. There may be something in this for them."

I was not surprised to hear he was in contact with the British Secret Intelligence Service and MI6. I wanted to know more but was late for a meeting.

*

Beck and Oster were already in Admiral Canaris's study when I arrived.

Beck looked up. "Friedrich, perfect timing. I was about to explain to Hans and Wilhelm that I approached key generals to ask if they would tender their resignations—*en masse*—to stop Hitler's invasion of Czechoslovakia. Many considered it. Some agreed. But in the end, not enough committed to move forward with our plan."

"What is their hesitation?" I asked.

"What it has been all along: every soldier is an *Eidträger*. An oath-bearer. They have sworn their loyalty to Hitler and are reluctant to get involved with politics. To do so would be an act of dishonor."

"Don't they realize," said Oster, "how horrendous war would be for Germany?"

Beck shook his head. "They have all experienced the horrors of war firsthand . . . as we have. But Hitler's continued assurance that England will not fight keeps many from siding with us."

Oster threw up his hands. "Apart from England, our people have talked to consuls, undersecretaries—even ambassadors—of other countries to warn them of Hitler's intentions to invade Czechoslovakia . . . all to no avail."

Canaris tapped his pipe on the table to get everyone's attention. "We are going about this the wrong way. Let's think this through. Until now, every German that has approached representatives of foreign governments has done so without suitable endorsements. They go armed with only a cautionary tale of what Germany's elected leader plans to do in the future. What upstanding nation would respond to someone without credentials? That is why our efforts to date have failed. The question, *mein Herren*: is there a German whom the British *would* believe? One we can send with proper endorsements?"

Canaris did not wait for a suggestion. He answered his own question.

"Ewald von Kleist-Schmenzin. He's the right person for this task. Kleist has been fighting the Nazis since the '20s. He has a stellar reputation and will be credible to the English."

Oster frowned. "He's a monarchist. If Kleist had his druthers, he would bring back the Kaiser."

"Are you forgetting the English are monarchists? The English will like that Kleist is an aristocrat. More importantly, they will understand that Kleist loathes Hitler. That he is an unconditional foe of the Nazis."

"Can Kleist get to Chamberlain?" Beck asked.

As Canaris relit his pipe, he tipped his head toward me. "The initiative has already been floated. Tell them, Friedrich."

I explained. "We all know Ian Colvin. His father who just passed was a highly regarded journalist in England. Senior Colvin was the lead writer for the *Morning Post*. Ian grew up in the business and knows the right people. He and I have had several meetings. When I told him that *x-tag* was September 28, he asked me to repeat it three times before he would accept it as true."

"If you are certain," Colvin said to me, "I will reach out to my British contacts. This will change minds that have, to date, been intransient to your fellow countrymen who continue to beseech our help."

"But you haven't answered my question," Beck repeated, "Can Kleist get to Chamberlain?"

"Before I answer that General Beck," I said, "I need to read you excerpts from Colvin's letter." I opened my leather case and retrieved the copy he made for me, knowing it would be needed at this meeting. I read the heading and then selected key paragraphs.

Highly Confidential. The situation in Germany appears as follows. Several military attachés here fear that a coup on Czechoslovakia will occur after the Nuremburg Rallies, which end in mid-September.

I have now learned from a German source in the High Command that September 28 has been chosen and fixed as "*x-tag*," which is the equivalent of "zero day" in British terminology. Only a select few in Hitler's inner circle know about this. The commanding generals have not yet been made aware of this resolution.

As a result of these developments, I ask that you receive a German emissary, a good friend of mine, when he travels to London to find support that Great Britain will intervene. He is a courageous and upright gentleman, though under suspicion by the Nazis. Great pains should be taken to receive his representations for Britain to avert a world war. Once I hear your disposition on this matter, travel arrangements will be forthcoming.

Yours very sincerely,
Ian G. Colvin.

I looked up from the papers. "This letter was sent to Lord Lloyd. At the time, he didn't mention Kleist by name in case the communiqué was intercepted. Lloyd knows who the emissary is now. And with your permission, I will meet with him to make the final arrangements."

"Why Lord Lloyd?" asked Oster. "We need to get to Chamberlain."

"With Lord Lloyd's help we will. Before he wrote this letter, Colvin put feelers out to Chamberlain. The Prime Minister was prepared to receive Kleist out of courtesy until the British Ambassador to Berlin—Nevile Henderson—got wind of it."

"That bastard is a Nazi-lover," explained Admiral Canaris. "If he could, he would be a card-carrying member of the Party. Henderson turned Chamberlain's head against receiving anyone from Germany, even a monarchist like Kleist."

I picked up the thread. "Which is why Colvin contacted Lord Lloyd. Lloyd will set up a meeting between Sir Robert Vansittart and Kleist."

"This goes from bad to worse." Oster smacked his knee out of frustration.

"On the contrary," I answered "Vansittart has been involved in the Foreign Service in one capacity or another since 1902. In 1930, Vansittart became permanent under-secretary in the Foreign Service. A few months ago, he was appointed chief diplomatic advisor to His Majesty's Government. He answers to Halifax and Halifax to Chamberlain. There, *mein Herren*, is your connection. Colvin's entreaties have worked their magic. Vansittart has been quite vocal against appeasing Hitler. He has agreed to receive Kleist."

"I appreciate your efforts," Beck started, "but how could you take it upon yourselves for Colvin to make these inquiries without discussing them with us first?"

Canaris started to answer; I held up my hand. "We're sorry for going around you, but most Brits don't want any part of us . . . if they can help it. Isn't it better to know that we finally made inroads? That Colvin's letter was well-received than not? If it were not for Colvin's valued voice being heard, we would have nothing. No hope. Little chance to succeed. Now we do."

Canaris cleared his throat. "There is one drawback: Kleist doesn't speak a word of English. He is fluent in French. I have no doubt he will manage to get our points across."

"Hearing your reasons, I can appreciate why you made the overture when you did," Beck said, "but we can't risk sending Kleist if he can't speak their language. Every word is critical. We need someone who speaks fluent English."

"Under any other circumstance, Ludwig, I would agree," I said. "But it won't be an issue because in a few weeks Carla has a show of her photographs in London. I have already laid the groundwork with Hitler that I will accompany her." I jerked my thumb at my chest. "*I* will be Kleist's translator."

Canaris filled his pipe. "Then are we in agreement, *mein Herren?* We send Kleist to London, and Friedrich is his translator."

Oster and Beck nodded as Canaris struck a match.

As we turned to leave, Beck cornered me. "Tell Kleist if he brings me certain proof that England will fight should Czechoslovakia be attacked, I will make an end to this regime!"

*

I telephoned Ian Colvin. "It's all arranged. We have been given the green light."

"As soon as our man is able to leave his estate, we can meet in a private room at the Casino Club," Colvin said. "And Friedrich . . . when we do meet, don't wear your uniform. Our guy hates everything Nazi."

"I hope you told him I am not a Nazi."

"He will know."

Some days later, I sailed through the revolving brass doors of the Casino Club into a bustling lunchtime crowd. I asked for Colvin. The host said I was the last guest to arrive. I followed as he zigged and zagged through tables to a warren of rooms meant for privacy.

Colvin and Kleist stood as I entered. To my surprise, there was a young man with them.

"Friedrich," said Ian Colvin, "may I introduce Ewald von Kleist-Schmenzin."

We shook hands. "Baron, it is a pleasure to finally meet you. I have admired you from afar, and heard much about you from Ian."

"Given who you are, *Obergruppenführer* Richard, I take that as a compliment."

While there was no edginess or subtext when using my title and surname, Kleist was not ready to embrace me.

Kleist-Schmenzin's reputation was renowned. He had railed against Hitler and the Nazis ever since the putsch in '23. In 1929, he published a manuscript on the evils of National Socialism. He was erudite. Dignified. Articulate . . . and committed to fight the Nazis. When Hitler came to power, Kleist-Schmenzin refused to fly the Nazi flag above his house. The fact that he remained a free man, albeit under watch, astounded all who knew him.

"Who is this dashing young man?" I asked.

"Allow me to introduce my son, Ewald Kleist-Schmenzin."

The father had a prominent forehead, gaunt features, and a look of perpetual concern. In contrast, young Ewald had a full head of blonde hair, a ready smile, and a twinkle in his pale blue eyes.

"Let me guess. You appear to be about fifteen," I said.

"I turned sixteen last month." Young Ewald puffed out his chest as he answered.

I looked from the boy to the father to Colvin. "Can we talk freely?"

Senior cracked a thin-lipped smile. "Ewald is one of us," explained the father with pride.

Sixteen. One of us.

The lad brushed a lock of blond hair off his forehead. "I have hated the Nazis from the moment I was old enough to understand how evil they are. Ever since they tried to kill my father during the Röhm Putsch, I have hated them even more."

"During the purge, I was in Berlin making certain nothing happened to Papen," I explained to the father. "I didn't know you were on the list. How did you survive the twin terrors: Himmler and Heydrich?"

"A friend hid me in Berlin for two weeks. Once Hitler became *Führer*, rendering me silent was no longer foremost on his mind."

"*Herr* Kleist-Schmenzin, so many of you have the same name. Your cousin was one of the thirteen generals Hitler dismissed in that February bloodbath. How can you be differentiated from each other?" I asked the elder Kleist.

He elaborated. "By our middle names. My full name is Ewald Albert Friedrich Karl Leopold Arnold von Kleist-Schmenzin. My cousin is General Paul Ludwig *Ewald* von Kleist-Schmenzin."

I turned to his son. "And yours?"

"Simpler. I am Ewald-Heinrich von Kleist-Schmenzin."

The father cleared his throat. "On a more serious note, you need to appreciate how hard it was for us to get here. The Nazi district officer in Belgrade informs the Gestapo whenever we leave the estate. Then we bob and weave as needed to meet someone without the Gestapo's knowledge."

"*Herr* Colvin arranged for us to enter through the kitchen door," said young Ewald. "It lessens the chance of being seen by suspicious eyes."

I looked at young Kleist. "You definitely belong here." Then I asked the father, "How did you and Ian meet?"

"Admiral Canaris recruited me early on. I met Ian through him."

"Admiral Canaris made the right choice," I said. "We need your standing and reputation to persuade the British to challenge Hitler. If the Brits step up, Beck will get the support he needs to convert wavering generals."

Kleist frowned.

"What is your concern, Baron?"

"As much as I would like to help, I am not allowed to leave the country."

"The admiral has assigned one of the *Abwehr* lawyers—Fabian von Schlabrendorff—to provide you with documents and make the necessary arrangements for your stay in London."

Kleist smiled for the first time. "I've known Fabian for many years. He's part of this?"

I nodded. "There are many more with us, Baron. What else concerns you?"

"Other than German, I can speak French. No English, I'm afraid."

"You can relax. The admiral already warned me. I will be by your side."

Chapter 51

August 17, 1938

"I don't see him." Carla peered out the window of the seventeen-passenger, trimotor Junker 52 parked at Tempelhof Airport. Its polished corrugated duralumin silver-metal skin glistened in the morning sunlight. "They are about to close the door."

"Canaris assured me that Kleist would have no problem at passport control. Schlabrendorff personally delivered the corresponding documents with his new name to him."

"Maybe the Baron got stuck at currency control," she said.

As she said this, a black sedan screeched to a halt on the tarmac in front of the plane. General Kleist, the Baron's cousin, in dress regalia with medals in full display despite having been forced out of the army, hopped out from the driver's side and opened the passenger door. Kleist emerged, nattily dressed in a steely-colored summer suit.

So far, so good. But I would not breathe normally until Kleist was onboard with the plane door locked.

Kleist took the seat in front of me.

"You made it," I whispered.

Kleist peered out the window and muttered, "Not until we get in the air."

*

The flight to Croydon airfield was uneventful. One hurdle remained: Kleist needed to get through British passport control. We had no general in full uniform to help here. Carla and I queued behind him as British screening proceeded at a snail's pace. I shifted from foot-to-foot. By the time Kleist reached the passport officer, my shirt was stuck to my back. But Kleist was the epitome of calmness as he approached the agent.

A letter poked out from Kleist's passport. The agent surreptitiously took it, read it, studied Kleist's face, handed it back, and stamped his passport.

Safely inside, I asked, "What was in that letter?"

Kleist shrugged. "Oh, that? I could only count on Canaris for so much. Colvin arranged for Lord Lloyd to provide a letter that stated, 'Let the civilian in the gray suit pass without interference.' It always helps to have the right friends," he said, as someone accustomed to privilege. "I only hope this foretells the success we will have for this mission."

Lord Lloyd arranged more than a smooth entry into England for Kleist, his translator, and the translator's photographer girlfriend. He had us stay at the Art Deco hotel—the Park Lane—on Piccadilly that overlooked Green Park.

As Carla unpacked, I asked if she would mind if I spoke with Kleist? Our rooms were next to each other.

"When will you meet Lord Lloyd?" I asked inside Kleist's room.

"This evening. Lloyd reserved a private room at the Claridge's for dinner."

"Shall we go together?" I asked.

He dismissed the offer. "No need. According to Ian, Lord Lloyd speaks fluent French. You and Carla enjoy yourselves. I am sure she has plenty to do before her show begins."

"She is meeting her agent tonight. She'll be happy to hear I can join them. Have you thought about what you will say to Lord Lloyd?"

"Lord Lloyd heads the British Council that is tasked with improving England's image in a host of different countries, especially in the Middle East and the Balkans. Lloyd answers to the foreign secretary, Lord Halifax. There will be no ambiguity on my part. I will tell him that Hitler's plans for mobilization are complete. As you know, the German army commanders have now been given their orders. Zero day is confirmed for September 28. Unless Britain delivers an open warning, nothing will stop this conflagration. Could I be any clearer?"

I agreed. "That is exactly how they need to hear it."

"Precisely. Tomorrow, I want you to join me when I breakfast with Sir Robert Vansittart. Although he speaks German, I need another pair of ears to help determine that he understands every nuance of the message he must give Chamberlain. Don't hesitate to clarify anything. There can be no room for misinterpretation."

"Between your meeting with Lord Lloyd and our meeting tomorrow with Vansittart, the British cannot deny knowing when Hitler plans to go to war."

"We have to do more than convince them," Kleist said, "we must get them to raise their hackles and object in the strongest sense so Beck can carry out the military leaders' plans."

*

"Do you know the story of Restaurant Boulestin?" asked Carla's agent, Kurt Kornfeld, at dinner. Kurt was trim, with brown eyes, a shock of dark hair, and a thin, Hollywood-inspired moustache. Had he been an actor he could have worked as an extra or as a stand-in for Errol Flynn. But as a co-founder of the Black Star Agency, along with fellow ex-Germans Ernest Mayer and Kurt Safranski, Kornfeld was a star in a different world. "The restaurant was opened by Marcel Boulestin eleven years ago. Now it is the most exclusive restaurant in London."

Carla was aglow at the decor. "Circus murals on the walls. Curtains of yellow-patterned brocade. Rich fabrics on the chairs. Wine-colored carpet. Hanging silk balloon lights. This is a fantasy world."

"Which you deserve for your smashing success," said Kornfeld.

"Aren't you getting ahead of yourself?" Carla asked. "The show is not until tomorrow night."

"Oh, but your work has been up in the gallery for days now. The response has been fantastic."

"*Herr* Kornfeld. I . . ."

"Please. Call me Kurt. As for using German, well, I'm an American now. I prefer English."

Kurt and his partners were German Jews who had fled the Nazis three years earlier.

"I understand, Kurt. What I would like to know is how you arranged for Carla to show her work at the Zwemmer Gallery. I did a bit of research. Léger. Miró. Picasso. Zwemmer represents the giants of *avant-garde* painting. Never photography."

"I was waiting for someone to ask. As you know, mid-August is when most Europeans take vacations. Galleries are empty. Most close. Because of what my partners and I have accomplished in New York, Anton Zwemmer indulged me when I called about a fabulous new artist. Once he saw Carla's prints, he understood how dramatic and important they are."

"I'm flattered, Kurt. But still. Friedrich has a point," Carla said. "The Zwemmer gallery?"

"Stop there. My agency, Black Star, provides *Life Magazine* with most of its photographs. Our photojournalists are the best in the world, located wherever there is a story to tell. Robert Capa. Andreas Feininger. Bill Brandt. Henri Cartier-Bresson. The list goes on." He turned to Carla. "You are on par with them. You are that good."

Carla's cheeks reddened.

It was a smashing evening.

Chapter 52

August 18, 1938

Kleist and I met Sir Robert Vansittart in a breakfast nook at the Park Lane Hotel. At fifty-seven, Vansittart remained slim and in fine physical condition. More importantly, he was clear-minded.

After brief introductions, Kleist handed Vansittart letters from Lord Lloyd and Canaris. The admiral's letter explained that Kleist had a time-sensitive message of the utmost importance to deliver from the German military. The letter also introduced me as an interpreter . . . as needed. Lloyd's letter was as expected: he instructed Vansittart to take us quite seriously.

"You are one of the few people in this country to whom I can speak freely about the certainty of war coming," Kleist began. "Hitler intends to invade Czechoslovakia."

"My, you are not one to beat around the bush, are you, Baron Kleist-Schmenzin?" Vansittart said.

I couldn't tell if Vansittart said this out of respect for Kleist being forthright or was displaying skepticism about the message.

"Are you implying that this danger is upon us? That the men around Hitler are determined to attack?" asked Vansittart.

"The extremist is Hitler himself. Not the men around him," replied Kleist. "He has made up his mind to invade Czechoslovakia. The German generals are not behind this. Even his toadies do not support this. The fuse is set, Sir Robert, and we know precisely when the explosion will occur."

Vansittart's tan face grew shades paler. "Are you saying Goebbels and Himmler are not the ones pushing Hitler in this direction?"

"Discount them," answered Kleist. "Czechoslovakia is Hitler's decision and his alone. His belief that England will not fight fuels his resolve to move forward on this."

"Let me give you a better picture," I said, "Hitler announced his plans to invade Czechoslovakia to the military leaders at a special meeting eight months ago."

"How did they react?" asked Vansittart. "Were they in favor of it?"

"On the contrary, the ones against it have been removed from their posts. Others Hitler could not count on have been forced to retire or were transferred to distant posts."

"What about the number two in the Reich? Göring? I presume he was there. Where does he stand?" asked Vansittart.

"Göring would sooner avoid war . . . but even he cannot stop Hitler. Sir Robert, the British government must know, in no uncertain terms, that the majority of the German generals are dead set against invading Czechoslovakia. They believe it will lead to a world war. Worse than the Great War. The generals need your help to stop this insanity."

Vansittart stroked his chin. "When is the absolute last day Hitler can be stopped?"

"*X-tag* is September 28." Kleist answered. "You understand we can't wait until the last possible second if it is to be stopped."

It was vital that the Englishman knew what might await Kleist when he returned to Germany. "You need to know that the Nazis have already imprisoned the Baron three times. He came here with a rope around his neck. If Hitler learns he was in England, he would put him to death. A fate I would also suffer. I implore you on behalf of the officer corps and the German people, please take him seriously."

Kleist squeezed my forearm. "If this were about anything else, Sir Robert, I would ask that you excuse my young friend's exuberance. But he is right. Every day England delays a decision is a day that brings us closer to war. It will be a different kind of war, with faster and stronger and more powerful weapons that the world has never witnessed. Consider this, Sir Robert. More than my life being at stake, think of what it means that the German military leaders are risking their lives—let alone their careers—asking England to take a strong position so that they can put an end to this odious regime. I can't say it more clearly."

Vansittart made no comment. He remained stone-still.

"What will you do to help?" I asked.

His voice was flat. "Write a report." My chest tightened. I felt defeated by his dismal response. "I will give it to Lord Halifax, the foreign secretary, and then make certain Prime Minister Chamberlain sees it."

Is that the best he can do?

Kleist, on the other hand, maintained his equanimity. He ended the meeting saying, "We could not ask for more. Thank you."

Once Vansittart left, I said. "I thought he would show more support. More encouragement. You went easy on him, Baron. Frankly, I am disappointed."

"Don't be. We said what we came to say. Vansittart is a career diplomat trained to write an account exactly as the meeting played out. Give him a couple of days. His report will go through the chain of command and fall on Chamberlain's desk. That is when we will see what sort of backbone the British have."

I left the subject in the hope he had some special insight I didn't have. I asked, "What will you do the rest of the day?"

"I'm drained. Cool my heels until tomorrow's meeting. Will you join me? It's at Chartwell."

"Are you serious? Miss a meeting with Winston Churchill?"

*

I spent part of the day with Carla as she shifted the placement of some photographs before the show opened that night. When I was no longer needed, I made my way to a side street lined with small businesses in inner London. Egerton Road was in an area known as Stamford Hill, five-and-a-half miles from Charing Cross. Number fourteen was a small storefront made to look like a picture frame with glossy, black painted wood that caused the casual eye to track to the gold Gothic lettering centered on the window. I opened the door. A bell jingled.

No one was in sight. I hovered over a glass case that housed samples of expensive paper and a rack of exquisite pens, and then inspected a curio filled with imported leather products.

Feeling eyes behind me, I turned to see the smiling proprietor.

"I was waiting to see how long it would take for you to turn around," said Bernhard Weiss. We embraced. "Let me look at you," He stood back and studied me. "A little gray in the temples. A few wrinkles around the eyes. You look none the worse for wear, my friend. None the worse for wear."

I held onto his arm. I didn't want to let go. "When was the last time *you* were out in the sun? It's August. You look pale."

"That's the vagaries of owning a business. I have no one to help me. My wife is helping refugees the Brits did let in at the synagogue around the corner. Tell me, how goes it back home?"

I brought him up to date about the moving parts of the opposition to the Nazi regime, who was involved, and how much was at stake on Kleist's mission.

I finished by saying, "If Kleist succeeds, General Beck and the military leaders will take down the regime in Berlin . . . and we will be done with this madness."

"My remaining contacts in the department indicate that Police Chief Helldorff will support a military intervention. Many of his police are behind this, too," Weiss added.

Bernhard coughed. He swiped away colored sputum on a well-used handkerchief.

"What did the doctor say?"

"He tapped. Poked. Listened. In the end, he suggested a chest X-ray. I told him next time."

"Bernard, you need to take better care of yourself."

He promised he would. "More to the point," Bernhard continued, "let's pray Vansittart's report jars the PM to his senses. In the meanwhile, what time is Carla's show? I want to meet her," said Bernhard.

"At eight. Don't feel obligated," I said. "It may be too long a day for you."

"I'm determined to be there . . . even if just for a few minutes."

Chapter 53

I returned to the Park Lane Hotel, showered, changed into fresh clothes, and rather than walk to the gallery, hailed a cab so I would be on time. I walked through rooms filled with works by Robert Medley and William Coldstream; Ivon Hitchens, Rodrigo Moynihan, and Ceri Richards; Salvatore Dali and de Chirico. The distant thrum of gallery whispers drew me to an open, well-lit room filled with admirers of Carla's work. I stopped at the entrance, plucked a glass of Champagne from a waiter's silver tray and gazed at her surrounded by a clutch of admirers. I was a lucky man.

"How is Bernhard?" she came over as soon as she noticed me.

"It was good to see him, but I'm worried. He claims it's nothing, but he doesn't look well. Even so, he insists on meeting you." I turned to the room. "This is your moment! I am so proud of you. Look at all these people!"

Carla's face flushed. "One reviewer gave me the greatest compliment. He said that I was the next great female war photographer since Olive Edis. Do you know who she is?" I shook my head. "The British government commissioned her to document the impact of the Great War throughout Europe. The reviewer said my photographs were a portal into the human spirit of survival. Of hope. Of resilience."

I started to say something when she stopped me. "There's more. Kurt had to get back to New York, but guess what?" Her eyes danced with glee. "He asked me to be his agency's photojournalist in Germany. Document what I see. What they accept will most likely end up in *Life Magazine*. Isn't that amazing?"

I thought of the dangerous places this might take her. But I knew to be quiet, for now.

"Carla. I always said that your work was special. I am thrilled that you are being recognized."

At that moment, Bernhard Weiss appeared at the gallery entrance. Sallow and drawn. His wife by his side.

I broke out into a grin. "Carla, may I present my dear friend, Bernhard Weiss, and his wife, Lotte." Lotte and I kissed on both cheeks. The last time I had seen her was in their Prague apartment when I helped Bernhard escape Berlin after Goebbels ordered his arrest.

Bernhard bowed. "It is an honor to meet the woman who captured my friend's heart."

Carla snaked her arm through mine. "I have heard so much about you. It is a pleasure to meet you in person."

"In a way, we've met before. I was once called onto the set at UFA Studios for a small matter. You were filming *Der Hund von Baskerville*," his memory crystal-clear.

"I played the beautiful but disgraced Laura Lyons. Her cheeks were described as 'the dainty pink that lurks at the heart of the Sulphur rose.'"

"You were radiant," said Bernhard, "and now we properly meet. Congratulations on your show."

Carla gave Bernhard and Lotte a tour of her works before they bade us goodnight.

*

The following morning, after reading the smashing reviews of Carla's show, I set out with Kleist to Winston Churchill's country estate—Chartwell—in southeast England. We were ushered to the drawing room. Though announced, Churchill left us standing in the doorway while he continued to put the finishing touches on the canvas in front of him. Finally, he turned to us, cigar jutting out the right side of his mouth. "Mr. Churchill, we have come to speak with you on a grave mission," I said. "Baron Kleist and I . . ."

Churchill put down the paint brush, rested the cigar against the side of an ashtray, and gently tapped the end, waiting for the ash to cleave from its own weight. Satisfied, he lumbered toward us.

"Tea!" he shouted to no one we could see.

In no time, a servant placed tea, scones, and settings for four on a small table followed by a man in his late twenties with a strong chin and a penetrating gaze.

"Gentlemen, may I present my son, Randolph?" After we introduced ourselves, Churchill said, "With your permission, Randolph will take notes."

Kleist wasted no time. "We have followed your speeches and articles urging the British government to take a strong stand against Hitler. The time has come to put a foot on Hitler's neck before it is too late."

"I couldn't agree more. Yet, few seem to listen to me. That's what happens when you are a back bench MP from Epping."

"I beg to differ, Mr. Churchill," I said. "Your voice is important. You should know that anti-war sentiment is spreading across Germany. General Ludwig Beck heads the movement to bring down the regime."

"Quite courageous for a *Wehrmacht* general. What do you need from me?" asked Churchill.

"A letter that says there will be war if Hitler invades Czechoslovakia."

Churchill relit his cigar. Plumes of smoke surrounded him like an early morning fog. "I feel the chill of war approaching in my bones, gentlemen. Your trouble and mine is that my fellow Englishmen do not feel those icy winds. They believe they can reason with your Hitler. That is Chamberlain's view. Halifax is no different. Our ambassador to Berlin, Henderson, is worse. His reports lead us in the wrong direction."

"To your point, we thought Vansittart would have been more enthusiastic when we met with him," I said.

"Van has a notion you might be right, but he is too far down the ladder."

"He did say he would pass our message on to Lord Halifax," Kleist said. "We took him at his word."

Churchill chewed on his cigar. "Oh, he will pass it on all right and Halifax will apprise the prime minister . . . but it won't matter. Gentlemen, there are two reasons you won't succeed. The first is that Chamberlain already knows that the German military leaders oppose Hitler's expansionism. You are not the first from Germany to broach this. The problem you face is that Chamberlain, Halifax—the whole lot of them—may believe your words are both sincere and serious, but they don't know whom you represent. Look at it from their perspective. For all they know, you will replace Hitler with an equally repressive regime, and nothing will have changed but the names on the door. In fact, many in the British government don't like violent regime change. Some go so far as to believe you are treasonous. That's Chamberlain's view. To them, your General Beck and anyone else in this cabal of opposition is considered subversive to an existing nation. For them, the unwritten law is not to meddle in the internal workings of sister countries."

"Mr. Churchill, you must know that is not the case," said Kleist. "I have come at great peril to myself and my family. I expect to be arrested and, perhaps, executed when I return to Berlin. But the risk is worth it if England, the bastion of liberty, will rise to stop this maniac."

"You said there were two reasons we would fail. What is the other?" I asked.

"I didn't use the word fail. I said you will not succeed. Chamberlain and his minions are dedicated to appeasement. *They* fail to comprehend the benefit of threatening war to avert war and are hell-bent to avoid one at any cost. But that begs the answer to your question, doesn't it? The other problem you have is that Chamberlain does not take criticism well. As Dante said, 'A mind sequestered in its own delusions is to reason invincible.'"

I tapped Kleist on his arm and rose. "Thank you for your time, Mr. Churchill. We've taken up too much already."

"Poppycock. Sit down, young man. I will give you the letter you want, though I don't know what good it will do given my present status . . . or lack thereof. Who should it be addressed to?

"General Beck," I answered, grateful he would do this.

He turned to his son. "Randolph, take this down. In case the letter falls into the wrong hands, begin, 'My Dear Sir.'"

My Dear Sir:
I am sure that the crossing of the frontier of Czechoslovakia by German armies or aviation in force will bring about a renewal of the world war. I am as certain as I was at the end of July 1914 that England will march with France and that . . . the spectacle of an armed attack by Germany upon a small neighbour and the bloody fighting that will follow will rouse the whole British Empire and compel the gravest decisions. Do not, I pray you, be misled upon this point. Such a war, once started, would be fought out like the last to the bitter end, and one must consider not what might happen in the first few months, but where we should all be at the end of the third or fourth year.
Evidently, all the nations engaged in the struggle, once started, would fight out for victory or death.

Kleist and I dared not move as words flowed from Churchill. When he finished, he asked, "Randolph, did you get all of it?"

"Every word, Father."

"Bully good. *Herr* Kleist," Churchill said, "I wanted you to hear the sum and substance of this letter. After I review it, you will receive the letter along with a number of copies soon after you return to Germany."

*

Back in Berlin, exhilarated from her gallery showing, Carla wasted no time exploring the city as Black Star's German photojournalist. I used my nervous energy to clear reports that had accumulated as I waited for Churchill's letter to arrive in the diplomatic pouch at the British embassy.

Canaris alerted Frank Foley, a passport control officer in the British Embassy who was aligned with our goals, that when Churchill's letter arrived, he was to notify Fabian von Schlabrendorff. Schlabrendorff, a promising lawyer active in our conspiracy, would deliver the letter to Kleist's estate on the pretext of bringing a belated birthday present for young Ewald-Heinrich.

*

The following day, I met Colvin and Kleist at the Casino Club. Silence greeted me. Kleist handed me a copy of the Churchill letter. It weighed heavy in my hand.

"Well?" I asked as I unfolded it. "What's the verdict?"

"There are nuances and there are nuances," Colvin answered.

"What is that supposed to mean?" I asked.

"After you and the baron left, Vansittart reported to Chamberlain. We all expected he would."

"I take it that Lord Vansittart reached out to you after he did?" I said.

Colvin nodded. "Chamberlain was wishy-washy. He advised Vansittart that, and I quote, 'I think we must discount a good deal of what Kleist says.'"

"There is no surprise there," Kleist said. "Nevile Henderson made certain Chamberlain would not only refuse to see me but would discount anything I might have to said. It is clear to me that no one in London was prepared to make a public stand. Didn't they understand that we were not asking for more than that? We don't need more. Our military leaders were prepared to take care of the rest."

Colvin held up his hand. "Not so fast. Part of your message may have reached Chamberlain. The PM did decide that 'something should be done.'" He jabbed the paper I held in my hand. "As strong-willed as we think Churchill is, this letter was not only vetted by Chamberlain's people, but they made certain Churchill quoted an old Chamberlain speech. That is something, you know."

"How? The British are lost to us," Kleist said. He motioned to a passing waiter. "A round of your best scotch for me and my friends." When we were alone again, he added, "We tried."

"It's not like you to give up, Baron," said Colvin.

"*X-tag* is around the corner. What do you suggest we do?"

"Perhaps the British need to see the military leaders demonstrably move to overthrow the regime," answered Colvin. "Once they do, there is a chance they will jump to support it. It may not be what you hoped for, but it could be enough to turn the tide to your advantage."

*

I left the Casino Club and went straight to Canaris's office with Churchill's letter tucked in my breast pocket. His first words stopped me in my tracks when I entered his office.

"Beck resigned," Canaris said matter-of-factly. I could not credit my ears.

"How could Beck do that? He wanted a letter of support from the British. We got him a letter. From Winston Churchill, no less. What did Beck hope to accomplish by resigning?"

"Beck's goal was to jar more military leaders into opposing Hitler and the regime. Beck came to believe that no matter what Churchill wrote, it would not be enough to tip the balance for those unwilling to commit to our cause. Beck reasoned that if the chief-of-staff resigned, it would be the catalyst needed to rally them all," explained Canaris.

"That's not what happened, is it?" I asked.

Canaris shook his head. "Not a ripple. Hitler is clever. He accepted Beck's resignation on condition that it not be made public until October."

"And Beck accepted that?"

Canaris's voice dropped. "He had already resigned. He could not take it back. That made Beck's plan obsolete."

There was nothing more to say.

"Friedrich, don't look so long in the face. Beck will continue to work for the cause. The good news is that Colonel General Franz Halder will replace Beck. Halder is in our camp."

Halder was no Beck. We had lost the country's greatest soldier.

Canaris flipped open the Cherrywood humidor, tamped in a pipe-full of aromatic tobacco, and then tucked in the loose shards before striking a match. "Is Churchill everything they say he is?"

"If only *he* were the one in power." I sighed. "I came from meeting Kleist and Colvin. Both are clear that Churchill's letter is the only endorsement the British are willing to give . . . and it is not much of an endorsement."

"That concurs with bits of conversations my agents picked up at the British Embassy and, again, from high-ranking Brit officials in posh clubs," Canaris added. "England does not have the stomach to come to the aid of the Czechs."

I reached into my jacket pocket. "Here. For whatever it's worth, is Churchill's letter."

Canaris took the letter and stashed it in the back of his desk drawer.

"You're not going to read it?" I asked.

"Does it matter what Churchill wrote?" he answered. "We're on our own now. Our only alternative is to remove Hitler by force."

Chapter 54

September 1–15, 1938

Hans Oster threw his hands up. We were at the admiral's house to discuss Franz Halder, Beck's replacement as chief-of-staff. "Beck's timing was awful. Why didn't he wait until we were about to march into Czechoslovakia? *That* would have achieved the necessary effect."

"That's no longer an option," I said. "What about Halder? What's your assessment?"

"Halder is on board. He came to see me after he spoke with the admiral last week," Oster said. "Asked about preparations for the *coup d'état*. As the highest-ranking military man under the commander-in-chief, Halder becomes the new, *de facto* leader of our conspiracy. That's not all. Ernst von Weizsäcker, the state secretary of the Foreign Office, has joined our ranks. With those two, we have the top leaders in the Army General Staff and the Foreign Ministry with us."

I pointed to Canaris and Oster. "And you two are the top leaders of the *Abwehr*. With three weeks—more or less—to make this happen, we may yet pull it off."

Canaris did not share our optimism. "We are still missing a key member: Colonel General Brauchitsch, the commander-in-chief. If we have both the army's commander-in-chief *and* the chief-of-staff, then we have the two highest-ranked soldiers in Germany with us."

"Hitler sealed Brauchitsch in his back pocket when he bailed him out of a sad marriage," I explained. "Brauchitsch is a bought man."

"I'm not ready to give up on Brauchitsch," Oster said. "What might work for us, in the end, is that Brauchitsch is not a die-hard Nazi. You all know Erich Kordt. He's in charge of the Foreign Service under Ribbentrop. More importantly, he is Brauchitsch's friend. Erich tried to convince Brauchitsch to commit to us."

"Did he make any headway?" I asked.

"Brauchitsch didn't lean one way or the other. He listened . . . which offers a ray of hope," explained Oster. "When Erich left Brauchitsch, he said, 'In your hands, *Herr* General, lies the destiny of the German Army and thus the destiny of the German people.'"

"That should move him," I said.

"If only it would," shrugged Oster.

*

"I got my first assignment from the agency," Carla said when I returned from Canaris's house. Then her gaze dropped. "You may not approve."

"I'm your biggest fan." I poured two scotches; we sat on the couch. "What's the assignment?"

"They want me to go to Nuremberg. To document the rally. They expect close to a half-million people this year."

The Nuremberg rally had been held annually since the twenties. It was a week-long propaganda-fest orchestrated by Goebbels to extol the Nazi Party and Hitler. I gave a feeble excuse why I couldn't attend. The real reason—that I was too busy trying to overthrow the government—would not have been well-received.

"Will you be there the entire time?"

She put the drink down and wrapped her arms around my neck. "Would you miss me?"

We kissed longer than a peck.

"I like your answer," she said. "They do want me to document it from beginning to end. Will you mind?"

"Of course, I'll miss you. But this is good for your career. Don't worry about me. I will find things to keep me busy."

"Volunteering to help Kitty train those *SS* whores *cannot* be on your list. Are we clear about that? How is that going, by the way?"

"The career girls are having fun with this. The new ones, the few that qualified from Heydrich's ad, well, Kitty says there have been more than a few awkward moments."

"How awkward?" Carla asked.

"Very," was all I would say.

*

Halder knew time was running out. He arranged successive meetings with key members of the government and with the local Berlin army commander.

Hjalmar Schacht was first on the agenda. Until recently, Schacht had been the minister of economics as well as the president of the Reichsbank. Hitler dismissed Schacht from his ministerial position due to his continued criticism of Germany's rearmament and of Göring's failed Four-Year Plan. But Hitler understood that Schacht was a financial genius and retained him as head of Germany's central bank—the Reichsbank. Our group had a much larger position planned for him.

We were seated in Canaris's study. "Let me be blunt," General Halder said to Schacht. "If Hitler pursues this course of war, his regime will be overthrown. It cannot be avoided. Should this occur, are you prepared to take over the administration?"

Schacht was sixty-one. He parted his still-light brown hair in the middle. His graying sides and frameless glasses perched on the bridge of his nose without side temples to rest on his ears did much to create a professorial air. A three-piece suit, white shirt with wide stripes, and a gold collar-pin that propped up his knitted tie's knot, completed the image.

Schacht remained expressionless. Not even a blink of an eye. For a moment, I thought he did not hear Halder's offer.

"Let us be clear," Schacht finally said. "You are asking me to head the new government?"

Halder confirmed it.

"I accept."

*

Next, Halder, Oster, Canaris, and I met with General Erwin von Witzleben, who commanded the Berlin troops. The insurrection could not succeed without the area's military commander or his troops that would be needed to quell the fanatically loyal *SS* and the diehard Nazis. We learned that lesson from the Kapp Putsch that failed without the army's help, as did our own Beer Hall Putsch. Witzleben had been sick when we planned our first attempt. He was well now and committed to us.

There was no way to describe him other than he looked like a hawk about to swoop down on unsuspecting prey. His thinning hair was combed to the side and gelled in place to partially obscure a receding hairline. He had arching brows that did not extend the full length of his eyes, making him appear even more formidable. And the only other remarkable structure on his gaunt face was his narrow, pointed nose designed to sniff out the enemy.

General Witzleben took over. He was our fiercest warrior. I was glad he was on our side.

"For this to work," Witzleben said, "it is imperative to isolate key points in Berlin that must be identified and occupied. We must control access routes to the city and be clear about how we will take over the Chancellery building. The key Nazis must be neutralized."

"Could you be more specific?" Halder asked.

"Of course," answered Witzleben. "Count Brockdorff-Ahlefeldt commands the 23rd Infantry Division Potsdam garrison. He will support my troops in Berlin. General Hoepner commands the Third Panzer Division and will block any attempt by the *SS Leibstandarte* to leave Munich. And lastly, Count Fritz von der Schulenburg will secure the government sector of Berlin. The troops will occupy Gestapo Headquarters and arrest Himmler and Heydrich, and any upper echelon *SS* they find there. Simultaneously, we will take over all means of communication and arrest key Party leaders. President Helldorff, the chief of police, is with us and has placed his forces at our disposal."

"That leaves Hitler," I said.

"A special detail will surround the Chancellery and make certain no one escapes," Halder said.

"When we confront Hitler," Witzleben said. "I will demand that he dismiss the top SS leaders . . . which I expect he will refuse to do. When he does, we kidnap him and keep him hidden in a place known only to the opposition leaders."

"Then what?" I asked. "We are talking about Adolf Hitler. The eyes of the world will be watching every move we make. Arresting him is the first step. What do we do next?"

"We issue reports in those first hours revealing the crimes of the regime and proclaiming to the German people that Hitler is intent on dragging us into a World War," answered Witzleben.

"We have Dohnanyi's files," Oster said. "They are critical to proving our case against Hitler."

For the last four years, Hans von Dohnanyi had recorded—chapter and verse—the countless crimes committed by the Nazis.

Canaris cleared his throat. "General, you have presented your plans in a thoughtful, succinct manner. Now that Hans has brought up the Dohnanyi files . . ."

Canaris rang a bell meant for a butler. Moments later the door opened and Erika Canaris ushered in Dohnanyi and Werner Schrader.

Only thirty-six years old and an immensely talented lawyer, Dohnani had been transferred from the ministry of justice where he'd been Franz Gurtner's most trusted aide to Leipzig, where he was currently a Supreme Court judge. Once he became aware of the fabricated charges against Colonel General Fritsch, it fell to Dohnanyi to document the untold lawless crimes that Hitler and the Nazis committed. Thin lipped, with a full head of hair and wearing wireless glasses, Dohnanyi had the air of an always-serious professor.

After we greeted each other and everyone was seated, the admiral said, "I want to thank Hans and Werner for waiting patiently for us." Then he explained, "Not only does Hans have papers critical to trying Hitler in court, but Werner does as well."

"I have kept records of every illegal Nazi action in Vienna. They will be available when needed," Schrader added.

Unlike any of us, Werner Schrader had been incarcerated and beaten in a concentration camp soon after Hitler came to power for speaking against the excesses of the Brown-shirted Storm Troopers. He escaped from the concentration camp and was able to enlist in the *Wehrmacht* until his past was discovered. Canaris rescued Schrader before he could be rearrested and installed him in the *Abwehr*, posting him first in Munich and then in Vienna. Pudgy with jowls, Werner Schrader had wavy hair, was clear-eyed, and well-liked by all.

"With Hans's and Werner's accounting of the myriad Nazi transgressions, we can feel confident about a trial," Halder said.

"It won't be just any trial," Canaris said. "That's why Hans and Werner are here. I have papers in my possession that document Hitler's mental instability. I have entrusted them to Werner along with my diaries that I began years ago and continue to this day." He turned to Dohnanyi. "Hans, please explain the rest."

In his quiet voice, Dohnanyi said, "Some of you know I am married to Christine Bonhoeffer."

"Pastor Bonhoeffer's sister," I added.

Dohnanyi nodded. "Dietrich Bonhoeffer, my brother-in-law, along with Martin Niemöller and other clergy, founded the Confessing Church to oppose the Nazis efforts to unify all Protestant churches into a single, pro-Nazi Evangelical Church."

"Before you go further," Canaris said, "Let the others understand why the clergy have banded together."

"Of course, admiral. As you all know, Christian beliefs forbid the traditional instruments of rebellion: terror, violence, brutality, and, of course, fomenting anarchy. So besides being a counterweight to the evils of Nazism, these religious men have become a conduit to the rest of the world about the evils we suffer," explained Dohnanyi. "But the critical point here is that along with Wilhelm's secret material, I have compiled a description of every known illness Hitler has suffered including reports from military doctors regarding his sanity. I am bringing it to my father-in-law, Dr. Karl Bonhoeffer, who is the most noted neurologist in Germany. Our hope is that after he reviews these documents, he will declare that Hitler is insane. We could introduce that in court."

"I've heard enough." All eyes shifted to General Witzleben. "Should Hitler live, no matter what you declare his state of mind to be, he will be revered. Let's not fool ourselves. Hitler has carefully crafted his image as Germany's savior to the point that he is admired around the world. Keep in mind, the German people are unaware of his plans to go to war. They are unfamiliar with most of the regime's crimes. He must not survive."

I kept quiet. My mind was in conflict.

I know he should not survive. But . . . after all these years . . . how can I sanction assassinating Wolf? Even Napoléon was only exiled.

Halder jumped up as a heated discussion erupted. "What we do with Hitler does not have to be decided at this moment. We have everything in place to take down the regime. Do not lose sight of the fact that without a clear and immediate danger to the Fatherland, we will be committing acts of treason in the minds of young officers who swore their allegiance to the *Führer*. We *must* wait until Hitler gives the order to march into the Sudetenland."

I frowned.

"What's wrong, Friedrich?"

"General, your plan. The window of time is too narrow between Hitler's order to march and our ability to stop him."

"I've stayed up nights thinking about that," Halder answered. "Hitler's orders to invade must come through me. I have told him—and he has accepted—that once issued, we need forty-eight to seventy-two hours to get the army in place. I have built our opportunity into those orders. That's when we take down the regime."

Oster cautioned. "Let's not forget that Hitler must be in Berlin when we seize him. He's still at the Nuremberg rally."

"That ends September 12," I said. "That gives us two weeks and two days."

Halder looked from man-to-man. "September 28 must never happen."

Chapter 55

While I waited for Carla to return from Nuremberg, I read in the morning paper that Hitler, exhausted from the annual rally, traveled to Berchtesgaden to rest. The subtext known to me—and a few others—was that he wanted to spend time with Eva Braun. Unfortunately, that put our coup on hold.

"Welcome home," I said as the door swung shut.

Carla dropped her bags and ran to me. "I didn't expect you would be home this time of day. Is anything wrong?"

"Now that you are here, no." I answered.

I leaned to kiss her; she jerked back.

"What's wrong?" I asked.

"It's just that I have so much to tell you. I could not believe the pageantry. Cecil B. DeMille could not have planned it any better . . . or made it more spectacular."

"It was that good?" I asked with a raised brow.

"Better."

"What was the theme this year? Last year, it was a *Rally of Labor.* The year before, a *Rally of Honor.*"

"After the *Anschluss,*" answered Carla, "what else could it be? *A Rally of Greater Germany.* But the drama. The homage to the fallen heroes. I took so many pictures. I can't wait to send the best ones to my agency."

Though a bit too early in the day, I poured us both a scotch and sat back as Carla shared her experiences at the Party rally. The more she spoke, the more I became concerned.

"One day, there were fifty thousand girls in the youth corps dressed in white, from head to toe. They formed concentric circles that expanded and contracted on the *Zeppelinwiese.* Then, with spectacular fluidity, they transformed into kaleidoscopic images that gave the illusion of floating angels. Did you know why they call the field *Zeppelinwiese?* Because Zeppelin landed his airship there thirty years ago."

"I've heard," I said dryly. "Anything else impress you?"

"Forty thousand German male workers, two thousand female workers, and one thousand workers from Ostmark, marched past the *Führer* and renewed their oath to serve him and Greater Germany. That was something to see. Oh, and the labor corps! They marched in brilliant precision, with polished swords held off their shoulders. And the most unbelievable sight occurred when the lines of marchers turned right, in unison, as if they were one person. When they did, the sun glinted off their sabers like a thousand suns exploding. It was blinding. I was in awe that they worked the details of the march down to that exact second where the sun needed to be. Then there was Hitler's speech to the assemblage, with the Cathedral of Light as the backdrop, creating an aura about him. It was mystical. It made him appear godlike."

I found it difficult to speak. "From the sound of it, you had a religious conversion."

"Anything but. Hitler has tried his very best to make Nazism Germany's only religion, and he its god. Goebbels is a genius creating those images and working his magic. But that's just it, Friedrich, it's smoke and mirrors. Most Germans don't buy that nonsense. Admittedly, the spectacle lifts deflated spirits. It gives hope to the disenfranchised." She grabbed my hand. "You have nothing to worry about me becoming a flag-waving Nazi. No matter how he is portrayed, Hitler will always be the Devil to me."

Thank God!

"What did you do while I was away?" asked Carla.

"I kept busy." I shrugged. "Paperwork. Things like that."

"In that case, enough talk. We have *other* catching up to do."

*

What the participants were not focused on during the pomp and pageantry at Nuremburg was Hitler's fiery denunciation of Czech abuses against German-speaking Sudetenlanders. His vituperations triggered riots that necessitated the Czechs declare martial law.

The following day, Hitler ordered Halder to mobilize the German Army.

Our time was at hand.

There was one more step we had to take to finalize our plans.

*

The following morning, Beck, Oster, Witzleben, and I met in Canaris's office. "

"We need a driver we can trust," I said by way of a preamble. "Someone who will keep their eyes open and their mouth shut as they drive us to high priority sites in and around Berlin."

"It should be a woman," Oster added.

"Why female?" asked Canaris.

"To make it appear casual. As if we are sightseeing. We need to identify marshalling points for our troops. Buildings to serve as detention centers for the SS, the Gestapo, and any military that try to resist. A woman gives us the cover we need," Oster explained.

"Friedrich. Heidi would be perfect. Shall I call her in?" Canaris asked.

"No. No. No. No matter how innocent this car ride is supposed to look, it is still fraught with danger. I cannot take that risk with Heidi. If anything happened to her, I could never forgive myself. It must be someone else."

Canaris started to say something when Hans Dohnanyi was announced.

"Not to worry. I will find you a driver," said Canaris. "I am glad you will hear what Hans has to say." After we greeted Hans and he took a seat, Canaris wasted no time. "Well? How did Dr. Bonhoeffer view the medical records?"

"There was no doubt in Dr. Bonhoeffer's mind," explained Dohnanyi, "Hitler is not sane."

"But?" said Canaris, ever the skeptic.

"He can't proclaim Hitler insane without examining him. He says it's an ethical requirement."

"But if he says he's not sane," said Oster, "isn't that just as good as being insane?"

"It's not," answered Dohnanyi. "My father-in-law will make no diagnosis without an examination!"

*

The next day, I was the first to arrive at the Potsdamer *Bahnhof.* Oster and Witzleben arrived next. We were dressed as country bumpkins for a day of sightseeing in the big city.

I glanced at my watch. "Beck is late."

"A last-minute change," Oster announced. "Canaris arranged for Beck to meet former Chancellor Joseph Wirth in a Basle hotel. Wirth is bringing a high-ranking French diplomat with him."

"Beck's wasting his time. The French will do nothing," I said.

"Until Hitler issues the final orders to invade Czechoslovakia, we have to explore every possible option to stop this madness . . . no matter how remote the chance," Oster replied. "To that end, Halder sent a former Reichstag deputy to the American Embassy in Berlin to ask them to encourage the French and British to be firm with Hitler."

As he said that, a large touring car driven by a middle-aged woman rolled up. After she identified herself, Witzleben took the front seat. He drew his cap down; Oster and I slouched in the back.

"Where to first?" the driver asked.

"Let's start with the government buildings on *Wilhelmstraße*," answered Witzleben. "Then Carinhall, where Göring lives. After that, the *SS* barracks at *Lichterfelde* and the *Königs Wusterhausen* radio station."

As we drove, I asked General Witzleben, "Which group will be tasked to take over the Chancellery?"

"I have a handpicked commando party of sixty men, ready to raid on a moment's notice. Oster and I agreed that they need to be a cross-section of Germans, not all soldiers. We do have young officers, but also students and expert workmen so this will not come off as a military putsch. Everyone will see normalcy restored by a cross-section of anti-Nazis," Witzleben explained.

"Who is leading the group?" I asked.

"Friedrich Wilhelm Heinz," answered Witzleben. "He was my adjutant for years until he joined the *Abwehr*."

"I've also assigned Helmuth Groscurth to shadow Halder. We can't afford Halder to get cold feet at the last moment," explained Oster.

"Is that necessary?" I asked.

Oster answered with a question. "Would you leave anything to chance at this late moment?"

Witzleben turned around. "Tell me, Friedrich, what sort of resistance can the men expect when they enter the Chancellery?"

"Thirty-nine *SS* men are assigned to guard the Chancellery. They work in three shifts. At any given time, there are no more than fifteen in the building."

"Perfect," said Witzleben. "I want to make one thing clear: I arrest Hitler. No one takes that from me."

*

The next day, Hitler ordered German troops to mass at the Czech border.

X-tag was about to occur.

The conspirators were alerted.

Our generals readied their men.

Weapons were distributed.

Helldorff's police took their positions.

Halder met with Brauchitsch, the commander-in-chief of the army, in a last-ditched effort to sway him to our side.

Brauchitsch leaned toward joining us.

It was midday, September 28.

Brauchitsch went to the Chancellery to confirm that the orders to attack Czechoslovakia were about to be given.

Witzleben waited by the phone for confirmation.

The call would launch the coup.

The call never came.

Mussolini had intervened and offered to mediate with the Czech situation at the last moment.

We had to temporarily stand down.

The following day, Chamberlain, Mussolini, Daladier, and Hitler met in Hitler's Munich apartment. No Czech was invited. There, seated on the couch in Hitler's living room, the British prime minister capitulated to the *Führer's* ultimatums. The Sudetenland would become part of Greater Germany; the Czechs would leave the area immediately; and the Hungarians and Poles would get their respective slices of the hybrid country born of the Treaty of Versailles that was less than twenty years old.

A triumphant Chamberlain left Munich clutching the agreement. When he landed in England, he waved the "Munich Agreement" with Hitler's signature in the air, proclaiming to the people of England and Europe, "I believe it is peace for our time."

At that moment, Hitler's prestige and person became untouchable.

He was catapulted beyond our reach.

There was no alternative.

We pulled the plug on our conspiracy.

*

As German troops moved into the partitioned Czechoslovakia, I met with Oster, Beck, Witzleben, Schlabrendorff, and Dohnanyi at the admiral's house.

"What I don't understand," said Schlabrendorff, "was how a god-fearing country like England lacks the backbone to stand up to this false god?"

"More to the point," I said, "all Chamberlain had to do was to declare that if Hitler took one step into Czechoslovakia, England would go to war. If he did that, England would not have had to mobilize, and we would have taken the tyrant down."

At that moment, his dachshunds, Seppel and Sabine, nosed their way into the room. Canaris lifted both on his lap before he continued. "The one contingency we didn't account for, the one no one dreamt of, was that Chamberlain was so determined to shine with his personal diplomacy that he lost all perspective of what he was doing. Rather than 'peace for our time,' Chamberlain has made another great war inevitable."

"Let me end this meeting on a positive note," said Witzleben. "We've been derailed. But nothing has gone to waste. We are yet unknown to Hitler. We are intact. We will prepare for next time."

Fabian von Schlabrendorff raised his hand as though swearing an oath. "I will do everything in my power to keep our plans alive. No matter what it takes."

While I did not doubt the spirit of my colleagues, in my heart I knew there was nothing more we could do to stop Hitler, who just added another triumph to his list. His standing among the German people was near mythical.

He was now beyond our reach.

*

October 6, 1938

"Did you read Winston Churchill's speech in Parliament yesterday?" Carla peered over the top of the morning paper.

"Read me what he said."

Carla mumbled over words as she read the most powerful parts:

I will begin by saying what everybody would like to ignore or forget, but which must nevertheless be stated;

namely that we have sustained a total and unmitigated defeat . . . we have sustained a defeat without war . . . The utmost my right honourable friend, the Prime Minister, has been able to secure, by all his immense exertions, for Czechoslovakia in the matters which were in dispute, has been that the German dictator, instead of snatching the victuals from the table, has been content to have them served to him course by course.

Carla's lips moved, uttering an intelligible word or two until she said, "The last two paragraphs. Listen."

They should know that we have passed an awful milestone in our history, when the whole equilibrium of Europe has been deranged, and that the terrible words have, for the time being, been pronounced against the Western democracies. 'Thou art weighed in the balance and found wanting.' And do not suppose that this is the end.

This is only the beginning. This is only the first sip, the first foretaste of a bitter cup which will be proffered to us year by year unless, by a supreme recovery of moral health and martial vigour, we arise again and take our stand for freedom as in the olden time.

"Do you know where the phrase, 'Thou art weighed in the balance and found wanting' comes from?" I asked.

"Would it surprise you that I know the answer? One thing I never told you," Carla said, "is that I went to Bible school on Sundays. It comes from Daniel 5, when the Jews were captive in Babylon and mysterious handwriting appeared on the wall which foretold that the king and his kingdom would fall. Is Churchill that clairvoyant?"

"No," I said. "He's that smart. That objective. And, above all else, has been the only one in the British government who sees the handwriting on the wall."

PART VI

PART VI

Chapter 56

October 1938

I arrived at the US Embassy on *Bendlerstraße* filled with dread. Nothing bored me more, these days, than a cadre of diplomats and business leaders squawking about the state of world affairs. But the *Führer* insisted I attend this event. Hitler assumed I would want to meet Charles Lindbergh, the guest of honor, since I had been to America many times.

I climbed the stairs to the second floor of the three-story building. Guests milled about: ambassadors; German officers; airplane designers Drs. Ernst Heinkel and Willy Messerschmitt; assorted naval officers and members of the American delegation. Two round tables, large enough to accommodate every guest, were off to the right.

There was no formal reception line. I sidled up to the youthful man with the famous toothy smile, who, though tall, was shorter than I. In sharp contrast, his petite wife stood next to him. She could not have been more than five feet tall.

After I introduced myself, I said, "Welcome to Germany, Colonel Lindbergh. There are rumors that you and Mrs. Lindbergh plan to move to Berlin."

Mrs. Lindbergh replied, "I looked at a lovely house in the Wannsee district this morning while the colonel toured the airplane factories. Do you happen to . . . ."

Anne Morrow Lindbergh did not get to finish her sentence as the air was sucked out of the room when Hermann Göring strode in, wearing a new blue tunic of his own design. He shook everyone's hand before stopping in front of the guest of honor with a red box and a scroll clasped in his left hand.

Göring called for everyone's attention. After we gathered around him and the Lindberghs, he announced in his booming voice, "By order of the *Führer*, as previously awarded to

Generalissimo Francisco Franco and other international notables, it is my honor to present to you, *Herr* Lindbergh, the Service Cross of the Order of the German Eagle."

Applause and congratulations erupted around the room.

Göring handed Lindbergh two identical medals. One, full-sized, housed in a red felt-lined leather case. The other, more diminutive, dangled at the end of a silk ribbon that Göring clumsily pinned to Lindbergh's jacket. The medal was a Maltese cross surrounded by four eagles with a swastika embedded into the birds' talons. After another round of applause, we adjourned for dinner. Göring sat at the head of one table and Lindbergh at the other. I sat with the Lindberghs.

Lindbergh drew my attention. "Is it true, *Obergruppenführer* Richard, that . . ."

"Please call me Friedrich."

"Friedrich it is. But I do like the sound of *Obergruppenführer*. Friedrich, is it true that Jewish men must now take Israel—and the women, Sarah—for middle names?" Not waiting for me to confirm what he already knew, he continued, "I've learned, starting this month, that Jews can no longer own businesses, and Jewish lawyers can no longer practice their profession. If you ask me, Roosevelt should embrace these laws. It is widely accepted that Jews are the cause of our social ills in America. That's one reason Anne and I want to move here."

I scrupulously avoided the man by alternatively forking a steady stream of food into my mouth or making small talk with the dinner partner next to me. But it was impossible to dodge Lindbergh for the entire dinner.

I cringed when he uttered my name. "Friedrich, after my tour of your airplane factories, I can only conclude that America could not win a war against Germany."

The rest of the night was a blur. I couldn't wait to get away.

When I got home Carla asked, "Did I miss anything?"

"The only thing you missed was how a first-class jackass looks and sounds."

*

Two mornings after the Lindbergh dinner, as we had breakfast, Carla pointed to an article in the paper. "I can't believe Heydrich ordered the arrest of Polish Jews living in Germany. This is horrible. They've been here for years!" She handed me the paper.

I read it. "Heydrich is retaliating against Poland's new law that revoked the passports of their Jews who have lived in Germany for five or more years. They don't want them back. Ever."

"It says here thousands of Jews were taken from their homes with time to only pack one suitcase. They were shipped to the Polish border," said Carla. "The Poles won't let them in, and the Germans won't take them back. They are in the worst kind of limbo: stateless."

I tossed the paper down. "Over the years, fifty thousand Polish Jews came here seeking a better life. They never gave up their Polish citizenship and now their homeland will never take them back. The Munich Agreement dumped another twenty-five thousand Sudeten Jews in our laps. Each Hitler triumph has brought more and more Jews. Heydrich is simply unable to follow orders to remove all the Jews from Germany. The pressure is building . . . and building."

"Those poor people," Carla said. "How is this going to end?"

*

November 7, 1938

Carla and I arrived at *Hotel Vier Jahreszeiten* in Munich with a busy schedule planned. Tuesday, we were to tour the newly-built, neoclassical *Haus der Deutschen Kunst*—The House of German Art—that had selected four of Carla's photographs for display. This was a great honor. Wednesday, I planned to attend the fifteenth anniversary of the Beer Hall Putsch while Carla visited Ludwig.

As we registered at the hotel, a newspaper headline caught my eye.

Deutscher Gesandter in Paris von Juden erschossen

"Did you see this?" I pointed to the paper. "Some crazed, young Jew—Herschel Grynszpan—shot a German diplomat in Paris."

"Did he survive?" Carla asked.

I scanned the article. "He was sent for surgery. Nothing about his condition. The strange thing is that the shooter made no effort to escape. He waited for the police to arrest him."

"Why did he do it?" Carla asked.

"No motive is given."

"Maybe it was his way of committing suicide," she answered.

"Then point the gun at your own head. No need to shoot a German diplomat."

But something didn't ring true; I needed to know more. While Carla unpacked our clothes, I called a trusted member of our conspiracy, Erich Kordt in the Foreign Office in Berlin.

"You are the third one to call about this shooting."

"What can you tell me?"

"Are you calling from a secure phone?"

"The lobby of the *Hotel Vier Jahreszeiten* in Munich."

"Understood." Kordt took a deep breath. "The envoy's name is Ernst vom Rath. A third-level secretary at the Embassy. Rath had the misfortune of being available to see a young man who claimed to have documents he needed to deliver. When Rath asked about the documents, Grynszpan yelled out, 'You're a filthy Kraut. In the name of twelve thousand persecuted Jews, here is your document.' Then he brought out his gun and fired five times. Considering they were two feet apart, it's a miracle that only two bullets found their mark. Rath managed to crawl to the hallway for help and was rushed to Clinique de l'Alma, a nearby women's hospital. The sad part is that Rath's sympathies are with us. He is anti-Nazi through and through."

"Why did Grynszpan do such a thing?"

"His parents are among those Polish Jews stranded at the border."

"What is the official government response?" I asked.

"For the moment? Nothing. No comment. Rest assured when they do issue a statement, it will be measured against whether Rath lives or dies."

By the time I returned to the room, Carla had unpacked both bags. "You were gone quite a while."

"I caught up on the details from Paris. It was a lone shooter. Not part of a plot. Nothing to be concerned about." I rubbed my hands together. "How about a fancy dinner in the hotel tonight? I can't wait to see your work hanging in the museum tomorrow."

She grinned. "That makes two of us."

*

November 8, 1938

Carla posed for a picture in front of her photos. Later, as we stood in the lobby of the *Haus der Deutschen Kunst*, I said, "You must be so proud."

"I hate to admit that Goebbels did a good job assembling so many outstanding German artists under one roof." Carla lowered her eyes. "I was fortunate to be included. Is there any news about the Paris legation secretary? Did he make it?"

There was a phone off to the side. Erich Kordt reported that Rath was sitting up and was relatively comfortable. However, a bullet was lodged in a hard-to-reach place and required a second procedure to remove it. Kordt ended on a dire note.

"Dr. Amédée Baumgartner, the treating surgeon, discovered that Rath has advanced tubercular lesions in his stomach and intestines. Even if the second bullet is successfully removed,

Rath's days are numbered. Friedrich, you will never guess who is with Rath as we speak? Dr. Karl Brandt."

Karl Brandt was an accomplished physician specializing in head and spinal surgeries. While Hitler kept Dr. Morrell around for his voodoo medicine, Brandt was also part of Hitler's entourage. Despite his qualifications, I disliked Brandt because of the ease with which he performed countless "necessary" medical abortions on women deemed to have genetic disorders.

I learned later that when Brandt reported to Berlin that Rath could survive the second operation but would die from the tuberculosis, Hitler directed him to ask the French medical staff to leave the bullet in. "They are not to make mention of this," Hitler said. "For propaganda purposes, it is more useful to have Rath die from his wounds than prolong his life only to have him die afterwards from a dreaded disease."

The next day, Rath died.

Chapter 57

November 9, 1938

It was late morning. I hurried back to the hotel, praying Carla had not yet left to visit her brother.

I stormed into the room. "I need to return to Berlin."

"Where's the fire? Why are you out of breath?" I was panting hard. "How can you leave the meeting early?"

"It's probably okay to see Ludwig today," I managed to spit out.

"Friedrich, slow down. You are talking too fast. Why did you say that it was *probably* okay to see Ludwig? What's wrong?"

I drew in a deep breath and exhaled a slow stream of air. "I was with Hitler when he learned that that German diplomat died. He pulled Goebbels and Heydrich aside and told them that Rath's murder was part of a Jewish conspiracy. That the Jews needed to pay. Then Hitler left."

"What do you mean? Hitler left the meeting?"

"It's vintage Hitler. Don't you see? Ever since the Évian Conference, Hitler wanted an excuse to unleash violence against the Jews."

"Why not pack them up and ship them out the way they sent the Polish Jews to the border?" Carla asked.

"There is nowhere to send them. No one will take them. Évian settled that."

Carla grimaced. "What does this all mean?"

"Hitler just gave Heydrich the signal. Hitler never openly soils his hands. He remains behind the curtain. But the inner circle understands what 'Jews must pay' means. Goebbels will make the speech to rile everyone up. Heydrich will coordinate mass attacks on Jewish homes, businesses, and synagogues across the country. And Hitler's fingers will not be seen anywhere near this."

Carla's eyes widened. "They wouldn't dare!"

"Honey. I love you, but it pains me to say that you are naïve. From the moment the Nazis came to power, they have taken every legal step to drive the Jewish people from Germany. As harsh as they have made it, many Jews remained. The *Anschluss* in Austria generated a pogrom that taught the Nazis a lesson: violence works. The Jews have been fleeing Austria ever since. But not here. Not in the same numbers. Rath's death provides the Nazis an excuse to start a pogrom. For his part, Heydrich will keep the *SS* out of the direct action while hoodlums run through the streets and attack Jews at random. Ransack their shops. In the end, the Gestapo will be behind it."

Carla gasped. "Not here. My god. No!"

"I have a driver waiting for you. He is armed. If he feels it is too dangerous for you to go to the hospital, promise to listen to him and return to this hotel. You will be safe here. If you don't see Ludwig today, there is always another day."

"If there is going to be trouble, I want to be with you."

I took both her hands; her eyes were moist. "I will be fine. What I don't need is to worry about your safety. Now promise me you will vigilant. Do whatever the driver says. Do you promise?"

She held me tight. "Oh, Friedrich. I'm afraid for all of us."

"So am I."

*

I went straight to my house from the airport, changed out of my uniform, and called Canaris. I found him home. "What have you heard?"

Canaris's voice sounded strangled. "The police have been directed to do nothing . . . as long as Jews are the only ones assaulted."

"What about the smoke in the distance? There are scores of fires."

Canaris explained, "Synagogues, mostly. The fire departments have orders to standby as long as the fires do not jeopardize Aryan-owned buildings or businesses."

"Wilhelm? There must be something we can do?" I said, desperately.

"Friedrich, we are two men. We can't stop a country gone mad."

"We have to try."

But try what?

Then it came to me.

*

Words cannot describe what I witnessed on my way to *Oranienburger Straße*. Window after window of Jewish-owned stores were smashed, their insides looted. Jews ripped out of their homes. Women dragged by the hair. Men stomped on, clubbed, and taken away by the truckload to concentration camps. One woman jumped from her window and lay crumpled, her blood coloring the ground.

And the streets!

The streets were strewn with broken glass, crunching under the boots of the marauding mobs.

The screams.

The shrieks.

The crying.

Black and gray smoke bellowed from buildings. Tongues of yellow-blue flames shot out from apartment windows. Just as Canaris described, uniformed firemen stood near their trucks, some smoking, some laughing . . . doing nothing to fight the conflagration of Jewish shops . . . but ready to prevent fires from spreading to gentile properties.

The Berlin landmark I sought was in the distance. Its ornate gold-ribbed dome perched high above twin towers that highlighted a beacon of iconic brilliance: the Neue Synagogue. This was Berlin's main place of Jewish worship, with room enough for three thousand in its cavernous sanctuary. It had been Max's synagogue.

I sprinted.

As I neared, I scoured the Neue Synagogue for licks of fire.

There were none.

I charged inside. Three hooligans were smashing chair after chair and tossing the pieces into a pile in the center aisle. Dozens of thick, black-covered prayer books were added to the heap. A fourth thug held a torch aloft, waiting for the leader—a broad-shouldered, tall young man—to give the word to ignite.

I yelled, "This place is sacred. You can't burn it down."

Their eyes turned to their leader who stood on the front stage, holding a red fabric-covered chair above his head.

"Try and stop us, old man." Then he hurled the chair down onto the pile; it broke into pieces.

My first instinct was to tackle the man with the torch as he edged nearer the stack of splintered wood and sacred books. Instead, I bolted outside to grab the arm of a policeman across the street.

"What is your name?" I demanded.

"Lieutenant Otto Bellgardt."

"Quick. They are about to burn down the synagogue. It's a protected national monument." I pointed. "Order that fire brigade to bring their hoses inside before the fire not only destroys the synagogue but the nearby Aryan businesses, as well. Hurry."

I expected Bellgardt to protest. To his credit, he dashed to the firemen and barked orders that they needed to enter the building. They argued. He would have none of it. Whatever he said, moved them into action.

As I tore back inside, the leader of the pack ripped off the brocaded curtain that covered a deep-set alcove filled with ancient Torahs. These scrolls contained Biblical stories written on parchment wrapped around wooden staves whose ends were covered with silver crowns that jangled like holiday bells. Each Torah stood upright, cradled in its own holder.

The ruffian grabbed the closest Torah.

I shouted. "Put that down!"

I charged the stage at the same time the thug lowered the torch to the mound of books and broken chairs. Smoke rose from the pile. Wood crackled.

I stopped, torn as what to do.

Try to stamp out the fires or race to protect the Torah?

The thumping of firemen's boots, plus Lieutenant Bellgardt's shouting, made my decision.

The guy holding the Torah jumped from the stage to toss it into the rising flames when I barreled into his gut. He toppled backwards.

I scooped up the Torah.

"You'll be sorry you did that, old man." He rubbed the back of his head as he got to his feet. "We have our orders."

I stepped to within an arm's reach. "Orders to do what?"

"Burn down the synagogues. Rough up the Jews. Anything and everything to make them leave."

"Who ordered you?"

"Reinhard Heydrich." He scoffed, "You know who he is, don't you?"

He tried to brush past me; I shoved him back . . . hard.

"What the hell?" He whipped out a revolver. "You're coming with me . . . that is, after *you* toss that Torah into the fire."

I glanced at the fire knowing his gaze would follow mine. Without a hint, I drove my knee hard between his legs. He collapsed to the floor, clutched himself, and then rolled to the side retching from the pain.

I snatched up his gun. "What gives you the right to hide behind Heydrich's name?"

Still curled in the fetal position, he managed to gasp, "I am *Oberscharführer* Rudolf Hampe."

"A lieutenant? You should know better. Heydrich meant for the *SA* to riot against the Jews, their businesses, and their synagogues. Not the *SS*."

"What makes you such a know-it-all, old man?" Hampe staggered to his feet.

This prick is off base. Exceeded his orders. What to do with him?

"Don't move," I shouted above the din.

A smug look was plastered on Hampe's face as I returned the Torah, keeping his gun trained on him with every step.

When I returned, I said through bared teeth, "Is that how an *Oberscharführer* stands? Where's your respect?"

"Respect for you, old man? Don't make me laugh. It hurts too much."

I drew out my *Ausweis*. "Attention, you fool."

He struggled to his feet.

I thrust my card into his sweaty palm.

"*Obergruppenführer*! But . . . but . . . why aren't you in uniform?"

"I could ask you the same thing, Hampe. Be in my office tomorrow. Nine a.m. sharp."

Chapter 58

Carla called from Munich soon after I arrived home. She was crying.

"It's horrific, Friedrich."

She saw countless Jews rounded up. Synagogues set on fire.

"Stay in Munich," I said. "It's safer."

"For how long?"

"Until I can make certain it is safe to travel." When she started to protest, I told her I loved her and had to go.

The following morning, I stopped at the Kaiserhof Hotel on my way to my office. I needed to offer condolences.

"Even I could not have imagined anything that bad," Bernhard Weiss said when I reached him. "Are you safe? Carla?" Before I could reassure him that we were, he rattled off facts from the morning papers. "Ninety-one Jews murdered. Thirty thousand rounded up and sent to concentration camps. Seventy-five hundred of the remaining nine thousand Jewish-owned businesses destroyed. Two hundred and seventy-one synagogues burned to the ground. Hundreds more badly damaged by fire. Cemeteries desecrated. The only thing that stopped this madness is that they ran out of Jewish things to destroy. Friedrich, they are calling it *Kristallnacht* . . . because of all the broken glass on the streets that glittered like crystals in the night."

"I'm sorry, Bernhard. For you and your people. Let's pray this is the end." My voice dropped off.

"You don't think it will be, do you, Friedrich?"

"It will only get worse. In the next few days, they will confiscate cars, make it illegal for Jewish children to go to school, forbid Jews to take public transportation, deny them medical care in the hospitals. And the ultimate humiliation? Heydrich will make the Jews clean up the remnants of the burned-out synagogues before the Nazis turn them into parking lots."

My words were met with silence.

"Bernhard? Bernhard? Are you there?"

I heard a soft sob.

My eyes misted.

I held on until he spoke again. I felt better when he told me he had seen his doctor and had a chest X-ray. His lungs were clear.

Then Bernhard said words that burned into my soul. "Friedrich, never forget the screams and smoke and human damage that occurred yesterday. I know you want to leave . . . more so than ever. But please, I beg of you, don't go. Don't abandon us. Continue the journey you began in Prague five long years ago. I pray that you are able to stay the course."

*

My office phone rang. I glanced at the clock: eight-fifty-nine. If nothing else, Hampe was punctual.

He gave the Hitler salute. I ignored it.

I pointed to a chair. "Sit."

"What am I doing here?" he asked.

"You called me an old man, yesterday. Do you remember? Think of it as someone from my generation wanting to understand your generation," I answered. "You were not supposed to be in that synagogue yesterday, Hampe. Why were you there? It was not an *SS* action."

"I didn't want to miss the fun."

"Fun, you say? Rudolf, is it? I don't understand how destroying something holy to others can be fun for you or anyone. I don't get it."

Hampe studied me. "Why do you care? Jews are not people. It doesn't matter what we do to them."

"Not every German feels that way," I said.

Hampe's face wrinkled in confusion. "I found out about you before I came here, *Obergruppenführer* Richard. You've been at the *Führer's* side from the beginning. They say you were one of the founders of the *SS*. Why are you talking like this?"

I went to Munich to find a friend. In the process, I helped create a world gone insane.

"Let me remind you, Hampe, this chat is about you, not me. It's about discipline. Obeying orders."

"I've earned commendation after commendation. I joined the Hitler Youth when I was eleven and rose through the ranks. Five years ago, I carried a torch past the Chancellery window the night the *Führer* became chancellor. It was my proudest moment. I became a Brown Shirt before joining the *SS*. Always obeying orders."

"That still doesn't explain your actions last night," I said.

"Last night was about patriotism. About making Germany *Judenfrei*."

"How old are you?"

"Twenty-three."

How could his hate be so deep-rooted?

"Are your parents Party members?"

Hampe turned solemn. "I never knew my father. He left for the war when my mother was pregnant. He never returned."

"Sadly, that story was repeated many times over. You didn't answer about your mother. Is she a Party member?"

He scoffed. "My mother? No. She wouldn't hear of it. She was upset that I joined the Youth."

"Then why did you?"

"Because my friends joined. The uniforms. The marching. The songs. The camping. It felt good to belong to something. To follow a path. And . . ."

"And what?"

"And for me . . . it made up for not having a father."

I felt a wave of pity for the boy. I lost any desire to punish him.

I was still thinking about what he said when he asked, "Is that it? May I go?"

"Yes, Rudolf. You may go."

As he stood to leave, he knocked over the picture on my desk. He jerked back. "Sorry." He picked it up. Before setting it upright, he blanched.

"What's wrong?" I asked.

He stared, mouth agape. He ran his fingers over each face in the photograph. Then looked at me. Perplexed.

"Why do you have this?" He gazed at me. Bewildered.

"I've carried it since the war," I answered. "Why?"

"It's a picture of my father, my aunt, and my grandparents. I have this *identical* picture in my home." His breathing grew shallow. His face perplexed.

At first his words didn't register. I reached for the framed picture; he pulled back.

It's a picture of my father, my aunt, and my grandparents. I have this identical picture in my home.

I looked at him as if for the first time. I studied his face. His cheekbones. His eyes. His lips. The part in his hair.

Who are you, Rudolf Hampe?

I began slowly. "When I was in the army, a wounded soldier knew he was going to die. He pressed this picture in my hand. Made me promise to tell his family that he carried it all during the war . . . and that he loved them. I've kept his picture ever since." I pointed to the frame. "See the date? My girlfriend is a professional photographer. She touched up the original and gave me this copy as a gift."

He looked up with puddled eyes. His voice cracked. "Did you get to keep your promise?"

In a daze, I asked, "What promise?"

"To tell the family that the soldier loved them?"

"I never had the chance. He was about to tell me his name when a shell exploded. I was blown to pieces. In a coma for a week. When I woke up, I was in the hospital, and that soldier . . . that soldier . . . that soldier was gone . . ."

What else can I say . . . my son?

Epilogue

Time Magazine

1938 Man of the Year

New York, New York

The greatest single news event of 1938 took place on September 29, when four statesmen met at the *Führerhaus*, in Munich, to redraw the map of Europe. The three visiting statesmen at that historic conference were Prime Minister Neville Chamberlain of Great Britain, Premier Edouard Daladier of France, and Dictator Benito Mussolini of Italy. But by all odds, the dominating figure at Munich was the German host, Adolf Hitler.

Führer of the German people, Commander-in-Chief of the German Army, Navy & Air Force, Chancellor of the Third Reich, Herr Hitler, on that day in Munich, reaped the harvest of an audacious, defiant, ruthless foreign policy that he had pursued for five-and-a-half years. Hitler had torn the Treaty of Versailles to shreds. He had rearmed Germany to the teeth . . . or as close to the teeth as he was able. He had stolen Austria before the eyes of a horrified and, apparently, impotent world.

*

These events shocked the nations that had defeated Germany on the battlefield only twenty years before, but nothing so terrified the world as the ruthless, methodical, Nazi-directed events which, during late summer and early autumn, threatened a world war over Czechoslovakia. Without loss of blood, he reduced Czechoslovakia to a German puppet state, forced a drastic revision of Europe's defensive alliances, and won a free hand for himself in Eastern Europe by getting a "hands-off" promise from powerful Britain and, later, France.

Adolf Hitler is, without doubt, 1938's *Time Magazine's*, "Man of the Year."

Authors' Notes

Sins of the Fathers encompasses November 1934–November 1938 and is the sequel to *Wolf* (1918–1934). Like its predecessor, most of the persons encountered in *Sins of the Fathers* were real people who largely lived the lives depicted. Only Ludwig, Max, Marta and Heidi, Rudolf Hampe, Sabine Stark, and the two concentration camp guards—Jüttner and Querner—along with our protagonist—Friedrich Richard—are fictitious.

For example, Kitty Schmidt did own the fashionable brothel Pension Schmidt. Kitty was caught at the border smuggling currency out of Germany (in 1939 rather than as represented in 1938). She agreed to Reinhard Heydrich's demands to change the name of her establishment to Salon Kitty, use girls trained by the SS, and allow the bedrooms to be electronically bugged to avoid being sent to a concentration camp.[1]

Other examples of "lives depicted" in *Sins* include Lilian Harvey, first introduced to the reader in *Wolf,* who was an international German film star ranked with the likes of Dietrich and Garbo. Lilian did return to Nazi Germany after Hollywood and was briefly arrested and interrogated for helping a homosexual artist escape the clutches of the Gestapo. Harvey left Germany for good as conditions deteriorated.

Carla Bartheel,[2] Friedrich's love interest, was as real as Lilian. Carla was an actress. She did appear in a film with Conrad Veidt (who was the model for Friedrich's plastic surgery in *Wolf*), and did become an accomplished photographer, publishing two books of photographs. Carla was not the photographer who submitted the photo of the Jewish child, Hessy Levinsons, who Joseph

---

1 Additional information on Kitty Schmidt and Salon Kitty post 1938 may be found at https://allthatsinteresting.com/salon-kitty.
2 https://en.wikipedia.org/wiki/Carla_Bartheel.

Goebbels selected to be the perfect Aryan baby in posters and magazines. Hans Ballin, a well-known Berlin photographer, took Hessy's picture and submitted it as a ruse. Hessy's family fled Germany in 1938. As of this writing, she is a retired chemistry professor in the United States.

More can be learned about other characters that appeared in *Sins* that were first introduced in *Wolf* including Maria Reiter, Lilian Harvey, General Erich Ludendorff, Franz Gürtner, and various Nazis, by visiting www.NotesOnWolf.com.

In writing *Sins*, we used major and minor events as they happened. In some instances, historians dispute their veracity. One example is the Ludendorff letter to Hindenburg that predicted the Reich President would regret the appointment of Adolf Hitler as chancellor. This was chronicled in *Wolf* on p. 414 and in *Sins* on p. 136. The letter originated in a book written by Hans Frank, Hitler's lawyer, as he awaited execution for war crimes: *Im Angesicht des Galgens* (In the Face of the Gallows). Some believe his account of the telegram is accurate. Others think it a forgery. We accepted it on its face value given Hitler's conduct at Ludendorff's funeral in deferring to Blomberg to give the state's tribute.

Franz Gürtner deserves special mention. In *Sins*, it was reasonable for Friedrich to appeal to Gürtner for justice for Max's killers at that time. Gürtner was the lone cabinet holdover—Reich minister of justice—from the previous administration when Hitler became chancellor in 1933. Readers of *Wolf* may recall that while not a Nazi, Gürtner—as Bavarian minister of justice—had been helpful during Hitler's trial (in 1924) for treason after the Beer Hall Putsch. It was Gürtner who permitted Hitler's early release from jail after his conviction. And it was Gürtner that aided Hitler after his half-niece and lover—Geli Raubal—committed suicide in Hitler's Munich apartment.[3]

---

3 Chamberlain executed the "Munich Agreement" in that apartment, on the same couch Hitler used to entertain Eva Braun. Eva did comment to a friend about "the goings on" that couch had seen after seeing the photo of Chamberlain sitting on it during the Munich Conference.

Nevertheless, in 1935 and 1936, Gürtner tried to maintain the rule of law, even in the concentration camps. Gürtner fought to bring justice to the concentration camp guards who abused prisoners. His letter to Deputy *Führer* Hess, quoted in *Sins* (p. 8), is accurate. Gürtner once prosecuted twenty-three guards at Hohenstein concentration camp. He not only won convictions against those guards but also against the camp commandant, *SS Standartenführer* (full Colonel) Jächnichen.[4] Those efforts ended, as Gürtner told Friedrich, when Himmler transferred jurisdiction over *SS* conduct in concentration camps to *SS* courts.[5] What little voice of reason was expressed by key cabinet members in the early years of the Nazi regime, eroded over time. In 1939, Gürtner crumbled. He made certain that his courts permitted the state to euthanize the mentally ill and other "useless eaters." But that was beyond the time of *Sins*.

Many individuals courageously tried to help victims of Nazi oppression. Many succeeded, oftentimes at great peril to themselves. Lilian Harvey saved the life of a choreographer and famously refused to provide names of Jewish actors and directors to the Gestapo. Lieutenant Otto Bellgardt, who appeared in *Sins*, deserves mention. With considerable risk to himself, Bellgardt drew his pistol to stop the destruction of Berlin's main synagogue—the Neue Synagogue—during *Kristallnacht* and ordered the fire department to save it from the flames. Had he not intervened, the synagogue would have been lost. (The synagogue was severely damaged by Allied bombing in November 1943). Later, during the war, Bellgardt forged identity cards and, when he could, warned Jews about imminent deportation.[6]

---

4   *Trial of War Criminals Before the Nuremberg Military Tribunals,* Volume III, The Justice Case, U. S. Government Printing Office, 1951.

5   Gürtner was something of a moderating influence in the Nazi regime. For example, he shielded Hans von Dohnanyi who worked for him in the Ministry of Justice. And it was Gürtner who made sure that Fritsch got his trial before a Military Tribunal.

6   https://www.museum-blindenwerkstatt.de/en/ausstellung/themen/the -helpers-circle-around-otto-weidt/police-officers-from-police-station-16/.

But *Sins of the Fathers* is not the story of isolated individual acts against tyranny. It is the story of German military leaders and civilians who conspired to overthrow Hitler in 1938; their appeal to the Chamberlain government to make a public stand against Hitler invading Czechoslovakia; and Winston Churchill's attempt to help the conspirators with a letter of support, a portion of which is reproduced in *Sins* (p. 326).

Adolf Hitler is the central historical character in both *Sins* and *Wolf.* He was unquestionably the most malevolent and destructive figure of the twentieth century, if not in all recorded history. And yet, for all that has been written about him—more than one hundred thousand books and counting—an accurate profile of this tyrant is elusive.

Why is there a lack of historically accurate profiles of Adolf Hitler? Perhaps it is because no one wants to "hear a good word" about this man and, therefore, no one wants to write a word that could be taken as one. And so, we are frequently presented a cutout caricature of a screaming, ranting gargoyle or of a cold, unfeeling human who is incapable of normal relationships, particularly with women. These cartoon images have become ensconced in readers who take comfort in this false picture.

But Hitler did not rise from the bottom of Austrian society—a penniless, street scene artist, residing in a ramshackle men's dormitory—to become the most powerful man in Europe without considerable personal and interpersonal assets. Willful blindness of those assets skews the view of the man we purport to study . . . and the times he so dramatically influenced.

As quoted in *Wolf's* Authors' Notes (www.NotesOnWolf.com):

> There was a real Hitler, a real person. It is not that we cannot find him. Rather, we prefer to create an image of Hitler that fits preconceived notions in order to explain Hitler's monstrous acts.[7]

---

7 "Hitler Studies, A Field of Amateurs," Ben Novak, HAOL, Numio (Primavera, 2006) pp. 157–168.

For example, Sir Ian Kershaw, today's most acclaimed Hitler biographer explains Hitler this way:

> Hitler . . . is the emptiness of the private person. He was, as has frequently been said, tantamount to an '**unperson.**' There is perhaps an element of condescension in this judgment, a readiness to look down on the **vulgar**, uneducated upstart **lacking a rounded personality**, the outsider with half-baked opinions on everything under the sun, the **uncultured** self-appointed adjudicator on culture . . . it remains the case that **outside politics Hitler's life was largely a void** . . . a biography of an '**unperson**,' one who has as good as **no personal life or history** outside that of the political events in which he is involved, imposes, naturally its own limitations.[8] (Emphasis added)

This evaluation could not be further from the truth. Murderer though he surely was, Hitler was not uncultured, not ignorant of the arts, and certainly not vulgar. He was passionate about all forms of art. He was a Bohemian; an artist; a painter; and an aficionado of architecture whose studies allowed him to know the interiors of Parisian classic buildings before he stepped foot in them in 1940.[9] Hitler wrote poetry. An opera lover, he was a devotee of Wagner whose librettos and operas he knew by heart. Hitler loved to consort with artists, performers, and architects like Paul Troost and Albert Speer, and film directors like Leni Riefenstahl. The list goes on. True, Hitler was self-educated. But by dint of an enormous amount of reading, aided by a phenomenal memory, he was far from ignorant. And his manners, reported by *all* who knew him, were impeccable—in the Viennese manner of the late nineteenth century.

---

8   *Hitler: 1889–1936 Hubris*, Ian Kershaw, W.W. Norton, London, 1998, p. XXV.

9   See www.NotesOnWolf.com, p. 58.

Much of this can be witnessed in readily available home movie clips. To be sure, he was a ferocious enemy, but he was also a faithful friend. In fact, he had many friends—particularly those who date to the earliest days of what he regarded as his "struggles"—that he would entertain at the *Berghof*. There were men and women he picnicked with in the woods before there was a *Berghof*. This is the Hitler we attempted to profile in *Wolf* and continued to portray in *Sins*[10] as his personality darkened and his mental condition spiraled downward.

In continuing the story from *Wolf* through *Sins*, characters both real and imagined grew. That is the way of life. As Friedrich rebounded from Marta to Lilian to Trude and finally to Carla, Hitler moved from Lotte Bechstein to Maria Reiter to his half-niece Geli Raubal and finally, to Eva Braun. Hitler's relationships were accurately portrayed in *Wolf* and *Sins*. In 1935, Eva did attempt suicide a second time for lack of Hitler's attention, after which he became quite devoted to her. Though they would not marry until April 1945 shortly before their joint suicide, Hitler did execute a will in 1938 in which he named Eva Braun a beneficiary.[11]

Hitler did have—embarrassingly for him—the meeting in a restaurant with Eva's parents dramatized in *Sins*;[12] and Fritz Braun did send a letter protesting Hitler's relationship with his daughter, requesting that she be returned to her family. The letter was indeed diverted[13] and Eva continued to use the house

---

10 It was Cromwell who commanded his portrait be accurate, warts and all. We attempted to present Hitler's warts to be sure, but the rest as well.

11 This is different from his will of April 29, 1945, the day before they committed suicide.

12 *San Francisco Examiner*, September 17, 1949, interview with Fritz Braun. "Hitler was very embarrassed we were there. He kept offering my wife more sugar for her tea. He piled her place with sugar. He wouldn't look me in the eye. I was astounded at how many cakes he devoured. It was very strained."

13 *Eva Braun: Hitler's Mistress*, Nerin E. Gun, Meredith Press, New York, 1968, pp. 105–6.

Hitler provided for her and her sister Gretl, paid for by Hitler's old friend and photographer, Heinrich Hoffmann.

By 1936, Eva Braun, though anonymous to the German people, presided over the Berghof as a wife would. Around the same time, Eva had use of a small apartment in the Reich chancellery. And the Brauns—father Fritz, mother Franziska, and sister Gretl—became the *Führer's* extended family. When Gretl Braun married *SS Gruppenführer* Hermann Fegelein, Hitler held the wedding at the *Berghof.* However, Eva's older sister, Ilse, who worked for a Jewish doctor, did not associate with Hitler to the same degree.

The difference between Friedrich and Hitler in our novels is that Friedrich is a fictional person with fabricated relationships; Hitler's relationships, on the other hand, were with real women and authentically depicted in *Wolf* and *Sins* in contrast to the inaccurate and distorted profile of Hitler's sex life presented by historians.[14] As a young man, Hitler did court older monied women, like Helene Bechstein and Elsa Bruckmann, who financed him and the Party in the 1920s, while having affairs with young girls at the same time, including Bechstein's daughter, Lotte.

As Hitler ages in *Sins*, he maintains steadfast loyalty to old comrades—*Alte Kämpfer*—like Emil Maurice and Herman Esser, both who figured prominently in *Wolf* even when they injured him.[15] And to what may surprise many, Hitler was loyal to the Jewish Dr. Eduard Bloch, who was referred to in name

---

14 See www.NotesOnWolf.com; For example, in a recent biography, *Hitler,* by Peter Longerich, Oxford, London, P. 163 (2019): "In view of Hitler's personality, it seems plausible that his life was asexual; any intimate relationship would have simply been incompatible **with his arrested emotional development with regard to other people and with his self-perception as a public figure through and through with an extraordinary historic mission . . ."** (Emphasis added). This evaluation, while breathtakingly inaccurate, is symptomatic of the overwhelming number of historians who—without any basis—make assumptions about Hitler's personality disorders, and, like Longerich, ignore the evidence of Hitler's treatment by Dr. Forster.

15 See www.NotesOnWolf.com pp. 3–8.

only in *Wolf*, but became a character in *Sins*. Bloch was the Hitler family physician when the young Adolf grew up in Linz, Austria. Bloch treated Hitler's mother during her final illness. When Klara Hitler died in 1907, eighteen-year-old Adolf paid a special visit to the Jewish doctor, took his hand, and said, "I shall be grateful to you forever."[16] When Hitler moved to Vienna, he sent postcards to Dr. Bloch, conveying his good wishes, respect, and gratitude.

As dramatized in *Sins*, Hitler protected Dr. Bloch after the *Anschluss*. Unlike other Jews, Bloch was permitted to practice medicine; did not have to display the Jewish star; did not have his passport stamped with the red *J*; and was allowed to sell his house at market rates. He emigrated to the United States in 1940. In Bloch's own words, "Favors were granted to me which I feel sure were accorded to no other Jew in all Austria or Germany."[17] On the other hand, Hitler made the *SS* retrieve the two postcards that remained in Bloch's possession.

Hitler was loyal to past lovers. He did not have to "pay them off" or threaten them to remain silent. Perhaps the best example was Maria "Mimi" Reiter. Though she attempted suicide after he abandoned her, Hitler sent a silver cup as a wedding present when she married with his name, "Wolf," engraved on it.[18] (A photograph of the cup with Hitler's engraved signature, "Wolf," can be found in www.NotesOnWolf.com.) When Hitler took up with her again in 1931 after Geli's suicide, his lawyer, Hans Frank, helped with her divorce. Years later, when she wanted to marry George Kubish, an *SS* officer, Hitler intervened to reverse Kubish's poor evaluations in his *SS* personnel file.[19] And when Kubish fell in France in 1940, Hitler sent Maria one hundred roses.

16 *Adolf Hitler: Volume I*, John Toland, Doubleday & Company, New York, 1976, p. 31.

17 Two-part interview of Dr. Bloch in *Collier Magazine*, March 5 and 22, 1941, after he arrived in United States Dr. Bloch was also interviewed by the OSS in 1941 and 1943.

18 See www.NotesOnWolf.com p. 10.

19 *Die Frauen der Nazis* (The Women of the Nazis), Anna Maria Sigmund, Verhagsgruppe Random House FSC, 1998.

Far from rare, these were examples of how Hitler treated former paramours, including Eugenie (Jenny) Haug and Suzi Liptauer. Liptauer was Hitler's girlfriend in 1921. When she discovered his infidelities, Liptauer attempted suicide. Ultimately, she returned to her native Vienna.[20] This was confirmed by Heinrich Hoffmann[21] without mentioning Suzi by name:

There is another woman, too, of whom the world knows nothing, who tried to end her life because of unrequited love for Hitler. In 1921, when Hitler was quite unknown, this woman tried to hang herself in a hotel room; but fortunately, she was found in time.

Many years later Hitler brought her, now a happily married woman, to my studio to have her photograph taken.[22]

There are more examples of Hitler's unbending loyalties, but one deserves special mention due to its historical significance: Benito Mussolini.

Hitler was passionate for Germany to annex his birthplace: Austria. *Sins* accurately describes Hitler's rapture as he triumphantly paraded into a cheering Austria. Eva and her mother did follow him to Vienna against his wishes and he did have to bail them out of their hotel charges.[23]

20 See the account of Herman Esser, www.NotesOnWolf.com p.14.
21 Hoffmann and Hitler were friends since 1920. Eva Braun worked in Hoffmann's photography shop in 1929 where the future couple was first introduced. Hoffmann was with Hitler when they learned of Geli's suicide in 1931 and was a frequent guest of the Berghof. Hitler designated Hoffmann as his official photographer, making Hoffmann a multi-millionaire.
22 *Hitler Was My Friend*, Heinrich Hoffmann, London, 1955, p. 510, electronic version by Frontline Books, S. Yorkshire, 2011. Interestingly, Hoffman (p. 478) also confirms Anni Winter's account (the housekeeper) that Geli found a note from Eva Braun in Hitler's jacket the day she committed suicide.
23 Interview Franziska Braun. Musmanno Collections: Interrogations of Hitler's Associates. Gumberg Library, Duquesne University, April 9, 1948, pp. 15–18.

Here is the critical point. Four years earlier, in 1934, when Hitler launched a preemptive coup against Austria, murdering the Austrian chancellor Dollfuss, Mussolini massed Italian troops along the border which forced Germany to back down (*Wolf,* p. 522). The next four years witnessed Hitler's romance of Il Duce. The reason? To remove Italy as an impediment when he moved again to takeover Austria.

Then, in 1938, poised to fulfill his longtime dream, Hitler could not give the order to invade Austria without Mussolini's positive response to a hand-delivered message asking for his consent. Would Il Duce prevent an invasion a second time? When he learned that Mussolini could not care less what Hitler did to Austria, the *Führer* went into effusive paeans of fidelity to the Italian dictator. Hitler's verbatim statements in *Sins* (p. 222–223) are taken from the exhibits introduced in the trial before the International Military Tribunal at Nuremberg. This portion is historically significant:

> I will never forget it, whatever happens. If he should ever need any help or be in any danger, he can be sure that I shall stick with him whatever happens. **Even if the whole world is against him.**[24] (Emphasis added)

The consequences of Hitler's extravagant promises to stand by Mussolini, even against the "whole world," were disastrous to Germany during World War II.

During WWII, British forces were sent to North Africa to confront the Italian invaders where the British were prevailing. Hitler diverted *Wehrmacht* troops and formed the *Afrika Korps* under the leadership of Rommel to aid the Italians. The British would rout them in the battle of El Alamein.

More disastrous and with greater consequences for Germany was Hitler's decision to delay invading Russia (Operation

---

24 *Munich: The Price of Peace*, Telford Taylor, Vintage Books, New York, 1979, p. 366.

Barbarossa)—scheduled for mid-May 1941—by five weeks to help the Italians floundering in their invasion of Greece. This cost the Germans weeks of good weather that became their undoing in their effort to take Moscow in 1941.

Finally, when the Italians rebelled and arrested Mussolini in 1943, Hitler sent an SS team headed by Otto Skorzeny to free Mussolini, who was imprisoned in Gran Sasso, and bring him to Hitler in his *Wolf's Lair* near Rustenburg.

Contrary to the myth of a man who had no friends and could feel no sense of loyalty, Hitler was intensely loyal, demanding loyalty in return. Simply put, Hitler was a man who was often too good to his friends and, almost always, far too terrible to his enemies.

The Hitler we presented in *Wolf* and *Sins* was a man who could well understand Friedrich's emotional commitment—even to a Jew like Max—and forgive him for taking personal vengeance against the SS men who tortured Max to death. (*Sins* p. 68). That is not to evaluate Hitler as a good man or a bad one, but rather the man that he was, inconsistencies and all.

*

The second and more important evaluation is of Hitler's mental state. Was he sane or insane—whatever those terms mean—or something in between?

Until 1972, what was generally known and accepted regarding Hitler's mental health was that he was capable of monstrous acts and that he lacked some fundamental element of humanity. Perhaps this could better be described as missing a mechanism for moderation or, at the very least, a sense of boundaries and proportionality. For example, Hitler's anti-Semitism was genuine, intense, and predicated on the belief that Jews were not another religion but a diseased race that infected the societies in which they lived. With this unbending view, Hitler was prepared to go to any and all lengths to rid Germany of all Jews.

Hitler's "personality disorder" was "inferred" by historians from his criminal conduct. They knew of no mental examination of Hitler by any physician.

That changed when historian John Toland obtained the declassification of the 1943 OSS interview of Dr. Karl Kroner in 1972. Dr. Kroner was the staff physician who admitted Corporal Adolf Hitler to Pasewalk Hospital with a complaint of blindness due to a gas attack in October 1918. According to Dr. Kroner, Hitler was diagnosed as a "psychopath" in the throes of "hysterical" blindness. Dr. Kroner also reported that Hitler was treated by psychiatrist Dr. Edmund Forster, not by an eye doctor. Dr. Forster headed the Berlin University Nerve Clinic and served as consultant neurologist to the military hospital at Pasewalk. Toland would publish details of the Kroner interview . . . but not until 1976.[25]

Enter Rudolf Binion, chaired professor at Brandeis University. Binion was fluent in German. He became aware of a novel by Ernst Weiss, *Der Augenzeuge (The Eyewitness)* written in 1938 but only published in the late 1960s. It employed a thinly veiled protagonist who received psychiatric treatment for hysterical blindness during WWI. Binion realized Weiss's book was about Hitler. But Binion had no way to separate fact from fiction in Weiss's novel: Weiss, who had fled Germany, killed himself as the Germans entered Paris in 1940. If Weiss's book were true, speculated Binion, who was the psychiatrist depicted in the novel that treated Hitler? Binion was stymied until John Toland contacted him. Both Toland and Binion were deep into researching their respective works on Hitler . . . but from different standpoints.[26]

Toland shared what he had learned from the declassified Kroner interview. An excited Binion wrote Toland on June 22, 1972:[27]

25 See www.NotesOnWolf.com p. 68; *Adolf Hitler*, John Toland, Doubleday, Inc., Garden City, New York, 1976, p. xv.

26 *Adolf Hitler*, John Toland, Doubleday, Inc., Garden City, New York, 1976; *Hitler Among the Germans*, Rudolph Binion, Elsevier, New York, 1976.

27 FDR Library, Hyde Park, NY: Toland Collection, Box 39.

62 Pinckney Street, Boston 02114.

22 June 1972.

Dear John:

That Navy Intelligence report was a tremendous boon: all my thanks! I did not know the identity of Hitler's doctor at Pasewalk--and now I am hot on the fellow's trail. His right name, by the way, is Forster (Edmund), not Foerster as in Kroner's version--and while I am at it, his university at his death was Greifswald, not Greifewald. I'll give you the whole story when I get it. Meanwhile, just one question: do your notes cover all the substantive points in the original (or did you have to limit yourself)?

Armed with Forster's name as Hitler's treating psychiatrist, Binion located and interviewed Forster's son Balduin. Balduin, a physician, confirmed that, according to his mother, his father did treat Hitler. Another lead brought Binion to Switzerland where he interviewed Walter Mehring. Mehring had been present when Dr. Forster gave his treatment notes to novelist Ernst Weiss in 1933.[28] This was the validation Binion sought. A detailed version of how Professor Binion's journey ferreted out truths about Hitler's sanity appears in www.NotesOnWolf.com on pages 72–76.

Reviewing how Hitler's mental diagnosis became known is essential to understanding the importance of the corroborative evidence we encountered in researching *Sins*. [29]

It was not a coincidence that Ian Colvin is a character in *Sins*. Ian Goodhope Colvin did begin his career in Berlin as a journalist

---

28 *Die verlorene Bibliotek: Autobiographie einer Kultur* (*The Lost* Library, the Autobiography of Culture), Walter Mehring, Ullstein Werkausgaben 1980, p. 268. Originally published by Secker & Warburg, London, 1951.

29 There is no mention of Kroner's interview by such popular authors as Ian Kershaw (*Hitler 1889–1936 Hubris*, W. W. Norton, London, 1998) and Volker Ullrich (*Ascent 1889–1939*, Alfred A. Knopf, New York, 2016). Ignoring Kroner permits historians to avoid the diagnosis and ramifications of why Hitler was in Pasewalk Hospital.

writing for the *News Chronicle*. He helped establish communications between the anti-Nazi German military generals and the British government during 1938–39 until he was expelled from Germany. In *The Gathering Storm*, Winston Churchill wrote, "Ian Colvin plunged deeply into German politics and established contacts of a most secret character with some of the important German Generals, and also with **independent men of character and quality in Germany who saw in the Hitler movement the approaching ruin of their native land**."[30] (Emphasis added).

It is likely that Churchill's post-war flattering reference to men like Kleist, Bonhoeffer, Dohnanyi, and others as "men of quality and character" may have been, at least in part, to make amends for Chamberlain's labeling them as traitors whom he refused to meet.

Colvin was an eyewitness to the significant events depicted in *Sins*. Indeed, he assisted Canaris and the conspirators by facilitating Kleist's trip to London. After the war, he wrote a biography of Admiral Canaris titled *Master Spy*.[31] The following passages are critical to understand Hitler's mental state as early as 1918, and that they were available to historians by 1952:

> Colonel Schrader, an intimate friend of Canaris, had committed suicide immediately after the insurrection of July 20 (1944) had failed. He (Walther Huppenkothen) interrogated his driver; the man could not think of any reason why his master should have been implicated— he lived a quiet life and did not see many people—but the driver did remember certain files entrusted to him, for which Colonel Schrader had enjoined him to give particular care.

---

30 *The Gathering Storm*, Winston Churchill, Penguin, London, 1985 edition, p. 74.

31 *Master Spy*, Ian Colvin, McGraw-Hill Book Company, New York, 1952. Colvin also wrote a biography of Vansittart which contains important first-hand observations. *Vansittart in Office*, Ian G. Colvin, published by Victor Gollancz, London, 1965. Pages 3607-3610 in Kindle version, *Master Spy*, Eumenes Publishing 2019.

Where were they? The S.D. (*SS*) searched his home, the War Ministry offices in the Bendlerstraße, and then Army H.Q. citadel at Zossen. There, after some weeks, they discovered Colonel Schrader's steel box and broke it open. The box contained a miscellany of papers. **There were the medical-history sheets of Corporal Adolf Hitler, containing the observations of the commandant of military hospital at Pasewalk in Pomerania, where Hitler had lain gassed after World War I. The remarks referred to his symptoms of hysterical blindness and suggested a psychiatrist's report on his sanity.** (Emphasis added)

Colvin—an eyewitness to the plot in 1938—wrote those words **twenty years before** Dr. Kroner's statement to the OSS had been declassified.[32]

There is another highly corroborative eyewitness. Otto John's account was written in 1969, three years before the Kroner interview was declassified. See Fraenkel and Manvel, *The Canaris Conspiracy*, Pinnacle Books, NY (1972).

Manvel and Fraenkel wrote a compelling account of how the conspirators who sought to depose Hitler attempted to enlist the help of Professor Bonhoeffer, a leading German neurologist, to declare Hitler insane.[33] The authors were able to meet and interview Otto John, who verified that Hitler's medical records were reviewed at this 1938 meeting.[34] We shall shortly return to this account.

Unless one is prepared to believe that Dr. Kroner lied to the OSS in 1943; that Mila Forster lied to her son in 1933 that his

---

32 *Auszug aus dem Geheimdienstbericht von* 1943. OSS Research Analysis Branch, "Regular" Reports, 7i6 31963 [entry 16] Record Group 226, National Archives Washington.

33 *The Canaris Conspiracy*, Roger Manvell and Heinrich Fraenkel, Pinnacle Books, N.Y. (1972), ©1969 by Hennerlon and Heinrich Fraenkel, reprinted Skyhorse, 2018. p. 71 Kindle version.

34 Ibid, p. 295 Kindle version.

father (her husband) treated Hitler; that the September 16, 1933 account in the *Das Neue Tage-Buch* of the meeting with Forster in Paris (www.NotesOnWolf.com, p. 74) was false; that Walter Mehring—who was present when Dr. Forster revealed his treatment notes on Hitler to Weiss—lied when Binion interviewed him in 1975 as well as in his writings that describe meeting Forster along with Weiss; that Colvin's 1952 account of his fellow conspirators' intention to use Hitler's psychiatric records once he was captured is false or inaccurate; and that Otto John's eyewitness account of Professor Bonhoeffer's review of Hitler's medical records is false; then it is certainly true that Hitler suffered from a psychiatric problem that manifested in hysterical blindness in 1918. It is also true that Hitler was diagnosed as a psychopath and that Dr. Edmund Forster, a psychiatrist—not an eye doctor—treated Hitler in Pasewalk Military Hospital in October and November 1918.

Dr. Foster's Pasewalk treatment record of Hitler has never been found. We now have an understanding as to why: the *Abwehr*, under Canaris, took them, intending to expose and depose Hitler at the right moment. This will be revisited in connection with the conspiracies of 1938.

Before moving from the Kroner-Forster-Hitler 1918 connection, we need to explore *why* historians and bloggers often reject Kroner's statements to the OSS in the face of Binion's corroborative investigation: the fear that accepting Hitler's 1918 diagnosis as a psychopath will be tantamount to furnishing a defense for his monstrous crimes.

Let's dissect Ambruster's and Theiss-Abendroth's conclusion found in *Deconstructing the Myth of Pasewalk: Why Adolf Hitler's Psychiatric Treatment at the End of World War I Bears No Relevance*:

Conclusion

The reticence as shown by the majority of historians concerning Hitler's stay at Pasewalk military hospital continues to be more than appropriate. After all, with the medical sheet missing, there is no way of substantiating that he was ever treated by Edmund Forster.

Moreover, even if it were true, it wouldn't signify more than a marginal episode in Hitler's biography for a historical assessment of his person. On the one hand, it reduces Edmund Forster to having been Hitler's therapist, which does not do justice to his personality and achievements. On the other hand—and this weighs more heavily—it diminishes and relativizes Hitler's responsibility for his acts. In the opinion of the historian Ian Kershaw, it minimizes the complex developments that led to the mass murder of Jews to the alleged trauma of one single person in 1918. And last, but not least, this indirectly follows the logic of Hitler's *Mein Kampf*, where he describes the shift his life allegedly took during his hospital stay, including his decision to become a politician.[35]

We have no way of knowing if these authors were aware of Ian Colvin's book that accounted for Hitler's missing medical file or of the eyewitness account of Otto John, who corroborates Kroner and Binion. What is clear is that the points Armbruster and Peter Theiss-Abendroth make are self-contradictory on their face.

They write that, if it were true that Forster treated Hitler, it would *not* be significant. Then they argue that such treatment would *be* significant because it would diminish Hitler's responsibility for his monstrous crimes, presumably suggesting a defense of insanity. Then they would have us disbelieve that Forster treated Hitler because it would diminish Forster's other accomplishments. Lastly, we are told not to believe Hitler had such treatment

---

35 *Deconstructing the Myth of Pasewalk: Why Adolf Hitler's Psychiatric Treatment at the End of World War I Bears No Relevance.* Jan Armbruster, and Peter Theiss-Abendroth, Archives Clinical Psychiatry 43 (3), May-June 2016, pp. 56–59.

at Pasewalk because that would validate Hitler's own account in *Mein Kampf*[36] that his life was changed when he was there!

This bevy of self-contradicting objections to discredit Dr. Kroner's account, while ignoring all of its corroboration, is revelatory of the primary defect in the historiography of Hitler: the overwhelming need to believe all derogatory information/statements about Hitler and to discredit anything that "sounds" positive.

Ironically, these authors seem to miss that the last thing Hitler wanted anyone to know was that he was diagnosed as a psychopath and treated by a psychiatrist for hysterical blindness. In this same vein, he would not want it known that he was "kind" to former paramours, because that would reveal they existed . . . despite all precautions to keep their existence secret.

As for what he wanted and why? That is plain. Hitler well knew he was not only a political figure but an historical one as well. He did not want the public to know him, or for posterity to record who he actually was. Hitler dealt in optics. He went to great lengths to create and maintain an aura of godliness, of celibacy, of selfless self-denial for immediate political reasons and for his historical legacy.

To unmask Hitler and reveal the truth about his many affairs with young girls, that he drove four to attempt suicide, and that he was treated by a psychiatrist for anti-social personality disorder (ASPD), which is another term that defines a psychopath,[37] is to do exactly what he would not want—as if any such consideration mattered in searching for the truth.

Anni Winter, Hitler's housekeeper for sixteen years, from 1929 to 1945, speaking to a reporter in 1953, explained it perfectly:

---

36 *Mein Kampf*, Adolf Hitler, Kindle version, White Publishing, 2014, unabridged, p. 93. One of the authors of *Wolf* and *Sins* has spent six decades within the Administration of Justice. In his view, the notion that any defense of Hitler's conduct on the ground of insanity would be simply ludicrous.

37 https://www.healthline.com/health/psychopath.

Reporter: Why did he keep his private life a secret?
Anni Winter: He said it would have upset the picture of a political God above known human frailties.[38]

Anni Winter's words remind us that Adolf Hitler made himself into a godlike leader, challenging Germans to forget the moral teaching of their Christianity. He was celibate for them. Hitler was their new God and Nazism their new religion.

November 5, 1937—The Hossbach Memorandum

The storyline in *Sins* hinges on the meeting at which Hitler declared his determination to invade both Austria and Czechoslovakia. Indeed, it may very well have been the hinge upon which World War II turned.

Sins described the November 5 meeting with great accuracy thanks to Colonel Friedrich Hossbach, Hitler's military adjutant who kept detailed notes that history has labeled "the Hossbach Memorandum."[39] Over the years, scores of historians have debated the significance of these notes. Some believed them inaccurate. Most, today—and we are in this camp—believe they are quite reliable.[40]

At issue is whether Hitler announced an immediate plan to invade Austria and Czechoslovakia at the risk of a looming war . . . or presented long-range goals that needed to be accomplished by 1943–1945. These later dates are when Hitler posited that England and France would narrow the arms gap with Germany. In 1961, A.J.P. Taylor wrote, "Hitler's exposition was, in large part daydreaming, unrelated to what followed in real lives."[41]

---

38 www.NotesOnWolf.com p. 15 and the *London Daily Mail*, March 14, 1953.
39 https://avalon.law.yale.edu/imt/hossbach.asp.
40 Perhaps the best exposition of this, *Munich: The Price of Peace*, Telford Taylor, Vintage Books, New York, 1979, pp. 302–307.
41 *Origins of the Second World War*, A.J.P. Taylor, published by Hamish Hamilton, London, 1961, pp. 131–133.

We do not agree. We stand with historian Telford Taylor who wrote:

> Three months after the conference of November 5, Blomberg, Fritsch, and Neurath were all out of office. It would be easy to infer that their opposition at the meeting was the direct cause of their downfall. Especially in the case of Blomberg, this may well be an oversimplification. Beyond question, however, the impressions that Hitler gathered at this meeting were a powerful contributing factor in the political convulsion which was about to grip the Third Reich.[42]

When the events that followed the November 5 meeting are analyzed, and the actions taken by Beck and other military leaders are put in perspective, there is little room for debate as to what Hitler's true intentions were that day. Within three months Blomberg, Neurath,[43] and Fritsch were "gone." Chief-of-Staff Ludwig Beck was so incensed that he sent Hitler a memo in opposition to the *Führer's* bellicose plans. For their part, German military leaders understood that Hitler's intentions were intractable and formed plots to depose him.

On February 4, 1938, Hitler fired thirteen generals and reassigned forty-four senior officers, abolished the position of minister of war, and took direct control of the entire military, removing Blomberg, Neurath, and Fritsch from their posts. Four months after the November 5 meeting, Hitler invaded Austria (in March 1938), absorbing it as a region of the newly formed Greater Germany. On September 29, 1938, six months after removing Austria from world maps, Hitler was handed the German-speaking Sudetenland in western Czechoslovakia. Thus, almost

---

42 Taylor p. 307.

43 Neurath reported the shock of the conference so great that three days later he suffered a heart attack. https://www.cvce.eu/en/obj/verdict_of_the_international_military_tribunal_1_october_1946-en-21b7397c-9afd-411d-9158-f2ffba73fe0c.html p. 37.

all of the Hitler objectives announced on November 5, 1937, had been accomplished in less than twelve months. The last remaining objective—the "total destruction" of Czechoslovakia—was completed by March 1939.

Perhaps the most important debates among historians concern the motivations of men like Fritsch, Beck, Canaris, Oster, Witzleben, and the others to organize resistance after the November 5 conference. With some exceptions, historians' points-of-view depend on whether they are American/British or German. This is particularly germane in the early years following the war when British and American historians did not see the German resisters as heroes. Such historians point to the fact that some conspirators had previously supported Hitler and those that objected to Hitler's November 5 program did so for military reasons . . . and not on moral grounds. And it is true that generals like Fritsch and Beck did oppose Hitler in terms of potential military defeat.

But is that what they meant?

The continued opposition of men like Kleist, Schlabrendorff, Oster, the Bonhoeffers, Dohnanyi, Witzleben, and Schrader— through early German victories as well as later defeats—validates their moral position. Knowing that the *Führer* had no morals in the conduct of public policy, it is hardly surprising that they chose to lobby against German aggression in terms of military defeat . . . as the argument to deter Hitler on his road to war.[44]

---

44 For example, Hitler stated to the November 5 attendees:
   . . . the annexation of Czechoslovakia and Austria would mean an acquisition of foodstuffs for 5 to 6 million people, **on the assumption that the compulsory emigration of 2 million people from Czechoslovakia and 1 million people was practical**. The incorporation of these two states with Germany meant, from the political-military point of view, a substantial advantage because it would mean shorter and better frontiers, the freeing forces **for other purposes**, and the possibility of creating new units up to a level of about 12 divisions, that is 1 new division per million inhabitants.
   Italy was not expected to object to the elimination of the Czechs, but it was impossible at the moment to estimate what her attitude on

Perhaps Professor Harold Deutsch, a Harvard PhD in history who studied at the Universities of Paris, Vienna, and Berlin during these critical years 1936–37, and who later became history department chairman at the University of Minnesota, put it best:

> Students of the period have at times remarked critically on the total absence of any moral tone in the protest raised [at the November 5th meeting]. By November 1937, however, those present knew the chief of state sufficiently well to recognize the utter hopelessness of influencing his policies by advancing considerations of right and wrong. The form and spirit of the discourse he had addressed to them that very day were proof enough that he would reject with scorn any discussion on such a plane. . .[45]

Firstly, the attendees at the November 5, 1937, meeting—and those they confided in—well understood that Hitler's declaration to act no later than by 1943 or the latest, 1945, was meant to obfuscate his real intentions and that they had to *immediately* coalesce into a resistance movement to prevent war. That is exactly what they did under the initial leadership of Colonel General Ludwig Beck, Admiral Wilhelm Canaris, and Colonel Hans Oster, along with other senior officers, civilians, and clergy.

To be sure, some conspirators were military officers who had been attracted to Hitler's party in earlier years, particularly

---

the Austria question would be; that depended essentially upon whether the Duce were still alive. (Emphasis added) https://ghdi.ghi-dc.org/sub_document.cfm?document_id=1540 p. 6.

These statements, from a moral point of view, are outrageous. Where were three million people to go after being ejected from their homes? And what were those "other purposes" of the Armed Forces, enhanced by 12 new divisions? Once the tenor of this meeting circulated among the senior 12 leadership of the army, finger waving in moral disapproval was hardly an option. Instead, a significant group went into resistance.

45 *Hitler and His Generals, the Hidden Crisis, January-June 1938*, Harold Deutsch, University of Minnesota Press (1974), pp. 64–65.

to its criticism of the unfairness of the Treaty of Versailles. But by 1938, men like Canaris and Beck had turned resolutely from Hitler and all he stood for. They would remain in opposition to him during the next six years until most lost their lives in the July 20, 1944, attempted assassination of the *Führer* spearheaded by Claus von Stauffenberg.

Baron Ewald von Kleist-Schmenzin, as depicted in *Sins*, had been opposed to Hitler since the 1920s. When Hitler came to power in January 1933, Kleist refused to fly the Nazi flag from his estate or give the Hitler salute.[46] His activities in the conspiracy are accurately described in *Sins*, as were Ian Colvin's. Colvin was indeed instrumental in arranging Kleist's meetings with Robert Vansittart, Lord Lloyd, and Winston Churchill.[47]

We presented Kleist as we believe that he was: a nobleman (read: noble man) not by birth but by his conduct. He was executed on Hitler's orders when the investigation of the July 20, 1944, conspiracy revealed a copy of Churchill's 1938 letter in Kleist's desk and the latter's role in the 1938 conspiracy. We did fictionalize the presence of his sixteen-year-old son, Ewald, at the meeting in the Casino Club. It was done to honor the younger Kleist, who in January 1944, as a junior officer, volunteered for a suicide mission to blow Hitler up along with himself. Explosives were hidden in a briefcase; the appointment with

---

46 *The Secret War Against Hitler*, Fabian von Schlabrendorff, Westview Press, (1994) p. 44. (First published Pitman Publishing Corporation, New York, 1965.

47 Schlabrendorff, p. 91. "A good opportunity to get in touch with leading English political circles came through Ian Colvin, an Englishman then living in Berlin. He was a member of the Casino Society . . . by arranging a visit to England by Ewald von Kleist, one of Hitler's most unbending adversaries, Colvin helped to establish a truly effective contact"; *None So Blind*, Ian Colvin, Harcourt, Brace & World, New York, 1965 p. 218–221. Colvin's letter to Lord Lloyd of August 3, 1938, warns that the invasion of Czechoslovakia has been set for September 28, 1928, wishes to set up a meeting with Kleist, and gives the intelligence that the *Abwehr* is opposed to the regime's plans. Part of the letter is reproduced in *Sins* (p. 308–309).

Hitler confirmed. The plan, blessed by his father, was frustrated when Hitler changed the scheduled appointment.[48]

In our view, Colvin's books are significant in that they represent first-hand accounts by a person who was on the scene and who knew many of the actors in the unfolding resistance.

Another such person was Fabian von Schlabrendorff.

As a law student before the Nazis came to power, Schlabrendorff already opposed National Socialism. By 1938, he was an active member of the resistance. Indeed, it was he who picked up Churchill's letter from the diplomatic pouch at the British Embassy in Berlin and passed it onto Kleist.[49]

Schlabrendorff's activities on behalf of the resisters were extraordinary. In 1939, Canaris sent him to England to meet with Churchill in yet another fruitless attempt to head off war.[50] In 1943, he attempted to kill Hitler by turning two bottles of Cointreau into bombs and placing them in Hitler's plane. When they did not go off, he boarded the next plane to Rastenburg in East Prussia and retrieved the bottles before they were discovered.[51] Schlabrendorff was exposed and arrested after the July 20, 1944 assassination attempt failed. He was brutally tortured but miraculously escaped execution.[52]

Lt. Colonel Werner Schrader was another who resisted the Nazis from the moment they ascended into power in 1933 until he committed suicide in 1944. His early anti-Nazi activities landed

---

48 https://www.youtube.com/watch?v=5MnuPYN0KLk

49 Schlabrendorff, p. 95. There is a contradictory account. Colvin states that Kleist received Churchill's letter and presented it to Canaris. Canaris, Kindle edition, location 1145. We favor Schlabrendorff's account as it is firsthand.

50 Schlabrendorff, pp. 97–8. There were continued efforts by the senior German military to stiffen England's spine, even after the Munich Agreement and prior to the full German takeover of Czechoslovakia.

51 Schlabrendorff, pp. 235–237. While a team of operatives contributed to "Operation Flash," it was left to Schlabrendorff to retrieve the unexploded "bombs."

52 The infamous and feared chief judge of the Peoples Court (*Volksgerichtsof*), Roland Freisler, was killed in an American bombing raid in 1945 holding Schlabrendorff's file in his hand.

him in one of the new concentration camps in 1933 from which he escaped a year later. Canaris recruited Schrader into the *Abwehr*. It fell to Schrader to maintain the archive of the resistance, including a history of Nazi crimes and *SS* atrocities. Of particular significance, Schrader was given the records of the mental assessment of Hitler by military doctors.[53] The conspirators intended to use those documents at Hitler's trial once he was overthrown.

Unfortunately for Canaris, and his 1938 co-plotters, the admiral kept a diary of their activities. These were also entrusted to Schrader. It was a mistake that cost Canaris his life, and the lives of many of his 1938 confederates, who had remained undetected until the failure of the 1944 plot, and the *SS* discovery of Schrader's cache of records.

When Hitler survived the blast intended to kill him in 1944, Schrader knew he would be arrested. His suicide note read, "I will not go to prison. I will not let them torture me . . ."

When Hitler read the Schrader documents, he was furious. He ordered the brutal executions of the 1938 conspirators. Kleist was tried and hung. Canaris and Oster were made to march naked to the gallows upon which they were hung.

These were some, but by no means all, of the key leaders of the conspiracy—or, more accurately, conspiracies—in 1938, that attempted to depose Hitler and save the world from the horrors of an impending conflagration. These were the same men Chamberlain dismissed as traitors to their own country when he refused to credit or even meet with their emissary, Baron Ewald von Kleist.

The heart of *Sins of the Fathers* is the story of the three stages of the conspiracy that evolved after November 5, 1937:

1. When the conspirators tried to spark a rebellion based on Hitler's false charges against the commander-in-chief of the army, Colonel General Fritsch.
2. When Baron Ewald von Kleist flew to England to persuade the British government to threaten Germany with

---

53 Colvin, Kindle edition, location 3601–3612.

war to prevent Hitler from crossing the frontier into Czechoslovakia. This also included the meeting with Winston Churchill.

3. The "Final Conspiracy" in 1938. This fell to Halder, who replaced Beck as chief-of-staff, to help formulate and direct the plan to arrest Hitler the moment troops were ordered into Czechoslovakia: Hitler would be either executed on the spot or put on a public trial that would reveal his insanity.

Had any of these efforts succeeded, the world would have been spared the largest military and civilian bloodbath in the history of warfare in which seventy-five million people died, including six million Jews in extermination pits in Russia and gas chambers in Poland.

The first effort—tied to the humiliation of Fritsch—failed because of Hitler's triumph in Austria. His popularity insulated him from any repercussion that may have resulted from the false accusations against Fritsch.

The second effort failed because the Chamberlain government refused to accept Kleist and his mission for what it was: an effort by decent men to rid their country of a demonic tyrant.

After the failed Kleist mission, the conspirators, recognizing that they were on their own, planned to launch the *coup d'état* the moment Hitler ordered Czechoslovakia to be invaded. As portrayed in *Sins*, Chamberlain's insistence on personal diplomacy culminating in the gift of the Sudetenland to Hitler at the Munich Conference pulled the rug out from under the conspirators yet again. They could no longer use the threat of imminent war to justify their revolt either to their junior officers or to the German population that now idolized a *Führer* who had delivered both Austria and the Sudetenland within six months without firing a shot.[54]

---

54 *The Oster Conspiracy of 1938*, Terry Parsinnen, Harper Collins, New York, 2003, pp. 166–167. It was General Witzleben who said it best: "If

The Blomberg/Fritsch Chapters

The two highest ranking members of the *Wehrmacht*—Blomberg and Fritsch—opposed Hitler's November 5, 1937 program. Both were out of office by February 4, 1938. Their cases were different. Blomberg did himself in—with help from Göring—while Fritsch was the victim of totally false charges engineered by Himmler and Heydrich.

Blomberg did marry a woman with a criminal record on Göring's birthday. Göring and Hitler did leave Carin Hall to be witnesses. Göring knew of *Frau* Blomberg's checkered past before the wedding; Hitler did not. The latter expressed genuine shock when he found out about the "marriage of the head of the German armed forces to a whore." A shocked Hitler said, "If a German field marshal will marry a whore, then anything can happen in the world."[55] This ended Blomberg's career and removed his opposition to Hitler's November 5 plans.

But Hitler did not stop there. He abolished the cabinet post of minister of war and assumed the role of head of armed forces which Göring coveted. In this way, Hitler outmaneuvered both his military enemies and his Party friends. There would never again be a professional soldier or, for that matter, a civilian politician standing between Hitler and the German armed forces.

Fritsch's story was different. In 1935, Reinhard Heydrich used claims by a petty criminal—Otto Schmidt—to accuse Colonel

---

we tried to do something now, history, and not just German history, would have nothing else to report about us than that we refused to serve the greatest German when he was the greatest, and the whole world recognized his greatness."

55 *To the Bitter End*, Hans Bernd Gisevius, Houghton Mifflin, Boston, 1947, Kindle edition Pickle Partners Publishing, Auckland, New Zealand, 2014, location 3805; *1938: Hitler's Gamble*, Giles MacDonogh, Basic Books, Philadelphia, 2009, p. 325; *The History of the German Resistance 1933–1945*, Peter Hoffmann, 3rd Edition, McGill-Queen's University Press, 1996, p. 39. (First published in West Germany, 1969 by R. Piper & Co.); *Hitler and his Generals*, Harold C. Deutsch, University of Minnesota Press, 1974, p. 106.

General Fritsch of homosexuality.[56] Hitler, who never much cared about homosexuality in his confederates while prosecuting it as a national policy, ordered Heydrich's report suppressed as garbage. But Heydrich kept the file.[57] After Blomberg's downfall in '38, Himmler and Heydrich resuscitated and enhanced Otto Schmidt's recollections.

It is indisputable that Himmler and Heydrich suborned Schmidt's perjury with the full knowledge that Bavarian Joe's (Joseph Weingärtner) liaison in 1933 was with retired Calvary Captain Achim von Frisch, not the commander-in-chief of the army, Colonel General Fritsch. The confrontation where Göring arranged the face-to-face between Schmidt and Fritsch in the presence of Hitler in the Reich Chancellery occurred as depicted in *Sins*. So, too, was Fritsch's shock and his initial supine reaction. Defense attorney Goltz did discover the existence of the old cavalry captain. He was able to show that the *SS*, under direct control of Heydrich and Himmler, brought charges against the commander-in-chief *with full knowledge* that it was retired Captain Frisch who had the sexual encounter with Joseph Weingärtner, not Colonel General Fritsch. Indeed, Weingärtner was interviewed by the *SS* and he told them the truth.[58]

The conspirators' plan to use the false prosecution and expected exoneration of Fritsch to unmask Himmler's and Heydrich's villainy and topple the Gestapo to end the regime was accurately depicted. But the plan foundered when Fritsch unexpectedly resigned before trial, and the trial was postponed by the imminent invasion of Austria. When the trial resumed, though Fritsch was acquitted, the conspirators lost all advantages due to Hitler's Austrian triumph. As a postscript, rather than rehabilitate Colonel General Fritsch to his position as commander-in-chief of the army, Hitler made him an honorary colonel of his former regiment.

---

56 Hoffman, p. 39; Parssinen, p. 24
57 Parssinen, p. 24; Gisevius, Kindle version, location 3939.
58 Parssinen, p. 26.

To our knowledge, no verbatim transcript of the Fritsch trial exists.[59] But we do know that Goltz—Fritsch's defense attorney—became a prosecutor of a sort by exposing Schmidt's perjury. It is also correct that Heydrich had the Gestapo arrest Germany's great athlete, the world-famous tennis player Gottfried von Cramm, who was on Schmidt's list of homosexuals, to bolster Schmidt's credibility against Fritsch.[60] Cramm—an ancillary victim of the Himmler-Heydrich plot—was convicted and incarcerated.

*

Reinhard Heydrich is often under-appreciated as one of the greatest villains in history and, as such, played a prominent role in many of the evils portrayed in *Wolf* and *Sins*.

We first met Heydrich in *Wolf* in 1931 after he had been cashiered from the navy for breaking an engagement with the daughter of a friend of Admiral Raeder. Through an intermediary, Heydrich had come to Hitler's attention. The *Führer* asked Himmler to interview Heydrich to take charge of the SS Security Office. Heydrich impressed Himmler and was hired. By April 1934, Heydrich headed the security branch of the Gestapo and played a prominent role in butchering scores of *SA* men during the Night of the Long Knives, also known as the Röhm Putsch. It is true that he organized the 1936 Berlin Olympics, and he did convert Pension Schmidt into Salon Kitty.

Heydrich became the most feared and powerful member of the SS. By the time of *Kristallnacht*, November 1938—which he launched and supervised—it would be difficult to find a historical figure in any age that exceeded him for cruelty and malevolence. His persecution of the Jews, homosexuals, Gypsies, and other groups alone is sufficient to so distinguish him. Yet, in the years after *Kristallnacht*, he exceeded these combined villainies.

---

59 Deutsch, p. 135.
60 Taylor, p. 319; Deutsch, p. 301

As malevolent as we describe him, Heydrich was also multi-faceted. He was a talented violinist and a champion fencer. Heydrich was no coward. Despite being one of the most powerful men in Germany and an *SS* general, he flew numerous combat fighter missions during the invasion of Russia. After he was shot down and barely escaped capture, Hitler ordered him grounded. In many ways, Heydrich and Hitler present the same dilemma: how to comprehend—much less account for—the barbarities of men who otherwise present the accomplishments of civilized human beings.[61]

Kleist's Mission to London

Having swallowed Austria, Hitler did not waste time to make Czechoslovakia his next meal. Perhaps one reason for his haste was his hypochondria.[62] Hitler did not expect a long life. We should recall what began the November 5 conference as his political testament: "To be regarded in the event of his death, as his Last Will and Testament."

By mid-March 1938, with Austria rolled into Greater Germany and the Fritsch military tribunal over, Hitler was ready for the second prong he announced on November 5, 1937: the conquest of Czechoslovakia. Hitler promptly met with Konrad Henlein, leader of the Sudetenland Germans. Henlein was ordered to make demands that the Czech government could not possibly fulfill.[63] The stage was set for invasion. For their part, the resisters were convinced that a strong public threat by Britain to go to war would be enough to deter Hitler

---

61 An interesting sidelight is the fate of Otto Schmidt. After the trial, Schmidt was sent to Sachsenhausen Concentration Camp. He lived there until shortly after Heydrich's assassination, when he was shot.

62 Dr. Theodor Morell became Hitler's personal physician in 1936. For a first-hand accounting of Hitler's health, hypochondria, medical treatment, and medicines, read Dr. Morrell's interview by Michael Musmanno: https://digital.library.duq.edu/digital/collection/mussinter/id/1074/rec/6.

63 Taylor, p. 380.

from invading Czechoslovakia. After all, the British navy ruled the seas and France not only had a larger and better trained army than Germany but had signed a pact with Russia to protect Czechoslovakia. German generals had been saying all along that if Germany went to war in 1938, it would be defeated. For these reasons and more, German military leaders reached out to the British government to persuade England to threaten war in order to prevent one. Kleist was their emissary. This launched the second phase of the conspiracy.

Colvin used his considerable contacts for Kleist to meet with Prime Minister Chamberlain and Lord Halifax, secretary of the Foreign Office. A letter from Colvin, dated August 3, 1938, advised the British government that September 28 had been set as *X-tag* or zero-day for the Czech invasion.[64] We reproduced that extraordinary letter on pages 308–309. Colvin, armed with military information from the conspirators, was able to provide the highly secret date set for the invasion while Canaris provided Kleist the false documents needed to leave Germany. Before Kleist departed in mid-August, Chief-of-Staff General Beck told him, "Bring me certain proof that England will fight if Czechoslovakia is attacked, and I will make an end to this regime."[65]

Armed with the necessary papers and a commitment by the chief-of-staff to bring down Hitler once Britain publicly threatened war, Kleist flew to England. He was driven to the airport by his cousin, General von Kleist. But it was not to meet Chamberlain and Halifax. Instead, Kleist met with Lord Lloyd and Vansittart. This change of actors came at the behest of England's ambassador to Berlin, Nevile Henderson, who was sympathetic to the German regime. Henderson counseled Chamberlain not to meet with Kleist or any people Kleist represented.

Vansittart, who had been the permanent undersecretary of state for foreign affairs for nine years and recently promoted "up"

---

64 *None So Blind*, Colvin, pp. 218–221.
65 Ibid, 223.

to a less meaningful position, did meet with Kleist. He reported his conversation in a note to Lord Halifax:

> August 19, 1938
>
> I spoke to you this morning about Herr von Kleist . . . I came to the conclusion that it would be a mistake to refuse to see him, and I therefore did so . . .
>
> I said, "Do you mean to say that the extremists are now carrying Hitler with them?"
>
> He [Kleist] said: "No, I do not mean that. There is only one real extremist and that is Hitler himself . . ."
>
> [Kleist]: ". . . Hitler has made up his mind for himself, all the generals in the German army who are my friends know it for a certainty and know the date on which the mine is to be exploded . . ."
>
> In conclusion, he said that his exit from Germany had been facilitated by his friends in the army . . . they had taken the risk and he had taken the risk . . . he had no illusions as to the fate that awaited him if he failed; but he made it abundantly clear, as I have said earlier, that they alone could do nothing without assistance from the outside on the lines he had suggested.[66]

Halifax forwarded Vansittart's memorandum to Chamberlain the next day. Chamberlain's response was to dismiss Kleist as a traitorous German interested in sowing rebellion:

> I take it that von Kleist is violently, anti-Hitler and is extremely anxious to stir up his friends in Germany to make an attempt at his overthrow. **He reminds me of the Jacobite's at the Court of France in King Williams' time, and I think we must discount a good deal of what he says.**

---

66 Ibid, 223–224.

>   Nevertheless, I confess to some feeling of uneasiness,
> and I don't feel sure that we ought not to do something.
> His . . . (Kleist's request), that one of us should make a
> speech or give an interview in which we should, in Van's
> phrase, **'be more explicit.'** . . . **I reject.**[67] [Emphasis added]

While Chamberlain was inclined to make "some warning
gesture," he specifically "rejected" what Kleist was sent to
England to obtain.

Churchill was another matter.

Kleist did meet with Churchill. To be clear, though Churchill
acted as a "has-been" politician put out to pasture with no
sway in the government, he met Kleist with the full knowledge
and approval of Halifax and Chamberlain. Churchill, for his
part, did report his visit with Kleist to Halifax. And Churchill
did provide Kleist with a letter, penned by him *alone*, that predicted war if Germany crossed the Czechoslovakia frontier.
(*Sins*, p. 326). Nonetheless, all *dramatis personae* understood
Churchill was speaking without authority to define the British
position.

Churchill was handcuffed in what he could write:

>   As **I felt** you should have some definite message to take
> back to your friends in Germany who wish to see peace
> preserved and who look forward to a great Europe in
> which England, France, and Germany will be working
> together for the prosperity of the wage-earning masses,
> **I communicated with Lord Halifax. His Lordship
> asked me to say on his behalf that the position of His
> Majesty's Government in relation to Czechoslovakia
> is defined by the Prime Minister's speech in the
> House of Commons on March 24, 1938.** The speech
> **must be read as a whole** and **I have no authority** to
> select any particular sentence out of its context; but I

---

67 Ibid, 228.

must draw your attention to the final passage on this subject . . .[68](Emphasis added)

It seems likely to us that while Churchill was authorized to meet with Kleist and, while he wished to do more, he was limited to quoting from a five-month-old Chamberlain speech. This fell far short of Britain threatening war if German troops crossed into Czechoslovakia.

Two critical questions remain.

1. Why was it so important to the conspirators that England provide a clear statement that an invasion of Czechoslovakia would mean war with England and France against Germany?
2. Why was Chamberlain's government so unwilling to make common cause with the German resisters? After all, England was not being asked to fight. With their public statement, the German military leaders would overthrow the government. There would be no war.

Fabian von Schlabrendorff, a conspirator who survived WWII, offered an answer to the first question:

Foreign support was vital because the hard core of resolute, determined men within the German resistance was hopelessly outnumbered, and besides was forced to push, pull and carry along many lukewarm, hesitant and vacillating people at the edges of the conspiracy who were nevertheless needed because of their influential positions.[69]

The German military leadership needed England to threaten war in order to justify their rebellion to the lower ranks. This

68 Churchill's complete letter plus the reference to Chamberlain's March 24 speech can be found in Manvell and Fraenkel, p. 75–76.
69 Schlabrendorff, p. 90.

would gain the junior officers' support to depose Hitler as the only alternative to war. Chamberlain's government, on the other hand, was reluctant to support the conspirators' request because they saw little difference between the resisters and the Hitler government that they opposed.

As Professor Terry Parssinen states:

> Vansittart and his colleagues did not understand that German conservatives and nationalists might be moral and religious men who were appalled at the lawlessness, brutality and inhumanity of the Nazis. It was a profound failure of analysis that led Vansittart and the foreign office to dismiss Kleist and his message so cavalierly.
>
> Churchill's response to his meeting was altogether different from Vansittart's. He urged Halifax to take the conspirators seriously, predicting that their planned coup would bring "A new system of government within 48 hours. Such a government, probably, of a monarchist character could guarantee stability and end the fear of war forever." [70]

Nothing was accomplished in England. Kleist returned to Germany to discover that Beck had resigned in protest over Hitler's intention to invade Czechoslovakia. Beck had expected significant numbers of the general staff to resign with him. Without generals, there would be no leaders of the army. Ergo, no war. But that failed when Hitler ordered Beck to delay announcing his resignation for two months. Unexplainably, Beck agreed.

Thus, the second major plot keyed to a threat of war by England came to nothing. The conspirators knew they could not expect support from the Chamberlain government. They were on their own. Nonetheless, they prepared to go forward and remove Hitler upon his order to attack Czechoslovakia.

---

70 Parsinnen, p. 76.

The Last Conspiracy of 1938

Colonel General Franz Halder became chief-of-staff of the German army after General Ludwig Beck resigned at which time he joined the conspirators' rapidly coalescing plan. It was left to Canaris, Oster, Schlabrendorff, and most importantly, Erwin von Witzleben—general of the infantry and commander of the troops in the military district of Berlin—to seize Hitler. Witzleben was an anti-Nazi officer who protested the Night of the Long Knives in 1934. He also was a close friend of General Fritsch. Unfortunately, Witzleben was ill when the nascent conspiracy was sparked by the humiliations of Blomberg and Fritch. The conspirators understood then that a coup would not be possible without troop support in Berlin . . . and Witzleben was unavailable at that time.

Witzleben, now recovered, prepared to remove Hitler. He was far from alone. Key senior officers within and without his command joined the "Last Conspiracy of 1938."

As depicted in *Sins*, the conspirators formulated a detailed plan to seize control of Berlin and arrest Hitler. Witzleben's subordinate, Major General Count Brockdorff-Ahlefeldt, commander of the 23rd infantry division at nearby Potsdam, would enter the city, secure Gestapo headquarters, and arrest Himmler and Heydrich along with their top staff. Witzleben demanded the right to personally arrest Hitler. Lieutenant General Erich Hoepner's First Light Division was poised to confront the *SS* regiment, the *Leibstandarte* Adolf Hitler, if it tried to move from Munich to Berlin, and Major General Paul von Hase, commander of the nearby Fiftieth Infantry regiment, was also ready to "spring into action."[71] General Hase was Dietrich Bonhoeffer's uncle and would continue to be part of the resistance, losing his life after the 1944 assassination attempt.

The conspirators formulated a careful, well-thought-out plan and assembled a capable and willing attack force to carry it out.

---

71 Parsinnen, p. 112; Schlabrendorff, p. 100.

The plotters were not limited to military personnel. Others participated. Count Wolf Heinrich Graf von Helldorf, chief of the Berlin Police, though an unlikely participant given his long history with the *SA*, the Nazi Party, and his rabid anti-Semitism, joined the conspirators. Civilians including Hans von Dohnanyi; his brother-in-law, Dietrich Bonhoeffer; Carl Friedrich Goerdeler, the former mayor of Leipzig; Hjalmar Schact, head of the Reichsbank; and many others were involved in the 1938 coup. Schlabrendorff and Dohnanyi participated in the 1943 assassination attempt as well. Nearly all lost their lives after the July 20, 1944 plot failed when their participation in the 1938 conspiracy was revealed.

Witzleben, slated to be the new commander-in-chief of the army after the coup, was arrested, tried before Roland Freisler in 1944, and hung from a meat hook by piano wire in the first group of conspirators to be executed.[72]

We have honored most of these men in the dedication of *Sins* for risking their lives to stand up to tyranny. A few, such as Helldorf and Hoepner, had either pre-war records or acts during the war that made such recognition distasteful.

The conspirators were divided as to what to do with Hitler if their 1938 putsch succeeded. Some, like Oster, argued for immediate execution. In his view, it was too dangerous to keep Hitler alive. Others, like Canaris, believed Hitler should be put on trial. To that end, Dohnanyi, who worked under Gürtner in the Ministry of Justice, kept exhaustive records of Nazi abuses as did Schrader at Canaris's request. Canaris kept diaries that he entrusted to Schrader which, when discovered, led to the arrest and execution of many 1938 conspirators and 1944 collaborators.

The conspirators intended to demonstrate that Hitler was insane—or at the very least, not sane—at his trial. To that end, they assembled Hitler's army medical records and presented them to one of Germany's leading neurologists: Dr. Karl Bonhoeffer,

---

72 Parsinnen, p. 180.

the father and father-in-law of two conspirators. The following is the first-hand account of what occurred:

> Here he would be prosecuted for endangering the safety of Germany. It was intended that part of the case should consist of a medical report on the defendant which provided him to be insane.
>
> . . . Hans von Dohnanyi became one of those detailed to prepare the case for the prosecution, while his father-in-law, Professor Karl Bonhoeffer, perhaps the most distinguished neurologist in Europe, was asked to endorse the medical evidence demonstrating Hitler's insanity.
>
> A meeting took place with the professor; Dohnanyi **accompanied by his friend Otto John**, another civilian member of the conspiracy, went to see him. They produced a report describing every known illness from which Hitler had suffered compiled from reports made by **official military doctors. Professor Bonhoeffer studied the reports carefully.** All he would say afterwards was, 'From this it would seem very **probable that the man is not quite sane.**' Dohnanyi and John hoped to persuade the old man to give them a medical certificate of Hitler's insanity. But the Professor was unable to sign any form of certificate concerning Hitler's mental condition without a thorough examination.[73]

Chamberlain's trip to Munich culminating in the gift of the Sudetenland to Hitler ended the last conspiracy of 1938 to depose Hitler. His latest triumph made him untouchable. On October 5, 1938, Chamberlain received accolades in Parliament for signing the Munich Agreement. After much adulation, Churchill rose to blast the agreement. "I will, therefore, begin by saying the most unpopular and most unwelcome thing .

73 Manvell and Fraenkel, p. 68–9; Manvell and Fraenkel, p 274 "We are most grateful to Otto John for giving us this account of the meeting with Professor Bonhoeffer **at which he was present**." (Emphasis added.)

. . what everyone would like to ignore or forget but which must nevertheless be stated, namely that we have sustained a total and unmitigated defeat, and that France has suffered even more than we have."

Perhaps the most astonishing aspect of Churchill's speech—which has been totally overlooked—was his oblique reference to the German resisters. It was oblique enough to protect their safety. But clear enough to anyone who knew of the Kleist Mission six weeks earlier.[74]

Persecution of the Jews

Beginning in 1920, Hitler and his Nazi Party repeatedly announced when they came to power they would eliminate Jews from Germany. From the moment they were given control of the country on January 30, 1933, the Nazi government implemented stringent legal steps with the express goal to make it next-to-impossible for the Jewish population of Germany to remain.

---

74 France and Great Britain together, especially if they had maintained a close contact with Russia, which certainly was not done, would have been able in those days in the summer, when they had the prestige, to influence many of the smaller States of Europe, and I believe they could have determined the attitude of Poland. Such a combination, prepared at a time when the German dictator was not deeply and irrevocably committed to his new adventure, **would, I believe, have given strength to all those forces in Germany which resisted this departure, this new design. They were varying forces, those of a military character which declared that Germany was not ready to undertake a world war, and all that mass of moderate opinion and popular opinion which dreaded war, and some elements of which still have some influence upon the German Government. Such action would have given strength to all that intense desire for peace which the helpless German masses share with their British and French fellow men, and which, as we have been reminded, found a passionate and rarely permitted vent in the joyous manifestations with which the Prime Minister was acclaimed in Munich.** (Emphasis added). Parliamentary Debates, 5th Series, Volume 339 (1938).

Medical and law schools were closed to Jews. Insurance funds were not permitted to reimburse services of Jewish doctors. Jews were forced to leave the universities. In time, Jewish students could no longer attend school. Laws were passed to eject Jews from the civil service. The passage of the Nuremberg Race Laws in 1935 deprived Jews of their civil liberties. Businesses were Aryanized. If Jews had names of "non-Jewish" origin, a 1938 law ordered men to take "Israel," and women to take "Sarah," for middle names.

Yet by the end of 1938 a surprising number of Jews remained in Germany. There were a variety of reasons for this. One was the tenacity of many Jews who regarded Germany as their homeland. They were reluctant to leave in the hope that the Nazi nightmare would pass. Jews that did want to leave Germany were prevented because the Nazis, while demanding they leave, also demanded steep exit fees for departure.

But perhaps the most compelling reason for Jews to remain was that most had no place to go. Throughout the world, barriers to immigration effectively prevented them from leaving Germany. The day Hitler became chancellor there were some 525,000 Jews in Germany. By March 1938, the Austrian *Anschluss* added more Jews to Hitler's domain than he found when he came to power on January 30, 1933. When the Évian Conference convened July 6–15, 1938, Czechoslovakia was on Hitler's horizon . . . and, when it would be absorbed, another 357,000 Jews would come under German rule.[75]

As described in *Sins*, President Roosevelt convened the Évian conference to deal with Europe's refugee crisis, which was a euphemism for "stateless Jews" . . . a phrase not mentioned in Évian. Thirty-two countries were invited to send delegates. Germany was excluded. Twenty-four voluntary organizations were invited as guests. Golda Meir did represent the British Mandate Palestine but was not allowed to address the conference. As reflected in

---

75 https://encyclopedia.ushmm.org/content/en/article/jewish-population
  -of-europe-in-1933-population-data-by- country

Sins, the conference was a failure. No attending country loosened its immigration laws to accept displaced refugees. The delegates who were quoted in *Sins* said what was attributed to them. The article quoted from the *Völkischer Beobachter* in *Sins* (p. 304) after the conference, did appear in that Nazi Party newspaper.[76] And Hitler did make a public offer—no doubt tongue in cheek—to provide first-class tickets out of Germany to the "criminals" (his term for Jews), if countries would accept them.

> I can only hope and expect that the other world, which has such deep sympathy for these criminals, will at least be generous to convert this sympathy into practical aid. We for our part, are ready to put all these criminals at the disposal of these countries, for all I care, even on luxury ships.[77]

By the end of September 1938, after being handed the Sudetenland, Hitler had more Jews under his authority than ever before. From the Nazi perspective, their laws, boycotts, and ruthless discriminatory practices had been ineffective in removing Jews from German lands.

In their warped way of thinking, they were forced to do something drastic if they were to rid themselves of the "vermin." Everything else had failed. Their answer began with *Kristallnacht*, which was a national physical assault on Jews, their property, and to their places of worship. A line was crossed that night: violence preempted economic and legal pressure to force Jewish emigration.

It is against this understanding and background of history as presented in *Sins of the Fathers*, that we conclude the Authors' Notes with Hitler's famous address to the Reichstag on January 30, 1939, celebrating the sixth anniversary of his coming to power.

---

76 http://learning-from-history.de/sites/default/files/books/attach/perspective -nazi-germany.pdf; "No One Wants to Have Them," Völkischer Beobachter, July 13, 1938.

77 *The Nazi Holocaust*, Ronnie S, Landau, I. B. Tauris, 2006, pp. 137–140.

This occurred six months following the Évian Conference, less than three months after *Kristallnacht*.

Many are familiar with Hitler's often quoted line from this speech:

> If the international Jewish financiers in and outside Europe should succeed in plunging the nations once more into a world war, then the result will not be the Bolshevization of the earth, and thus the victory of Jewry, but the annihilation of the Jewish race in Europe!

Few are aware of the context in which he shouted these words. What is missing is Hitler's fury at the failure of the Évian Conference to unburden him from his Jews. With the same relentless logic that they imposed on the purification of their own people—from sterilizations to abortions to the euthanasia of "useless eaters"—the Nazis were intent to purify their country of Jews. Discriminatory laws did not work. Outbreaks of violence were not enough. Ghettoization could contain only so many. And then, when millions of Polish and Russian Jews fell into their hands in the early years of World War II and there was no place to warehouse them, they turned to extermination.

Consider the following: when Hitler spoke in front of his black- and brown-shirted audience in the Reichstag on January 30, 1939, he was also addressing the "hypocrisy" of the attendees to the Évian Conference who attacked Germany's Jewish policy while they refused to accept Jewish immigration into their own countries:

> . . . it is a shameful spectacle to see how the whole democratic world is oozing sympathy for the poor tormented Jewish people but remains hard-hearted and obdurate when it comes to helping them which is surely, in view of its attitude, an obvious duty. The arguments

that are brought up as an excuse for not helping them actually speak for us Germans and Italians.

For this is what they say:

1. "We," that is the democracies, "are not in a position to take in the Jews." Yet in these empires there are not 10 people to the square kilometer. While Germany, with her 135 inhabitants to the square kilometer, is supposed to have room for them!
2. They assure us: We cannot take them unless Germany is prepared to allow them a certain amount of capital to bring with them as immigrants.

With diabolical adroitness, Hitler addressed the reluctance of other countries to accept Jews who brought no money with them. He explained why Jews should leave Germany virtually penniless:

For hundreds of years, Germany was good enough to receive these elements, although they possessed nothing except infectious political and physical disease. What they possess today, they have by a very large extent gained at the cost of the less astute German nation by the most reprehensible manipulations.

Then, with dripping sarcasm, the *Führer* excoriated the many countries that criticized Germany's treatment of the Jews while, at the same time, refusing them entry:

. . . If the rest of the world cries out with a hypocritical mien against this barbaric expulsion from Germany of such an irreplaceable and culturally eminently valuable element, we can only be astonished at the conclusions they draw from this situation. For how thankful they must be that we are releasing these precious apostles of culture and placing them at the disposal of the rest of the world. In accordance with their own declarations, they cannot find a single reason to excuse themselves for refusing to receive this most valuable race in their own countries. Nor can I see a reason why the members of this race should be imposed upon the German nation, while in the States, which are so enthusiastic about these "splendid people," their settlement should suddenly be refused with every imaginable excuse . . .

It was at this point that Hitler shouted his prophecy to the cheers of the packed Reichstag:

In the course of my life I have very often been a prophet and have usually been ridiculed for it. During the time of my struggle for power it was in the first instance the Jewish race which only received my prophecies with laughter when I said that I would one day take over the leadership of the State, and with it that of the whole nation, and that I would then among many other things **settle the Jewish problem**. Their laughter was uproarious, but I think that for some time now they have been laughing on the other side of their face. Today I will once more be a prophet: If the international Jewish financiers in and outside Europe should succeed in plunging the nations once more into a world war, then the result will not be the Bolshevization of the earth, and thus the victory of Jewry, but the annihilation of the Jewish race in Europe![78] (Emphasis added)

It is unfortunate that most histories quote only the "prophecy" of the "annihilation of the Jewish race in Europe" without its

---

78 *The Speeches of Adolf Hitler,* April 1922–August 1939, Volume I, N. H. Baynes, ed., Oxford University Press, London, 1942, pp. 737–741.

context: Hitler's demand that the rest of the world relieve his Reich of its Jewish population.

For some, the "Holocaust" began in 1933, with the legal pressure brought to bear on Jews to leave. For others, it began the night of November 9–10, 1938, with the violence of *Kristallnacht*. Still others place it when the Germans entered Russia on June 22, 1941, and began the mass killings. For us, when the Holocaust began is relative to its definition. The inescapable fact is that Hitler was determined to rid Germany of Jews from the time of his first public statements in 1920. Year after year, he espoused and shouted what he was going to do to them.

He wrote about it in *Mein Kampf*. And when he became chancellor, his rhetoric turned more vitriolic as law after law was passed to force the Jews to leave Germany. And still, most stayed. Simultaneously, he preached that Germany could not be restored to its former greatness without more land. *Lebensraum*. But his territorial gains came with an unacceptable price: more and more Jews that no one would take off his hands.

Less than three months after *Kristallnacht*, his "prophecy" could not have been clearer: the Jewish population of Greater Germany, that now included Austria and the Sudetenland, would not be permitted to remain, much less continue to grow. And if the "democracies" continued to refuse to take his Jews, he prophesied he would provide his own solution to the "Jewish Problem."

Which he did.

—Herbert J. Stern and Alan A. Winter, July 2021

Acknowledgments

Writers do not write in a vacuum. They need the tender loving care, understanding, tolerance, help, and criticisms from those that surround them. We acknowledge, here, those that made this work possible.

Once again, we would like to thank Thomas White, the University Archivist at Duquesne University, who assisted us with access to the Musmanno Papers. Noted author Michael Ridpath was generous not only with his time answering our many questions but with sharing his research about Ian Colvin and Baron von Kleist-Schmenzin. If that were not enough, it was Michael who opened our eyes to the critical role Fabian von Schlabrendorff would play in this story. Our gratitude to Clare and Andrew Colvin, who read both the early and final manuscripts of *Sins* and offered valuable comments about their father's role.

Our thanks to our team at Skyhorse Publishing—Tony Lyons, Mark Gompertz, Caroline Russomanno, and Kathleen Schmidt—who always maintained their professionalism, exhibiting inexhaustible patience and grace for two compulsive writers. And to Meryl Moss, of Meryl Moss Media, who did everything possible to bring *Sins of the Fathers,* along with *Wolf,* to public attention.

No words can adequately acknowledge Denise Penna Shephard's contribution to *Sins of the Fathers.* From typing and retyping our many versions of the manuscript, to helping with research and correspondence, and keeping files that a work such as this requires . . . she was always there with a smile and the ability to make it happen. Thank you, Denise.

Special thanks to those who toiled over the manuscript, making key suggestions along the way: Michael Mandelbaum and Hew Pate who were among the first; and to Clyde and Otto

Feil whose amazing editing kept us on course. And then there were those who read and critiqued along the way: Bill Boyd, Paul Feuerstein, Stephen Foreman, Ken Gantz, Jayne Gumpel, Marc Himmelstein, Bill Jaffe, Brian Machler, Madelene Magazino, Alan Marcus, Ruth Maron, Mark McGivern, Bob Recine, Daniel Rosen, Donna Dodson, Larry Rubin, Irv Schecter, Jim Smith, Peter Sudler, Shaun Tully, Olga Vezeris, Marc Wein, and David Zornow.

Finally, and most importantly, we acknowledge the two people who sacrificed the most to make this work possible: our wives Lori and Marsha.

—Herbert J. Stern and Alan A. Winter
September 2021